# Effie Mae
# The End

By

Patty Mitchell

ISBN-13: 978-0-578-56579-8

# Acknowledgements

It is with great gratitude that I like to acknowledge Jacqueline Munn-Hall, my neighbor in the 90's that served as my initial reader during which time I decided to write my very first novel, entitled "Black Roses."But through multiple changes and writing style, it became "Effie Mae." Jacqueline found great pleasure in reading my written works and believed in my ability as a Writer. Thank you, Jackie.

I also thank Articia Johnson-Hunter for the support, feedback and encouragement she provided to me in reading my manuscript.

Once again I'd like to thank my daughter Ashley for helping me to pull my book together as a whole.

And as always, I thank God for anointing me with the gift of writing, giving me the ability to envision a story in my head then be able to transpose that story onto paper. It is truly a blessing! Thank You Lord.

# Contents

# Chapter One

Effie Mae awakened early Saturday morning. She watched Anthony as he slept and thought how lucky she was to have gotten a second chance in his life—her life. She also thought of Blue and how much she loved and missed him. Her eyes moistened as her thoughts drifted to the day she told Blue she would be leaving New York, returning to Mississippi, and marrying Anthony.

Her thoughts were cut short when Anthony awakened. He pulled her in his arms and romantically kissed her then abruptly stopped and stared at her. Effie Mae watched in awe as he rolled over towards the night stand and opened the top drawer, removing a roll of breath mints, popping two in his mouth and again taking her in his arms, passionately kissing her. He intimately slid one of the sugary flavored breath mints from his mouth into hers. She giggled.

"I still can't believe you're here with me Baby." Anthony said applying light kisses to her neck and shoulders.

"Anthony?"

"Yes Baby." He replied as his mouth made its way back to Effie Mae's lips. He again kissed her.

"What did you just do?" Anthony continued intimately kissing her lips, shoulders and neck.

"You mean the breath mint?"

"Yeah Anthony I mean the breath mint." He stopped.

"Oh that!"

"Yeah that."

"Did it offend you Baby? I just thought that—"

"I actually enjoyed it." A pleasurable smile displayed on Effie Mae's face. "It's just that all the time we was together I don't remember you ever doing that before.

"Well I've kissed a few women since then and it was like kissing spoiled, raw meat." Effie Mae's mouth flung open.

"Is that how it felt when you kissed me Anthony?"

"Well Baby it wasn't the best kiss we've ever had." Her mouth again opened.

"Anthony!"

"No Baby this time it was me." He swirled the breath mint around in his mouth. "I had onions and cheese on the hamburger I ate for dinner yesterday before leaving Jackson."

"Anthony you can eat a skunk and your kisses gon always be sweet to me." Effie Mae said wrapping her arms around his neck, kissing him. He embraced her in his arms and romantically kissed her.

"Baby, where are the kids?"

"Why Anthony?" She giggled. "You ready to have a good time?"

"Yes Baby I am." Anthony seductively kissed her on the neck and lips. Effie Mae pulled him over on top of her.

"Wait!" Anthony's eyes widened as he looked over at the open door.

"I thought you said you was ready to have a good time Anthony?"

"I am Baby, but don't you think we should lock the door first?"

"For what Anthony?"

"Baby, what if the kids—" Effie Mae chuckled.

"Boy I'm just teasing you, Annie Mae came by and got my babies yesterday so we could have some time together." She kissed him softly on the lips.

"I love you Baby." Anthony said, again kissing her. "Sometimes it seems unreal—you being here with me."

"Well Anthony I am!" Effie Mae stated, placing a tantalizing kiss to his awaiting lips. "So are we gon have a good time or what boy?" An enormous smile appeared on Anthony's face. They passionately kissed then engaged in intimacy.

———————————

Arriving home from work, Pete entered the house slowing when seeing Effie Mae's children sitting at the kitchen table eating dinner yet again. He shifted his eyes to Annie Mae then shook his head in frustration, continuing down the hall to the bedroom, slamming the door after entering. Millie shited her eyes over at her children then looked at Annie Mae, concerned.

"Child go talk to your husband." Millie whispered.

"What? Annie Mae said seeing the worried look in her momma's eyes. "Pete didn't say he wanted talk to me Momma."

"Annie Mae you been married to that man all these years and you still can't read him?"

"What Momma?"

"Just go talk to your husband child, I'm sure Pete's got plenty he want to say." Annie Mae stood stationary. "And he ain't gon wait all day to say it."

"I'm going Momma." She said walking slowly down the hall, clueless of what to expect from her infuriated husband. Annie Mae swallowed the nervous lump in her throat as she arrived outside the closed bedroom door—hesitating before entering.

"You want to see me Pete?" He stared at her.

"Is Effie Mae over here Annie Mae?" He asked unbuttoning and removing his work shirt.

"Naw but—" He cut her off.

"Then why's her kids over here?"

"Anthony came home last night and I thought maybe they needed some time alone."

"What about us Annie Mae, we don't need time alone?"

"You know my sister's been through a lot—" He again interjected.

"Effie Mae made her own bed hard for the most part." Pete said taking off his work boots. "Now I know you love your sister Annie Mae, but you married to me." He hesitated. "You still love me don't you Annie Mae?"

"Yeah Pete." He walked over and embraced her in his arms then romantically kissed her.

"Now I'm gon bathe and put on some clean clothes then we gon leave here and go to the Cozi-T." Annie Mae's jaw dropped. "And we gon act like we did before we got married and had all these kids." She blushed.

"What am I gon tell Momma?"

"Tell her we going to the Cozi-T—it's okay Annie Mae we married!" She remained speechless. "Go on now girl." He released her then unbuckled and dropped his pants. Annie Mae opened the door to leave. "Hey!" She turned seeing the enormous smile on his face as he stood wearing only his boxers. "You know that tub's big enough for the both of us." His smile widened.

"Pete!"

"What . . . it is!" Annie Mae blushed then exited the room closing the door behind her.

———————————————

"I love you Baby." Anthony said coddling Effie Mae in his arms as they leaned against his car the following Sunday morning before his return trip back to Jackson.

"I love you too Anthony." They intimately kissed.

"Are you pregnant yet?"

"What?" She said looking at him with widened eyes, surprised by his out of the blue question. "Anthony getting pregnant can take time." Effie Mae said uneasy by the subject.

"Baby we didn't have a problem making Lil' J.R. and we hadn't been together in six years."

"Just give it a little more time Anthony." She said masking her true feelings about giving birth to yet another child. "I'm sure it ain't gon be long before I'm pregnant." He placed a quick kiss on her lips.

"Okay Baby, I'll be patient." They again kissed. "I'll call you as soon as I get back to Jackson okay Baby."

"Okay Anthony." He looked across the street at Ms. Dawson's house—now babysitter to Effie Mae's many children. Anthony briefly watched as they ran throughout Ms. Dawson's front yard, porch and stairs in a playful game of tag.

"Bye kids!" He waved.

"Bye Anthony!" They shouted, vaguely looking up as they continued running up and down Ms. Dawson's stairs. Anthony again turned to Effie Mae. They kissed.

"Bye Baby."

"Bye Anthony." Effie Mae said forcing a smile, masking her distress from Anthony's request for another child. He climbed in the car and started the engine before sharing an intimate kiss with Effie Mae through the open window.

"Be sure to call me Baby if you need anything okay?"

"I will Anthony." She smiled, watching as Anthony backed onto the dirt road to begin the long drive back to Jackson. Effie Mae now felt convinced that resuming her relationship with Anthony had been the right thing to do.

· _____

Effie Mae put the last of the breakfast dishes away before going upstairs to check on her children as they prepared for church the following Sunday morning, after Anthony had once again left for his return trip back to Jackson.

"Y'all hurry up now . . . Pete gon be here to pick y'all up for church in a minute." She said walking across the hall to Lil' J.R.'s room.

"You almost ready Lil' J.R.?"

"I wanna stay with you Momma." He whined attempting to button his starch white dress shirt.

"Where your tie at Lil' J.R.?" Effie Mae asked looking around the room, discovering the navy blue tie lying on the floor next to the bed. She picked it up. "Do you still want to grow up and be a preacher like your Daddy, Lil' J.R.?" He nodded.

"Yeah." She buttoned his shirt and adjusted the tie around his neck. "Then you need to go to church and listen to Rev. Hill so you can learn how to preach, okay baby?" Effie Mae said admiring her young son. He nodded. "Look at you Lil' J.R." He smiled "You look so handsome!" A big smile stretched across his small face. "Now come on let's go downstairs before Pete get here . . . he probably already pulling in the driveway."

"Okay Momma." Effie Mae kissed him on the cheek, taking hold of his hand as they exited the room. "That's my big boy." The sound of Pete's honking horn rung out from the driveway.

"Y'all ready Mahalia?" Effie Mae said on her way down the stairs.

"Yeah Momma." Mahalia said exiting her room, hurrying down the stairs. She pushed open the front door and leaped off the porch.

"Hi uncle Pete." She stated before climbing in the bed of Pete's truck, joining her multiple male cousins.

"Lena, Billie, Sarah!" Effie Mae called out. "Come on babies." The three girls rushed from their room, adorned in their colorful church dresses then scurried down the stairs, passing Effie Mae and Lil' J.R. along the way. They burst open the front door joining Mahalia and their cousins in the back of Pete's truck.

"I don't wanna go Momma." Lil' J.R. whined. "I wanna stay here with you."

"Don't you want to see Granny and Annie Mae?" Effie Mae asked. He nodded. She pick him up and carried him out onto the front porch then kissed him on the forehead and put him down.

"Come on boy!" Pete shouted. "You do this every Sunday!"

"Leave my baby alone Pete." Effie Mae said in defense of her spoiled son. Pete watched as Lil' J.R. dragged his feet then impatiently honked his horn.

"I wanna stay with you Momma." Lil' J.R. stated looking back at her. Pete threw the gears in reverse.

"Pete don't you leave my babye!" Effie Mae hollered out.

"Then he better bring his butt on!" He yelled as Lil' J.R. walked slowly down the porch stairs. Pete shook his head then quickly climbed out his truck—picking Lil' J.R. up, carrying him over to his truck and putting him in back with his sisters and numerous cousins.

"I wanna stay with you Momma." Lil' J.R. said with tear-filled eyes.

"I'm gon cook you some French fries when you get back from church, okay baby?" His eyes lit up. He nodded.

"Okay Momma." She waved.

"Bye Lil' J.R."

"Maybe one of these days you'll come to church with us!" Millie called out from the passenger side window.

"Momma you know I ain't living right, all that's gon do is give them Ol' nosey folks something to gossip about—especially Ms. Sissy!"

"Maybe you ought to start living right then."

"Bye Momma."

"Bye child." Millie said displeased with her eldest daughter's living arrangements. Effie Mae waved at her many children as Pete backed onto the road and drove away. Her attention suddenly drew to Ms. Dawson peeping through her closed living room drapes. Effie Mae quietly chucked then waved—taunting her.

"Ol nosey busy-body." She said thinking out loud. Ms. Dawson slightly pulled back the curtain and watched as Effie Mae entered the house closing the door. Effie Mae looked around the childless home and suddenly missed her life in New York, the taste of scotch—and Blue. She walked swiftly in the kitchen in search of an alcoholic beverage, preferably scotch as her anxiety increased, and her resistance for alcohol decreased. She opened the refrigerator then abruptly closed it when seeing only food. She returned to the living room, walking over to the window and looking out seeing the empty country road and the peering eyes of Ms. Dawson now sitting on her front porch. Effie Mae turned away and began pacing—sporadically looking at the phone, desperately wanting to call the man who'd always come to her rescue—Blue. No longer able to resist, she picked up the phone and dialed Blue's number.

"Blue's Jazz Club . . . Blue speaking." Effie Mae's eyes moistened at the sound of his voice.

"Hey Blue."

"Hey Baby girl!" He said, elated. "How you doing?" She burst into tears.

"I need you Blue."

"What wrong Baby girl?"

"I just need to see you." A huge smiled stretched across his face, delighted in knowing Effie Mae still needed him.

"Okay, just let me talk to Melvin and let him know I'll be gone for a few days."

"Hurry Blue!"

"Baby girl you gon be alright until I get there?"

"Yeah Blue, just hurry!"

"I'm on my way."

"I knew you still loved me Blue."

"Always you know that."

"Bye Blue."

"Bye Baby girl . . . I love you."

"I love you back Blue." Effie Mae said comforted as he once again rescued her from herself.

————————————

"Momma?" Mahalia said entering the kitchen from the living room where her sibling watched cartoon on television.

"Yeah baby." Effie Mae said looked adding brown sugar to the candied yams simmering on the stove. She looked briefly at her young daughter noting the sad look on her round face. "Mahalia baby you alright?"

"I want to go home Momma."

"Home?" Effie Mae's stomach filled with butterflies. "What you mean baby—this is your home, I told you last month we was gon be living here with Anthony." Mahalia eyes erupted with tears.

"I don't want to live with Anthony, Momma . . . I want Daddy!" She began crying.

"Don't cry baby." Effie Mae said as her head pounded. "Let me call your daddy so you can talk to him, okay?"

"Okay Momma." Effie Mae turned the burners down underneath the pans on the stove then opened the oven to check the readiness of the pork chops and gravy as she tried not to emotionally crumble in front of her daughter. She took hold of Mahalia's hand and exited the kitchen, entering the living room.

"Come on baby." Effie Mae said picking up the phone, calling J.R. Millie Ann answered.

"Hello."

"Hey Millie Ann, how you doing baby?"

"Momma!" She said, excited. "Daddy letting me cook supper today, I made some mashed potatoes and—" Effie Mae interjected.

"Millie Ann baby, put your Daddy on the phone."

"Okay Momma—I love you." Millie Ann said sensing her Momma's agitation. "Daddy telephone!" She yelled. "It's Momma." A concerned look entered J.R.'s eyes as Millie Ann handed him the phone. He knew for certain Effie Mae's call would be troubling.

"Uh, Effie Mae."

"Hey J.R." She said trying to mask her distress.

"Is uh, everything okay?" She remained momentarily silent. "Effie Mae?" J.R. repeated. She burst into tears, handing the phone to Mahalia.

"Daddy I want to come home and live with you and Millie Ann." She cried out as tears streamed down her face.

"Mahalia . . . let me uh, speak to your momma." She handed Effie Mae the phone—both weeping.

"Effie Mae?" J.R. said, worried. She gave no reply. "Effie Mae!"

"What J.R.?"

"What's wrong?"

"I can't do it J.R."

"Calm down—tell me what's going on."

"I can't do it."

"Where's Anthony?"

"He in Jackson." Effie Mae's agitation grew. "He always in Jackson!" She shouted.

"Uh, okay." J.R.'s mouth dried. He coughed—now worried if agreeing to let Effie Mae take the children with her to Mississippi had been a mistake. "You need me to come get the children?"

"I don't know J.R." She stated ambiguously. On the one hand she knew caring for the children had proven to be too much for her. On the other, she wanted desperately to prove she could do it.

"I'm here Effie Mae—talk to me." He said concerned she might be drinking again. "Tell me what's going on."

"I keep wanting to drink J.R."

"Uh, okay." He inhaled blowing it out through his nose. "Do you know what's making you feel that way?"

"I miss Blue!" Effie Mae blurted. A lump formed in J.R.'s throat, disheartened by her unexpected reply.

"Uh, okay . . . have you talked to him?"

"Yeah J.R., he said he gon be here tomorrow." J.R. swallowed the seemingly growing lump. "

"Have you uh, talked to Anthony about Blue coming there?"

"I can't do that J.R.!" She shouted. "Anthony ain't gon understand that—he ain't like you."

"Effie Mae you sure getting back with Anthony was the right thing to do?"

"Anthony's good for me J.R."

"I remember you saying that but—" He briefly moved the phone away from his ear, upset by his wife's continued relationship with Blue. "So uh, what's gon happen when Blue get there?"

"What you mean what's gon happen J.R.?"

"Effie Mae—" J.R. said knowing for certain she understood what he meant.

"If you asking me if I'm gon be with Blue—" She silenced refusing to answer. He shook his head in disappointment. "I love Blue!"

"Effie Mae—"

"What J.R.?" She yelled.

"What about Anthony?"

"What about him?" Effie Mae stated without guilt. "And why you worrying about Anthony?"

"So uh, what is it you need me to do?"

"My baby Mahalia saying she want to go live with you and Millie Ann."

"Of course she can I love my daughter and I uh, have no problem with—" Effie Mae interjected.

"I love my baby too J.R.!" Effie Mae said raising her voice.

"I uh, never said you didn't Effie—"

"You ain't never thought I could take care of my babies  no way J.R.!"Effie Mae yelled. He took a deep breath before again speaking.

"Effie Mae—" J.R. took a deep breath before speaking. "—if that's what my . . . our daughter wants and it's gon take some pressure off you, I can pick her up this weekend."

"Thank you J.R." Effie Mae said calming down.

"Have you uh, received any mail from here recently?" He asked, slightly nervous.

"Mail? What kind of mail J.R.?"

"Uh, don't worry about it . . . it ain't important right now." He hesitated. "I uh, guess I'll see you this weekend."

"Okay J.R."

"Uh, okay." He paused. "I uh—" Effie Mae blushed, amused in knowing her estranged husband wanted to say *I love you.* She quietly giggled.

"What J.R.?"

"You uh, take care Effie Mae and uh, me and Millie Ann send you our love." She again blushed.

"You know J.R. for a minute it sound like you was gon say you love me."

"Would it be a bad thing if I did?"

"Nope, right now hearing you say that wouldn't be a bad thing at all."

"Ahem!" J.R. cleared his throat. "I uh, I love you Effie Mae." He whispered. She giggled.

"Thank you J.R." They remained momentarily on the phone then both simultaneously hung up.

# Chapter Two

Millie looked in the direction of the front door when she heard it open—seconds before the house filled with the chatter of her grandchildren.

"Hey Momma!" Effie Mae said walking over and hugging her.

"Hi Granny." The children all greeted as Millie sat at the kitchen table peeling potatoes for supper. She smiled as each of her grandchildren applied a kiss to her chocolate cheeks.

"Where Pete Jr. and them, Momma?" Effie Mae asked.

"They out there somewhere."

"Y'all gon outside and find your cousins—go play." Effie Mae said preparing to again leave them in the care of Annie Mae. Lil' J.R. pushed open the back door and scurried outside in search of his cousins. The other children followed. "Where Annie Mae at Momma?"

"Now Effie Mae I hope you ain't brought them children over here wanting your sister to watch them again."

"Annie Mae don't mind watching my babies, Momma." Millie rose from the table then walked over to the refrigerator removing a large black pot, carrying it over to the stove placing it on one of the four burners.

"Well Annie Mae's husband do."

"Who—Pete?" Effie Mae looked inside the pot. "Momma is that gon be enough turnip greens to feed all them babies?"

"I guess Pete thinking her watching your children taking her time away from him." Millie chuckled.

"What?" A baffled look appeared on Effie Mae's face. "Momma, Pete and Annie Mae got babies here too—my babies ain't but a few more." Millie raised an eyebrow.

"A few more?"

"Well Momma can you watch them then?" Millie looked at her with suspicion.

"Now I know Anthony's at work in Jackson and you ain't working nowhere, so tell me child what you doing you needing somebody to watch them children?"

"Momma promise me you ain't gon get mad." Millie's forehead wrinkled with frowns in anticipation of the words Effie Mae would say next. Her attention suddenly drew to the front door when hearing footsteps coming up the stairs, ending at the screened door. Millie's eyes widened when seeing Blue standing on the other side. She lowered herself back into her chair then looked at Effie Mae with disappointment before again turning to Blue. Effie Mae's face lit up when she looked in the direction of the door in response to her momma's gaze—seeing Blue. She hurried over and opened the door. Blue beamed as he entered, taking her immediately in his arms and passionately kissing her.

"I missed you Baby girl." He said applying light kisses to her lips and neck before engaging in a romantic kiss. "Thank you for letting me come and see you." Blue said again kissing her. "You just don't know how much I've missed you." His jaw suddenly dropped when seeing Millie sitting at the table watching, a disapproving look on her face. He nervously swallowed. "How you doing Ms. Reed?" He said shifting his eyes to Effie Mae and back to Millie. "I'm sorry Ms. Reed I didn't see you sitting there." Millie continued her stern gaze. "I didn't mean you no disrespect, it's just that seeing Baby girl—" He released Effie Mae from his embrace.

"Excuse me Blue . . . I need to talk to my daughter in private." Millie said getting up from the table, walking in the direction of her bedroom. Effie Mae followed. The mother-daughter duo entered the bedroom, but not before Millie flashed Blue a look of displeasre. He lowered his eyes as a scolded child as Millie closed the bedroom door. "Effie Mae you and J.R. still married?"

"As far as I know Momma, why?" Millie ignored her naive response. "Momma I'm still waiting on J.R. to do whatever he gon do—" Millie cut her off.

"You and Anthony still living in sin?"

"Momma!"

"Don't momma me."

"Momma you know I can't marry Anthony until me and J.R. get divorced."

"So then tell me this child . . . where do Blue fit into all this mess?"

"Momma right now I need Blue."

"Need him?" She looked at Effie Mae with disciplining eyes. "Need him for what Effie Mae?" Millie asked before thinking  about the open-ended question. She raised an eyebrow. "Never mind, I don't want to know."

"That ain't it Momma." Effie Mae said disappointed by the judgmental look in her momma's eyes. "When I lived in New York, Blue was always there for me Momma when I needed help."

"Well you ain't in New York!" Millie yelled. "You home in Mississippi."

"I know Momma, but I still need help."

"Help with what child?"

"Coming home ain't been easy Momma." Millie ignored her passive words. "I ain't lived here in a long time, but if I'm gon marry Anthony—" Millie interjected.

"Marry Anthony?" She looked Effie Mae in the eyes. "Tell me this Effie Mae—how you gon marry Anthony when you still married to J.R.?" A confused looked appeared in Effie Mae's eyes.

"And the only home my babies know is New York—" Millie's agitation lessened when thinking of her grandchildren. "And seems now they wanting to go home."

"Them children ain't got no business being caught up in all this mess anyway!" Millie said upset as she thought how Effie Mae had made a disaster of her life and how she had included her children.

"I spoke to J.R. yesterday Momma and he gon be here this weekend to take Mahalia back home to live with him and Millie Ann." Millie's eyes widened.

"Effie Mae you think you ought to be bringing men up in that boy's house?" Effie Mae giggled.

"Momma I ain't getting ready to take Blue in Anthony's house."

"Well you sure ain't laying up in here with him!" Millie said raising her voice. "Tell me child, how Blue being here gon make anything any better?"

"I don't know Momma it just will." Effie Mae said smiling as she thought of Blue waiting in the living room. "It's just that when I'm with Blue—" She blushed. "—he always make everything seem right."

"Then why didn't you just stay in New York with Blue then Effie Mae?" Millie scolded.

"You know why Momma." Effie Mae lowered her eyes. "Blue got that jazz club—"

"The one been feeding you all that liquor?"

"Yeah Momma . . . and we both know what happen when I start drinking." Effie Mae looked in her momma's agitated eyes. Millie gave no reply, disturbed with Effie Mae's alcohol addiction. "Momma you gon watch my babies for me?"

"Tell me you ain't getting ready to go lay up with that man Effie Mae!" Millied scowled. Effie Mae blushed.

"Momma I ain't seen Blue in six months, you really want me to answer that?" The sour look on Millie's face amplified.

"I guess if you wasn't faithful to J.R. and he your husband, I can't expect you gon be any more faithful to Anthony." Millie shook her head. "Who ain't!"

"Momma when J.R. left, Blue was like a husband to me—" Millie cut her off.

"But he wasn't your husband Effie Mae and he still ain't!" She said agitated.

"I know that Momma but—"

"But what Effie Mae?" Millie tried to ignore the pleading look in Effie Mae's hazel brown eyes.

"Please Momma."Millie reluctantly relented. "I guess you gon be wanting them children to stay all night?"

"Can they Momma?"

"Go head on child." Effie Mae's eyes lit up.

"Thank you Momma." She hugged Millie then applied a kiss to her cheek. Millie felt ambiguous about her decision to participate in Effie Mae's immoral behavior. On the one hand, she knew it was wrong. On the other, she could see how much being with Blue meant to her complicated daughter.

"So what's gon happen when J.R. get here this weekend Effie Mae?" Millie raised an eyebrow. "And what's gon happen when Anthony get home and find both him and Blue in his house?"

"Momma, Anthony can't stop J.R. from coming to get his baby and he ain't even gon know Blue was here." Millie gasped. Effie Mae giggled.

"Effie Mae!"

"What Momma—he won't and J.R. ain't trying to be with me like that."

"Why not he a man ain't he? And don't forget he still your husband."

"Yeah Momma, but J.R. different." Millie raised an eyebrow.

"Is he?"

"Yeah Momma he is." Effie Mae said, amused. "If I tried to be with J.R., that man wouldn't touch me Momma." Millie listened, unconvinced.

"If that day ever come child I think you gon find J.R. don't function no different than Blue or Anthony."

"Momma!"

"Go head on." Millie chuckled. "You and Blue have fun." Effie Mae's jaw dropped, shocked by her momma's words.

"You mean that Momma?" Effie Mae said giggling.

"You know what I meant child." Millie shook her head. "Bye Effie Mae."

"Maybe you didn't mean it that way Momma, but me and Blue gon do just that." Effie Mae burst into laughter then again kissed Millie  on the cheek. "Bye Momma."

———————————

Effie Mae lay in Blue's arms at the Cozi-T-Motel with a huge smile on her face. He kissed her gently on the lips then gazed in her eyes and smiled.

"What Blue?" She blushed.

"I never dreamed, well maybe I did dream . . . but I never thought, well maybe I did think—" Effie Mae giggled.

"Thought what Blue?"

"I'd be with you again Baby girl." His smile grew. He suddenly began coughing.

"You alright Blue?"

"Yeah Baby girl I'm alright." He said through his persistent coughing. "I got this bad cold after you left and it don't seem to want to go away."

"You been to see the doctor Blue?" Effie Mae asked, alarmed by the forcefulness of his cough.

"Yeah, he gave me some pills and some cough syrup, but they ain't helping much." Blue stated through his vigorous coughing. "It don't do nothing but put me to sleep."

"Blue baby maybe you need to go back to that doctor."

"I am." He said rolling over to the side of the bed and picking up his pants, removing a bottle of pills. Blue dropped a couple in his hand and tossed them in his mouth, swallowing using only saliva to wash them down. He rolled back over and again enveloped Effie Mae in his arms, nestling her head onto his chest then placing a gentle kiss on her forehead as his coughing gradually ceased. "I'll call and schedule another appointment when I get back home." Effie Mae took hold of his hand and rubbed it softly against her cheek.

"Thank you for coming Blue, I just needed to see you."

"Baby girl you know all you had to do was call and I'd run from New York to Mississippi just to get to you girl!" She giggled as he lovingly gazed at her. "Baby girl if you were in a volcano I'd jumped in and burn up trying to get to my baby."

"Well I hope I ain't ever fool enough to jump in no volcano Blue."

"Me too, because that would be the wrong time to find out if I had that kind of courage." They laughed then stared intimately into each other's eyes then passionately kissed. Blue continued his gazed. Effie Mae blushed.

"What?"

"Baby girl I cried a whole week straight after you left." Effie Mae's mouth slightly opened.

"Blue Tyrell Lee Jones, I know you ain't cried like that over me!"

"Yeah Baby girl I did."

"A whole week Blue?" She said, humored.

"Yeah Baby girl—a whole week." Effie Mae blushed. He kissed her softly on the lips. "But wait until I tell you this." Effie Mae's blushing smile widened.

"What Blue?"

"It got so bad one night when Huck was in the club—" Blue shook his head. "—that man had to come up on stage to comfort me!" Effie Mae burst into laughter.

"You lying Blue!" She said continuing to laugh. "Huck—Henry Lee White comforted you when you was crying over me?"

"I ain't lying Baby girl, he did!" Effie Mae tilted her head.

"Is that right?" She said mocking Huck. "Sound like Henry Lee White done got a little soft since Effie Mae Reed left." They continued laughing. "Because I remember it was a time when it looked like Huck was gon kill you Blue." His eyes widened.

"Yeah at one time Baby girl I thought he was too." A perplexed looked showed on Blue's face. "But you know what Baby girl—"

"What Blue?" She placed a light kiss on his lips.

"I swear it felt like I was comforting him jist as much as he was me." Blue said grinning. "Baby girl I swear I saw tears in that man's eyes." Effie Mae's jaw dropped.

"Tears?" She again burst into laughter. "You lying Blue!"

"Baby girl you know that man love you just as much as I do." Blue said placing an intimate kiss on her lips, delighted to once again have Effie Mae in his life.

"Blue Tyrell Lee Jones, I know y'all grown butt men wasn't crying over me like that." Effie Mae said flattered at the thought.

"Baby girl you know you one in a million." He said again kissing her on her lips. "I'm in love with you Effie Mae . . . you know that?" She blushed.

"Yeah Blue I know that." She gazed in his peaceful eyes.

"I said I love you Baby girl." Blue repeated, waiting to hear her captivating response.

"I love you back Blue." He beamed. They passionately kissed then engaged in a night of intimacy.

———————————————

Anthony looked with inquisitive eyes at the two unfamiliar cars parked in his driveway as he arrived home for the weekend. Uneasy by the vehicles blocking his path, he pulled on the front lawn and parked, glancing inside each car as he walked in the direction of the house hoping for a clue that might identify his mysterious guests. His curiosity grew as he stepped on the front porch and opened the door then entered. Anthony's eyes quickly drew to Lil' J.R. sitting on J.R.'s lap, appearing to be sharing a father and son bonding moment. He continued his visual search, politely smiling at Millie Ann seated next to her daddy on the sofa before turning his attention to the strange man comfortably lounged in his brown leather recliner appearing to be somewhat ill at ease by his presence.

"How's everybody doing?" Anthony asked looking throughout the downstairs in search of Effie Mae. He walked over and extended his hand to J.R. "It's good to see you again J.R." The two men shook

"How you doing Anthony?"

"I'm not sure." A bewildered look displayed on Anthony's face. "Are you here to get—" J.R. interjected.

"Effie Mae? No I'm uh, here to take Mahalia back home to live with me and Millie Ann, Effie Mae seems to think she's having trouble adjusting to the south." J.R. said, slightly humored.

"Oh!" Anthony said surprised. "Effie Mae didn't say anything about that to me." He again shifted his eyes to the man sitting in his recliner, uncertain if he and J.R. were together. "A friend of yours J.R.?" Anthony asked hoping J.R.'s answer would be yes. Blue quickly stood.

"Uh, my name is Tyrell." He glanced nervously over at J.R. then back to Anthony, extending his hand. They shook. J.R. watched the awkward exchange chuckling underneath his breath.

"I don't believe I know you Tyrell, do I?" Anthony said.

"You uh, probably know me as Blue."

"Blue!" Anthony's eyes widened. "Effie Mae's friend Blue from New York?" A shocked look appeared in his eyes in response to Blue being in Mississippi—and in his home. Blue again shifted his eyes to J.R. then back to Anthony, apprehewnsive about what would happen next.

"Effie Mae!" Anthony called out.

"She uh, upstairs." J.R. said holding back his laughter. Anthony again looked at Blue then headed up the stairs.

"Effie Mae?"

"Yeah Anthony." She said, answering from her daughter's bedroom, sorting through clothing as she packed Mahalia's suitcase. Anthony walked over and took Effie Mae in his arms and kissed her then stared into her eyes.

"Baby are you leaving me?"

"Naw Anthony why you ask?" She suddenly remembered her special guest downstairs. "Oh, Blue."

"Yes Baby—Blue." Anthony said bothered by his presence. "Baby why is he here?"

"Blue's still my friend Anthony." Effie Mae said in a matter of fact tone. "He wanted to come see me Anthony, so I told him he could."

"So Baby when did he get here?" Anthony asked certain it wasn't today.

"A few days ago, why?"

"A few days ago?" His anxiety heightened. "Has he been staying here?"

"Naw Anthony I wouldn't do that."

"I've been calling you for the last few nights and you didn't answer either night—were you here?"

"What you asking me Anthony?"

"I guess what I'm asking is did you and Blue—"

"Let me get my baby's clothes packed so she can go back home with J.R. then we can talk."

"It sounds like we need too." Effie Mae silently looked at him. "What Baby?"

"I can't finish packing my babies clothes Anthony if you holding me."

"Oh, okay." He kissed her quickly on the lips then looked at her with curious eyes. "Remember Baby . . . we're trying to have another baby—not you and Blue." Effie Mae quietly chuckled as Anthony released his hold and walked away headed to his bedroom to bathe and change. He stopped and stared briefly at her then entered his room.

· · · ·

"Bye Momma!" Mahalia said hugging her. "Bye, Anthony!" She waved at him then hurried from the house heading over to her daddy's car, opening the back door of the burgundy, mid-size Sport Wagon and getting in—being seated behind Millie Ann already sitting up front. J.R. put his young daughter's suitcases in the rear trunk then closed the hatch, walking around to the driver's side where Effie Mae and Anthony stood intimately embraced.

"I uh, guess I'll stop by Ms. Millie's and say hi to her and the rest of my children before I head back home to New York."

"Since you going that way J.R. can I ride with you? I need to pick my babies up from Momma's." He subtly shifted his eyes to Anthony then back to Effie Mae. He knew from past experience Blue would somehow be in the equation.

"Uh, sure."

"Thank you J.R."

"Well Anthony—" J.R. said extending his hand. "—it was uh, good seeing you again and uh, thank you for helping Effie Mae take care of my children."

"I love Effie Mae J.R., so taking care of the kids and my son Lil' J.R. was my pleasure." J.R. glanced over at Effie Mae bothered by Anthony's biting words. The two men exchanged a final uncomfortable handshake before J.R. again turned to Effie Mae.

"I guess if you uh, riding with me you should get in the car?" He said opening the driver's side door and getting in. "Uh, Millie Ann get in the back so your momma can sit up front."

"Okay Daddy." She quickly climbed out and got in the back joining Mahalia as J.R. discreetly watched as Effie Mae kissed Anthony lightly on the lips. "I'll be right back Anthony."

"Okay Baby." They again kissed. "Don't be too long I have a surprise for you when you get back."

"A surprise?" Effie Mae's eyes widened. "Tell me Anthony!" She said with childlike excitement as they held hands and walked around to the passenger side of the car. Lil' J.R. followed. Anthony opened the door as he and Effie Mae gazed intimately into each other's eyes. J.R. watched with disbelief as she climbed inside. He thought what little regard Effie Mae had for his feelings considering he remained her legal husband.

"Come on Lil' J.R." She said lifting him up, sitting him on the seat between her and J.R. before turning her attention back to Anthony. "A surprise huh?" She said smiling.

"Yes Baby, so hurry back." J.R. gazed through the windshield attempting to ignore the passionate kiss they shared.

"Ahem!" He cleared his throat as the kissed prolonged. Effie Mae and Anthony's lips slowly pulled apart in response to J.R.'s subtle signal. Effie Mae giggled, humored by J.R.'s obvious jealousy as Anthony closed the car door and again applied an affectionate kiss to her lips.

• • • •

J.R. shifted his eyes to Effie Mae when seeing Blue's car parked in the driveway as they arrived at Millie's house. She turned to her two daughters sitting in back, electing not to discuss J.R.'s opinion of her less than desirable behavior in the presence of their children.

"Y'all run on in the house and say bye to your Granny." Effie Mae said opening her door allowing Lil' J.R. to climb across her lap and get out. Millie Ann and Mahalia burst open the back doors exiting from opposite sides of the car then raced towards the house, running up the stairs and onto the front porch. Lil' J.R. lagged behind. J.R. watched as they scurried through the front door of their granny's house then turned to Effie Mae.

"What J.R.?" She said in response to his judgmental gaze.

"Sometimes I uh, feel like I never really knew you." He looked at her with perplexed eyes. "Is it that easy for you to just get out of one man's bed and into another's?"

"Why you asking me that?"

"It's just that you live with Anthony then you call Blue down here and uh, I'm pretty sure you and he—" She cut him off.

"Why you worried about what me and Blue doing?" His eyes widened in response to her insensitivity. "What J.R.—you think only men got the right to get out of one bed and in another?"

"A right?" J.R. said raising his voice. "That ain't what I'm saying Effie Mae!"

"Then what you saying J.R.?" She asked, agitated by the chastising look in his eyes. "What—you jealous? Is that what it is J.R.?" Effie Mae said verbally lashing out. "Cause I ain't in your bed too?"

"That's not what I said Effie Mae."

"So if I got in your bed J.R., you telling me you wouldn't touch me?"

"As your husband I'm the only man that's got that right." She thought of Millie's words and laughed to herself.

"What?"

"I guess Momma know men better than I thought she did." Effie Mae giggled then looked at her estranged husband with intrigue.

"What?"

"You know J.R., I might take you up on that one day." She placed a kiss on his cheek.

"What was that for?" He asked looking at her with peculiarity.

"For making me see you ain't no different than no other man." She giggled.

"Huh?"

"Let me go say bye to Blue." J.R. watched as she opened the door and got out then walked over to Blue's car and climbed in. Effie Mae slid over next to Blue as he put his arm around her, laying her head on his chest. They passionately kissed. J.R. looked briefly through the windshield of Blue's car as he walked pass on his way to the house, throwing up his hand waving as he stepped on the porch, disappearing through the front door.

• • • •

Effie Mae gave no thought to Anthony waiting for her to return home as she found comfort in Blue's intimate embraced. They romantically kissed. Blue stared in Effie Mae's eyes dreading his departure back home to New York.

"When am I gon see you again Baby girl?" Blue asked as his eyes moistened.

"I don't know Blue."

"Baby girl will you promise me you'll call me every day?"

"Is it alright Blue if I call you just through the week? Anthony come home on the weekend—last thing that boy gon want to see is me calling you." She lightly chuckled. Blue quietly stared at her. Effie Mae blushed.

"What?"

"I wanted to wait before asking you this because I'm scared what your answer might be."

"What is it Blue?" Effie Mae asked raising her head from his chest, looking in his frightened eyes.

"Baby girl you and Anthony married?" She again laid her head on his chest and listened to his  pounding heart.

"Naw Blue—me and Anthony ain't married yet." Effie Mae half-heartedly giggled. "I'm still married to J.R." A smile stretched across Blue's face, delighted by the news.

"Then come back to New York with me Baby girl!"

"Blue I'm still engaged to Anthony." His heart sank into his stomach as his hope faded. "I still want to be with Anthony, Blue . . . it's just that he always in Jackson and—" She silenced when seeing him hang his head.

"Blue—Anthony want us to have another baby."

"I wish I had been able to give you a child, Baby girl."

"A Tyrell Lee Jones Jr.?" Effie Mae said giggling. "I would love having you a son Blue." She noted hopelessness in Blue's eyes. "What's wrong Blue?"

"Baby girl I can't have kids."

"Why you say that Blue?"

"Because I can't."

"How you know Blue?"

"When I was thirteen I came down with the mumps. After I got so sick they thought I was gon die, the doctors told Momma I would probably never have kids." He looked in Effie Mae's hopeful eyes. "I guess that doctor was right."

"Naw Blue he wasn't right." She said as her eyes dampened. "Cause we gon have us our own baby one day Blue." Effie Mae said determined. "And I'm gon name our baby boy Tyrell Lee Jones Jr." Blue blushed then raised her hands to his lips and kissed them.

"Tyrell Lee Jones Jr." He said grinning. "Okay, I'll see what I can do." Effie Mae giggled.

"It's gon happen Blue—you gon see!" She said desperately wanting to create a child with him.

"What about Anthony, Baby girl?"

"You let me worry about Anthony." They romantically kissed. "You know Blue—" She thought for a moment. "—I always wondered why I never got pregnant by you or Huck."

"I don't want to hear about you and Huck, Baby girl okay?"

"I'm sorry Blue, I was just thinking maybe that's why we never—" He interrupted.

"Naw Baby girl, Huck's got kids!" Effie Mae's mouth abruptly opened, surprised by Blue's news.

"What? Huck got babies, Blue?"

"Yeah he got a son and a daughter."

"You lying Blue!" Effie Mae said, shocked. "You telling me Henry Lee White got babies?"

"Yeah, they about eighteen or nineteen—I think."

"Blue, Huck got babies?" Effie Mae said humored by the thought.

"Yeah Baby girl he do—they live in Buffalo somewhere that's where he from you know."

"Naw Blue I didn't know that."

"That's where his momma, daddy and all the rest of his brothers and sisters live."

"What? You telling me Huck got a momma and a daddy?"

"Baby girl of course that man got a momma and a daddy." Blue chuckled.

"Huck ain't ever said nothing about his family to me, how you know so much Blue?"

"We grew up together." Blue paused. "Huck's my brother, Baby girl." Effie Mae's jaw dropped. "Well, my half brother."

"What?" She yelled out. "Blue, you and Huck brothers?"

"Yeah we got the same daddy but different mommas." Effie Mae remained speechless, overwhelmed by Blue's disclosure. "Daddy's got kids all over Buffalo by at least six different women, Huck's momma was the only woman he ever married though." Blue quietly chuckled.

"Why you laughing Blue?"

"Me and Henry Lee been competing over girls every since we were young, so when I got you he was mad as hell!" Blue said continuing to laugh.

"I'm glad you got me Blue." Effie Mae said blushing. She kissed him lightly on the lips. He gazed in her hazel brown eyes.

"I'm glad I got you too Baby girl." They romantically kissed. "You the best thing to ever happen to me Effie Mae you know that?" Blue said placing a gentle kiss to Effie Mae's lips. "Come back to New York with me Baby girl."

"I would love to go back with you Blue, but you know what happens whenever we together."

"We don't have to live at the jazz club Baby girl!" He said, pleading. "We can get us a place somewhere else."

"Blue it ain't just the jazz club."

"I know Baby girl." He said confirming his understanding of her alcohol addiction. "Damn!" He yelled. "I wish I had never gave you that first drink." Blue said angry at himself.

"It ain't your fault Blue, I didn't have to drink it." She listened to the rhythm of Blue's heart as her head continued resting on his chest. "You take care of yourself Blue."

"I wish you was coming back with me Baby girl." He said placing another kiss on her lips. "If somebody call you on weekends and just sit on the phone it's me Baby girl just needing to hear your voice." They again shared an intimate kiss. Their eyes filled with tears.

"Bye Blue."

"Not Bye Baby girl, I'll see you again." She looked in his tearful eyes and smiled.

"If you say it Blue I believe it."

"I love you Baby girl."

"I love you back Blue." Tears rolled down each of their faces as they held one another. Effie Mae kissed his wet lips then slid over to the door and opened it. She looked in Blue's tear drenched eyes, using her hand to wipe his tears away. He watched with pain in his heart as she got out of the car, drying her own eyes before hurrying away, entering the house. The front door again opened. J.R. rushed out walking quickly past Blue's car then climbed inside his own, startin the engine then backing out allowing Blue to pulled onto the road, honking his horn twice as he drove away in tears on his way back home to New York without Effie Mae.

# Chapter Three

"I thought you were bringing the kids back?" Anthony said as they looked at each other from across the dining room table eating dinner.

"I let them stay at Momma's house since you said you had a surprise for me." He looked at her but gave no reply. "My babies wasn't ready to come home and Momma wasn't ready for them to leave." Effie Mae quietly chuckled while waiting for Anthony to tell her of his surprise. "Millie Reed loves her grandbabies and they love her." She said trying to contain her eagerness. "You gon tell me what your surprise is Anthony or am I gon have to try and guess?" She stated no longer able to hold her excitement. Anthony reached across the table and took hold of her hands.

"You think Ms. Reed can watch the kids for about a week?"

"A week!" Effie Mae's enthusiasm heightened. "Anthony my babies would love that, but I got to check with Momma first—Annie Mae and Pete got babies living there too and Momma said Pete been complaining 'bout my babies being over there so much."

"Baby it'll only be for one week." A girlish smile displayed on Effie Mae's face.

"What you up to Anthony?"

"I'm taking you back to Jackson with me." Effie Mae's eyes widened with childlike anticipation. "I don't like coming home and finding both of my fiancée's ex's sitting in my living room and especially Blue." She giggled, amused by Anthony's jealousy of Blue. "Plus if we're going to have another baby we probably need to spend a little more time together." Effie Mae snatched her hands away.

"Is that the only reason you taking me to Jackson with you Anthony?" She asked, disappointed.

"No Baby of course not!" He noted the let down look in Effie Mae's eyes. "Come here Baby." Anthony said opening his arms. Effie Mae slowly stood then walked around the table and sat on his lap. He intimately embraced her in his arms, kissing her on the lips. "I know it's difficult talking about us having a baby after what Mr. Daniel and his wife did to you." Effie Mae's eyes dampened.

"My baby boy don't even know me Anthony." She said crying.

"Shhhhh, I know Baby." Anthony rested her head on his chest. "Stop crying Baby."

"I want my baby Anthony."

"I know you do Baby and you'll have him one day." He said gently stroked her wavy, black hair. "Mr. Daniel and his wife are too old to be raising a baby and one day they'll realize it."

" I ain't seen my baby boy since I moved back home Anthony."

"I know Baby."

"I don't know if he crawling or what he doing." Tears erupted from Effie Mae's eyes, running down her cheeks.

"Stop crying Baby." Anthony said picking up a napkin off the table, wiping her tears. "If you don't feel comfortable talking about us having a baby while we're in Jackson, we won't okay?" She nodded. He kissed Effie Mae on the forehead as her crying lessened. She noticed the enticing smile on Anthony face. She blushed.

"What?"

"Baby can we go upstairs now and make pretend we're working on that baby?" Effie Mae's mouth slightly opened in response to his unexpected question.

"Anthony!"

"What?"

"Come on boy." She placed a quick kiss on his lips and giggled then rose from his lap to go upstairs and *make pretend*.

---

"Meet me in the room Annie Mae!" Pete said, demanding when entering the house from work seeing Effie Mae's children sitting at the kitchen table—Annie Mae helping them, in addition to their own children, with homework. He stared at her with angry eyes then shook his head. Annie Mae shifted her eyes over at him, ignoring his irate gawk.

"What?"

"You heard me . . . I ain't gon wait all day either!" He said walking hastily down the hall, storming in the bedroom then slamming the door. Millie hurried from her room in response to the thundering noise.

"What was that?" She asked startled by the loud sound awakening her from her nap.

"That was Pete Momma I guess he mad." Frowns formed on Millie's forehead in response to the continued discord between her son-in-law and daughter.

"What's going on with you and Pete, child?"

"Ain't nothing going on with me Momma—I don't know what Pete's problem is." Millie looked over at the children and cautioned Annie Mae with her eyes not to discuss it in front of the children.

"I remember the day that boy marry you Annie Mae." Millie said troubled by their now rocky union. "Told both me and his Momma it was the happiest day of his life." Millie looked over at her many grandchildren and smiled. "And look at all them beautiful children y'all made." Millie suddenly noticed Pete Jr. looking and listening. "But that ain't something we need to be discussing around them children."

"Ain't nothing to discuss Momma—" Annie Mae said dismissing her marital problems. "—if Pete—" Millie cut her off.

"We can talk in my room."

"Momma I'm helping the kids." Millie walked away and headed for her bedroom.

"You got ten minutes before I go back to sleep." She stated. Annie Mae watched as her momma entered her room leaving the door open.

"Pete Jr.—keep a eye on the kids until I get back."

"Yes ma'am." He said looking at with worried eyes. Annie Mae left the kitchen, joining her momma. Millie stared at her young daughter as she entered, disturbed by her and Pete's obvious ongoing marital issues.

"What's wrong with you child? You trying to throw your marriage away like your sister done?"

"Momma, Pete know how Effie Mae is—" Millie interjected.

"Your sister's—" She shifted her eyes over at the opened door and lowered her voice. "—over there with one man that ain't her husband, laying up with another while she got a husband that love her despite her adulterous ways." Millie shook her head with displeasure. "Pete's a good man Annie Mae--"

"Momma if Pete want to leave, let him go I don't care!" Millie's eyes widened. She hurried over and quickly closed the bedroom door.

"You don't mean that child!" She said upset. "Now you think about what you got to gain by letting your husband walk out that door." Annie Mae's eyes displayed defiance.

"That's all I been thinking about Momma." Millie's jaw dropped, shaken by her young daughter's consequential words. "Momma when me and Pete got married I was only sixteen, and it seems all I been doing since then is raising Pete's kids."

"Pete's kids!" Millie said raising her voice in agitation. She stared at Annie Mae, troubled by the words coming from her mouth. "Where all this mess you speaking coming from Annie Mae?"

"Momma I'm tired of just being Pete's wife." Annie Mae said looking in her momma's aggravated eyes. "And I ain't sure that's what I want no more."

"Then you tell me Annie Mae—" Millie glared at her with angry eyes. "What you gon do without him?"

"I been thinking about that too Momma." Annie Mae said briefly lowering her eyes. "And I been thinking I might want to go to New York like Effie Mae done."

"Hush!" Mille yelled. "Just hush your mouth!" She said looking in her naïve daughter's confused eyes. "So you think the grass is greener on the other side Annie Mae?" Fury raged in Millie's eyes.

"I didn't say that Momma." Annie Mae said confused. "All I know is I want something different than—" Millie interjected.

"Than what!" Millie again raised her voice. She looked at Annie Mae with pleading eyes. "Go talk to your husband Annie Mae." She said refusing to discuss the matter any further. "Tell him what you just told me."

"Momma, Pete don't want to hear that! He probably won't even listen to me."

"Go on child."

"Momma!"

"I'll keep an eye on the children while you work things out with your husband." Millie dismissed Annie Mae's adolescent words. "Go talk to Pete—tell him how you feel, that boy loves you child he'll listen." Annie Mae momentarily stared at her then reluctantly exited the room on her way to talk to Pete.

• • • •

Annie Mae continued down the hall in anticipation of speaking with her frustrated husband. She stood outside the bedroom door once arriving and wondered if talking would be a waste of time, but knew her momma wouldn't let up until she did. She glanced down the hall when sensing Millie's peering eyes then opened the door and entered, closing it behind her.

"You want to see me Pete?" She asked avoiding eye contact. He stared at her before speaking.

"Annie Mae do you still love me girl?"

"Why you ask me that Pete?" She said ambiguous. On the one hand she truly believed she wanted out of the marriage. On the other, Annie Mae still loved Pete and deep inside feared what life would be like without him.

"Sometimes I feel like you spend so much time with them kids 'cause you don't wanna spend time with me." Annie Mae gave no reply. Pete's heart raced in response to her silence. "Am I right?"

"I still love you Pete." She said uncertain if she should tell him how she really felt. "But—"

"But what Annie Mae?"

"I don't know if it's the same as it was." Pete looked at her—lost for words then shook his head, hurt by her heart-piercing admission.

"So what you want me to do Annie Mae? Because it ain't gon be no divorce—I tell you that now!" He said raising his voice.

"Do you still love me the same as you did when we first got married Pete?"

"More!" His eyes moistened. "When Momma asked me how I knew what I felt for you was love the day I asked her and daddy if I could marry you—" Tears ran down Pete's coffee brown cheeks. "—I told her if you needed a heart I'd give you mines even if it meant I had to die to do it." Her eyes watered. She walked over and laid her head on her husband's warm chest. "Girl I love you so much—why you want to hurt me like this Annie Mae?"

"I didn't mean to hurt you Pete." She said crying.

"What can I do to get us back to where we was?"

"I don't know Pete." An indecisive look showed on her face. "Sometimes I feel like my life is missing something Pete." He kissed her on the lips, wiping away her tears.

"I guess Momma and Daddy's marriage was so messed up it was bound to have an effect on mines and Jimmy's." Pete shook his head as he thought about it. "Jimmy and Rosetta's over there getting along so bad if he knew Effie Mae was in town, he'd be ready to throw Anthony out his own house." Pete lightly chuckled. "Or throw Rosetta out of Momma's."

"That's the last thing my sister need Pete."

"Annie Mae that boy so crazy in love with your sister—don't look like no woman gon ever be able to take Effie Mae's place in Jimmy's heart."

"You didn't tell Jimmy, Effie Mae was living back here did you?"

"What for? They both got enough troubles already, and from what I can see ain't either one of them got room for no more." Pete and Annie

Mae looked in one another's eyes then romantically kissed her. "Tell me what I need to do Annie Mae to make you love me again?"

"I don't know Pete." She said thinking about his question. "What did we do before we got married that we ain't doing now?"

"Everything's still good between us ain't it?"

"Maybe that's what's wrong." Pete looked at her, puzzled by her confusing words.

"What you mean Annie Mae?"

"It seem like we still doing the same things we was doing when we first got married."

"Then tell me what is it you want me to do?"

"Don't just tell me you love me Pete, show me."

"Show you? How?"

"Do things like take me out to dinner, a movie or something."

"We got too many mouths to feed to waste money going out to eat or a movie."

"Then let's just go for a walk and hold hands, even that would be something different . . . and it's free!"She giggled. "And romance me Pete." A seductive smile displayed on his face. "That ain't what I'm talking about Pete."

"Then tell me what you mean Annie Mae."

"Surprise me like you did when you took me to the Cozi-T."

"I thought you said that ain't what you was talking about."

"It ain't."

"Girl you confusing me."

"And I want to go on a real vacation."

"A real vacation like what?"

"I don't want going to the Cozi-T to be the closest thing we get to having a real vacation." They both laughed. "But it was fun though." Annie Mae blushed. They smooched.

"Where you wanna go Annie Mae?"

"I don't know?"

"We got family living somewhere in Texas maybe we can go—".

"And stop being so mean Pete!" His eyes widened, surprised by her opinion of him.

"Mean? You think I'm mean Annie Mae?"

"Yeah Pete I do—sometimes you talk to me like I'm a child." She pouted. "In case you ain't noticed Pete, I ain't sixteen no more."

"I'm gon change all that Annie Mae." Pete said desperate to restore their marriage. "I love you too much girl to lose you." He kissed her gently on the forehead then affectionately on the lips. Annie Mae smiled. "But give me time Annie Mae people don't just change overnight."

"I know that Pete." She looked at him with loving eyes. "I love you Pete Parker." He beamed.

"I love you too Annie Mae Parker." They looked in each other's eyes then intimately kissed. "You don't need a heart do you?" They again laughed.

---

"Well, this is where I live when I'm working." Anthony said as he and Effie Mae entered his *company paid* apartment. Her eyes sparkled as she looked around his spacious, beautifully decorated, two bedroom abode.

"I love it Anthony." Effie Mae said excited. "Is this where you been kissing spoiled raw meat?" She asked remembering his comment after they'd kissed. His eyes slightly widened when remembering he'd shared that information with her. Anthony noted the insecure look on Effie Mae's face.

"Baby, you were married and living in New York."

"I didn't say nothing Anthony."

"So what's the status of that anyway? Have you and J.R. discuss the divorce?"

"Nope . . . far as I know J.R. ain't done nothing yet."

"Baby are you sure J.R's going to give you a divorce?"

"I don't know Anthony." Effie Mae said hoping her estranged husband would be in no rush to do so. "He never said."

"Do you need me to talk to him Baby? I want to make you my wife before Blue makes you his." Effie Mae giggled. Anthony embraced her in his arms and kissed her.

"Anthony?"

"Yes Baby." He said applying repeated kisses to her neck and lips.

"Do you feel threatened by me and Blue's relationship?"

"Should I be?"

"Nope." Effie Mae said thinking of her recent rendezvous with Blue—she blushed. "I still love Blue, but I'm here with you Anthony." He placed an intimate kiss on her lips feeling secure by her spoken words.

"You feel like going out for a romantic dinner this evening Baby?" Effie Mae's eyes lit up, feeling loved by Anthony's special treatment.

"I would love that Anthony!"

"So how does this sound Baby . . . we have a nice steak dinner, a bottle of red wine, a little dancing then we come back here and get started on making Lil' Anthony." Effie Mae's mouth opened.

"Anthony!"

"I was just teasing Baby." He said, humored. "I told you we wouldn't discuss Lil' Anthony and we won't—not tonight."

"Anthony!"

"Okay Baby." Anthony placed a quick kiss on her lips.

"It's gon happen Anthony just wait." Effie Mae said forcing a smile as she tried to think of an excuse to bypass the wine at dinner for fear of a possible intoxication.

"Well just in case I'm already pregnant maybe I should skip the wine Anthony." She said electing to keep him in the dark about her past alcohol addiction.

"You're right." Anthony again kissed her. "We want Lil' Anthony to be a healthy baby boy."

"That's right!" Effie Mae said trying to keep up the front.

"I love you Baby." Anthony said gazing in her eyes before placing an romantic kiss on her lips. "You ready?"

"Yep." Effie Mae said convincing herself that whatever occurred before her and Anthony's reuniting, would be shared on a *need to know* basis. Anthony opened the door as they prepared to leave—his plan being to return home after they'd shared a bottle of wine and begin working on Lil' Anthony.

## *Chapter Four*

Daniel pulled up to the curbed outside of J.R.'s house and parked, there to pick up Millie Ann. He honked his horn twice and waited. J.R. walked over to the back door and looked out.

"Millie Ann."

"Huh Daddy?" She answered from her bedroom. A solemn look displayed on J.R.'s face.

"Uh, Cousin Daniel's here."

"Okay Daddy."

"How old is uh, Cousin Daniel's son now?" He asked continuing to look out the back door, staring at Daniel's car.

"He's seven and a half months old Daddy—he's crawling too!" J.R. cracked a half smile.

"He is?"

"Yeah, sometimes he try to pull his self up to the living room table, but he always fall back down and start crying then Mr. Daniel pick him up and hug him. J.R. replied merely responding to Millie Ann's voice. "Ms. Geraldine calls him Mr. Daniel's twin because he looks just like him." Millie Ann said continuing to get ready. J.R. suddenly envisioned his wife sharing in intimacy with his cousin.

"Uh, let's not keep Cousin Daniel waiting okay?" Millie Ann hurried from her room into the kitchen. "Uh, have a good time with your baby brother and uh, I'll see you when you get home." J.R. said trying hard to mask his disdain for his cousin from his young daughter.

"I love my baby brother so much Daddy." Millie Ann said speaking just above a whisper.

"That's good Millie Ann." J.R.'s mind drifted to thoughts of Effie Mae's relationship with Blue.

"Bye Daddy."

"Uh, have a good time with your—" Millie Ann interrupted. "Daddy!" J.R.'s concentrated thoughts abruptly broke.

"Huh?"

"You said that already."

"Oh, did I?" Mille Ann approached him with opened arms, requesting a hug. He lovingly embraced his eldest daughter then opened the back door.

"I love you Millie Ann."

"I love you too Daddy." J.R. watched as she rushed out of the house and climbed in the car with her cousin Daniel on her way to visit the brother created by her momma and her daddy's cousin.

• • • •

Millie Ann hurried ahead of Daniel, quickly entering the house where Ms. Geraldine awaited her arrival.

"Hi Ms. Geraldine!"

"Hey Millie Ann! How you doing baby?"

"Fine."

"I cooked your favorite foods today." She said hugging Millie Ann. "I have barbeque spare ribs, mustard potato salad, macaroni and cheese, fried cabbage, cornbread and for dessert caramel cake." Millie Ann's eyes lit up.

"Ooooh! Thank you Ms. Geraldine." She said rushing in the living room in search of her baby brother, not finding him his playpen. "Where's D.J.?"

"Right now that little boy's sleep." Ms. Geraldine said chuckling. "He just about ran me and Daniel ragged today!"

"Ooowee!" Daniel said entering the house. "That boy's got more energy than me and Geraldine put together!" He laughed.

"Can I get him up?"

"Noooo!" They both stated in unison.

"He can wait." Ms. Geraldine said headed in the living room being seated on the sofa. "Come sit down with me Millie Ann I want to talk to you."

"Okay." Millie Ann said entering the living room. Ms. Geraldine shifted her eyes quickly to Daniel then turned her attention back to Millie Ann as she sat down next to her.

"He should be waking up in the next fifteen minutes anyway."

"Then can I go get him Ms. Geraldine?" Daniel intervened.

"Yeah Millie Ann then you can go get him."

"Oooh okay."

"That boy's sure gon love seeing you Millie Ann!" Daniel stated shifting his eyes briefly over to his wife as he waited to hear what she wanted to speak with Millie Ann about.

"Daniel told me you just got back from Mississippi from seeing your momma." Ms. Geraldine said probing.

"Yeah and we brought Mahalia back with us to live."

"You did?" She said glancing in the kitchen, looking in Daniel's angry eyes as she continued her questioning. "Why didn't you bring her over here with you? I would've loved to have seen her."

"She was sleep."

"Sleep? Is she feeling alright?"

"Yeah . . . she just tired from not sleeping last night."

"Not sleeping, you sure she's not sick?"

"Yeah she's just miss momma." Ms. Geraldine again shifted her eyes to Daniel then turned back to Millie Ann. "Daddy said she don't know what she want to do, she cried because she wanted to come live with me and Daddy—now she's crying because she want to go back to Mississippi and live with Momma and Anthony." Daniel turned away when seeing his wife look at him, attempting to observe his reaction. "She just need to get use to living here again, she'll be alright." Millie Ann said repeating her daddy's words.

"How's your momma doing Millie Ann?" Ms. Geraldine asked leading up to her intended conversation.

"She's doing good." Millie Ann unsuspectingly replied. "My Momma's friend Blue was there too when me and Daddy got there."

"He was?" Ms. Geraldine said looking quickly in the kitchen at Daniel, taking pleasure in hearing of Effie Mae and Blue's continued involvement. He ignored her pettiness as he scooped a spoonful of potato salad from the large yellow bowl sitting on the counter, hesitating before putting it in his mouth when sensing her unrelenting gawk. Daniel stared back, aggravated by her spiteful attempt to throw Effie Mae's *love life* in his face.

"Geraldine don't be asking Millie Ann about her momma's business!" Daniel said raising his voice. "What Effie Mae do is her business not yours!" Ms. Geraldine took satisfaction in seeing his obvious hurt. "Stop meddling Geraldine!" Daniel shouted momentarily staring at her before shoving the spoon of potato salad in his mouth then dipping the spoon in the pan of macaroni and cheese on the stove. He removed a spoonful and ate it.

"All I was doing Daniel was asking Millie Ann how her momma was doing." Ms. Geraldine said trying to sound innocent. "How is that meddling?"

"Geraldine you already know when you ask Millie Ann about her momma she gon tell you everything she know." He turned to Millie Ann. "Millie Ann I don't think your momma want you telling Geraldine all her business baby, okay?"

"Okay Mr. Daniel." He stared at his bitter wife then shook his head, displeased with her using Millie Ann for her vindictiveness.

"Let me fix me a plate so I can go out here on this back porch—get away from you and all that mess." Daniel said washing his hands at the kitchen sink before removing a flowered patterned plate from the cupboard, his head pounding in response to Millie Ann's words about her momma and Blue.

"You don't have to do that Daniel . . . I'll fix it." Ms. Geraldine said looking into his contemptuous eyes as she rose from the sofa. He glared at her with fury, his gawk ending when hearing the cry of his toddler son awakening from his nap.

"I'm sure my food's gon taste a whole lot better without having to hear your mouth while I'm eating it!" Daniel stated impatiently waiting for her to fix his plate. Ms. Geraldine looked at him and smirked then turned her attention back to Millie Ann.

"If you want to go get D.J. now Millie Ann go ahead, I'm sure he's ready to eat." Millie Ann hurried from the living room and through the kitchen then down the hallway. Daniel looked his wife with enraged eyes as she entered the kitchen to fix his plate.

"The truth hurts don't it Daniel?" She stated with bitterness. He flashed her a look of resentment then stormed out the back door slamming it.

"He's wet Ms. Geraldine." Millie Ann said startling her when suddenly appearing in the dining room from the hallway carrying her baby brother. "Can I change him?"

"Yeah that's fine Millie Ann, but you watch that little boy—" Ms. Geraldine said dropping three spoons of potato salad on Daniel's plate between the spare ribs and macaroni and cheese. "—because the minute you take his diaper off, that little boy seems to always want to pee." Ms. Geraldine looked over at him. "Don't you D.J.?" He smiled in response to her baby talk then giggled.

"Come on D.J. let me get this wet diaper off you." Millie Ann kissed him on the cheek then hurried back down the hall. Ms. Geraldine dropped a square piece of cornbread on top of Daniel's food and prepared to go out on the back porch. She pushed open the back door and headed over to Daniel. He watched with angry eyes as she approached.

"Here's your food Daniel."

"Why the hell you in there asking Millie Ann about her Momma's business Geraldine?" He asked snatching the plate from her hand. "You don't give a damn about how Effie Mae's doing—we both know that!" Daniel visually inspected his plate to ensure it contained each of the dishes prepared before resuming his chastisement. "You ain't doing nothing but looking for something you think you can hurt me with, that's all."

"Do it hurt Daniel hearing Effie Mae's still seeing Blue?" Ms. Geraldine said taunting him.

"If it did Geraldine I wouldn't tell you."

"You betrayed me for a woman who's in love with another man." She said reminding him of his affair with Effie Mae, a little over a year and a half ago. "That girl probably hasn't thought about you once since she left here."

"Leave me alone Geraldine!" Daniel said giving warning. She continued.

"You around here acting like some love sick teenager—" Ms. Geraldine abruptly silenced when seeing Daniel sit his plate on the chair next to him, a look of fury burning in his eyes.

"Geraldine I ain't ever laid one hand on you!" He said inhaling and exhaling with rage. "But if you don't get the hell out of my face trying to make me feel like a damn fool—" She interjected.

"I'm not the one making you look like a fool Daniel—" Her eyes widened with fear when seeing him swiftly stand to his feet.

"Say one more word Geraldine!" Daniel shouted trying desperately not to strike her. "Say one more damn word!" Ms. Geraldine hurried away, frightened by his volatile demeanor and the sound of wrath in his voice. He watched with incensed eyes as she quickly entered the house, closing the door and locking it—terrified of the possibility of him hurting her.

———————————

Effie Mae fixed Anthony's usual breakfast of toast, coffee and orange juice as he dressed for work in the bedroom. After adjusting his tie, Anthony reached for his briefcase sitting on the dresser and prepared to leave the room. In his haste, he accidentally knocled Effie Mae's purse onto the floor—its contents scattering. He knelt down and began picking up the many items from the floor, stuffing them back inside the purse. His eyes widened and his mouth flung open when seeing a chronologically correct, half empty pack of birth control pills. Anthony quickly retrieved the pack of pills from the floor then stormed from the bedroom and into the kitchen. He vigorously grabbed hold of Effie Mae arm startling her. She looked at him with frightened eyes in response to his painful grasps on her arm and the incensed look in his eyes.

"What the hell is this Effie Mae?" He yelled holding up the pack of pills, clasped in his right hand. "Why would you keep this from me?" He shouted. "I know you said it might take a little time for you to get pregnant, but birth control pills Effie Mae!" Anthony suddenly raised his fist in fury.

"Ahhhhhhh!" Effie Mae cried out in anticipation of his impending blow. He abruptly stopped, lowering his fist and turning away when seeing the look of terror in Effie Mae's eyes.

"So tell me Effie Mae—" He said again facing her. "—were you just going to keep on lying to me, letting me believe you were trying to get pregnant when you had no intentions on us having another child?" Anthony asked, again grabbing her by the arm. She cringed with fear. "Don't you think I had a right to know you were on birth control pills Effie Mae?"

"I'm sorry Blue!" She yelled out, incoherent with fear.

"Blue!" Anthony shouted looking at her in disbelief. "No Effie Mae, I'm not Blue . . . I'm Anthony your fiancé." An increased state of confusion showed in Effie Mae's eyes.

"What? I didn't—" He cut her off.

"Is that who you want to be with Effie Mae—Blue?" Her fear accelerated, terrified by Anthony's out of control temper. He suddenly glanced down at his watch. "Great!" He yelled. "Now I'm running late for work, but you can bet we'll be discussing this when I get home!" Anthony released her arm then clasped hold of her chin staring into her frightened eyes. "That should give you plenty enough time to think of how you're going to explain these!" Effie Mae shifted her eyes to the birth control pills still gripped in his right hand. She watched in fear as he threw them on the floor then returned to the bedroom retrieving his briefcase. He again entered the kitchen stopping directly in front of her looking momentarily at her without speaking before walking out and slamming the door. Effie Mae rushed from the kitchen into the living room and picked up the phone. She called Blue.

"Blue's Jazz Club—"

"Let me speak to Blue!" She yelled into the phone.

"Blue's busy right not Effie Mae."

"What you mean he busy? Tell him it's me Melvin and I need him!" She abruptly hung up. Two minutes later the phone rang. Effie Mae quickly answered.

"Blue!" She burst into tears.

"What's wrong Baby girl?" He asked, alarmed.

"I just needed to hear your voice Blue."

"I'm here Baby girl calm down and tell me what's going on."

"Anthony found my birth control pills Blue."

"Baby girl I thought you said you and Anthony were trying to have another child? How you gon do that if you on the pill?" He asked rationally.

"Who said I wanted another child, Blue!" She screamed.

"Calm down Effie Mae, did you tell Anthony you didn't want another child?"

"What you think Blue?"

"Baby girl you gon have to be honest with that man if you expect for y'all to make it."

"Is that what you want Blue?" Effie Mae shouted. "For me and Anthony to make it? I thought you loved me Blue." She began crying.

"I do Baby girl you know that." Blue's anxiety heightened as he attempted to calm her down. "I just want for you whatever you want —" He began coughing.

"What's wrong with you Blue?" She yelled as his coughing persisted.

"Effie Mae this is Melvin —"

"I don't want to talk to you Melvin, put Blue back on this phone!"

"Blue's gon have to call you back Effie Mae he having another one of them coughing spells."

"You tell Blue he don't ever have to call me ever again!" She screamed into the phone.

"Effie Mae wait —" She slammed down the phone.

# Chapter Five

"I really enjoyed your sermon today Rev. Smith." A well dressed, attractive fortyish female stated flirtatiously as J.R. stood at the front entrance of his church saying his customary farewells to the members of his now sizeable congregation.

"Uh, I'm glad you enjoyed it Ms.—"

"Taylor, but you can call me Yolanda." She batted her eyes. J.R.'s mouth abruptly dried. He coughed.

"Well uh, Ms. Taylor I hope I said something that uh, might have possibly made a difference somewhere in your life." He stated apprehensively.

"It's Yolanda—and you did." She said gazing in his eyes. "Do you mind if I ask you a question Rev. Smith?"

"Uh, question?" J.R. said, uneasy by her seductive approach.

"I see you're wearing a wedding ring, but I've never seen a wife is she deceased?"

"Uh no, my wife is uh, very much alive." J.R.'s mouth again dried. He coughed.

"Is she ill?" Ms. Taylor asked, unconvinced by the gold wedding band displayed on J.R.'s finger.

"Uh ill, no she's not ill."

"Now Mahalia looks like you, but Millie Ann she's a really pretty girl . . . does she look like her mother?"

"Uh yes, as a matter of fact Millie Ann looks just like her momma." A brief smile appeared on J.R.'s face as he thought of Effie Mae.

"I see." Ms. Taylor said continuing to smile as she sized up her competition, deeming J.R.'s alleged wife as a her rival, if indeed she did exist. "I guess you're probably wondering why I'm asking such personal questions." She said flirtatiously. His uneasiness magnified when seeing the starry look in her eyes.

"You uh, are a quite curious?"

"Just a little." She girlishly giggled. "I think you're a very handsome man Rev. Smith, and I guess you can see by me not wearing a wedding ring like you . . . I'm also unattached."

"Daddy when we leaving?" Millie Ann asked startling him as she walked towards him and Ms. Taylor. "Mr. Daniel's coming to pick me and Mahalia up so we can go see D.J."

"Uh, Millie Ann this is Ms. Taylor." J.R. said relieved by her interference.

"Yolanda." Ms. Taylor stated correcting him.

"Did you uh, say hello Millie Ann?"

"Hi Ms. Taylor."

"Hi Millie Ann." A clever look showed on Ms. Taylor's face. "I was just asking your father about your mother—" J.R. intervened.

"Uh, Ms. Taylor—" He said trying to end her intrusiveness. "—it's always good speaking to the members of my congregation and I truly do appreciate the feedback I receive—" She cut him off.

"Just so you know Rev. Smith if you ever need a home cooked meal and a little female companionship—" J.R. shifted his eyes to Millie Ann embarrassed by Ms. Taylor's suggestive words.

"Uh, Millie Ann why don't you uh, go find your sister so we can get ready to leave."

"Okay Daddy." Millie Ann hurried back into the sanctuary in search of Mahalia. Ms. Taylor grabbed hold of J.R.'s hands and gazed into his nervous eyes.

"Uh, Ms. Taylor I uh, don't think—"

"I'm a really good cook Rev. Smith." She stated, softly caressing his hand. "Maybe you can let me cook you dinner one evening." A suggestive smile displayed on her face. "And breakfast the next morning?" J.R.'s eyes widened, stunned by her unexpected offer. She gently squeezed his hand, looking at the ring on his finger. He swiftly pulled his hand away.

"You uh, have a nice evening Ms. Taylor." J.R. said unnerved by the awkward conversation.

"Yolanda."

"Huh?"

"Call me Yolanda." She stated, seductively smiling.

"I uh, guess I'll uh, see you next Sunday—Ms. Taylore." J.R. stated trying to end their uncomfortable chat.

"Yolanda and count on it Rev. Smith." She winked. J.R.'s mouth dreid. He coughed. He watched in awe as Ms. Taylor walked away, looking back at him and waving before exiting the church. J.R. remained frozen as he collected his thoughts.

"That was uh, interesting." He said to himself, rattled by Ms. Taylor's forwardness, yet he somehow felt flattered.

Effie Mae ran from the living room when hearing Anthony insert his key and unlock the door. She rushed in the bedroom and laid on the bed, pretending to be asleep.

"Baby!" Anthony called out as he opened the door and entered. He proceeded to the bedroom when not seeing her in the living room or kitchen. A smile formed on his face when discovering her lying on the bed, her back facing the door. "Baby?" Anthony said, gently shaking her shoulder. Effie Mae remained silently still as he gently pulled her hair away from her shoulder and neck, applying a seductive kiss just below her ear. Effie Mae giggled then turned over and looked into Anthony's smiling face.

"Hi Anthony . . . you still mad at me?" She asked in a childlike manner. He kissed her intimately on the lips.

"A little."

"I'm sorry Anthony, I know I should've told you I was taking birth control pills, but you was so excited and I felt bad about you not being there when Lil' J.R. was born—" He interrupted her with a kiss on the lips.

"No Baby I'm the one who's sorry."

"I didn't mean to lie to you Anthony." Effie Mae said sitting up in bed. Anthony positioned himself next to her, lying her head on his chest. "I thought if I told you the truth—" He cut her off.

"I don't want you to ever think you can't talk to me about anything Baby, okay?" He said placing a light kiss on her forehead.

"Okay Anthony." He looked Effie Mae in the eyes.

"I guess I owe you an apology too Baby."

"For what Anthony?"

"Baby I should've never let myself get so angry that I put my hands on you." Anthony's eyes expressed regret. "When I saw the frightened look in your eyes—" He shook his head with remorse. "—I felt like such a monster!" He again placed a kiss on her forehead. "That's not who I am or who we are." Effie Mae saw sincerity in his eyes. "I am sorry Baby, do you forgive me?" She looked at Anthony and wondered if she could ever trust him again—given his unforeseen display of violence. Effie Mae quickly convinced herself that she could.

"Okay Anthony I forgive you."

"Thank you Baby." They romantically kissed. "Well now that we've gotten that out of the way, I have some good news and some bad news, which one do you want to hear first?" She looked at Anthony with childlike eyes.

"That depends on how bad the bad news is and how good the good news is Anthony." She giggled.

"Well the good news is good and the bad news is bad and getting worse the longer we sit here."

"Anthony!" Effie Mae playfully pushed him. "Just tell me." He placed a quick kiss on her lips.

"Okay Baby." His excitement increased. "Today our firm landed its largest account ever!"

"That sounds good Anthony." Effie Mae said clueless to what Anthony's good news actually meant.

"Baby it's great! And since I'm one of the lead accountants assigned to the account, from now on we're going to be on easy street."

"I ain't really sure what that mean Anthony, but it must be good you seem to be real happy about it."

"I am Baby and all you need to know is that it means more money for me—for us!" Anthony again applied a quick kiss to her lips.

"You said you had some bad news too Anthony."

"Yes Baby I did." Effie Mae tried to read the unreadable look on his face.

"Tell me Anthony!"

"Are you sure you really want to know Baby?" He teased.

"Yeah Anthony tell me!"

"Okay Baby, but remember you asked." Anthony cleverly smiled. "Well to celebrate our firm's great achievement were having a soiree." A puzzled looked appeared on Effie Mae's face.

"A what?"

"A soiree." Anthony repeated. "That's French for a party."

"Then why you just didn't say party Anthony?"

"Now for the bad news—" Effie Mae listened with apprehension, unsure of how bad Anthony's bad news could be. "We're late . . . the party started fifteen minutes ago."

"Anthony, I ain't got nothing to wear to a—" Effie Mae tried to remember the correct pronunciation. "What was that word you said Anthony?"

"Party." He said humored.

"Anthony!" She again playfully pushed him. "That ain't what you said."

"Yes it is Baby."

"No it ain't Anthony." Effie Mae giggled.

"I said our firm was having a soiree—a party."

"So what kind of clothes do you wear to a—"

"Soiree?" He said completing her question. "Don't worry Baby I picked you up something on my way home from work, you'll love it." He silently gazed at her. Effie Mae blushed.

"What Anthony?"

"I have more bad news."

"Anthony!" Effie Mae pouted. "I don't know if I can handle all this bad news but tell me anyway."

"We're going to have to get dressed in Stewart's bathroom once we arrive at his home." A suggestive smile displayed on his face.

"Boy there you go with that smiling again." Effie Mae said blushing. "We don't have time for that do we Anthony?"

"Now that we've kissed and made up and we're already late, a few more minutes won't hurt." Effie Mae looked at him and again blushed.

"A few minutes Anthony?"

"Well, maybe a little more than a few." He looked at his watch. "Why don't I run outside to the car and get your dress and shoes that way you can get dressed right after we uh, you know—" Effie Mae giggled. Anthony hurried from the room and out of the apartment door on his way to his car to retrieve Effie Mae's formal attire.

---

"There you are Anthony!" Stewart said when seeing him and Effie Mae arriving—an hour and fifteen minutes into the celebration. "And who is this lovely lady you have with you?" He asked slightly intoxicated.

"This beautiful woman is my fiancée, Effie Mae." Anthony stated proudly. Stewart extended his right hand while holding an alcoholic drink in his other.

"Well hello Effie Mae!" Her eyes shifted to the glass of liquor held in his hand as they shook. "My name is Stewart and I'm proud to say I'm a colleague of Anthony's." Effie Mae discretely watched as he turned the glass of alcohol up to his mouth and took a swallow. "And I must say Anthony's one of our firm's brightest accountants—in fact, it's due in part to Anthony's genius we're celebrating here today." Effie Mae smiled as she tried to resist her sudden craving for scotch.

"Hey buddy!" Phil, another one of Anthony's associates said as he approached. "We were just about to make a toast." He slurred. "So why don't you and that beautiful gal you have on your arm go ahead and grab a glass of champagne and join us." Effie Mae's anxiety accelerated as she thought of how to respectfully decline Phil's offer—or even if she could.

"Well Baby—" Anthony said turning to her. "—I guess since you're not pregnant a glass of champagne won't hurt." Effie Mae forced a smile as she again elected not to inform him to her alcohol addiction. Anthony took hold of her hand, escorting her over to the bar located in the rear of the sizeable, elegantly decorated dining room radiating with the delightful smell of hors d' oeuvres. Effie Mae's eyes visually searched the various types of liquor stocked in the bar to include several bottles of scotch then shifted her eyes to the hired bartender as he poured both her and Anthony a glass of champagne. Her stomach bundled with nerves as she and Anthony picked up their glasses and returned to the enormous living room where his many colleagues and their spouses awaited their arrival—all slightly inebriated.

"A toast!" Phil said raising his glass. "To Chapman & Hill on its success in obtaining one of our largest accounts in the history of the firm."

"Here, here!" Stewart second. Effie Mae looked around the room as the multitude of glasses turned up to the mouths of its holders. She watched as Anthony too raised his glass of champagne and drank.

"Go ahead Baby—drink." He stated when seeing her glass still full. "One glass of champagne won't hurt." Effie Mae forced a smile as she looked in Anthony's urging eyes, hesitating before turning the glass up to her mouth—consuming its contents.

"You don't mind if I steal your fiancé for second do you Effie Mae?" Stewart asked tugging on Anthony's arm.

"I'll be right back Baby." Anthony kissed her quickly on the lips. "Go mingle."

"Anthony don't—"

"I won't be long." He said giving her a smooch on the lips. Effie Mae watched with frightened eyes as he walked away with Stewart being accompanied by two other men from the firm, all congregating in a corner to discuss business. She looked around the people-filled room, everyone seemingly drinking alcohol. Effie Mae again shifted her eyes to Anthony as her craving for scotch grew and her resistance diminished. She slowly walked in the direction of the bar, driven by her alcohol addiction. She again look over at Anthony, still deep in conversation then resumed her journey across the room ending at the bar—and the scotch.

"Can I get you something ma'am?" The bartender asked as Effie Mae approached. "Another glass of champagne?" Her locked onto the bottles of scotch.

"Scotch."Effie Mae stated—her mouth slightly watering.

"One scotch coming up." The bartender stated. Effie Mae watched with eagerness as he opened a bottle of scotch and poured the brownish colored liquid in a shot glass, placing it in front of her. Her hand slightly trembled as she picked it up and quickly emptied its contents into her mouth.

"I guess you must really be thirsty." The bartender joked. "Would you like a refill?"

• • • •

"Well Stew—" Anthony said looking at his watch, realizing it had been forty minutes since he'd abandoned Effie Mae. "—I guess I'd better rejoin my fiancée."

"Okay Anthony, but be sure to follow-up with me on that concept tomorrow at the office."

"Stew . . . you've seen my beautiful fiancée." A cunning smile formed on Anthony's face. "She's only here for a week, how about we discuss that first thing Monday morning?" Stewart grinned and winked.

"Monday morning's fine Anthony—"

"Anthony." Phil said as he staggered over.

"Yes Phil?"

"It looks like your fiancée's having a little difficulty handling her liquor."

"Effie Mae's not exactly a drinker—" Anthony stated with confidence. "—but I'm sure she should be able to handle a glass or two of champagne." Phil burst into laughter.

"Champagne! She's drinking something a lot stronger than champagne." He slurred. "Hell the bartender said she's already drank half a bottle of scotch." Anthony's jaw dropped.

"Are you sure Phil?" He asked visually searching the crowded room for Effie Mae's whereabouts. "I've never known Effie Mae to drink anything stronger than root beer, so I couldn't imagine her drinking something as strong as scotch?" Anthony stated skeptical of Phil's report. His eyes suddenly widened when seeing Effie Mae intimately embraced in a corner of the room with his drunken colleague Chuck. Anthony watched in horror as the two engaged in cheek to cheek dancing—Effie Mae's arms seductively wrapped around Chuck's neck as his lips sporadically kissed her on the shoulders and ears.

"Excuse me Stew—" Anthony said embarrassed and upset by Effie Mae's behavior. "—I think perhaps I need to go rescue my fiancée." He said swiftly walking away in pursuit of a drunken Effie Mae. "Baby?" Anthony said removing her arms from around Chuck's neck. "Let's go Baby."

"Hey Anthony!" She said attempting to again embrace Chuck as he continued slow dancing by himself. Anthony took hold of Effie Mae's reaching arms as she tried for a second time to rejoin her dance partner.

"Come on Baby it's time to go." Anthony said seeing his colleagues and their spouses watching as Effie Mae for a third time reached for Chuck. "No, no Baby—no more dancing we're leaving."

"No Anthony I ain't ready to leave!" She said raising her voice. "I want to stay here at the soiree." A proud look showed on Effie Mae's face. "See Anthony I even said it right this time." She said slurring her words thenlosing her balance. Anthony quickly caught hold of her arm breaking her fall.

"Get your hands off me Blue!" She shouted, snatching her arm and pulling away. He stared at her—lost for words when hearing her again reference to him as Blue. He glanced around the room, looking in the gaping eyes of his peers, all focused on his drunken, out of control fiancée.

"Effie Mae—baby it's me Anthony." He said trying to contain his anger. "Come on Baby I'm getting a little tired and I want to go home so we can go to bed and I need you there to tuck me in okay." He kissed her lightly on the lips. Effie Mae smiled.

"You love me Anthony?"

"Yes Baby—now let's go." A seductive smile displayed on her face.

"Are we gon have a good time when we get home Anthony?"

"Don't we always—" He shifted his eyes to his colleagues and half-heartedly smiled, humiliated by Effie Mae's unacceptable behavior. Anthony again turned to her. "—but we have to get there first Baby." He firmly took hold of her arm. "Well goodnight everybody." Anthony said masking his shame.

"She's going to have one hell of a hangover in the morning!" Phil hollered out.

"Do you need help getting her out to the car Anthony?" Stewart asked.

"No, we'll be fine but thanks for offering Stew." Anthony put his arm around Effie Mae and escorted her out the door.

• • • •

Anthony stood next to the bed the following morning and watched Effie Mae as she slept, not yet awakened from her over indulgence on scotch.

"Effie Mae!" He called out. She slowly rolled over on her back, gradually opening her eyes.

"Hey Anthony." He stared at her trying to hold back his rage.

"Baby, do you remember anything about last night?"

"Last night?"

"Yes Baby—yesterday."

"I remember meeting some of your friends Anthony." She said feeling the effects of her hangover as she tried to remember. "And drinking some champagne?" Effie Mae's stomach bundled with nerves as she noted the wrath in Anthony's eyes. "But from the way you looking at me I guess I must've had too much of it."

"Champagne? No Baby—not champagne." Effie Mae slightly cringed as she waited to hear the outcome of the soiree. "It wasn't the champagne Effie Mae." Her heart pounded in her chest. "It was that half bottle of scotch you drank when I stepped away for only a few minutes to speak with my colleagues—" Anthony raised his voice. "—people I have to work with everyday!" He shouted. Her mouth slightly opened as fear entered her reddened eyes, frightened by Anthony's growing rage.

"Scotch? I didn't drink no scotch Anthony." Effie Mae said with uncertainty.

"Yes Baby you did." Her eyes drew to her suitcases sitting by the bedroom door. "Yes Effie Mae you're going home."

"Why Anthony?" She asked innocently. "I don't want to go home, I'm sor—" He cut her off.

"I think it's best that you do."

"I want to stay here with you Anthony."

"I don't think that's a good idea Effie Mae."

"Why? What I do—tell me?" He momentarily stared at her.

"I think you first need to figure out who I am!"

"Huh?"

"Last night was the second time in one day you called me Blue." She looked at him with tear-filled eyes.

"I didn't call you Blue, Anthony."

"Yes Effie Mae, you did." He looked over at her luggage. "I think you need to go back home and decide if it's me you want to be with or Blue." Effie Mae looked at him with confused eyes. "Get up!" He yelled.

"Noooo Anthony!" Tears ran down Effie Mae's face. "I don't want to go back home . . . I'm sorry Anthony."

"Get up—I'm taking you home!"

"I want you Anthony not Blue."

"Get up Effie Mae!" Anthony demanded." He watched as she climbed out of bed and headed towards the bathroom. "Don't worry about bathing." He stated eager for her to leave. She looked at him with defiance. "I think the sooner you're out of here the better." Effie Mae ignored Anthony's bitter words as she entered the bathroom and slammed the door.

---

Blue stood on stage at the jazz club playing his saxophone during an afternoon practice session with his band members. Ten minutes into the session he began coughing nonstop. His horn dropped from his hand as he gasped for air and the room appeared to be spinning. He tumbled over onto the bass guitar player standing to his left, collapsing. The bass guitarist quickly caught Blue, breaking his fall, lowering him onto the floor.

"Somebody call an ambulance!" He shouted, kneeling at Blue's side, his guitar still strapped over his shoulder. "Blue passed out!" Melvin rushed from the kitchen in response to the call for help. He hurried over to the bar area and picked up the phone up off the counter and called the operator.

"We need an ambulance down here at Blue's Jazz Club!" Melvin shouted in the phone, panicked. "My cousin Tyrell Jones just passed out—hurry!" He hung up then rushed over to Blue. "Man what happened?" Melvin asked frightened. The base saxophonist shook his head and humped his shoulders indicating he had no idea.

"He just fell man!" The bass guitarist stated—his forearms still supporting Blue's upper body. Melvin looked helplessly down at his motionless cousin and watched as Blue appeared to be clinging on to life through the shallow breaths he took.

---

Effie Mae stood at the mailbox gathering yesterday's mail after seeing her children off to school. She flipped through the multitude of envelops that mainly consisted of bills. Her attention drew to the large white, oblong envelope with the name of an attorney's office in New York City. She also noted an envelope sent from Daniel.

"Effie Mae?" She looked up, startled by a man's voice coming from inside of a red Ford Mustang, recognizing the driver as Kenny. "You living back here now girl?"

"Yeah Kenny I am." Effie Mae said as her eyes locked onto the mysterious white envelope.

"Is this where you live?" He asked looking around to see if she was alone.

"Yeah Kenny it is." She stated gently rubbing her fingers across the letter from Daniel exploring the contents of the closed envelope through touch. Her responses to Kenny's probing words, minimal.

"Who you live here with your husband?"

"What?" She said distracted by the two pieces of mail. "What you ask me Kenny?"

"I'm glad I ran into you." A huge smile stretched across his face. "Some of the kids we went to school with having a barbecue tonight." His eyes slowly explored her body. "If you and your husband ain't busy maybe y'all can stop by—"

"My husband?" Effie Mae looked up and into Kenny's roaming eyes and lustful smile. "Oh, you mean Anthony?" Her curiosity grew as she again turned her attention to the letters examining the square shaped object in the envelope sent from Daniel.

"Anthony? Is that your husband's name?"

"I can't Kenny—Anthony works in Jackson and he don't come home until the weekend." Effie Mae said as her mind remained occupied on the two envelopes.

"Then you can come with me." Kenny stated flirtatiously.

"Anthony call me every night and if I ain't here—"

"So it's like that huh?" He cunningly grinned. "I can understand that fine as you are." Kenny's white teeth highlighted the enormous smile on his face. "If you was my woman I'd keep tabs on you too." He said continuing to grin.

"Plus Kenny, I got four babies I got to feed and put to bed when they get home from school." Effie Mae again fixated on the letter from the New York attorney.

"Well here—" Kenny said searching inside his car for something to write on. "—let me give you my number in case you change your mind after you get your babies to sleep." He chuckled. "We gon be there late into the night anyway so—" He picked up a matchbook from the Cozi-T Motel lying on the seat and jotted his number on the cover. "Here you go." Effie Mae reached inside the car and removed the matchbook from his hand without looking at it.

"It was good seeing you again Kenny." She said resuming her gaze at the large white envelop.

"I still got that sheet if you want it." He seductively smiled as he locked his eyes on her upper body. "But if you want it—" He cunningly grinned. "—girl you gon have to come get it!" Kenny's smile widened.

"Bye Kenny." Effie Mae said turning her attention from the white envelope, back to the letter from Daniel.

"Bye Effie Mae." Kenny stared at her—smiling. "Oh, if I ain't at that number when you call just leave a message I'll get it." He watched with anticipation as Effie Mae walked away. His mind racing as he thought of how he'd seduce her into a night of intimacy. He cleverly grinned then sped away. Effie Mae's eyes remained fixated on the mail as she stepped on the porch and again entered the house, dropping the additional pieces of mail on the coffee table before opening the envelope from the attorney's office. She reached inside and slid the multitude of papers out looking them over. Her eyes moistened with tears when identifying the documents as divorce papers from J.R. Effie Mae hurriedly picked up the phone and frantically called him.

"Hello."

"You don't want me no more J.R.?" She yelled into the phone. He assumed she'd received the divorce papers.

"What?"

"You heard me!" She said weeping. "You don't want me no more?"

"Effie Mae you were the one who wanted—"

"You go to hell J.R.!"

"Effie Mae if you uh, want to hold off on the divorce we can wait—" She cut him off.

"First Anthony then Blue—now you!" She continued sobbing. "I don't care if don't none of y'all don't want me!" She yelled. "All y'all can go to hell—"

"Effie Mae what's going on—you and Anthony having problems?" J.R. asked trying to understand her rage.

"Don't you worry about what's going on with Effie Mae Reed." She shouted.

"Effie Mae are you drinking?"

"I bet you one thing J.R. Smith—" Effie Mae said ignoring his question. "—I bet you Huck still want me."

"Effie Mae do I need to come get my children?"

"You stay away from me and my babies J.R.!" She screamed.

"Effie Mae go talk to Ms. Millie—" She slammed down the phone, tossing the legal documents from her hand—they scattered onto the floor. J.R. repeatedly called back worried about her fragile state of mind. Effie Mae stared at the ringing phone, refusing to answer. She hurried over to the coffee table and picked up the letter from Daniel, ripping it open—it's contents falling on the floor. She clasped her hand over her mouth when seeing a picture of Daniel holding D.J. in his arms.

"Give me my baby!" Effie Mae cried out, dropping to her knees, hysterically weeping. She crawled over to the phone—the photo of her baby boy held against her heart. Effie Mae snatched the phone off its base and called Blue.

"Blue's Jazz Club—Melvin speaking."

"Melvin this is Effie Mae, I called Blue two weeks ago why he ain't calling me back—did you even give him my message?"

"Blue ain't here right now Effie Mae he's—"

"What you mean he ain't there?" She yelled. "He live there!" Melvin hesitated.

"Effie Mae I need to talk to—"

"I don't want to talk to you Melvin I need Blue!" She shouted. "Tell him to come get me—take me away from this place!"

"Effie Mae, Tyrell's in the hosp—" Effie Mae slammed down the phone. "Effie Mae!" Melvin called out trying to tell her about Blue's recent illness. "Effie Mae—hello!"

"Where you at Blue?" She said sobbing. "I need you." She slowly got up off the floor then briskly swept her right hand across the coffee table, thrusting the items on top onto the floor, including the mail she'd just brought in. Effie Mae looked down at the strewn documents from J.R.'s attorney. "You go to hell J.R.—you think I'm drinking then that's just what I'm gon do." She looked around the living room. "I know Anthony got something around here I can drink." She said talking to herself as she dragged the oblong sofa pillow off onto the floor. "Well I guess it ain't nothing under there." She half-heartedly laughed then walked over to the floor model color television in front of the window and blew at it. "Look at all that dust!" Effie Mae said thinking out loud. "Sending me back here to live in this dusty house . . . he need to come clean this place up!" She screamed walking away and entering the kitchen. She snatched open the refrigerator, hoping to find a beverage containing alcohol. She knelt down and explored both shelves, discovering a bottle of red wine tucked away on the very bottom shelf in a back corner. "They don't have to want me, none of them!"

Effie Mae stated walking over to the cupboard, pulling open the multitude of kitchen drawers, rummaging through Anthony's neatly arranged silverware tossing forks, spoons and knives onto the floor before finding a cork screw. She stabbed the corkscrew into the cork and vigorously twisting and pulling until it finally popped.

"What you got to say now J.R. Smith?" Effie Mae said continuing her self talk as she raised the bottle of red wine up to her lips, emptying its entire contents into her mouth. She dropped the bottle in the sink then returned to the living room slightly inebriated but not yet drunk.

"Let me call Kenny tell him I'm going to this barbeque with him." Effie Mae staggered around the living room in search of the matchbook, finding it lying on top of the fallen mail. "There it is." She picked the matchbook up and dialed Kenny's number.

"Hey Kenny!" She slurred.

"Effie Mae?" He said smiling with delighted. "Girl is that you?"

"Yeah Kenny it's Effie Mae Reed." His lustful smile widened. "What time did you say that party was?"

"It don't start until around seven, but if you want to hang out with me before then—"

"Come get me Kenny."

"Girl I'm on my way!"

"Bye Kenny." Effie Mae hung up then stumbled out the front door, staggering down the stairs as she headed across the street to Ms. Dawson's house. She stepped up on the front porch and began pounding on the door. Ms. Dawson hurried in the living room and peeped out of her curtains. Her eyes widened when seeing Effie Mae standing at the door slightly unbalanced. She cracked open the door, curious of Effie Mae's unexpected visit and unsteady gait.

"Did you need something Effie Mae?" Ms. Dawson asked looking at her with suspiciousness.

"How you doing Ms. Dawson?"

"I'm doing fine Effie Mae, how you doing?" Ms. Dawson asked grimacing from the smell of alcohol radiating from Effie Mae's breath.

"Right now Ms. Dawson I don't know how I'm doing." Effie Mae said slurring. She observed Effie Mae's effort in trying to maintain her balance.

"Is everything alright Effie Mae?"

"Nope." Effie Mae giggled. "It sure ain't."

"You need me to call Anthony or Ms. Millie?"

"Nope." Effie Mae said looking into Ms. Dawson's judgmental eyes. "I need you to see 'bout my babies when they get home from school — and keep them." A peculiar look appeared on Ms. Dawson's face.

"Keep them?" Effie Mae half-heartedly laughed.

"I mean watch my babies and — stay all night with you?"

"You know I don't mind letting them youngins stay over here Effie Mae —" Ms. Dawson said curious of Effie Mae's reason for needing her to watch the children. " — you and Anthony going somewhere?" She asked noticing Effie Mae's reddened eyes. "I was only asking, you know, just in case I need to reach you."

"Call my momma!"

"Okay Effie Mae, but —"

"Thank you Ms. Dawson." Effie Mae stumbled off the porch and again crossed the streets, faltering as she stepped back on her porch. Ms. Dawson watched with suspicious eyes as Effie Mae entered the house.

"Poor Anthony, he outta to take that piece of mess right back to wherever he got her from."

• • • •

Ms. Dawson hurried to her living room window twenty minutes later when hearing the sound of a honking horn out front. Her jaw dropped when peeping through the drapes, seeing Effie Mae's risqué apparel. She scowled.

"Lord have mercy Poor Anthony . . . look like I'm gon need to give Betsy a call let her know about this mess her son done moved in his house." She shook her head with disgust. "Gal ain't nothing but a Jezebel."

Kenny gawked with pleasure as Effie Mae walked towards his car wearing a short red striped skirt, red sleeveless button down blouse and a pair of red high heel shoes, highlighted by the black fishnet stockings she wore. He reached over and opened the passenger side door — his eyes fixated on her thighs exposed from underneath the hip high skirt.

"Thank you Kenny." Effie Mae said climbing in and closing the door.

"Uh-uh, thank you!" Kenny replied through the huge smile on his face. Ms. Dawson watched in awe as the red car sped away — with Effie Mae.

_____

"Effie Mae!" Millie shouted standing over her as she lay passed out drunk on the living room floor, the lower half of her body draped with a sheet. Effie Mae slowly opened her eyes, looking in the furious face of her momma.

"Momma?" She said hung over. "What time is it?"

"It's time for you to call J.R. and tell him to come get his children before you do something, gon bring you more trouble than you can bear."

"What you doing here Momma? Did Ms. Dawson call you?"

"What's wrong with you child? Dragging in here last night so drunk you like to been scared that poor woman half to death!" Millie yelled. "And who was that you brought up in this boy's house—got him staying in here with you all night?"

"What? Ain't nobody stayed in here with me last night Momma." Effie Mae said trying to recollect last night's events. "Kenny brought me back here after the party then he went home."

"Kenny?"

"Yeah Momma you remember Kenny don't you? We went to school together."

"He went home alright, after he'd done had his way with you." Millie raised an eyebrow.

"Who told you that Momma?"

"Ms. Dawson called me—said she saw a man leaving out this boy's house this morning around sun-up—"

"What?"

"Said the man had to pick you up off the porch last night and carry you in the house being you couldn't seem stand on your own two feet!"

"She wrong Momma." Effie Mae said unsure. "I ain't done nothing with Kenny."

"How you know Effie Mae?" Millie's attention suddenly drew to the sheet covering Effie Mae. "Is that my sheet?" Effie Mae gave no reply as she tried to recall exactly what happened after her and Kenny arrived at the party. "Was you so drunk child you don't know who done what—" Millie silenced when seeing Effie Mae's red skirt shoved underneath the four-legged end table—her panties wrapped partially inside.

"Look underneath that sheet—" Millie said certain her accusations about Kenny was right. "—that ought to tell you just what Kenny done or didn't do while you was laid up in here drunk out your mind." Effie Mae's mouth flung open as she peeped underneath the sheet.

"Momma that boy had his way with me!" Millie raised an eyebrow.

"Let's just hope he ain't get you pregnant."

"I'm on the pill Momma."

"The pill?" A confused look formed on Millie's face. "I thought you told me you and Betsy Lewis' boy was trying to have another child Effie Mae."

"That's a long story Momma." Effie Mae said giving no further details. "Well if Kenny did have me at least I know somebody want me." Millie's eyes widened.

"What you talking 'bout child? Anthony want you or you wouldn't be staying in here in this boy's housem especially after the way you shamed him in front of them folks he work with."

"Do he, Momma?" Effie Mae rose from the floor covering the bottom half of her body with the sheet then walked over and sat down on the sofa. "Right now Momma, Anthony so mad at me—" Millie interjected.

"What you expect Effie Mae—you embarrassed that man!"

"It ain't that Momma, he found my pills." Millie shook her head in frustration, bothered by her eldest daughter's dishonesty.

"Why didn't you just tell that man you was on them pill Effie Mae?"

"If Anthony hadn't been going through my purse he would've never found them pills in the first place." Millie listened, disappointed to hear Effie Mae placing blame on somebody other than herself.

"Momma my baby ain't even a year old yet, and—" Effie Mae silenced when realizing she'd disclosed her secret regarding D.J.

"Baby? What baby child?" Effie Mae looked into her momma's inquiring eyes, momentarily lost for words.

"Momma I got a baby boy in New York—" Millie gasped then lowered herself into Anthony's recliner. "—and I don't even know if he mine or not." A confused look formed in Millie's eyes.

" Effie Mae . . . child is you still drunk? Cause what you saying ain't making a bit of sense!"

"Naw Momma I ain't drunk." Guilt showed in Effie Mae's eyes. "You asked me about D.J. when me and J.R. came here looking for Anthony—"

"And I recall you saying that boy was J.R.'s cousin's child."

"He is Momma—" Effie Mae hesitated, fearing her momma's judgment.

"I don't understand what you saying then Effie Mae."

"Mr. Daniel's D.J.'s daddy, and I'm that boy's momma." Millie's jaw dropped. She gasped.

"Effie Mae!" She said unable to close her mouth, stunned by Effie Mae's lack of judgment.

"Momma, me and Mr. Daniel got together—" Millie interjected, frowning.

"What you mean y'all got together?"

"You know Momma." Millie thought for a second and gasped.

"Effie Mae ain't that man got a wife?"

"Yeah Momma—Ms. Geraldine." Effie Mae's eyes slowly watered. "Momma that woman stole my baby."

"Stole your baby—what you mean she stole your baby Effie Mae?"

"She did Momma!" Effie Mae said wiping her tears with the sheet. "Right after Ms. Ida had done pulled that boy out of me, Ms. Geraldine stole him—" Millie interjected.

"Stole him?" She said raising her voice, troubled by Effie Mae's unclear statement. "What you mean she stole him? I ain't understanding you Effie Mae!"

"She gave Ms. Ida money to say he was my baby boy's momma, and Ms. Ida done what she told her—putting Ms. Geraldine's name on my baby boy's birth record." Millie sensed Effie Mae's hurt. "And then Momma that woman wouldn't even let me go near my baby boy." Millie remained silent as she thought how Effie Mae had once again brought unnecessary chaos into her life.

"Do J.R. know about your child with Mr. Daniel?"

"Yeah Momma he know." Effie Mae again wiped her tears with the sheet then looked at Millie with remorseful eyes. "But you know how J.R. is Momma."

"That man loves you Effie Mae."

"I know that Momma." Effie Mae suddenly laughed.

"I wished you'd tell me what's so funny?" Millie said upset by her out of place laughter.

"I ain't laughing 'bout that Momma." Effie Mae continued chuckling. "I was just thinking how J.R. still ain't speaking to Mr. Daniel because of that." Millie looked at her, unamused. "If it wasn't for my friend Huck telling Mr. Daniel he was gon kill Ms. Geraldine—" Millie gasped.

"Kill her!"

"Huck wasn't really gon kill Ms. Geraldine, Momma." Effie Mae giggled. "But he was gon hurt her." Millie's jaw dropped.

"I may be just a old country woman Effie Mae, but I ain't stupid . . . if your friend Huck said he was gon kill that woman that's exactly what he planned on doing."

"She shouldn't have took my baby from me Momma then kept me from seeing my baby boy." Effie Mae stated in defense of Huck's criminal behavior. "Momma that woman called a Social Worker on me and they wouldn't let me see none of my babies!"

"Can you blame her Effie Mae?" Millie said sympathizing with Ms. Geraldine. "You gave birth to that woman's husband child!"

"I know that Momma, but still—" Millie cut her off.

"You hurt that woman Effie Mae."

"I know that Momma but—"

"Ain't no but about it!" Millie chastised. "You laid down with that woman's husband and got up with his son."

"I know that Momma." Effie Mae's sadness increased in response to her momma's lack of support.

"That's got to be one of the worse kinds of hurt a woman can have." Effie Mae lowered her head with guilt. "But keeping that child from you ain't no way for one woman to be acting towards another—even if it is a husband child."

"I know Momma that's why Huck did what he done." A concerned look displayed on Millie's face.

"What kind of person is this Huck anyway? Sounds like somebody you don't need to be running around with."

"You should've seen Mr. Daniel and Ms. Geraldine, Momma—" Effie Mae laughed. "—Huck like to been scared the life out of both of them!"

"Talk like that would scare anybody halfway got any sense."

"They should've never tried to keep me from baby boy, Momma." Millie shook her head in response to the look of satisfaction on Effie Mae's face. "Maybe one day Momma you can meet my friend Huck." Millie's eyes widened.

"Meet him? I hope not." Effie Mae giggled.

"I know Huck can be a little dangerous Momma, especially when it came to Blue—"

"Your friend Huck sound like some kind of gangster to me."

"Momma Huck ain't no gangster." Effie Mae said electing not to tell her momma of her near death experience at the brutal hands of Huck. "Huck wasn't doing nothing but looking out for me."

"You don't need nobody looking out for you in that way."

"Mr. Daniel sent me a picture of my baby boy Momma." Effie Mae said redirecting the conversation from Huck. A warm smile formed on Millie's face.

"He did?"

"I guess he thought I was gon be happy seeing it—" Effie Mae's eyes moistened. "—but all that done was made me miss my baby boy even more." She lowered her head. "Then all I could think about Momma was drinking—scotch." Effie Mae's eyes suddenly lit up. "You want to see my baby boy Momma?"

"Awww Effie Mae I sure would." Effie Mae looked down at the sheet covering her naked bottom half.

"Momma you gon have to get me my purse." Millie raised an eyebrow.

"Where is it child?"

"I hope it's over there under the table with my clothes."

"Let's just hope Kenny didn't leave here with that too." Millie again raised an eyebrow. She rose from the recliner and walked over to the end table then picked up the skirt seeing Effie Mae's purse lying underneath. "Look like Kenny took only what he came here for—you." Millie handed Effie Mae the purse then sat next to her on the sofa. Effie Mae's excitement heightened as she removed the photo, looking at it before handing it to Millie. A grandmotherly smile spread across Millie's face as she admired the grandson she never knew existed.

"Awww Effie Mae, look at this beautiful baby." A puzzled look formed on Millie's face. "This old man holding him is that Mr. Daniel?"

"Yeah Momma that's him."

"Child how old is that man?"

"I don't know Momma, I guess he probably 'bout Ms. Sissy's age." Millie raised both eyebrows.

"He a good looking man, but he too old for you."

"Momma!" Effie Mae looked at her, surprised by her statement. "I didn't know you looked at men like that."

"Why not? I'm still a woman ain't I?" Millie grinned. "I may be a old woman but I ain't too old to appreciate a good looking man." She giggled.

"I want my baby Momma."

"Have you talked to Mr. Daniel about that Effie Mae?"

"As long as Ms. Geraldine's alive he ain't gon let me have my baby boy, Momma."

"I'd advise you not to say in front of your friend Huck." Millie raised an eyebrow. Effie Mae chuckled then lowered her eyes in despair.

"What am I gon do Momma?"

"Keep your friend Huck away from Mr. Daniel and his wife!" Effie Mae giggled. A smile remained on Millie's face as she continued to admiring her grandson. "Only thing I can say Effie Mae . . . that's a question you should've thought about before you laid down with that woman's husband." Millie paused. "And your husband's cousin."

# Chapter Six

Blue lay in the hospital medically sedated—an IV in his arm and an air mask covering his mouth and nose. Huck and Buckeye entered his room. Huck walked over and looked down upon his half brother then shook his head, fighting back his tears.

"Huck man you gon be alright?" Buckeye asked when seeing his old friend's emotional state diminishing.

"Yeah Buckeye, I'm alright." He said reaching over, taking hold of Blue's hand. "I know I never told you this Buckeye, but Blue's my half brother." Buckeye eyes widened.

"He's your what man?" Buckeye said raising his voice, shocked by his old friend's admission. "Man I had to stop you from killing that man one night—now you telling me he's your brother?"

"Naw Buckeye I wasn't gon kill him." Huck lightly chuckled. "Daddy would've killed me if I'd done that." He said shifting his eyes to Buckeye then back to Blue. "Blue's Daddy's favorite . . . the son he loves."

"Huck man I'm sorry about—"

"Ain't no point in worrying about all that Buckeye." Huck gently squeezed Blue's hand as his eyes moistened with tears. "Daddy married Momma—stayed with her because she was pretty, didn't want nobody else to have her." Huck shook his head with displeasure. "But Tyrell's momma—Ms. Jones, she was the woman Daddy really loved." Huck shifted his eyes over to Buckeye then turned his attention again to Blue. "Ms. Jones wasn't the best looking woman in the world, but Daddy didn't care, he loved him some Ms. Jones." Huck half-heartedly grinned. "But because Momma loved a man that didn't love her in the least, it led her to that bottle." He again turned to Buckeye. "On Effie Mae's drunkest days Buckeye, she couldn't out drink Momma." Buckeye's jaw dropped.

"Damn!" Huck man we grew up together and I never even knew Ms. Rita even drank."

"How often did you see my momma, Buckeye?"

"Not that often."

"You ever wonder why?"

"I always thought she was working."

"Yeah Momma was working alright—working on that bottle of scotch." Buckeye's jaw again dropped. "And whenever she got drunk she started in on me." Buckeye listened with an open mouth. "I don't know if you remember Buckeye, but I look just like my momma—"

"Yeah man I remember"A huge smile formed on Buckeye's face. "Ms. Rita was fine!" He said continuing to smile. "Man I had the biggest crush on your momma!" Huck tilted his head and grinned.

"Is that right?"

"Yeah." Buckeye cunningly grinned. "Ms. Rita was real easy on the eyes—I thought I was gon grow up and be your daddy man!" They both laughed.

"Yeah Buckeye a lot of my friends had a crush on Momma." Huck stated. "But me looking like Momma wasn't always a good thing." He recalled his childhood. "Momma hated herself and she hated me for reminding her of herself." Buckeye looked at his old friend with pity.

"Huck man I didn't know—" Huck cut him off.

"Don't worry about it Buckeye the damage already been done." He looked Buckeye in the eyes then turned back to Blue. "And I'm it." Huck again glanced over at his old friend. "I guess deep down inside Buckeye I envied Ol' Blue." Tears rolled down Huck's face. "He had a momma and daddy—my daddy, and Henry Lee White Sr. loved his son Tyrell Lee Jones." Buckeye listened, sympathetic to Huck's hurt, but surprised to hear him reveal his heartfelt story. "I think sometimes I even hated Ol' Blue for that—" Buckeye interrupted.

"I know it ain't right man, but I can understand how you could feel that way." Huck shook his head with regret then turned to Blue.

"But I never wanted this."

———————————

J.R. watched from the back door as Daniel drove up to the curve and parked. His curiosity peaked when seeing him get out of the car and began walking towards the house, stepping up on the porch and ending his journey at the back door. The two men stared one to the other on opposite sides of the screened door.

"Ahem!" Daniel cleared his throat. "How you doing J.R.?"

"Cousin Daniel." J.R. said showing little emotion. Daniel looked at him loss for words trying to swallow as his mouth quickly dried.

"I thought it was time we talked." Daniel said as his anxiety magnified. "But now—" He nervously chuckled. "—I don't know what to say to you J.R."

"Maybe you can start by explaining why you laid down in bed with my wife." Daniel lowered his eyes with guilt, he slowly looked at J.R.

"Can I come in?" J.R. glared at his disloyal cousin then stepped aside allowing him to enter.

"Millie Ann!"

"Huh Daddy?"

"Cousin Daniel's here." J.R. said continuing his eye to eye gawk with his cousin. "Why don't you and uh, Mahalia go out to the car and wait for him there so we can talk." Daniel's heart pounded in anticipation of answering J.R.'s unexpected question.

"Okay Daddy." Millie Ann hurried from her bedroom and entered the kitchen. "Hi Mr. Daniel!" She said hugging him.

"Hey Millie Ann . . . the doors are already unlocked, I'll be right out."

"Okay." Millie Ann hugged her daddy. "Bye Daddy!"

"Bye Millie Ann." He watched, smiling as his eldest daughter pushed open the back door then headed for Daniel's car. J.R.'s attention shifted to Mahalia as she entered the kitchen.

"Hi Mr. Daniel!"

"Hey baby you coming over to the house too?" He hugged her.

"Yeah."

"Geraldine's sure gon love seeing you." A cheerful smile appeared on Daniel's face. "She got Sunday dinner already cooked and waiting."

"Oooh!" Mahalia rushing out the door, hurrying down the sidewalk to join her big sister.

"Slow down Mahalia." J.R. yelled.

"Okay, Bye Daddy."

"Bye Mahalia." Fatherly pride displayed on J.R.'s face. His attention again turned to Daniel.

"Geraldine know she loves having those girls come over." Daniel said chuckling. J.R. gave no reply as he waited to hear his cousin's reasoning for his adulterous affair with his wife. A lump formed in Daniel's throat in response to J.R. quietness.

"You know J.R.—" Daniel swallowed the seemingly growing lump in his throat. "—answering that question ain't that simple." He nervously scratched his head. "I guess I could always say I'm sorry J.R.—and I am." Daniel noted the hurt look in J.R.'s eyes. "But—" J.R. cut him off.

"But what Cousin Daniel?"

"What happened between me and Effie Mae was just me giving into lust." He shook his head with remorse. "I knew it was wrong J.R., but—"

"But what Cousin Daniel?"

"Ain't nothing I can say or do gon ever make up for how I hurt you and Geraldine." Daniel's eyes momentarily displayed a hint of guilt. "And if you want to hit me I won't try and stop you."

"Hit you?" J.R. said puzzled by the volatile offer. "Why would I want to hit you Cousin Daniel?"

"I hate things happened the way they did J.R., but I'd be lying if I said I regretted it." J.R.'s mouth flung open—he found himself unable to speak. "Truth is, I wouldn't change it if I could." J.R.'s mouth dried. He coughed then turned and walked away. He stared angrily out the back door, looking at his daughter's waiting in their cousin Daniel's car as he resisted the urge to take his cousin up on his offer to throw a right punch.

"Don't keep my daughters waiting." J.R. said turning briefly to his cousin then again looking out the back door. The house filled with silence as J.R. prayed within himself before he again faced his remorseless cousin. "As a man how I feel right now—" J.R. took a deep breath. "—I could tear you apart for climbing in bed with my wife."

Daniel squinted then raised his hands in defense as J.R. walked towards him.

"Wait a minute now J.R.—" He said slightly choking on his own spit.

"But that wouldn't change a thing now would it?"

"Naw J.R. you right, it sure wouldn't so—" J.R. cut him off.

"As a man of God—" He said looking intently at his two-timing cousin. "—I have to forgive you just like I have to forgive my wife."

"That's right J.R." Daniel nervously agreed.

"But be thankful you wasn't standing in front of me when I heard about you being in my bed with my wife." J.R. shook his head then turned and walked back over to the door looking out. He again faced Daniel, looking in his guilt-ridden eyes. "Being a man of God would've been the last thing on my mind." Daniel swallowed. "I know walking out on Effie Mae and my children was the wrong—" He said trying to remain calm. "But it sure as hell didn't give you the right to have her."

"You right J.R., it didn't."

"And knowing Effie Mae I'm sure she didn't make your decision to be with her a difficult one." Daniel felt slightly redeemed when hearing those words.

"We gon be alright J.R.?" He asked hoping their talk had repaired the damage.

" Maybe over time we can have some kind of relationship." J.R. said gradually calming. "I uh, guess we have too we're family."

"I can accept that J.R."

"I also know how much my children love their Cousin Daniel and his wife Geraldine and I would never do anything to hurt that relationship." J.R. thought about the bad blood between Effie Mae and Ms. Geraldine. "Maybe one day Geraldine can even forgive Effie Mae, give her back her son." The two cousins looked one to the other.

"Thank you J.R."

"For?"

"For hearing me out, I know that couldn't have been easy for you." J.R. gave no reply. "I also want to thank you for not punching me in the nose." Daniel half-hearted laughed as he walked over to the back door and prepared to leave. J.R. cracked a half smile.

"Can I ask you something J.R.?"

"Uh, ask me something? Okay."

"How's Effie Mae doing? Everything okay with her and Anthony?" J.R. hesitated before answering.

"Why don't you call her Cousin Daniel? Let her know how her son's doing."

"You gon be alright with that J.R.?"

"Yeah Cousin Daniel I'm gon be alright with that." J.R. slightly chuckled. "But I can't speak for Anthony." He said amused.

"I hope everything's okay." Daniel stated with worry. "I sent her a picture of D.J. a couple weeks ago and I ain't heard back from her yet." J.R. smiled.

"That explains the call I got from her."

"Huh?"

"Looks like I need to call Effie Mae myself, see how she doing and let her know you'll be calling her."

"I'd appreciate that J.R."

"Well uh, you take care Cousin Daniel."

"You too J.R." The two men awkwardly embraced before Daniel turned to leave.

"Uh, Cousin Daniel?"

"Yeah J.R.?"

"Try not to keep my girls out too late, they have school in the morning."

"I'll try J.R." Daniel chuckled. "But you know how Geraldine is when it comes to them girls—hate to see them leave!" He continued chuckling, feeling slightly vindicated, relieved to be leaving his cousin's house—without injury.

———————————

Anthony pulled in the driveway returning home from Jackson for the weekend. Ms. Dawson hurried out her front door trying to catch him before he entered the house.

"Anthony!" She called out, quickly approaching him.

"How are you Ms. Dawson?"

"Is your wife home?" She asked peering at his front door.

"I'm not sure Ms. Dawson I'm just getting home. "He noticed her suspicious behavior. "Is there something wrong?"

"I would hate to cause problems between you and your wife?" She said in a questioning tone.

"Problems? Did something happen Ms. Dawson?"

"Well since you asked me—" She again looked over at Anthony's house. "—is your wife a drinker?" She whispered.

"A drinker? I don't know what you mean." Anthony's concern grew in response to her probing questions.

"About a couple or so she asked me if I would watch them youngins—now you know I don't mind watching them cause they ain't ever been a problem for me to watch." Ms. Dawson's eagerness increased in anticipation of revealing Effie Mae's indiscretion. "They got some hardy appetites though." She said subtly complaining. "But that's alright cause I always cook a lot of food anyway." She half-heartedly chuckled and again shifted her eyes over at Anthony's house hoping not be seen by Effie Mae before she could give her full report.

"Would you like for me to give you money to replace the food the kids ate Ms. Dawson?" Her mouth quickly opened.

"Is that what you thought I was doing Anthony, asking for money?" She said forcing a look of surprise on her face. "Noooooo, I wouldn't hear of it!" Anthony removed his wallet from his back pocket.

"How much do you want Ms. Dawson?"

"You know I could never take money from you for caring for them youngins Anthony." He put his wallet back in his pocket. "Twenty or thirty dollars should be enough, but only because you asked me." Anthony again removed his wallet.

"My momma always said Dafanetta—" Anthony interrupted.

"Dafanetta?"

"I do have a first name you know." She stated sarcastically. "My momma said Dafanetta since you never know who gon be dropping in for supper it's always best to cook more than you need than not to have enough and leave folks hungry." She shifted her eyes to Anthony's wallet. "You understand what I'm trying to say don't you Anthony?" He opened his wallet and removed two twenty dollar bills. She quickly reached over and eased the money from his hand.

"Yes Ms. Dawson I think I do know exactly what you're saying."

"Anthony?"

"Yes Ms. Dawson?"

"I guess your wife must've forgot she was suppose to pay me for watching all them youngins too, but I ain't said nothing cause I knew you'd take care of it." She chuckled. Anthony again removed another twenty dollar bill from his wallet and handed it to her then quickly returned his wallet back inside his pocket. "I also wanted to ask you—" He abruptly cut her off.

"No more money Ms. Dawson."

"Is that what you thought I was fixin to say Anthony?" She chuckled. "What I was gon say is I was wondering—"

"Wondering what Ms. Dawson?" She leaned towards Anthony's ear. "Do your wife have a brother, cousin, or some other male kinfolk living round here in these parts?"

"A brother? No . . . Ms. Reed has only the two daughters everybody knows that, why?"

"I don't mean to cause problems between you and your wife? It's just that a young man came by one evening and picked her up." She stared at Anthony observing his response to her *tattling*. "I figure that must've been the reason why she wanted me to watch them youngins— all night?" She said instigating.

"All night?" Anthony said curious. Ms. Dawson nodded confirming her words then waited for his reaction to the news of Effie Mae spending the night with another man.

"Now you know yourself Anthony I ain't ever had a problem with watching them youngins for your wife?" She looked over at 0Anthony's front door. "Naw not one bit, like I said they ain't ever gave me no trouble, eat a lot though, especially that little boy—Lil' J.R.?"

"You said that already Ms. Dawson."

"Oh, did I?" She chuckled. "Is that your boy Anthony?"

"Yes Ms. Dawson that's my boy."He stated proudly.

"Then how it is y'all come to call him Lil' J.R.?" She peered at him with questioning eyes. "Is he named after you?" Anthony redirected the conversation.

"I believe you were asking me if Effie Mae drinks."

"Oh yeah—well like I was saying, after she left here with that young man—" Ms. Dawson continued observing Anthony's response to Effie Mae's possible adulterous act. "—when he brought her back home looked to me she was drunk." Anthony maintained his silence as he absorbed her words. "Like I said, I don't mean to cause no problems between you and your wife?"

"Well, Ms. Dawson it brings me great comfort to know that you're not trying to cause me and Effie Mae problems."

"That's why I ain't said nothing 'bout how that young man carried her in the house when he brought her back in the wee hours of the night." A troubled look appeared on Anthony's face.

"Carried her?"

"Seen it with my own eyes!" Ms. Dawson quickly added. "But like I said, I don't want to be the cause of nobody's marriage ending in divorce." She shifted her eyes across the street to Anthony's upstairs window when seeing the curtain slightly move. "Did I mention he was in there with your wife—all night?" She again stared into Anthony's eyes and tried to read his thoughts.

"Well thank you Ms. Dawson for sharing that gossip with me." Anthony stated underneath his breath.

"Huh? Did you say something Anthony?"

"I was just saying thank you for watching and feeding the kids."

"Like I said—" He cut her off.

"Goodbye Ms. Dawson."

"I finally had to call Ms. Millie to come see 'bout that poor child."

"If you'll excuse me, I think I need to go speak with Effie Mae to get a better understanding of what's going on." Anthony walked away removing himself from Ms. Dawson's aggravating meddling. She watched with satisfaction as Anthony walked up on his porch and entered the house.

"Maybe now he'll get that Ol' Jezebel out of his house and out of this God fearing neighborhood."

• • • •

"Effie Mae!" Anthony called out.

"I'm upstairs Anthony."

"Come down Baby, I think we need to talk."

"Okay." He curiously watched as she hurried down the stairs, romantically wrapping her arms around his neck trying to kiss him. He subtly pulled away.

"I spoke to Ms. Dawson, Baby—" Effie Mae interrupted.

"I already know what she told you Anthony."

"Okay since you already know why don't you explain it to me?"

"You ain't gon kiss me Anthony?" Effie Mae said puckering her lips, waiting for a kiss. Anthony placed a quick kiss on her lips then awaited her explanation. "While you were gone Anthony I got J.R.'s divorce papers in the mail—" He quickly interjected.

"Divorce papers? Okay Baby that's great news." Anthony's optimism heightened. "Now we can start planning our wedding." He again kissed her.

"Then I got a picture of my baby boy from Mr. Daniel."

"How did that go?" Anthony asked, certain the outcome wasn't good.

"It didn't Anthony and I ended up doing something that's gon make you mad."

"Something like what Baby?"

"I know I should've told you this but—"

"That doesn't sound good Baby."

"I kind of got a problem with scotch."

"Problem? What kind of problem?"

"When I start drinking it Anthony I can't stop!" His jaw dropped.

"Baby are you telling me you're an alcoholic?"

"Yeah Anthony that's what I'm telling you."

"Okay—" He said recalling his company's soirée. "So tell me Baby when did this happen? And why am I just now hearing about it?"

"J.R. took my babies from me Anthony!"

"Okay, J.R. took the kids, what does that have to do with you drinking scotch?"

"I started being down at Blue's jazz club—" Anthony interrupted.

"Blue?" He stared at her. "Baby has anything good ever come from you being with Blue?" Effie Mae giggled then kissed him. She kissed him a second time then a third.

"What's going on Baby? What's with all the kisses?"

"You promise you won't get mad at me Anthony?" She said kissing him again.

"That doesn't sound good Baby." He blocked her as she again tried to kiss him. "Stop with all the kisses and tell me what's going on."

"It's something I need to tell you Anthony."

"Something like what Baby?"

"I still been seeing Blue." Anthony's mouth abruptly opened.

"Seeing Blue?" A disappointed look displayed on his face. "Why Baby?"

"I'm sorry Anthony."

"Do you love me Baby?"

"Yeah Anthony I do."

"Then tell me why is Blue still in your life?"

"I don't know Anthony."

"Baby before we left New York I thought you said goodbye to Blue?"

"I did Anthony."

"Then why is it every time I turn around there he is?"

"I'm here with you Anthony not Blue."

"Baby are you sure this is where you want to be?"

"Yeah Anthony." She looked in Anthony's doubting eyes. "But if you want me to leave I'll go." Effie Mae pulled out of Anthony's hold and began walking away.

"Where are you going Baby?"

"J.R. said he wouldn't divorce me if I didn't want him to." Anthony opened his arms.

"Come here Baby." Effie Mae gradually entered his awaiting embrace. "I'm sorry if it seems like I don't understand, but with everything that's been happening it's like I'm actually getting to know you for the first time." Anthony stated kissing her gently on the forehead. "I guess I'm still seeing you as seventeen year old Effie Mae Reed and you're not."

"Is that a problem for you Anthony?"

"I wish I could say it wasn't but—"

"I'll go call J.R. and tell him to come get me."

"No Baby you're not calling J.R." Anthony said placing a reassuring kiss on her lips then laying her head on his chest. "We can work this out Baby . . . it just seems we need to get to know each other all over again as adults." He kissed her lightly on the lips. "So is there anything else I need to know about you that I don't know?" Effie Mae giggled.

"Remember Anthony you asked!"

"Oh no, that doesn't sound good Baby."

"Anthony would you believe me if I told you I was once a whore?" He chuckled.

"Yeah Baby, I kind of remember your reputation."

"Naw Anthony I mean a real live whore!"

"Baby tell me you're joking."

"Naw Anthony I ain't joking."

"A paid for whore?" He looked at her with disbelief.

"Yep, I had my own entertainment room and everything!" She giggled.

"Next you'll be telling me Blue was your pimp?"

"Nope, but he was one of my customers."

"Baby you're kidding right?"

"Nope." Effie Mae continued giggling. "Huck was my pimp!" Anthony's jaw dropped. "But I didn't know it until later."

"Huck!" He looked at Effie Mae, overwhelmed by her truth. " Your friend Huck?" Anthony again opened his mouth to speak, but nothing came out. He looked at Effie Mae, momentarily loss for words. "Yes Baby . . . it definitely looks like we have a lot of catching up to do."

"You mad at me Anthony?" Effie Mae asked pouting.

"Mad no . . . shocked definitely." Anthony took a moment to reflect on Effie Mae's confession. "Baby, a whore?" A large smile suddenly formed on on Antony's face.

"What Anthony?" Effie Mae asked in response to his abrupt smile.

"I guess I have to admit I've picked up one or two of those in my life, but I would never have considered marrying one." Effie Mae playfully pushed him then looked at him, her eyes displaying seriousness.

"Thank you Anthony."

"For not sending you back home to J.R.?"

"For understanding why I ain't ready to have another baby yet."

"Baby you said yet!" She kissed Anthony gently on the lips seeing the excitement in his eyes.

"I would love for us to have another baby Anthony, but when I'm ready."

"I can accept that—" They intimately kissed. "—for now." Effie Mae giggled. "So Baby which one of us is cooking dinner tonight?"He asked.

"Let's both do it?"

"Okay Baby." They again kissed. Anthony suddenly noticed the absence of the children.

"Baby where are the kids?"

"Momma took them home with her after she came over here this morning and found me passed out drunk again on the living room floor." Anthony's jaw dropped.

"Baby tell me you're kidding."

"I'm just giving you what you want Anthony—the truth."

"Am I going to be sorry I asked?"

"Naw, you can handle it." They laughed then headed for the kitchen.

———————————

Pete entered the house after work carrying a colorful bouquet of assorted flowers. Millie silently chuckled when seeing him.

"How you doing Ms. Millie?" He asked uncomfortable by the amused look on her face.

"I'm doing just fine son."

"Where Annie Mae at?"

"She went over to her sister house, but she gon be back here shortly." Pete looked down at the flowers in his hand then walked over and handed them to his mother-in-law.

"Here you go Ms. Millie—enjoy them." A defeated look showed on his strong face.

"Pete?"

"Yeah Ms. Millie?"

"The flowers are beautiful." Millie said smiling. " But I know you ain't bought them for me son." She raised an eyebrow. "Now take these flowers and go give them to your wife. If you want Annie Mae to give you time to change you gon need to do the same for her as well."

"You right Ms. Millie but—" Millie handed him back the flowers.

"It's gon be alright son." An reassuring smile showed on her face. "It's gon take some doing, but you and Annie Mae gon work things out." Pete nodded in agreement then walked down the hall headed for his bedroom. "You going the wrong way ain't you son?"

"Naw Ms. Millie I'm gon go bathe, put on my best clothes then I'm going out here to Anthony's house and get my wife, take her to dinner, a movie—something." Pete's enthusiasm increased

"Do that mean you gon need me to watch the children all night?" Millie giggled.

"I sure would appreciate that Ms. Millie." Pete said as he proceeded down the hall. He abruptly stopped. "Thank you Ms. Millie." She smiled as he continued down the hall, carrying the bouquet of flowers on his way to prepare for a romantic evening with his wife.

# Chapter Seven

Blue remained hospitalized—two and a half weeks later. Asleep in bed, he gradually opened his eyes when hearing the sound of footsteps entering his room. He slowly brought Huck's face into focus. He shifted his eyes to Buckeye then again to Huck.

"Hey Blue, how you feeling little brother?" Blue chuckled. "Why you laughing?"

"You ain't called me that since we was kids."

"What you want me to call you—Tyrell?" Huck teased.

"Then that means I'd have to call you Henry Lee?" The two brothers laughed.

"I'm sure I'll be hearing enough of that when Daddy get here."

"Daddy?" A surprised look formed on Blue's weakened face. "You called Daddy?"

"Naw, Ms. Jones." Blue's eyes dampened. "You know if anything happened to you Blue and I didn't call your momma, Ms. Jones would never forgive me." Knots filled Huck's stomach as he masked his emotional hurt as his concern over Blue's condition consumed him. "You know she got you spoiled like that Tyrell!" The two brothers again laughed.

"I guess she do—her and Daddy both." A boyish smile displayed on Blue's face. Huck's humor diverted to envy then to fear as thoughts entered his head regarding the extent of Blue's sickness.

"What your doctor saying Blue?"

"He saying I got lung cancer man." Huck took a deep breath and shook his head, devastated by the seriousness of Blue's diagnosis.

"Damn shame." His eyes slightly moistened. "How you know what that doctor telling you is right Blue?"

"Man if you knew how many test they put me through—" Blue abruptly stopped.

"You alright Blue?"

"Yeah I'm just thinking how I'm gon tell Baby girl." He stated, knowing the extreme devastation she would endure when learning of his impending death.

"That's gon damn near kill that girl Blue." Huck said shifting his eyes over at his old friend. Buckeye shook his head with sorrow. "You know she act like she can't live without her Blue." Huck humorously laughed, concealing his own brokenness over the imminent demise of his brother.

"She shouldn't have to!" Blue stated in anger. "If I had known this was gon happen I would've married Baby girl and moved to Pennsylvania like we talked about before Anthony came and took her away." Huck suddenly laughed.

"What?" Blue said puzzled by Huck's laughter.

"I was just thinking about all that time me and you spent fighting over that girl then some old boyfriend stepped in the picture and took her away." He continued laughing. "Damn shame, but I know Effie Mae . . . she ain't fitting into that life."

"Go get her for me Huck." Huck slightly tilted his head.

"Go get her?" He shifted his eyes briefly to Buckeye. "Think about what you saying Blue! You think Anthony's just gon let Effie Mae leave and come here to be with you?" A smile of confidence appeared on Blue's face.

"He couldn't stop Baby girl if he tried." Huck again shifted his eyes to Buckeye the back to Blue. "The only reason she didn't come back to New York with me when I went down there to see her—" Huck cut him off.

"You been to Mississippi Blue?"

"Yeah, Baby girl called and I went running like always." Blue chuckled. "I spent two good nights with her too before Anthony came home and caught me and J.R. up in his house."

"J.R.?" Huck grinned. "I see that girl is still something else."

"Yeah she is." Blue said chuckling. "Baby girl said he was there to get one of their daughters to bring her back here to New York." Blue suddenly quieted. "They ain't giving me but six months Huck."

"Six months?" Huck's stomach bundled with nerves as he again shifted his eyes to Buckeye. "Damn shame."

"And I want to spend every second of them six months with Baby girl."

"Give me a couple days Blue I'll get her here—n" Huck paused. "—if I can."

"She'll be here." A look of certainty showed on Blue's face. "I'll bet my jazz club on it." Buckeye's eyes widened in response to Blue's costly wager. Huck glanced briefly over to Buckeye then again turned to Blue.

"You know me Blue, it ain't too often I'd turn down a bet like that." He said shifting his eyes to his old friend. Buckeye's eyes widened, enticed by Blue's bet. "But somehow Blue—" Huck said looking him in the eyes. "—I think if I bet on that Blue I'd lose."

---

Effie Mae followed her children out onto the front porch, watching as they climbed on the bus for school. She taunted Ms. Dawson with a wave when seeing her sitting on her front porch watching.

"How you doing this morning Ms. Dawson?" Effie Mae said on her way to the mailbox.

"I'm doing fine and you?" Effie Mae thought for a second before answering her neighbors subtle, snooping question.

"I'm sober right now, but I sure could use a drink! You got any scotch over there?" She said continuing to taunt her nosey neighbor. Ms. Dawson's mouth quickly opened. She hurried inside her house, slamming the door behind her. "Old busy-body." Effie Mae said to herself laughing as she opened the mailbox and looked inside, removing yesterday's mail, sorting through the many envelopes seeing nothing of importance. She prepared to re-enter the house.

"Hey Effie Mae." She abruptly stopped. Her heart raced as she slowly turned in the direction of what sounded like the familiar voice of Huck.

"Huck!" She screamed dropping the mail on the ground. Ms. Dawson rushed to the window and peered through her half opened curtains in response to Effie Mae's squeal. Effie Mae hurried over and entered Huck's awaiting arms. He kissed her lightly on the lips. Ms. Dawson's eyes widened when seeing the intimate exchange.

"How you been doing girl?" He asked as they continued their embrace.

"Before or after Momma found me in the house passed out drunk on the floor naked from the waist down." An enormous smile displayed on Huck's handsome face. He tilted his head.

"Is that right?" Effie Mae giggled. "It's a good thing your momma found you and not me." Effie Mae'

"Huck!" She blushed.

"What Effie Mae? All you left me with was memories." He seductively grinned.

"If your brother hadn't stopped taking my calls that would've never happened and Momma—" Huck cut her off.

"Brother?" He looked at Effie Mae with questioning eyes. "Blue told you that?"

"Yeah he said something about it when we was talking about us having a baby."

"A baby? You and Blue?" Huck slightly titled his head. "Is that right?"

"Not like that Huck!" Effie Mae giggled. "Me and Blue was talking and I was thinking bout the two men I never had babies with—Blue was one and you was the other." She again giggled. Huck's attention drew to the slightly moving curtain across the streets at Ms. Dawson's house.

"You think we need to be talking about that out here on the streets?" He shifted his eyes over to Ms. Dawson's. "Your neighbor been watching for the last ten minutes—she ain't gon call the police is she?" He joked.

"Naw, but she gon have an ear full for Anthony when he get home this weekend." Effie Mae laughed.

"Come on—let's go in the house so that woman can give her eyes a rest." Huck again looked over at Ms. Dawson's house. He waved then quietly laughed to himself. Ms. Dawson quickly closed her curtain and hurried to the front door, opening it to a crack then peeping out.

"Kiss me." Huck said smiling.

"What?"

"Kiss me."

"Huck you know Ms. Dawson over there watching."

"So let's give Ms. Dawson something to look at." Effie Mae giggled as Huck romantically embraced her then passionately kiss her. Ms. Dawson's jaw dropped.

"Lord have mercy." She said continuing to watch. "Now where did I put Ms. Millie's phone number?" She quickly closed the door and hurried through the house in search of the number. "Look like she gon need to come see 'bout that daughter of hers—Ol' Jezebel." Huck put his arm around Effie Mae as they walked towards the house, stepping onto the porch. Huck looked around the impressively decorated home as they entered. He nodded with approval. "Not bad."

"So this where you and Anthony live huh?" Effie Mae smiled.

"Yep . . . this where me and Anthony and my babies live."

"How many of your babies you got living here with you now Effie Mae? I heard J.R. picked one up and brought her back to New York."

"That was my baby Mahalia." Effie Mae suddenly laughed.

"What?"

"You know Blue's got Anthony round here acting like you now." He tilted his head.

"Is that right."

"And just where is Blue? I been calling him for three weeks and all Melvin keep telling me is that he ain't there—I don't believe he even giving Blue my messages because Blue always call me back, even when he mad at me and I ain't heard nothing from—" Effie Mae abruptly stopped when seeing the troubled look on Huck's face. "What?"

"Blue in the hospital Effie Mae."

"What?" A frightened look formed on her face. "Is he alright Huck?"

"Naw he ain't alright."

"What you mean he ain't alright Huck?" Effie Mae's eyes filled with tears.

"I'll let him tell you." He stared at her. "Blue sent me here to get you." Huck thought about Blue's wager and subtly smiled as he waited to see if Blue's bet would have proven prosperous for him or Blue.

"Just let me run upstairs and pack some stuff." Effie Mae stated without hesitation. "Then I'm gon need to go by Momma's and ask her to look after my babies 'til I get back."

"Yeah you go do that Effie Mae, I'll be down here waiting." Huck stated silently chuckling as Blue's prediction proved true.

• • • •

"You gon be alright Effie Mae?" Huck asked sensing her fear as they sat in his car parked in Millie's driveway. Effie Mae looked at him then burst into tears. "Come here." He said pulling her towards him, laying her head on his chest.

"I can't live without Blue, Huck!" Effie Mae cried out traumatized by the thought of losing the only man she ever loved.

"Come on now Effie Mae, stop crying girl."

"I can't Huck!" She bellowed. "I don't want to lose Blue."

"I know you don't Effie Mae, I don't want to lose him either but—" Huck's eyes moistened as he combated his own weakening emotions. "You know this ain't how Blue want you acting girl." He said kissing her gently on the forehead. "My brother gon need you to be strong." Effie Mae suddenly chuckled. A perplexed looked appeared on Huck's face in response to her out of place laughter.

"What?"

"It sound funny hearing you call Blue your brother."

"He is!"

"Yeah, but I ain't use to hearing you say it." She continued laughing.

"Get on Effie Mae—go say bye to your momma."

"I'm going."

"Get on." She quietly giggled. Huck stared at her. "You still laughing about that?"

"Naw . . . I was thinking bout the first time Blue came here to Mississippi with me." Huck humorously watched as Effie Mae's laughing enhanced. "I got so drunk Huck, Momma threw me and Blue out of her house." Huck quietly grinned. "We ended up staying all night at the Cozi-T Motel." Effie Mae cried through her laughter as tears rolled down her cheeks. Huck looked at her with worried eyes—he wondered how she would continue life after Blue's death.

"You ready?" He said wiping her tears with his hands.

"I don't know Huck." Effie Mae said thinking how this would be her momma's first time meeting Huck." She giggled.

"What you laughing about now Effie Mae?"

"I can't wait for Momma to meet you!" An uncomfortable look appeared on Huck's face. He tilted his head.

"Is that right?"

"But let me warn you—" Effie Mae said amused. Huck looked in the direction of the house with mystery then turned back to her.

"Warn me about what Effie Mae?"

"Henry Lee White ain't no match for Millie Annabell Reed!" She said bursting into laughter. A look of unease showed on Huck's face in response to Effie Mae's depiction of her momma's toughness. He tilted his head and humorously smiled.

"Is that right?" Effie Mae continued laughing as she opened the car door and got out.

"Come on Huck I want you to meet my momma!"

"I don't know Effie Mae—"

"Momma ain't gon do nothing to you Huck." She said, giggling.

"You sure about that?" Huck joked.

"Yeah Huck I'm sure, now come on!" He peered through the windshield as Effie Mae hurried towards the house. He quietly laughed then opened the door and got out.

"I ain't gon have to call Buckeye am I?" He stated humorously.

"Naw Huck, you ain't gon have to call Buckeye—now come on." Effie Mae continued giggling as she walked up on the front porch. Huck followed uncertain of what awaited him inside.

"Momma!" Effie Mae called out as they entered.

Huck's attention drew to the opening bedroom door just off the livingroom. He curiously watched as Millie emerged from her room and entered the living room. She looked at him with unfamiliarity then turned to Effie Mae. Huck's eyes abruptly shifted to the female walking down the hall also headed towards the living room. Both women stood mute as they looked in awe at the well groomed, extremely handsome gentleman accompanying Effie Mae.

"Momma this my friend Huck."

"Huck!" Millie's eyes widened. "Not that man who was gon kill Mr. Daniel's wife?" Huck's mouth slightly opened, surprised by Millie's knowledge of his past criminal deeds. He looked at Effie Mae and titled his head then turned back to Millie.

"Momma you wasn't supposed to say nothing about that." Effie Mae said looking at Huck, giggling "And that little girl right there is my baby sister Annie Mae."

"How y'all doing? Ms. Reed, Annie Mae."

"I don't know Huck?" Millie said looking at him with mistrust. "Is that what your momma named you?" He shifted his eyes briefly to Effie Mae then back to Millie. Effie Mae looked at him and giggled.

"Momma, Huck's name is Henry Lee White."

"That sounds much better . . . how you doing Henry Lee White, and how you know my daughter?" Millie raised an eyebrow. Annie Mae intervened.

"Momma that man don't want you all in his business." She said captivated by his extraordinary good looks—from his navy blue and white leather shoes; pinstriped navy blue vest and pants complimented by his powder blue shirt and navy blue Stetson on top of his head.

"Momma, Huck was the first person I met when I moved to New York." Effie Mae looked at him and smiled. "He was also the one who introduced me to Blue."
"Did he also introduce you to all that scotch you was drinking?" Huck interjected. "Naw Ms. Reed, I love this girl too much to do that." Millie looked quickly at Effie Mae.

"Love?"

"It's a long story Momma." Effie Mae smiled. Huck blushed.

"I see you dressed mighty fine Henry Lee." Millie said scrutinizing his stunning attire. "What kind of work you do up there in New York?" He glanced over at Effie Mae amused at the thought of answering Millie's inquisitive question. His attention abruptly drew to Annie Mae's unrelenting gaze. Huck slightly lowered his head and blushed.

"Momma can you watch my babies for me?" Effie Mae said redirecting the conversation from Huck's occupation.

"Effie Mae!" Millie scowled.

"It ain't for that Momma." Huck looked at Effie Mae and silently grinned, humored by look of sour look on Millie's face.

"Huck taking me to New York Momma—" Millie interjected.

"New York?" A look of fear entered her eyes, uneasy by the announcement of Effie Mae's unanticipated travel. "Ain't nothing wrong with them babies is it?" Effie Mae's eyes moistened.

"Naw Momma my babies fine—it's Blue." She looked up at Huck. "He in the hospital Momma, he real sick." Huck intervened.

"Blue sent me here to get Effie Mae, Ms. Reed—take her back to New York."

"Get Effie Mae?" Millie said confused. "Get her for what?" Huck turned to Effie Mae and waited for her to answer her momma's question.

"Blue loves me Momma—" Millie interrupted.

"And what about Betsy Lewis' boy?" She said disturbed by Effie Mae abandoning Anthony to be with Blue. "He loves you too!"

"Momma—"

"Don't momma me." Millie said frustrated. "Effie Mae have you told that boy you leaving here to go be with Blue?" Huck again turned to Effie Mae, amused by Millie's straight forward questions, quietly chuckling as he waited to hear her reply.

"Momma this ain't got nothing to do with Anthony." Huck's attention again drew to Annie Mae's continuous gaze. He again lowered his head and blushed then turned to Effie Mae.

"I'm gon go ahead let you talk to your momma, Effie Mae—" He glanced over at Annie Mae. She blushed. "—and your sister, I'll be out here in the car waiting." Huck said trying to ignore Annie Mae's gawk.

"Okay Huck, I'll be out in a minute." He turned to Effie Mae and placed two fingers underneath her chin then slightly tilted her head, gently kissing her on the lips. Annie Mae's jaw dropped. Millie raised an eyebrow.

"Nice meeting y'all." He said still gazing in Effie Mae's hazel brown eyes. She blushed. Annie Mae watched with infatuation as Huck turned and walked away, exiting the Reed family home. Millie looked at Effie Mae and scowled, displeased by her obvious intimate relationship with Huck.

"I guess ain't no need in me even asking now is it?" She raised an eyebrow. Annie Mae's eyes lit up with inquiry.

"Well I'm asking Effie Mae—have you?"

"Have I what Annie Mae?"

"Been with Huck?" Effie Mae blushed as she ignored her young sister's snooping then turned her back to Millie. "Oooh Effie Mae he is so good looking!" Annie Mae's eyes beamed, captivated by Huck's attractiveness. Millie observed her married daughter's unusual interest in Effie Mae's extraordinarily handsome friend.

"Good looking or not—don't forget Annie Mae Parker you got a husband! You keep your eyes on Pete!"

"What Momma? All I said was he was good looking."

"You and Pete got enough problems with y'all marriage as it is!" Effie Mae swiftly turned to her baby sister, shocked by her momma's disclosure of her and Pete's marital discord.

"What?" Effie Mae said amused. "Perfect Pete and Annie Mae got problems in they perfect marriage?"

"We working on it." Annie Mae said in a childlike manner.

"How long you think you gon be in New York, child?"

"I don't know Momma." Effie Mae's eyes dampened. "Huck ain't telling me, but whatever's wrong with Blue it's bad Momma." Millie shook her head with sympathy.

"I sure hope you wrong Effie Mae."

"If Blue sent Huck here to get me—" Effie Mae quietly cried.

"Come here child." Effie Mae entered her momma's open arms. "Don't you worry none about them children."

"Yeah Effie Mae." Annie Mae intervened. "You know we love those kids and taking care of them ain't no problem." She joined in the mother—daughter embrace. "I don't care what Pete got to say." Millie looked quickly over at her and raised an eyebrow.

"What Momma?" Annie Mae stated defiantly.

"We can talk about that later."

"Thank you Annie Mae, Momma." Effie Mae said through her weeping.

"You just go see about Blue." Millie said laying Effie Mae's head on her chest. "I know you love that man, Effie Mae."

"Yeah Momma I do." She placed a comforting kiss on Effie Mae's cheek then mother and daughters ended their group hug. Effie Mae wiped her eyes with her hands, suddenly noticing her Momma's reprimanding gaze.

"What Momma?"

"Try to keep your mind on Blue." Millie hesitated. "And your body away from Huck." Effie Mae's mouth flung open.

"Momma!"

"Don't Momma me . . . you heard what I said." Millie raised an eyebrow. "Don't forget you still got a husband yourself."

"Effie Mae you know I ain't ever approved of you being with all those men—" A huge smile stretched across Annie Mae's face. "—but that man right there—"

"Annie Mae!" Millie yelled, hushing her youngest daughter. "Don't let your husband hear you talking like that child!"Annie Mae looked briefly at her momma—ignoring her words of warning then resumed her conversation with her big sister.

"You got my permission Effie Mae to be with Huck all you want!" The two sisters laughed. Millie flashed her two daughters a look of disapproval.

"Listen at you little girl!" Effie Mae said surprised by Annie Mae's apparent physical attraction to Huck. "I guess you and Pete is having problems." Effie Mae chuckled. "I didn't think you knew no other man existed besides Pete."

"It ain't!" Millie shouted glaring angrily at her young daughter. "Not for Annie Mae." Annie Mae silenced seeing her momma's chastising eyes.

"Look like Pete's gon have to keep his eye on you little girl." Effie Mae teased.

"What?"Annie Mae stated innocently. "I'm just looking." She pouted. "You know I love my husband."

"And you remember that!" Millie scolded.

"I am Momma."

"Come on little girl, give your big sister a hug." Effie Mae said extending her arms, amused by Annie Mae's out of character behavior. The two sisters hugged.

"You tell Huck I said drive careful now." Millie said. "And let me know how Blue's doing."

"I will Momma." Effie Mae released her baby sister. "Tell my babies I love them."

"I sure will do that Effie Mae."

"Bye Momma."

"Bye child." Millie said masking her worry.

"Bye Effie Mae."

"Bye little girl." Effie Mae forced a smile as her heart pounded in her ears and her thoughts drifted to the possibility of Blue dying.

# Chapter Eight

Effie Mae and Huck remained seated in his car parked in the emergency room parking lot of the hospital. They looked at each other, both at a loss for words.

"Get that off me." Huck said breaking the silence.

"What?" Effie Mae visually searched his clothes.

"You don't see that?"

"See what Huck?"

"Your sister's eyeballs." He said laughing. Effie Mae chuckled. "As hard as she was looking at me I know she left at least one of them on me." He said continuing to laugh.

"My baby sister did think you was the finest man she ever seen." Effie Mae giggled.

"Your sister married ain't she?"

"Yeah she married—her and Pete got married when they was just kids." Effie Mae silenced when seeing the peculiar gaze in Huck's eyes.

"What?"

"You trying to get me locked up Effie Mae?"

"Naw, why you say that Huck?"

"Telling your momma I was gon kill old Daniel's wife."

"I was just teasing with Momma."

"Do she know that?" He asked worried. Effie Mae giggled.

"Yeah Huck she know."

"I know you love me too much to see me behind bars, ain't that right?"

"Yeah Huck you know that." She suddenly laughed.

"What?"

"You know my baby sister gave me her permission to be with you." Huck tilted his head and blushed.

"Is that right?"

"I know you ain't blushing."

"Blushing? Naw what for?"

"What? You like Annie Mae or something?" Effie Mae said teasing him as she reflected on the time when he'd asked her the very same question regarding Blue. "Ain't that what you said to me the first time I met Blue?"

"Yeah, I wish I had never introduced you to him now—should've kept you for myself." He momentarily stared at her. "Come here girl." Effie Mae hesitated then slid over, her thoughts being only of Blue's impending fate. Huck embraced Effie Mae in his arms and romantically kissed her—abruptly releasing his hold when feeling rejected by her subtle resistance.

"It's three o'clock in the morning Huck, you think they gon let me in there to see Blue?"

"They know you coming all the way from Mississippi, so they said they'd make an exception." Effie Mae's stomach rumbled with butterflies. "You ready?" He asked. She burst into tears. "Naw you ain't ready, you want to wait and come back later?" Effie Mae shook her head no.

"I'm gon be okay."

"You sure Effie Mae?" She nodded. "You need me to come in with you?"

"Naw." She looked in his disappointed eyes. "I want to spend some time with Blue alone."

"Yeah you do that Effie Mae." Huck said glaring at her. "I ain't trying to see you and Blue kissing and carrying on no-way." He removed a handkerchief from his shirt pocket and forced it in her hand. "Dry your eyes, I don't want Blue seeing you all teary eyed."

"How am I gon hide my tears when I get inside Huck?" Effie Mae asked with defiance.

"I'll let Tyrell worry about that—" Effie Mae's tear filled eyes widened.

"Tyrell? Why you calling him that?"

"That's his name ain't it?" She stared at briefly at Huck, but said nothing further as she wiped away her tears. Effie Mae felt it best not to upset him any further. "Get on." He stated solemnly. "I'm giving you and Blue fifteen minutes then I'm coming in and I ain't trying to see you and him—" She cut him off.

"Then you may as well not even come in because as long as Blue want to kiss on me I'm gon let him." Huck looked away, staring angrily through the windshield.

"Call me at the Envoy when you ready." He said refusing to look at her. "I'll be back to get you." Effie Mae noted his childish behavior.

"Huck!"

"Get on now Effie Mae I said I'll be back."

"So I guess you mad?"

"What you think?"

"Kiss me." She said teasing. He blushed then took her in his arms and passionately kissed her.

"Where you staying tonight Effie Mae?" Huck asked gazing in her eyes. "Come stay with me."

"With you?" A humorous look displayed on Effie Mae's face. "And just where you staying Huck?" She asked giggling. An appealing smile showed on his handsome face.

"I got a place."

"Where? You staying at Ms. Norma's whore house now?" Effie Mae said laughing. Huck grinned. "You know my momma told me to keep my body away from you, Henry Lee." She said teasing him. He quietly grinned tilting his head.

"Is that right?"

"I'm probably gon be staying with J.R. and my babies."

"J.R.?"

"Yep."

"I thought y'all was divorced."

"Nope we still married."

"Do J.R. know you here Effie Mae?"

"Nope."

"Then get here tomorrow." She looked him in the eyes.

"Let me think about it."

"Yeah you do that Effie Mae." He momentarily stared at her then placed a quick kiss on her lips before releasing her. "Get on." Effie Mae got out the car and hurried in the direction of the hospital's entrance. Huck watched with envy as she disappeared through the emergency room doors.

• • • •

Effie Mae quietly entered Blue's hospital room walking over to his bed watching him sleep. She leaned over and kissed him softly on the lips. He gradually opened his eyes in response to her gentle kiss. A large smile formed on his weakened face when seeing her.

"Hey Baby girl!" Blue said as she sat down on the bed. He reached up and lovingly pulled her in his arms then intimately kissed her. "I knew you'd come."

"Of course I'm gon come Blue." He again kissed her. "What's going on Blue?" Effie Mae asked hoping his answer would be something non-life threatening.

"They say I got lung cancer Baby girl."

"What? Lung cancer? No Blue!" Tears erupted from Effie Mae's eyes.

"Yeah—" He said electing not to tell her of his life expectancy. Effie Mae's heart pounded with fear.

"But you gon get better ain't you Blue?"

"Where's Huck?" He asked changing the subject.

"He said he was gon be at the Envoy—" Effie Mae looked in Blue's eyes with worry.

"How was the trip up here?" He asked trying to avoid discussing his health.

"Tell me Blue."

"Baby girl—" Blue's agitation increased in response to Effie Mae's persistence.

"What them doctors saying Blue?" He briefly looked away and shook his head then turned back to Effie Mae and gazed into her eyes.

"They ain't giving me but six month to live Baby girl."

"Nooooo!" She cried out. "You can't leave me Blue!"

"Baby girl."

"What Blue!" She yelled. He gently laid her head on his chest.

"I don't want you crying."

"What else am I suppose to do Blue? In six months you ain't gon be here!"

"That's why I need you to help me enjoy whatever time I got left." Blue kissed her lightly on the forehead. "And you can't do that Baby girl if you crying all the time."

"I don't want to stop crying Blue!" Effie Mae shouted. He placed another kiss on Effie Mae's forehead then used his sheet to wipe away her tears.

"My doctor talking about letting me go home in a couple days." He looked into her eyes. "Baby girl will you be there when I get home?"

"How am I gon do that Blue?" She asked continuing to cry. "You know what happens whenever I live with you Blue."

"Yeah Baby girl I know." Blue stated recalling her excessive intoxication when living with him several times before. "But this time Baby girl we gon do this together?" He kissed Effie Mae lightly on the lips. "If that doctor's right you only gon have six months with me Baby girl—do you want to spend that time so drunk you won't even remember it?"

"You know I don't Blue—" He noted the look of defeat in her eyes. "—but I ain't sure I can do it."

"Yeah Baby girl you can." Blue said placing a kiss on her forehead. "You just need to believe you can." He looked into Effie Mae's frightened eyes. "We gon get through this Baby girl okay?"

"Okay Blue." She stated masking her doubt behind a smile.

"I ain't gon lie to you Baby girl, it ain't gon be easy." Effie Mae gazed in his peaceful eyes. They romantically kissed. "How's things working out with you and Anthony?" Blue asked hoping Huck prediction of her not *fitting in* held true. She giggled.

"You wouldn't believe it if I told you Blue." He grinned.

"Yeah Baby girl I would."

"Me and Anthony don't even know each other no more." A puzzled looked formed on Blue's face.

"What you mean y'all don't know each other no more?"

"When me and Anthony got together we was just kids Blue."

"Yeah Baby girl I remember you telling me that."

"So much stuff done happened Blue since then—in both our lives, especially mines—" She silenced, looking in the love filled eyes of the man who held her heart. "Can't nobody take your place Blue." He smiled. "And I think Anthony learning that." Effie Mae suddenly giggled. "That boy around there acting all jealous like Huck now!" Blue quietly laughed then looked at her with troubled eyes.

"What's wrong Blue?"

"Baby girl you didn't bring Anthony with you—did you? I got enough to deal with."

"Naw Blue." She kissed him gently on the lips. "He don't even know I'm here." Effie Mae noted the uneasy look on his face. "But I'm gon have to let him know Blue, I need him to bring me my babies."

"I love you Effie Mae—" He placed a smooch on her lips. "—you know that?" She girlishly smiled.

"Yeah Tyrell, I know that." She said gently rubbing his face. "And I promise you Blue I'm gon make these six months the best months of your life—" He intervened.

"Of our lives Baby girl." A wide smile stretched across his face.

"Thank you Baby girl." Blue stated applying another kiss to her lips.

"Why you say that Blue?"

"I tried to bet Huck my jazz club that you would be here." Effie Mae's mouth flung open, stunned by Blue's unbelievable wager.

"Well I'm glad I came Blue!"

"I didn't doubt for a minute that you wouldn't." He grinned then passionately kissed her. Effie Mae noted the odd look entering in his eyes as the kiss ended.

"You alright Blue?"

"I know Huck already made his move on you." He said not really wanting to know the answer. She blushed in response to Blue's subtle jealousy.

"You know how your brother is Blue, if he hadn't tried something it wouldn't be Huck." She giggled.

"What you gon do Baby girl?" Blue asked nervously awaiting her reply—certain he already knew. She looked away.

"I don't know Blue."

"You may as well Baby girl." Effie Mae's jaw dropped as she turned to him, surprised by his words.

"Is that what you want Blue?"

"You know it ain't Baby girl, but I can't stop him."Blue said feeling helpless. "I don't want that man hurting you—and you know he will!"

"I don't want to hurt you Blue."

"Don't worry about me Baby girl—"

"What you mean don't worry about you Blue?" Effie Mae asked as her eyes quickly watered with tears.

"Baby girl I know you ain't forgot what Huck did to you the last time you told him no." She looked in Blue's frightened eyes. "That man almost killed you girl!"

"I know Blue but—" He cut her off.

"After I get out of this hospital it's gon be just me and you okay?" Effie Mae blushed.

"Okay Blue." They romantically kissed. "I want you to know Blue I'm only doing this cause I don't want you up all night worrying about Huck hurting me." He nodded with understanding.

"I'll see you when I get home Baby girl." They again kissed. "Make sure you go over to J.R.'s and spend some time with your kids."

"I will Blue."

"You think Daniel's gon let you see your son?"

"Mr. Daniel will, but Ms. Geraldine would go to her grave before she let me lay one eye on my baby boy." Effie Mae said amused.

"Baby girl don't say that."

"It's true Blue—and that Ol' hateful woman ain't getting ready to leave this world."

"Maybe one day she'll change her mind."

"Her mind?" She laughed. "That woman would have to change her whole heart!" Blue momentarily chuckled then silently gazed at her. Effie Mae blushed.

"What Blue?

"Hey!"

"Huh?"

"I love you Baby girl."

"I love you back Blue." They stared briefly in each other's eyes then lovingly kissed. Blue gently stroked Effie Mae's shiny black hair as she rested her head on his chest and listened to the beats of his heart.

---

Geraldine stood at the stove preparing a dinner of chicken and dumplings—watching as Daniel played with his toddler son on the living room floor.

"Come back here boy!" Daniel said reaching for the active toddler as he crawled quickly away from his grasp. "Geraldine, I'm getting too old to be crawling around here on this floor chasing after this boy."

"Aww Daniel it does my heart good to see you and your twin playing like that." She chuckled. "That little boy looks more and more like you every day." She stated, masking her resentment as Daniel picked up his namesake and kissed his milk scented cheek.

"You daddy's big boy D.J.?" Daniel said speaking in baby talk. D.J. looked at his daddy's moving lips as he spoke then giggled, reaching for Daniel's mouth.

"Daniel you love that little boy so much you'd climb Mount Everest to get him if he crawled up it." Ms. Geraldine laughed, abruptly quieting when seeing her husband's lingering love for the mother of his son as he looked at the toddler. "How did Effie Mae like the picture you sent her?" Ms. Geraldine asked speaking from her hurt. "The one of you and D.J.?" Daniel shifted his eyes to her in the kitchen then sat D.J. on the floor. A look of agitation beaming from his eyes.

"Why you asking me about Effie Mae, Geraldine?" He asked, upset.

"I was looking for that picture one day, I wanted to put it in my picture book but I didn't see it anywhere." Her envy of Effie Mae heightened. "So when I didn't find it I figured you must have sent it to Effie Mae . . . without telling me."

"Geraldine—Effie Mae's this boy's momma and she got every right to see him!" Daniel yelled looking at her with contempt. He shook his head then prepared himself for another one of his wife's verbal attacks regarding Effie Mae.

"You know Daniel, I don't even think it was you and Effie Mae being together that hurt me the most—" He interrupted.

"Come on now Geraldine." Daniel took a deep breath trying to calm himself. "How long you gon keep throwing that up in my face?"

"I don't have to say one word Daniel—" She looked in the living room at D.J. sitting on the floor quietly watching them argue. "—that little boy right there will always be a constant reminder." Daniel got up from the floor, picking D.J. up and putting him in his playpen.

"Let me go out here on back porch—" He said looking momentarily at his toddler son. "—I ain't getting ready to listen to another one of your sermons Geraldine on how me and Effie Mae betrayed you." Daniel headed in the kitchen as he prepared to go out back. Ms. Geraldine quickly stepped in front of him—blocking his path.

"Leave me alone now Geraldine!" Daniel warned. She stared in his guilt-ridden eyes and refused to move.

"I think what hurt me most Daniel was knowing you let yourself fall in love that girl." He looked at her but gave no reply. "What Daniel? Did you not love me anymore? Is that what it was?"

"Geraldine I never stopped loving you!"

"Then what was it Daniel?" She said raising her voice.

"I don't want to hurt you Geraldine, so let's just drop it!"

"I can't do that Daniel I need to know." A grimacing look displayed on her face as she gripped the top of her head from pain.

"Alright then Geraldine I'll tell you, but remember—" He looked her in the eyes. "—you asked.

"I asked Daniel because I want to know."

"Okay then." Daniel hesitated before speaking. "When I married you Geraldine, yeah I loved you." She smiled with satisfaction. "But—" Her smile quickly faded.

"But what Daniel?" He shook his head with remorse.

"It never came a time Geraldine where I fell in love with you." Daniel said as his feelings of betrayal ate at him seeing tears emerge from his wife's bitter eyes, running down her cheeks. "You see Geraldine!" He shook his head. "I told you I didn't want to hurt you!"

"You don't want to hurt me!" She yelled. "The day you climbed out of my bed and in your cousin's wife's that's just what you done Daniel!" Daniel shook his head, refusing to bicker with her.

"Uh-uh Geraldine naw—I ain't getting ready to do this with you."

"Do you still love her Daniel?" Ms. Geraldine asked squinting in response to the severe aching in her head.

"Geraldine I told you now—"

"Told me what Daniel!" She shouted. D.J. jerked, frightened by her sudden outburst. He began crying.

"See what you done Geraldine!" Daniel said hurrying in the living room, removing the toddler from his playpen. "It's alright D.J." He said gently patting his son on his back. "Yeah it's alright daddy's here." Ms. Geraldine watched through scorned eyes as Daniel kissed D.J. lovingly on the forehead, gradually calming the toddler as he looked at Ms. Geraldine with frightened eyes before laying his head on his daddy's chest.

"You didn't answer my question Daniel." He looked at her, infuriated.

"Geraldine can't you see you upsetting this boy!"

"All you have to do is answer my question and I'll hush."

"Leave me alone Geraldine!" Daniel said in agitation as he rocked D.J. in his arms.

"Did you hear me Daniel?" He stared her angrily in the eyes.

"Okay Geraldine, but you remember—"

"Tell me Daniel!" Ms. Geraldine yelled. D.J. again jumped and pouted, startled by her alarming voice.

"I ain't gon keep letting you upset my boy Geraldine." Daniel said trying not to raise his voice. "One more time Geraldine—you got one more time to scare my boy then I'm walking out that door—for good!" She looked at him without responding as the pain in her head worsened. Daniel placed another kiss on D.J. forehead before answering his wife's pending question. "Yeah Geraldine I still love Effie Mae and I miss her like hell!" She quickly turned away. "But I would've never left you Geraldine, I couldn't hurt you like that." The throbbing pain in her head, and the hurt in her heart magnified.

"So what did you and Effie Mae talk about when you called her?" Daniel's eyes widened, shocked by her knowledge of his recent call to Effie Mae.

"What you doing Geraldine watching me?" He said staring at her.

"I think it's a little too late for that don't you Daniel?" His attention suddenly diverted from his wife's fury to the aroma of D.J.'s dirty diaper penetrating his nostrils.

"Smell like you need your diaper changed boy." Daniel said sniffing. "You stank boy." He stated playfully then placed a quick kiss on the toddler's cheek. "You know that Ol' stinky boy." D.J. giggled and cooed.

"You want me to change him Daniel? Ms. Geraldine asked turning off the burner underneath the pot of chicken and dumplings.

"Naw Geraldine I got it . . . it's my boy I'll clean him."

"Suit yourself." She stated turning up her nose. Daniel ignored his wife's sly remark, hoping to bring an end to their heated altercation.

"You just keep on doing what you doing." He retrieved a diaper and baby powder from the coffee table then reached inside the playpen taking out a receiving blanket laying it on the floor. "You think you can get me a wet towel from the bathroom and put a little soap on it?"

"You sure you don't want to do that yourself too?" She stated, sarcastically. Daniel dismissed her *baiting* words as he laid D.J. on the blanket then sat down on the floor and begin the diaper change. D.J. watched Ms. Geraldine handed Daniel the wet washcloth, he smiled. Daniel looked up seeing the sour look on his wife's face.

"What Geraldine?" He said trying not to raise his voice.

"Do you even regret what you done Daniel?"

"What you want me to say Geraldine?"

"The truth."

"Naw I don't regret falling in love for the first time in my life and having this boy right here!" He stated without repentance. "Nope I don't regret it at all." Ms. Geraldine's grimacing intensified from the excruciating pain in her head. "Look at this boy Geraldine . . . how can I regret him being here—I can't!" Daniel said completing the diaper change then picking his son up, kissing him on top of the head. "Daddy love you boy." A huge smile formed on the toddler's face. He giggled. Daniel reluctantly turned his attention back to his wife, watching him from the kitchen. "Now if you asking me if I regret hurting you the way I did Geraldine, yeah I do—now that hurts like hell!"

"Does it Daniel?"

"Yeah it do." He stated softening his tone. "You didn't deserve that Geraldine." Daniel shook his head with regret. "You always been good to me."

"Daniel—Daniel!" Ms. Geraldine called out as she tumbled on the floor. Daniel quickly stood, alarmed by her sudden fall. He quickly returned D.J. to his playpen then rushed in the kitchen to his wife's aid.

"Geraldine—Geraldine!" Daniel shouted shaking her shoulders. She remained unresponsive, but breathing. His eyes widened with fear when noticing her slightly twisted mouth and drooped left side of her face. Daniel hurried in the living room and called for an ambulance.

———————————————

"I probably should get some sleep and let you get some rest Blue." Effie Mae said as her head remained on Blue's chest.

"Thank you Baby girl." He kissed her gently on the top of her head.

"For what Blue?"

"For being you."

"That's the first time I ever heard anybody say that about me." She half-heartedly laughed.

"Then I'm glad to be the first one to say it." Blue grinned then gazed into Effie Mae's eyes. She blushed.

"What?"

"Effie Mae will you marry me?"

"Blue you asked me already and I said I would."

"Naw Baby girl I mean now." Effie Mae looked at him with confused eyes.

"I'm still married to J.R., Blue"

"I know Baby girl." Blue said placing a kiss on her forehead. "I want us to get married, have a ceremony and everything before—" He abruptly silenced. Effie Mae noted the look of enthusiasm on his face. "I want us to live together as husband and wife until—" Effie Mae interrupted.

"How we gon do that Blue?"

"I'll figure something out if you say yes." She lifted her head from Blue's chest and looked in him eager eyes, her own eyes moistening with tears as she realized this moment would never again be possible.

"Yeah Blue I'll marry you." A large smile stretched across his face.

"Thank you Baby girl." He kissed her repeatedly on the face and lips with excitement. Effie Mae rejoiced with ambiguity. On the one hand, she was elated about becoming Blue's wife. On the other, she wondered if it were even legal.

"How you feeling today Blue?" Huck said startling them both as he entered the room, after momentarily standing outside the door watching their intimate exchange, unaware of the reason for them rejoicing.

"Now that Baby girl's here I feel better already." Blue said wiping his tears with the sheet. Effie Mae sat up on the side of the bed and looked in Huck's envious eyes with concern.

"You ready Effie Mae?" He asked unable to mask his resentment.

"Yeah, just let me say bye to Blue." He glared at her, angered by her request to be alone with his rival.

"I guess Ms. Jones gon be here tomorrow." Huck said turnig his attention to Blue. "You still gon be here ain't you Blue?" He teased.

"That's the plan big brother."

"I guess I'll let you and Effie Mae say y'all goodbyes—then we gon move on." Huck shifted his lustful eyes to Effie Mae in anticipation of their impending intimate night then exited the room. Effie Mae's stomach bundled with nerves when seeing the hurt in Blue's eyes.

"Baby girl that man don't plan on letting you get no sleep tonight."

"It may be Huck I'm laying with Blue, but it's gon be you I'm thinking about." He embraced her in his arms then passionately kissed her.

"I love you Baby girl." Blue said trying to hold back his tears.

"I love you back Blue." Effie Mae said forcing a smile as she tried to prepare herself for an unwanted night of intimacy with Huck. "Bye Blue." She rose from the bed then slowly walked in the direction of the door to join Huck in the hallway. Blue smiled and winked.

"Bye Baby girl." Effie Mae exited the room seconds before tears erupted from Blue's eyes trickling down his face, dripping onto his sheets as he stared in the direction of the door. His heart pounded in his chest as thoughts of Huck making love to the woman he loved, haunted him.

––––––––––––––––––––

Effie Mae remained numbed as she envisioned her impending rendezvous with Huck.

"You gon be alright?" Huck asked seeing the stationary tears in her eyes.

"I'm worried about Blue." She said concealing the true reason for her tears. "He look so weak and—" Huck cut her off.

"I'll pull the car around to the door." He said ignoring her concerns over Blue. She shifted her eyes to the horizontal numbers located above the elevator doors—watching as the numbers lit up at each floor before stopping on number six. Effie Mae's anxiety mounted as she waited for the elevator doors to open. She hoped if at all possible she could talk Huck out of the intimate night he'd planned, despite Blue's terminal state. Her optimism shattered when seeing the lustful gaze in his eyes. Effie Mae knew without doubt in Huck's mind, their night had been *carved in stone*. She hurried onto the elevator seconds after the doors opened. Huck followed. He turned and faced her, romantically embracing Effie Mae in his arms.

"You ready?" He asked kissing her seductively on the lips. She forced a smile. For the first time in her life Effie Mae actually felt void of intimate feelings. Huck smiled as he gazed at her. "I want your mind and body on us." He placed a gentle kiss on her lips. "You can worry about Blue after we done." He briefly hesistate then romantically kissed her. The elevator doors opened to the main floor as Huck continued holding Effie Mae in his arms and the kiss persisted. They again closed.

"We gon stay on this elevator all night Huck or you gon let me go so we can get off?" Effie Mae teased. He cunningly smiled then released her before the doors again opened.

"Naw we getting off." Effie Mae clasped her hand over her mouth when seeing Daniel in the waiting room nervously pacing—D.J. held in his arms. She looked up at Huck, her eyes requesting his permission to go to her baby boy.

"Get on, but when I pull around you come on out." She nodded.

"Mr. Daniel!" Effie Mae called out walking quickly towards him. Daniel looked in the direction of the elevators in response to the sound of her voice—fixating his eyes on her face. Effie Mae's eyes lit up as she looked at her toddler son.

"Effie Mae!" Huck called out. She turned to him. "I'll be around in a minute—you be ready." He said shifting his eyes over to Daniel then back to Effie Mae.

"Okay Huck." She stated shifting her eyes back to her baby boy. Daniel watched as Huck exited through the sliding glass doors then turned to Effie Mae.

"How you doing Effie Mae?" He asked hugging her with his free arm. D.J. looked at his momma with unfamiliarity then smiled.

"You want to hold our boy?"

"Is that gon be okay with Ms. Geraldine?"

"Yeah take him." Daniel's eyes remained on Effie Mae's face as he placed D.J. in her arms. "He crawling now—boy getting into everything!" He said chuckling before noticing the frightened look in her eyes.

"Oh—naw D.J's fine . . . ain't that right daddy's boy?" He kissed the squirming toddler on the head, excited by his daddy's voice then again turned to Effie Mae before reaching for his daddy.

"Look like he want to go back to you Mr. Daniel."

"He'll be okay." Daniel said staring at her. Effie Mae blushed. "He just want you to talk to him that's all."

"Hey D.J.—hey my sweet baby." She stated. The toddler looked at her and smiled then giggled. "I love you D.J." He squirmed and cooed.

"That's all he wanted." Daniel said delighted in seeing Effie Mae with their son. "It's Geraldine—"

"Huh?"

"I had to call the ambulance to come get Geraldine from the house earlier today." Daniel's eyes displayed worry.

"Is she—"

"I don't know Effie Mae, I'm still waiting to hear something." He stated nervously scratching his head. "I think she might've had a stroke." Effie Mae's mouth slightly opened.

"You think so Daniel?"

"I ain't heard nothing from the doctor since the ambulance brought her in here." He looked intoEffie Mae's widened eyes. "She didn't look too good Effie Mae when they took her away from the house." His presence in New York suddenly dawned on him. "You back here now Effie Mae?"

"For a little while—" Thoughts of Blue's fate resurfaced in Effie Mae's mind. "—I came here to see about Blue."

"I guess that Ol' Huck brought you out here?" Daniel said making no attempt to mask his dislike for Huck.

"He came to Mississippi and got me."

"Mississippi?" Daniel's eyes widened. "It must be pretty serious then?"

"It is Mr. Daniel." Tears erupted from Effie Mae's eyes. Daniel embraced her as she held D.J. in her arms.

"I'm sorry to hear that Effie Mae I know how much Blue means to you."

"I love him Mr. Daniel!"

"I know you do Effie Mae." He said staring helplessly at her, the love he felr—evident in his eyes. "J.R. know you here?"

"Naw." Effie Mae slightly lowered her head, self consciously believing him to have concluded she'd be spending intimate time with Huck. "I'm gon go see my babies when they get home from school this evening." She looked in Daniel's love filled eyes as D.J. squirmed and cried, again reaching for his daddy.

"Come on boy!" Daniel stated. Effie Mae kissed the toddler on the forehead then handed him back to Daniel. "He just tired and sleepy." Daniel said resting D.J.'s head on his chest. Effie Mae kissed her baby boy on his spongy cheek.

"I love you baby." She stated. Daniel beamed as he imagined them as a family. "Mr. Daniel when all this is over can we talk about me seeing our baby boy?" Daniel's heart fluttered at the reality of him and Effie Mae spending time together with their son.

"Yeah Effie Mae—I'd like that." He slid his hand around her waist and kissed her lightly on the lips. "I still—" A serious look appeared in Daniel's eyes. "—girl I still ain't over you!" Effie Mae blushed. Her eyes shifted quickly over to the exits when hearing a honking horn.

"I guess I better get out here." She said turning back to Daniel. "I don't want Huck to have to come in here looking for me."

"I don't think either one of us want that." Daniel stated humor. "Call me Effie Mae when you ready to talk." She again shifted her eyes over to the exit.

"I will Mr. Daniel." He kissed her on the cheek.

"Say bye to your momma, D.J." He said raising the toddler hand, waving goodbye. Effie Mae smiled as her son looked briefly at her and smiled then closed his eyes, gradually going to sleep. She kissed him on the head.

"Bye my sweet baby." She said turning to leave. Daniel watched as Effie Mae rushed through the exit doors and climbed into Huck's car waiting at the door.

"Mr. Jones!" A nurse called out as she entered the waiting area breaking his stare at Effie Mae. Daniel turned and looked as she approached.

"Huh?"

"The doctor's on his way out to speak with you about your wife."

"Oh, okay—good." His mouth dried as he wondered what the doctor would say.

---

"What you and old Daniel talk about?" Huck asked breaking his prolonged gazed at Effie Mae as she sat on the burgundy, crush velvet sofa in the eloquently decorated living room of his two bedroom apartment.

"He was saying he think Ms. Geraldine had a stroke, but he wasn't sure." Huck shook his head with sympathy.

"Damn shame." Effie Mae's mind raced as her thoughts drifted to Blue, Ms. Geraldine, J.R. and Anthony then back to Blue."

"What he say about your son?"

"He said we could talk about me spending time with my baby boy." Huck noted the occupied look in her eyes.

"What he say got you looking all confused?"

"Nothing."

"Nothing?" He looked at her with suspicion. "It don't look like nothing to me."

"It's just with Blue being sick and now Ms. Geraldine—" Effie Mae tried to mask her lack of interest in sharing Huck's bed with him. "— then seeing my baby boy." A smile formed on her face when speaking of D.J. Huck took hold of Effie Mae's hand assisting her to her feet.

"Come on let's go to bed." She gave no reply as a sense of helplessness came over her, much like when she worked as a whore at Ms. Norma's whorehouse a few years back. Huck embraced her in his arms and intimately kissed her. "Don't tell your momma about this." He cunningly grinned. Effie Mae forced a smile as she thought only of Blue, as Huck led her into his bedroom to engage in intimacy.

# Chapter Nine

Effie Mae arrived at J.R.'s church that afternoon, dropped off by Huck. She entered the foyer seeing him inside the sanctuary accompanied by a female. Electing not to make her presence known, curious of the relationship between J.R. and the unfamiliar woman, she remained out of sight and listened.

"I'm still waiting on that dinner invitation Rev. Smith . . . or can I just call you J.R.?" Ms. Taylor asked flirtatiously.

"Uh, Rev. Smith is fine uh—"

"You never did say where your wife, what's her name again?" J.R.'s anxiety increased.

"Was there uh, something in particular you needed Ms. Taylor?" Effie Mae quietly giggled as she watched J.R. unsuccessfully *ward-off* Ms. Taylor's advances.

"Uh-uh J.R. . . call me Yolanda!" She said batting her eyes. "Now I keep seeing that wedding ring on your finger, but no wife." She seductively smiled then grabbed hold of J.R.'s hand. He shifted his eyes to his *hi-jacked* hand then noted the suggestive smile on Ms. Taylor's face.

"Uh, Sister Taylor I don't think uh—" She interjected.

"Now you wouldn't be wearing that ring trying to keep the women away would you—J.R.?" She girlishly grinned.

"Rev. Smith—just uh, call me Rev. Smith." J.R. said sliding his hand from her grasp.

"Now what did you say your wife's name was again—J.R.?" She asked, again taking hold of his hand. Effie Mae removed Anthony's engagement ring from her finger then reached inside her purse and took out her wedding ring—putting it on.

"Effie Mae!" She stated entering the sanctuary. J.R.'s mouth abruptly opened, shocked by her presence. "Hey J.R." Effie Mae said approaching him and his female suitor. Ms. Taylor's eyes widened as she looked at the woman running interference on her play for the reverend. Effie Mae brushed pass the persistent female then stood directly in front of J.R. Ms. Taylor remained momentarily silent, rendered speechless by the unexpected intrusion.

"Effie Mae?" J.R. said looking at her in astonishment, but delighted to see her. "When did you uh—" Effie Mae wrapped her arms around his neck and passionately kissed her estranged husband's compliant lips. Ms. Taylor's jaw dropped. She looked in awe at the unfamiliar female moving in on her territory. J.R. gazed into Effie Mae's eyes as the mouthwatering kiss ended. He marveled over her unanticipated, but most welcoming kiss. He blushed.

"Excuse me Miss—" Ms. Taylor said. "—I believe I was talking to Rev. Smith . . . I mean J.R."

"Uh, Sister Taylor—" J.R. said momentarily loss for words. "—this is uh, my wife Effie Mae." He stated. Effie Mae turned and faced her rival.

"How you doing Miss uh, did I hear J.R. say your name was Sister Taylor?" She looked at Effie Mae with displeasure, disturbed by her obvious existence. "I'm Effie Mae Smith." Effie Mae said rubbing Ms. Taylor's nose in it. "And like my husband said, I'm his wife and I been his wife for—" She turned to J.R. "—how long we been married sweetie?"

"Uh, fourteen years?" He said struggling to maintain a straight face, humored by the entire event as Effie Mae continued her woman-to-woman standoff with Ms. Taylor.

"So to answer your question Sister Taylor . . . J.R. is very married." Effie Mae extended her left hand, displaying J.R.'s wedding ring—again on her finger. "So my husband ain't wearing his wedding ring cause  he trying to keep women like you away, but because he love his wife." J.R.'s smile widened, pleased to see Effie Mae wearing his ring as she laid claim on him as her husband. Ms. Taylor rolled her eyes as she engaged in a *stare down* with Effie Mae. J.R. intervened.

"I uh—don't think uh, you ladies should be fighting over me." Ms. Taylor disengaged her stare with Effie Mae then turned to him.

"Shut up Rev. Smith!" She shouted. J.R. and Effie Mae's jaws dropped in response to Ms. Taylor's unexpected response. She shifted her angry eyes  again to Effie Mae then back to J.R. "I can't believe I've been wasting my time on you Rev. Smith!" Ms. Taylor said with contempt. "A sheep in wolves clothing that's what you are . . . in here in God's house preying on innocent young women." Effie Mae interjected.

"Innocent? Young?" She stated. Ms. Taylor glanced briefly at her then turned her attention back to J.R.

"I guess you can't trust nobody these days, not even a preacher!" She yelled. "I guess preachers ain't what they use to be that's for damn sure!" Ms. Taylor's looked at Effie Mae and again rolled her eyes then turned to leave. "Hah!" She scoffed walking hastily down the center aisle of the sanctuary and into the foyer. J.R. and Effie Mae silently watched as Ms. Taylor stormed out the front doors of the church, but not before flashing the *husband and wife duo* an ice cold stare. They looked at each other, astounded by what had just taken place then burst into laughter.

"I think you just lost a church member J.R." Effie Mae said laughing.

"I uh, I think you might be right." He said as their entertaining moment persisted. He looked through the glass doors when hearing screechin tires seeing Ms. Taylor as she sped away. "Uh, by the way I never said I was interested in her." J.R. said thinking out loud. He turned to Effie Mae and smiled. She blushed. "It's uh, good to see you Effie Mae." He said glancing briefly out the door expecting to see Anthony. "Is uh, Anthony with you?" He asked hoping he wasn't. Effie Mae suddenly remembered she'd not yet called him.

"Naw J.R." His optimism increased.

"Are the uh, children—"

"Momma and Annie Mae watching my babies for me while Anthony at work in Jackson." J.R.'s optimism diminished.

"Is uh, everything alright with you and uh—" She smiled.

"Everything's fine with me and Anthony, J.R." Effie Mae said amused by his obvious jealousy.

"Uh, okay." His mouth dried in response to her disappointing news. He coughed. "You uh, here to see the girls?" Effie Mae hesitated before answering. Her eyes moistened with tears.

"It's Blue, J.R."

"Blue? Is uh, everything okay?"

"Naw J.R. it ain't." He embraced Effie Mae in his arms.

"Uh—"

"Blue's doctor only giving him six months to live J.R." His eyes widened, shocked by her troubling news.

"I uh, I'm sorry to hear that Effie Mae—"

"J.R. I can't live without Blue!" She cried out as tears flowed from her eyes." J.R. swallowed the newly formed lump in his throat then laid her head on his chest.

"You uh, want to talk about it?" Effie Mae looked up at him and shook her head no. "Uh, okay so what do you need me to do?"

"I need you to bring our babies up here J.R. so they can live with you."

"Okay I can uh, do that." He delighted in the thought of reuniting with his children—and her. "When did you uh, need me to do that?"

"I can't keep leaving my babies on Anthony!" She stated through her weeping. Effie Mae suddenly silenced then chuckled.

"What uh—" J.R. said puzzled by her out of place laughter.

"I see my baby sister and Pete having problems in their perfect marriage." She said wiping her tears. J.R. looked at her with suspicion.

"You uh, didn't have anything to do with that did you?"

"Nope—it ain't had nothing to do with me J.R." Effie Mae continued laughing. "J.R. you should've seen how Annie Mae was looking at Huck—"

"Uh, Huck?"

"Blue sent him to Mississippi to get me." She blushed when thinking of Blue's recent marriage proposal. "When that little girl saw Huck she couldn't take her eyes off that man!" J.R.'s ears slightly deafened to Effie Mae's words as his curiosity of her travel from Mississippi to New York with Huck—nagged at him.

"So uh, when did you say you got here?" Effie Mae pulled from his embrace.

"If you asking me if I stayed the with Huck, yeah J.R. I did." She stated with defiance. "You may not want me no more, but that ain't ever gon happen with Huck." She began walking away.

"Effie Mae—wait!"

"Wait for what J.R.?" She said raising her voice.

"You was the one who didn't want to be married to me anymore—"

"Don't worry about it J.R., as soon as all this is over—" Effie Mae silenced when realizing, *it being over* meant Blue being gone."

"I only filed for divorce because you said you wanted to marry Anthony, but if you don't want—" She burst into laughter.

"Marry Anthony? I ain't sure bout that either."

"What?" J.R. said puzzled.

"J.R. so much done changed with me and Anthony, it's like we don't even know each other no more." J.R.'s hope for their reunification heightened. "It seems me and Anthony been so busy trying to pick up where we left off we ain't realized we ain't the same people we was when we was kids." J.R. grinned.

"I uh, don't think any of us are." A cunning smile suddenly stretched across J.R.'s face as he reminisced. "Wow . . . when I was sixteen life was a lot different, I can remember—" He abruptly quieted when noticing Effie Mae's dropped jaws and the look of shock growing in her eyes.

"J.R. Smith you telling me you ain't the innocent man Ms. Sissy think you is?"

"You were uh, saying you and Anthony have changed?" J.R. said redirecting the conversation.

"Yeah J.R. a lot." Effie Mae blushed. "But that boy know he still know how to have a good time—that ain't changed." She giggled. J.R. frowned.

"Effie Mae."

"What J.R., he do!" Her blushing smile widened.

"I uh, would rather not hear about that." Effie Mae's playful mood changed to a serious one.

"I know it take more than that to make a marriage J.R."

"Have uh, you and Anthony talked about this change?"

"A little."

"A little?"

"I need to call Anthony, let him know where I am—that boy probably done called Momma a thousand times since I ain't home answering the phone." She laughed. "You know he act like he got call me every night."

"I'm sure he's uh, just making sure you okay."

"Sometimes J.R. I don't know if Anthony checking on me to see if I'm alright or checking up on me to see if I'm with Blue." J.R. humorously smiled.

"What?"

"I thought you said Anthony didn't know you?" Effie Mae giggled and again laid her head on J.R.'s chest. He embraced her.

"Wouldn't it be funny J.R. if after all this time we got back together?" Effie Mae said smiling. J.R.'s heart raced as he listened to her unexpected words.

"Uh, funny?"

"When I got them divorce papers from your attorney—" She looked J.R. in the eyes. "—it scared me J.R." He listened, feeling hopeful. "I know I ain't ever acted like your wife, but in all these years J.R. that's who I been." He oddly appreciated her acknowledging herself as his wife despite being in town to be at her dying lover's side. "Not Anthony's, Huck's or even Blue's." Effie Mae smiled as she heard her own truthful words. "So I guess that make you more my husband than Momma's." A peculiar look showed in J.R.'s eyes.

"Huh?" She giggled.

"What I'm saying J.R.—" Effie Mae looked in her estranged husband's eyes then wrapped her arms around his neck. "—one day I might just choose you for myself." J.R. gazed in Effie Mae's eyes as she slowly pulled his mouth onto hers then intimately kissed him. He fondly remembered the love he felt the day Rev. Hill pronounced them husband and wife. He gradually opened his eyes following the mouthwatering kiss.

"Uh, about what you just said, I was hoping—" She cut him off.

"Right now J.R. all my love belong to Blue." J.R.'s bubble of promise burst when hearing her speak on her love for Blue.

# *Chapter Ten*

"Wake up boy!" A man's voice stated loudly. Blue slowly turned his head in the direction of the command and gradually opened his eyes bringing into focus his father—Henry Lee White Sr., six feet two, bronzed colored, sixtyish, handsome, well groomed and finely dressed. His hair salt and pepper in color.

"Daddy?"

"Yeah boy it's me—your no good brother told your mother you were sick."

"Daddy please don't get started on Henry Lee—" He cut Blue off.

"You know Henry Lee ain't no good Tyrell . . . he ain't ever been no good and he ain't ever gon be no good!" His father stated with contempt. "Just like that no good momma of his." Blue's anxiety increased in response to his father's cruel words regarding his half brother.

"Daddy I'm sick—my doctor ain't giving me six months to live and long after I'm gone Huck still gon be your son—" Blue suddenly began to cough.

"You alright Tyrell?" His father asked, alarmed by his vigorous coughing.

"Water Daddy—I need—some water." Mr. White quickly picked up the pitcher of water from the bedside table and filled the empty glass next to it. He raised the head of the bed and held the glass to Blue's mouth, watching as he took small sips before retrieving his inhaler lying on the nightstand, taking two quick puffs—inhaling and exhaling twice, looking in his father's worried eyes until his coughing gradually subsided and his breathing began to normalize.

"Where's—Mom—ma?" A smile formed on Mr. White face.

"Your mother's downstairs in the gift shop, she wanted to bring you some flowers and a card." He lovingly grinned. "You know how your mother is Tyrell—Rosalyn's a good woman that's why I love so much." He looked at Blue with regret in his eyes. "I just hate I never married her." Blue looked at him with questioning eyes.

"I always wondered about that Daddy, if you loved Momma so much what stopped you from marrying her?"

"My wife Rita!" Mr. White stated nonchalantly. "Crazy woman always said if I married Rosalyn she'd kill us both." A nervous look displayed in Mr. White's eyes. "And as crazy as she was and the way that woman could drank . . . I know she'd make good on that threat."

"How Ms. Rita doing anyway Daddy—is she okay?" Blue asked concerned. "Huck ain't heard from her in a few years."

"She's still a drunk if that's what you're asking." His father stated, shifting his eyes over in the direction of the open door, not wanting Blue's mother to hear his impending words. "Starting to lose her good looks too." Blue frowned, agitated by his father's unkind words.

"Daddy!"

"She is Tyrell." A bittler look showed on Mr. White's face. "When I met Rita she was beautiful!" He stated with enthusiasm. "Had to practically fight to keep other men away from her." He scowled. "Now I wouldn't look at her twice." He chuckled. "And once is too many."

"Daddy don't talk about that woman like that!" Blue said unamused. His attention suddenly drew to the door seeing his mother peering in.

"Hey Tyrell." Ms. Jones said entering the room, walking over towards him—sitting a bouquet of colorful flowers and a beautiful *Get Well* card on the night stand. "How are you feeling sweetheart?"

"I'm a lot better than I was Momma." Blue said delighted to see his mother. She leaned over and kissed him lightly on the forehead.

"Henry Lee told me you were sick." A boyish looked formed on Blue's face as his mother gently rubbed his head.

"They only giving me six months to live Momma." Her eyes saddened.

"Just broke my heart when Henry Lee told me." Ms. Jones said placing a kiss on his forehead a second time. Mr. White shook his head when thinking of his favorite son's fate.

"I didn't think your mother was ever going to stop crying." He said rubbing his longtime mistress softly on the back then placing a loving kiss on her cheek. Ms. Jones looked at him and smiled.

"Thank you Henry."

"Where's that's no good wife of yours Tyrell?" His father asked, upset. "And why is she not here?"

"You know I don't have no wife anymore Daddy." Blue said shifting his eyes to his mother. "Me and Daphne been divorced for fifteen years now." A look of disgust displayed on Mr. White face as he thought about her.

"Yeah that's right . . . caught her laid up with that no good brother of your didn't you?" Ms. Jones looked at him with chastising eyes in response to his insensitive words.

"Henry!"

"What Rosalyn—he did!"

"It wasn't just Huck, Daddy." Blue chuckled. "Daphne was like a doorknob—everybody got a turn." Blue's chuckle progressed into laughter. "Every member in my band had her!"

"But Henry Lee was your brother, Tyrell!" Mr. White said, angry. "He should've never touched Daphne he knew she was your wife."

"Henry!" Ms. Jones said scolding him. "Now why on earth are you bringing up all that mess?" He looked in her peaceful eyes and mellowed. "That's been so many years ago Henry it's hardly worth mentioning."

"Yeah you're right Rosalyn." He kissed her softly on the lips then seated himself in a corner chair, adjacent to Blue's bed saying nothing further. Ms. Jones turned her attention back to Blue.

"Do you have a special lady in your life Tyrell?" A huge smile stretched across Blue's face.

"Yeah Momma I do, she'll be waiting for me at home when I get there tomorrow." She shifted her eyes over to Mr. White with concern then again looked at Blue. "Her name is Effie Mae, Momma and I love her so much." Blue's eyes moistened as he spoke. "I asked her to marry me Momma!" Her eyes widened.

"Marry you?" She said stunned by his unexpected announcement. "My goodness Tyrell we haven't even met this girl." A distressed looked showed in his mother's eyes as she given his impending mortality. Mr. White intervened.

"I just have one thing to say Tyrell . . . if you want to keep her—keep her away from that no good brother of yours." Ms. Jones turned quickly to him, bothered by his statement.

"Henry!"

"Come on now Rosalyn you know how Henry Lee is."

"Well Henry maybe he's changed over the years."

"Changed!" Mr. White shouted looking at her with skeptical eyes. "If he ain't already had her—he will."

"Henry!"

"Alright Rosalyn I'm done." He said relenting. "I've said all that needs to be said . . . it's up to Tyrell to listen."

"You know Daddy, I wouldn't care if Huck did have her already." Ms. Jones' jaw dropped.

"Tyrell . . . surely you don't mean that!"

"Yeah Momma I do." Blue said as his frustration grew. "Huck was the one who introduced me to Effie Mae in the first place." Ms. Jones shifted her eyes to Mr. White. "He may have had her first, but it's me she loves Momma!" She again shifted her eyes to Mr. White, displeased with her son's unacceptable logic.

"Tyrell?" His mother looked at him with disappointed eyes. "Surely you're not serious about marrying a woman that's been intimately involved with your brother are—"

"Yeah Momma I am." Blue said dismissing her subtle objection. "That woman came all the way here from Mississippi just to be with me." A perplexed look entered Ms. Jones' eyes—she again glanced over at Mr. White, her eyes forbidding him to say one word of reprimand to her only son as she continued questioning him. "Mississippi . . . how can she be in a relationship with you Tyrell if she lives all the way in Mississippi?"

"Effie Mae used to live here Mommam but she moved back to Mississippi about six months ago."

"That still doesn't make sense Tyrell." Ms. Jones said uncomfortable with the long distance relationship. Mr. White looked at her with disapproving eyes as he continued to hold his peace. "So when do you get to see her Tyrell?" His mother asked finding the arrangement somewhat odd.

"I'm getting kind of tired Momma." Ms. Jones looked in Blue's tired eyes and relented.

"Alright Tyrell then I won't ask you anymore questions—today, but when you're feeling better I want to hear all about this Effie Mae."

———————————

"Yeah Buckeye, I started another girl over at Ms. Norma's the other day." A large smile appeared on Buckeye's face in response to Huck's new female find.

"Yeah man, Libby was telling me something about that the other day when I—" Huck cut him off.

"Libby?"

"Yeah—" Buckeye's smile widened. "—me and Libby still get together every now and then." Huck tilted his head.

"Is that right?"

"Huck man you know Libby gon always be my girl."

"You paying for that Buckeye?" Buckeyes' eyes widened.

"Man I thought—"

"I'm just messing with you Buckeye." The two men laughed as they walked through the hospital corridor on their way to visit Blue. "Yeah Buckeye my new girl, she ain't no Effie Mae but—" Huck abruptly stopped when seeing Ms. Jones sitting on Blue's bed. He walked closer to the room bringing his father into view, sitting in a chair next to Blue's bed. "How you doing Ms. Jones?" Huck said as he entered the room. She turned in response to his voice.

"Hello Henry Lee . . . and I'm doing just fine." She said shifting her eyes to Buckeye then back to Huck. "I see you're still just as handsome as ever." He blushed.

"Thank you Ms. Jones, I guess a man can't ever get tired of hearing that."

"But you always have looked just like your mother." Huck ignored her words regarding his mother. He also disregarded his father's presence in the room, turning his attention to Blue.

"How you feeling Blue?"

"Well let me get out of your way Henry Lee—" Ms. Jones said as she rose from the bed. "—I'll let you visit with your brother." She looked briefly at Buckeye as she walked pass him on her way to stand over by the door. Mr. White looked at his eldest son with disdain as the two brothers talked.

"I feel a lot better than when they first brought me in here man." Blue chuckled then looked at Buckeye.

"Hey Lawrence."

"Tyrell . . . you doing alright man?" Buckeye asked sensing the tension between Huck and his father. "I sure do miss seeing you down at the club man, standing up on stage blowing that horn." Buckeye laughed as he discretely shifted his eyes to Mr. White before turning his attention back to Blue.

"It looks like my horn blowing days might be over man!"

"You don't see me sitting over here Henry Lee?" Mr. White stated. Huck dismissed his father's words. "You hear me talking to you boy?"

"Huck did you see Daddy over there?"

"That's your Daddy, Blue." Huck said refusing to acknowledge him. "My Daddy left me and my momma the day he decided making thirteen kids with six different women was a better option."

"I see you still lowdown as ever." Mr. White stated callously.

"I guess if I am lowdown Mr. White—" Huck said keeping his back turned to his father. "—it's because I'm my father's son." Blue's anxiety heightened as the tensity between his father and Huck mounted. "When they talking about letting you out here Blue?" Huck asked shifting his eyes to Buckeye, preparing for the impending altercation he knew would ensue. "I can pick you up—take you home, make sure Effie Mae gets there." Blue smiled. "I dropped her off at J.R.'s church so they could talk."

"Henry Lee how's your mother?" Ms. Jones asked hoping to defuse the tension mounting between Huck and his father. He stared at Blue, his eyes giving warning of his displeasure with Ms. Jones asking about his mother.

"I don't mean you no disrespect Ms. Jones, but I don't think you got no place asking me about my—" Mr. White quickly intervened.

"Don't you talk to my woman like that boy!" He said raising his voice.

"Your woman?" Huck shook his head. "Damn shame. "It was you and your woman that drove my momma to drinking." He said turning defiantly to his father. "If your woman mean so much to you Mr. White why don't you go ahead and give my momma her divorce—free her." Mr. White and Ms. Jones looked at one another with guilt, neither replied. "Maybe then she can find a man more worthy than the one she spent her young years crying over and drinking then beating the hell out me after that scotch built up the devil's rage up in her." Mr. White rose to his feet.

"Sit your ass down Mr. White." Huck said staring him in the eyes before again turning to Blue—visually warning him of the battle he prepared to have with their father. "I don't like it when a man look like he trying to make a move on me Mr. White." He shifted his eyes to Buckeye.

"Well I'm not just any man Henry Lee—I'm your daddy boy!"

"Daddy?" Huck looked into Blue's frightened eyes. "Tell him Buckeye—tell him to sit his old ass down before I put him down." Blue's eyes pleaded with Huck not to do it.

"Mr. White—" Buckeye stated on his old friend's behalf. Mr. White slowly removed a large knife from the leather holster attached at his right side. Huck again turned and faced him when seeing the terrified look in Blue's eyes.

"You think I'm scared of that Mr. White?" Huck said looking at him, undaunted by the large weapon. "I've had bigger blades than that pulled on me in poker games." He again shifted his eyes to Buckeye then to Blue and again looked at his father. "I tell you what Mr. White—" Huck said maintaining his composure. "—if I was you I'd put that apple peeler back in your pocket before you beat Ol' Blue here to the grave." Mr. White took a step forwards, quickly stopping when hearing the hammer of a pistol cock. Ms. Jones' mouth opened and her eyes widened, horrified by the .38 caliber pistol held in Buckeye's right hand, aimed at the man she loved.

"Mr. White—" Buckeye said. "—me and Huck's been friends since we were kids and he's just like a brother to me." He glanced over at Huck then turned back to Mr. White staring him in the eyes. "And I think you should know I would die for this man, so if you don't get your ass out of here threatening my friend I'm gon use this pistol to put a hole you." Mr. White remained silent as he looked into the barrel of the pistol aimed at his heart. "You see Mr. White I ain't ever known my daddy— hell for all I know you could be him." Ms. Jones looked at Buckeye, visually searching for any resemblance to Mr. White. She quietly gasped.

"But if you are—" Buckeye continued his eye to eye gaze with Mr. White. "—I don't want to know because to me my daddy died same as my momma did from a heroin overdose." Mr. White's fear heightened when seeing rage burning in Buckeye's eyes. "You see . . . by me believing you ain't my daddy is the only thing keeping me from pulling this trigger blowing your ass away." Blue's terror progressed into panic. "Because if I thought for one minute you were the man that left me to be raised by my dope dealing uncle who put me out on the streets hustling and coning folks when I was only ten years old—" Buckeye's fury mounted. "—then ran out on me every time the law got close to catching up to his ass—"

"Stop!" Blue shouted. "This ain't right!" All eyes turned to Blue. "I'm in here dying and my family's turning my hospital room into a combat zone!" Huck looked at him with remorse in his eyes.

"You right Blue." He said apologizing. "This should've never happen." Tears streamed down Blue's face.

"Daddy I appreciate y'all coming, but I want you to take Momma and leave, I need to get some rest." Mr. White continued his stand-off with Huck and Buckeye.

"Let's go Henry!" Ms. Jones said anxious to distance them from the volatile situation. "It was good seeing you Henry Lee." She stated politely before quickly exiting the room. Mr. White remained stationary as he gave Huck a final look of disgust before sliding the large knife back in its holster then walking in the direction of the door.

"This ain't over Henry Lee!" He said shifting his eyes to the barrel of Buckeye's .38 caliber pistol cocked and drawn. Mr. White shifted his eyes momentarily at Blue then exited the room joining Ms. Jones in the hallway.

"Well Buckeye—" Huck looked over at him. "—I guess we can grieve together, seems my daddy died same as yours."

———————————

Effie Mae watched from the back door as J.R. got into his car, on his way to the church to conduct daily business. She girlishly smiled when thinking of Blue coming home from the hospital that day. Her smile widened as she recalled the love in his eyes when proposing marriage from his hospital bed. Effie Mae basked in the realization that she and her beloved Blue would soon be sharing in a wedding ceremony and uniting as husband and wife. Her glowing moment ended when remembering she still hadn't Anthony. She now worried how he would react to her plans to marry Blue, despite still being his fiancée. Effie Mae's apprehension increased when thinking of Anthony's excessive rage when discovering her birth control pills. Her thoughts scrambled when reliving the fear she felt when Anthony raised his fist to her. She stared nervously at the phone before picking it up and dialing Anthony's number.

"Hey Anthony."

"Baby where are you? I've been calling the house every night and you're not answering, is everything—"

"Anthony wait!"

"Okay."

"I'm in New York Anthony."

"New York!" He took a deep breath. "Baby why are you in New York—have you left me?"

"Anthony—listen!"

"Okay Baby I'm listening."

"It's Blue, Anthony."

"Blue?" He again took a deep breath. "So you have left me."

"Anthony Blue's dying."

"What?" His eyes widened in response to her unexpected news. "Baby are you alright?"

"Naw Anthony I—" He cut her off.

"Baby just tell me what you need me to do?"

"I need you to bring my babies up here to New York Anthony."

"Baby you know I don't mind watching the kids."

"Anthony how you gon watch my babies if you in Jackson all the time?"

"Okay, you're right I see what you're saying, so when do you want me to bring you the kids?"

"As soon as you can Anthony, Lil' J.R.'s already asking for me."

"Okay Baby . . . is this weekend good?"

"That's fine Anthony." Effie Mae briefly silenced. "When you bring my babies Anthony we need to talk."

"That doesn't sound good Baby."

"Blue asked me to do something Anthony."

"Do something—something like what?"

"Anthony . . . Blue only got six months to live, I can't leave him."

"Okay, so what does that mean for us?"

"That's what we need to talk about Anthony." The phone went silent. "You there Anthony?"

"Yes Baby, I'm still here."

"You need me to send J.R. to get my babies Anthony?" Effie Mae asked, hearing disappointment in his voice.

"No Baby, I don't want you to send J.R.—I said I'd bring them."

"You sure Anthony?"

"Yes Baby at least that'll give me a chance to see you."

"Thank you Anthony."

"You're welcome Baby." The phone again went silent.

"You there Anthony?"

"I love you Baby."

"You may not feel that way Anthony after we talk."

"Ouch that hurts."

"Bye Anthony."

"Bye Baby."

———————

Huck placed Blue's arm around his neck and assisted him from the car to the front door of the jazz club. Buckeye followed. The door swung open just as Blue prepared to knock—Melvin stood on the other side, a huge smile on his face.

"Welcome home man!" Melvin said embracing his cousin excited by his return home. "Last time I saw you Blue man . . . you wasn't looking too good!" Blue took a deep breath, slightly winded.

"I'm glad to see you too cousin, but it wasn't your face I was hoping to see when that door opened." Blue said laughing as he entered the people filled jazz club. His eyes moistened when seeing his many patrons, friends and family—all applauding his arrival home.

"I love you man!" Melvin said exchanging a brotherly hug with him, his own eyes dampening.

"I love you too cousin!" Blue said looking anxiously around the club in search of Effie Mae. Huck's attention drew to his father seated mid-center, left of the room watchin him with distrustful eyes.

"Come on so you can and sit down Blue." Huck said assisting him to a table in front of the stage where Ms. Jones awaited. Huck shifted his eyes to Buckeye signaling him with a nod of the head to keep an eye on his father. Buckeye nodded confirming he understood Huck's non-verbal cue then turned to their cohorts also present at the club, alerting them with his eyes to watch Mr. White. The three men replied with a single nod, indicating they're intent to act on the first signs of trouble.

"Where's Effie Mae, Tyrell?" Ms. Jones asked looking around the club. "I can't wait to meet her." Blue looked at Huck with questioning eyes. Huck winked ensuring him he'd already brought Effie Mae there.

"She'll be here Momma."

"Is she here Tyrell?" Ms. Jones asked eager to meet her possible future daughter-in-law.

"She coming Momma!"

"Are you sure Tyrell?"

"Yeah Momma I'm sure." Blue's attention drew to the stage as his band walked up, retrieving their instruments. Cued by the sound of the piano they began playing Blue's favorite jazz pieces. He looked up at his members and smiled then gratefully nodded. His eyes slightly watering when seeing the place where he once stood—now vacant.

"Hey Baby." Blue quickly turned in the direction of the stairs in response to the voice he'd been waiting to hear. A huge smile displayed on his face when looking into Effie Mae's hazel brown eyes.

"Help me up Huck." Blue stated trying desperately to stand. Huck took hold of his arm and assisted him to his feet. "I love you Baby girl!" Blue hollered out. Effie Mae's smile widened. Huck watched intently, unable to remove his eyes from Effie Mae as she walked down the stairs. Buckeye noted his old friend's unrelenting gaze and sympathized with his envy. He knew deep inside Huck harbored love for the woman whose heart belonged to his half-brother. Blue grasped hold of Effie Mae's pulling her into his arms the minute his hands were able to reach her. They passionately kissed. The group of onlookers stood to their feet and clapped.

"Momma this is Effie Mae."

"Well I guessed that much Tyrell." Ms. Jones said chuckling. "Hello Effie Mae!" She extended her arms and prepared to hug Effie Mae. "Tyrell, how am I supposed to hug her if you're wrapped all around her?"

"I'm sorry Momma, I just love this woman so much I don't ever want to let her go." He placed a loving kiss on Effie Mae's lips.

"I ain't going nowhere Blue." Effie Mae teased. Huck momentarily watched with resentment then intervened.

"You gon let Ms. Jones meet Effie Mae or what Blue?" He said trying to mask his jealousy. Blue reluctantly released her as he again sat down.

"Thank you Henry Lee." Ms. Jones stated before compassionately hugging Effie Mae, looking at Blue with approving eyes. "She's beautiful Tyrell."

"Inside and out Momma." Blue said easing Effie Mae on his lap seconds after her hug with his mother ended. She intimately kissed him on the lips then looked up when sensing Huck's vindictive gaze as he stood to the left of Blue. Her eyes pleaded with him to allow her and Blue to celebrate his return home. Mr. White watched from across the room, studying their non-verbal interaction as he surmised the relationship between his eldest son and Effie Mae had not concluded.

"I'm gon go ahead and make a move Blue, let you and Effie Mae enjoy y'all moment." Huck said continuing his gawk at Effie Mae.

"Hold up a minute Huck! I got an announcement to make." Huck tilted his head, curious of Blue's sudden pressing news.

"Hey everybody listen up. " Huck said bringing the chatter filled room to silence. "Blue here got something he want to say." Blue's smile widened as he looked at Effie Mae.

"Help me up man."

"Blue baby you think you need to be standing up like that?" Effie Mae said concerned. Melvin rushed over to him.

"Hold on Blue, let me get you a microphone man." He looked up on stage at the band. "Somebody hand me a mic." The pianist quickly removed a microphone from a stand and handed it to Melvin—he gave it to Blue. Huck shifted his eyes to Effie Mae and wondered if she knew what Blue was about to say. She looked brierfly at him then turned away. He again turned his attention to Blue and the huge glowing smile on his face as he looked around the club at his many guest.

"I know most of y'all here know this beautiful woman sitting on my lap." He looked at Effie Mae. She blushed. The room filled with nods and verbal replies. "Some of y'all even know the day I fell in love with this woman and how she stole my heart." Blue's eyes moistened as he and Effie Mae exchange a quick smooch. Ms. Jones smiled. Huck shifted his eyes to Buckeye, unnerved with suspense. "Y'all this woman has made me the happiest man this world has ever seen!" Tears erupted from Blue's eyes.

"Are you going to be alright Tyrell?" Ms. Jones asked in response to his intense emotional state.

"Yeah Momma."

"Blue Baby stop crying." Effie Mae said wiping his tears with her hand.

"I can't Baby girl I love you so much."

"I know Baby but you can't tell everybody our news if you crying." She kissed him lightly on the forehead. He looked up at Effie Mae, his eyes filled with tears as he held the microphone to his mouth.

"Y'all . . . I asked this beautiful woman to marry me and she said yes." Huck quickly shifted his eyes to Effie Mae then looked at Blue as the sound of applause for the newly engaged couple filled the room's acoustics. Blue enveloped Effie Mae in his arms and romantically kissed her. Huck shifted his envious eyes to Buckeye then again to Blue, lost for words. "So this Saturday y'all I'll be making Baby girl my wife right here at the club and I want all y'all to come out and join us." Blue's excitement amplified, overjoyed at the thought of him and Effie Mae being united as husband and wife. They passionately kissed. Huck gazed curiously at Effie Mae, puzzled by her agreeing to marry Blue when she continued to be a married woman.

"You look tired Blue . . . let me help you upstairs." He said wanting to confront him and Effie Mae away from the crowd.

"Huh?" Blue looked up seeing the demanding look in Huck's eyes. "Huck man I ain't ready to go—"

"Yeah, you ready." He stated, grabbing hold of Blue's arm.

"Are you leaving Tyrell?" Ms. Jones asked when seeing Huck assisting him to his feet. Effie Mae looked at Huck as she rose from Blue's lap.

"Yeah Momma I'm feeling a little tired." Ms. Jones gently rubbed his face.

"Then you go ahead and get your rest sweetheart." She smiled. "I guess I'll see you and that beautiful lady in the morning." An adoring smiled displayed on Blue's face as he looked at Effie Mae and lovingly smiled. She blushed.

"What Blue?"

"I love you Baby girl."

"I love you back Blue." Huck's anger magnied as Blue and Effie Mae exchanged an romantic kiss. Ms. Jones smiled. Mr. White scoffed, watching with suspicion as he carefully observed the trio.

"You ready Blue?" Huck asked eager to challenge his half brother on his unacceptable marriage proposal. He looked over at Buckeye then shifted his eyes to Mr. Whilte. Buckeye nodded then turned to Huck's cohorts . . . they likewise nodded ensuring they were ready to act if necessary.

"Tyrell I'm so glad you found Effie Mae." Ms. Jones said as Blue steadied himself. "She seems like such a wonderful girl."

"She is Momma."

"Let's go." Huck said escorting Blue over to the stairs, anxious to share his strong objections to his plan to marry Effie Mae. He abruptly stopped and looked back when realizing Effie Mae hadn't joined them.

"It was really nice meeting you Effie Mae." Ms. Jones said hugging her.

"It was good meeting you too Ms. Jones."

"I guess I should say congratulations!" Ms. Jones said, again embracing Effie Mae.

"Thank you Ms. Jones." Effie Mae's attention drew to Huck when sensing his intimidating stare. "I guess me and Blue gon see you in the morning then." She said shifting her eyes to Huck then back to Ms. Jones.

"I guess you will." Ms. Jones giggled then hugged Effie Mae a fourth time. "Goodbye Effie Mae."

"Bye Ms. Jones." Effie Mae walked swiftly away joining Huck and Blue over at the stairs. Mr. White continued observing as the three headed up the steps, disappearing as they neared the top.

———————————

"What you doing Blue?" Huck asked as he lowered Blue into a sitting position on the bed then took a step back and looked at him in awe—stunned by his announcement.

"How in the hell you gon marry Effie Mae and she already got a husband?" He stared at Blue with chastising eyes. "What? You doing this for Ms. Jones' sake?" Blue gave no reply as his agitation increased in response to Huck's disciplining words. "J.R. know you talking about marrying Blue, Effie Mae?" Huck asked watching as she walked over to the dresser and removed a pair of Blue's pajamas.

"Don't you worry 'bout what J.R. know." Effie Mae stated boldly. She turned her attention quickly to Blue when he began forcefully coughing. "You alright baby?" She asked frightened. He nodded then reached inside his shirt pocket and retrieved an inhaler holding it to his mouth taking two quick puffs—inhaling and exhaling deeply until his breathing normalized.

"Huck man I ain't got but six months to live." Blue said taking two additional puffs from the inhaler. "It's gon take longer than that for Baby girl and J.R. to get divorced!" Effie Mae ignored Huck as she unbuttoned and removed Blue's shirt replacing it with a plaid blue pajama shirt. "I know me and Baby girl can't do nothing but have a ceremony Huck—" Blue said raising his voice. "—and we okay with that!" Huck tilted his head.

"Is that right?" He said looking at Effie Mae. "What about Anthony, Effie Mae? He know what you and Blue talking about doing?" She glanced over at him but gave no reply. "Look here Blue, I tell you what I'm getting ready to do." Huck stated shifting his eyes to Effie Mae then again to Blue. "I'm gon get Ms. Jones up here let her finish getting you ready for bed then me and Effie Mae gon talk—"

"Naw man!" Blue shouted cutting him off. "Just let me spend one night with my woman!" A sarcastic look formed on Huck's face. He shook his head with objection.

"Your woman?" He looked at Effie Mae kneeling in front of Blue removing his pants then sliding a pair of matching pajama bottoms on his legs, Blue tightening the them around the waist with a string.

"Effie Mae's a married woman Blue." Huck said hoping to talk him out of the unethical marriage. Effie Mae shifted her eyes over at him, adjusting two pillows underneath Blue's head as he laid down. She gave no reply. Huck gazed seductively at Effie Mae and cunningly grinned. "It's a whole lot players in that game Blue."

"What you want Huck?" Effie Mae asked as she pulled the covers up around Blue's shoulders then placed a kiss on his lips. "I don't recall you worrying about J.R. or Anthony when I laid in your bed the other night!" He shifted his guilty eyes over at Blue, surprised by Effie Mae's unexpected admission of their recent intimacy. "I'm gon spend the night with my man just as he planned . . . and tonight I'm gon keep my mind and body on him." A huge smile stretched across Blue's face. "As for you, J.R. and Anthony—" She laid down next to Blue on the bed. He wrapped his arms around her and romantically kissed her. "—maybe I'll worry about y'all in the morning." Huck looked at her, challenged by her actions.

"Yeah you do that Effie Mae." He turned to Blue and sarcastically grinned. "You gon be able to handle that Blue?" He ignored Huck's insulting words. Huck gazed at Effie Mae then walked around the bed and sat down next to her. He aggressively pulled her up and in his arms looking over at Blue then passionately kissed her.

"Like I said Blue—" Huck said placing an intimate kiss on Effie Mae's lips. "—it's a whole lot of players in that game." He kissed Effie Mae a third time then turned to Blue grinning as he rose from the bed. Blue's anger accelerated as he lay in bed unable to defend himself or the woman he loved. He glared at his half brother with angry eyes as he walked over to the door and prepared to leave. "Bye Effie Mae." Huck said seductively looking at her then winked. He shifted his eyes to Blue and quietly grinned then exited the apartment.

---

Effie Mae arrived at J.R.'s house after he'd gotten their two daughters off to school. She stared at him from across the kitchen table, apprehensive about telling him of her plans to marry Blue. He noted her unusual quietness and wondered if it could be related to Blue's failing health.

"Uh, how's Blue?" He asked breaking the silence.

"J.R., Blue asked me to do something for him."

"Do something? Uh, something like what?"

"He want me to marry him J.R." Effie Mae stated without hesitation. His mouth abruptly dried. He coughed

"Uh, marry him?" He looked at her with confused eyes. "How Effie Mae when you still married to me?"

"It ain't no real marriage J. R. we just—" He interrupted.

"Ain't no real marriage? Is it some other kind of marriage I don't know about?"

"We ain't doing nothing but having a wedding ceremony J.R.—" He again cut her off.

"Wedding ceremony?" He said trying to remain calm, believing Effie Mae to be merely acting on her emotions in response to Blue's terminal illness. "Effie Mae—" She interjected.

"Then we gon live as husband and wife until—" Effie Mae silencened when seeing the hurt in his eyes. J.R. looked up at the ceiling and shook his head, disheartened by Blue's unbelievable request.

"Tell me something Effie Mae—"

"What J.R.?"

"The uh, other day at the church?" He said feeling foolish.

"What about it?"

"Have you uh, thought for one minute how it's gon affect the children—you living with one man while still married to their father?" She looked at him with unapologetic eyes.

"As long as Blue want me there J.R. I'm gon be there."

"And you expect me to do what Effie Mae—agree with that?" J.R. hesitated. "No!" He shouted. "I ain't gon agree to my wife marrying another man!" A blank stare displayed in Effie Mae's eyes. "What about the children Effie Mae? Do you expect them to understand you and Blue's so called marriage?"

"I don't care who don't understand what me and Blue doing!" She yelled. J.R.'s jaw dropped, shocked by her disregard for their children.

"Well guess what Effie Mae—" He said looking at her with disappointed eyes. "—you may not care how you pretending to marry Blue is gon affect my children, but—" She cut him off.

"My babies want whatever I want J.R.!"She yelled.

"Do you even know what you want Effie Mae?"

"Yeah I know what I want J.R., I want Blue!" His mouth dried. He coughed.

"Well don't expect me to give you my blessing."

"I don't need your blessing J.R.!" Effie Mae shouted. "And I'm gon marry Blue whether you like it or not!" J.R. rose quickly from the table and walked away, entering the living room. Effie Mae followed. "I don't need your permission to marry the man I love!" His head throbbed as he listened to her emotionally painful words.

"You go right ahead!" He shouted looking her in the eyes. "If that's what you want—"

"It is!" She yelled. J.R. turned away, pacing briskly throughout the living room as he tried to contain his anger.

"You call me crying because you thought I was divorcing you, now you telling me you getting ready to marry Blue . . . who you said didn't want you either!"

"Blue love me J.R.!" Effie Mae screamed.

"And so do I, but that don't seem to matter." She gave no reply.

"What about Anthony, Effie Mae?"

"What about Anthony?"

"Wasn't he the reason you left here in the first place saying he was good for you, now you standing there saying you marrying Blue?"

"Why everybody worrying about Anthony?" Effie Mae's eyes moistened as she thought only of Blue's inevitable death. "You let me worry about Anthony—I don't remember him asking nobody if he could marry me before he put his ring on my finger do you?" J.R. calmed when seeing her eyes filling with tears.

"Effie Mae I uh, I didn't mean to uh, make this time more difficult." He said reaching out to embrace her. She turned away. "What is it you want me to do?" J.R. asked sympathizing with her emotional hurt. "But if you expect me to congratulate you on marrying Blue—I can't do that."

"I didn't ask you too J.R.!" Effie Mae yelled as tears ran down her cheeks. "If you want to help then tell me how I'm gon go on living, once Blue is gone." J.R. reached out to embraced her. Effie Mae showed no resistence as he took her in his arms and comforted her.

---

"Effie Mae sure seems like a really nice girl, don't you think so Henry?" Ms. Jones said as she and Mr. White sat downstairs at the jazz club drinking coffee, waiting for Melvin to return with the breakfast he'd prepare. Mr. White gave no reply. "And Tyrell seems to be just crazy about her!" She chuckled. "I think Effie Mae's going to make a beautiful bride don't you Henry?"

"I hope I got everything y'all wanted." Melvin said as he approached with his homemade breakfast. "Auntie Roz . . . I got your lightly scrambled eggs, ham, hash brown potatoes, toast and a side order of sautéed onions—just the way you like them." He sat the plate of food on the table in front of her. "Mr. White let's see—you wanted fried eggs, over easy, four sausage patties, hash brown potatoes, biscuits and a ham steak." Melvin said placing the food on the table.

"Everything looks delicious Melvin." Ms. Jones said admiring the neatly arranged plates of food.

"Thank you."

"My pleasure Auntie Roz."

"I see you cook just like my brother did before he passed away." She stated.

"Taught me everything I know?" Melvin said proud of his father's cooking abilities.

"Yeah, I remember Ol' Calvin." Mr. White stated. "Use to cook every holiday." He chuckled. "Man could out cook any woman!"

"Even Momma!" Melvin said laughing.

"It sure hurt my heart when I heard about your mother's passing away last year Melvin." A heartfelt look displayed on her face. "My brother truly did love Cora.

"Yeah, I miss momma too." Melvin momentarily silenced. "Well y'all enjoy your breakfast."

"Thanks Melvin." Mr. White said as he tossed a sausage patty in his mouth. Melvin turned to leave.

"If y'all need more coffee just let me know—I just put a fresh pot on."

"We sure will Melvin." Ms. Jones sais as she mixed her scrambled eggs with the sautéed onions. Melvin walked away returning to the kitchen to begin preparing breakfast for Blue and Effie Mae.

"Did you see how Tyrell's eyes practically lit up when seeing Effie Mae?" Ms. Jones said speaking between swallows of food.

"I also saw how her and Henry Lee was looking at one another too."

"Well now remember Henry . . . Tyrell did say that Henry Lee and Effie Mae went together before he stole her away." She giggled. Mr. White stopped eating then stared at her.

"Rosalyn, does that sound right to you? Tyrell stealing a woman away from Henry Lee?" Ms. Jones mouth abruptly opened.

"Just what are you trying to say Henry?" She asked sitting her fork down on her plate. Mr. White nervously sipped his coffee.

"You know what I'm saying Rosalyn."

"No Henry, I don't think I do!" She said upset by his insulting words. "Are you trying to say because you and Rita's son's just a little more handsome than ours, Tyrell couldn't possibly steal his girl away?" Mr. White stared momentarily into his mistress' offended eyes then resumed eating.

"You know that's not what I meant baby!" He said trying to redeem himself. "But just think about it Rosalyn—" She cut him off.

"I am Henry, and I don't think I like what you're saying about my son!" She picked up her fork and continued eating.

"I'm just stating the truth Rosalyn."

"Who's truth Henry? Rita's?"

"Come on now baby you know I love Tyrell, but he ain't the most handsome man in the world."

"Henry!" Ms. Jones yelled. "You take that back."

"Take what back Rosalyn?" He said shoving a chunk of the ham steak in his open mouth. Ms. Jones quickly stood to her feet.

"Come on now baby." Mr. White subtly pleaded. "Sit down and finish your food."

"Don't baby me Henry . . . and I won't sit down!"

"Rosalyn—"

"I think maybe my breakfast will taste a whole lot better if I ate it upstairs with my handsome son and my beautiful daughter-in-law."

"Rosalyn—" Mr. White called out as he continued eating nonstop, watching as Ms. Jones picked up her plate and headed in the direction of the stairs on her way to Blue's apartment. "You know what I was trying to say baby!" He looked over at Melvin when sensing him observing the amusing altercation. "I'll take some more of that coffee when you get a chance Melvin." He said using a biscuit to sop up the egg yolk off his plate as he watched Ms. Jones continuing up the stairs. Melvin silently laughed.

---

Anthony arrived home Friday evening from Jackson. He stood at the mailbox retrieving his accumulated mail for the week then looked up when a car pulled around the corner and stopped in front of him. He leaned down and looked into the opened passenger side window, peering at the driver.

"Hey I'm Kenny is Effie Mae home—you Anthony?" Anthony looked at him with inquiring eyes.

"Do I know you?"

"Naw, I know your wife Effie Mae?" Kenny said smirking. "Yeah she told me how you like to keep tabs on her."

"Keep what?"

"Well you need to keep closer tabs." He said grinning. "Because a few days ago me and Effie Mae got reacquainted." He looked Anthony in the eyes. "In the biblical sense." A cunning smiled formed on his face. "If you know what I mean."

"No, I don't know what you mean." Anthony said perturbed.

"Ask Effie Mae . . . she know what it means." Kenny said grinning. "Is she here?"

"I don't think Effie Mae's whereabouts is any of your business." Anthony said as his intolerance heightened, angered by Kenny's rude conversation.

"Well just let her know Kenny came looking for her." He said cleverly chuckling. "Tell her I got a couple bottles of scotch." He shifted his car into gear. "Oh and uh, Anthony—let her know whenever she ready to bring that sheet back she got my number." He winked then sped off. Anthony watched as the red car disappeared down the road, perplexed by their odd exchange of words. He shifted his eyes over at Ms. Dawson's house when seeing her living room curtain quickly close.

"Busy body." He said thinking out loud as he walked onto the porch, visually sorting through the bundle of mail—perplexed by what had just taken place. Anthony entered the house dropping the multiple pieces of mail on the coffee table before going upstairs to bathe and change then picked up the phone in the bedroom and called J.R. in search of Effie Mae, uneasy by Kenny's insulting visit.

"Hey J.R. this is Anthony . . . is Effie Mae anywhere around?"

"Uh, not since this morning—was it uh, a message you wanted me to give her if I see or hear from her again today?"

"If you could just have her call me that would be fine." Anthony paused. "And J.R., would you please you let her know it's important that I speak with her?"

"Uh, okay—no problem Anthony."

"Thank you J.R."

"You're uh, welcome Anthony." J.R. hung up, curious of the mystery surrounding Anthony's unexpected call. He surmised from the tone in Anthony's voice, his impending talk with Effie Mae would not be a pleasant one. J.R. immediately phoned her at Blue's. She answered.

"Hello."

"Effie Mae?"

"Yeah J.R.?"

"I just uh, got a call from Anthony." He paused. "He wants you to call him."

"Okay."

"He said it was uh, important?" J.R. curiosity heightened. "Is uh, everything alright with you and Anthony?"

"Why you asking J.R.?"

"He uh, didn't sound too happy."

"We gon work it out."

"Uh—"

"Thank you J.R." She said, hanging up. J.R. continued holding the phone in his hand, puzzled by Effie Mae's evasiveness and abrupt hang up.

———————————————

J.R. rose from the table as he ate his Saturday morning breakfast of two boiled eggs, a couple pieces of toast and a slice of ham. His attention drew to the back door when hearing a knock. He stared at the shadowy figure with questioning eyes, recognized the silhouette on the curtain to be Effie Mae. J.R. took a deep breath as he wondered what new dilemma her unexpected visit would bring this time. He rose from the table and opened the door.

"Effie Mae." He stated dryly.

"Hey J.R." She said walking hastily pass him as she entered the house. J.R. looked at her with curiosity as she traveled through the kitchen and into the living room. His stomach bundled with nerves as he slowly closed the door and waited on an explanation for her early morning stopover.

"Can I uh, get you something to eat Effie Mae?" He asked, his eyes fixated on her face unreadable face.

"Where my babies?" She asked when noting the absence of her children.

"Uh, Cousin Daniel's . . . they uh, spent the night over there." He said rambling, trying to emotionally prepare himself for the altercation he knew would ensue. "I uh, thought you and Blue was getting—"

"Married." Effie Mae said completing his sentence. "Yeah J.R. we are." His mouth abruptly dried. He hoped her plans for her unethical marriage had changed. "I came to see if you still got my wedding dress." He coughed.

"Uh, your wedding dress?"

"Yeah J.R., the last time I saw it . . . it was laying over a chair at the Cozi-T." An amusing smile formed on Effie Mae's face as she reminisced on the day.

"As a matter of fact I do . . . I uh, kept it." A perplexed look formed on J.R.'s face. "I don't know why—I just did."

"You paid for it J.R. so I guess that make it yours."

"Are you uh—"

"Yeah J.R. I'm wearing it." He looked at her, distressed by her decision.

"Does this feel right to you Effie Mae?" J.R. asked frowning, "How can you stand there and make plans to marry another man when legally you still married to me?"

"J.R. please!" Effie Mae said raising her voice. "This hard enough as it is."

"Is it Effie Mae?"

"Yeah J.R. it is!" Effie Mae's eyes slowly began to water.

"Effie Mae I uh, didn't mean to—" He embraced her in his arms then placed a light kiss on Effie Mae's forehead. "It's just that I can't—"

"Can't what J.R.!" She shouted. "Understand what me and Blue doing?" His mouth again dried. He coughed. "Right now J.R. how you feel ain't important!" Effie Mae cried out. "I'm getting ready to marry a man who ain't got but six months left on this earth—so what you do or don't agree with ain't gon give Blue back one day of the life he losing now is it?" J.R. released her. He knew nothing he said at that point would change her mind.

"It's uh, hanging in my room in the closet covered in plastic."

"Thank you J.R." She said walking away. J.R. looked at her, frustrated as she headed in the direction of his bedroom. Effie Mae entered the room and walked over to the closet then retrieved the wedding gown hanging inside. She returned to the kitchen with the dress draped over her right arm and prepared to leave.

"I uh, see you found it." J.R. stated, not knowing what else to say.

"The ceremony's at two o'clock J.R. if you want to come." Effie Mae said ignorong the disappointed look on his face. "You the only family I got here besides my babies."

"Family?" He looked at her in disbelief. "I'm your husband Effie Mae!" J.R. said raising his voice. She ignored his anger.

"It's at the jazz club."

" Jazz club?"

"What J.R.?" She said noting his objection.

"Effie Mae think about what you—"

"Bye J.R." She said placing a kiss on his cheek before opening the back door to leave.

"Effie Mae—wait!" J.R. said relenting. "If you uh, want me there I'll uh . . . I'll be there, even though I don't agree with my wife marrying another man." He looked at her with surrendering eyes. "But I uh, do understand how you feel—I think."

"Do you J.R.?" Effie Mae asked as her eyes erupted with tears. "Then you understand better than me, because right now I don't understand none of this!" She yelled. J.R. removed the dress from over her arm and laid it across the back of a kitchen chair, embracing Effie Mae in his arms.

"Effie Mae you don't have to do this."

"You know J.R. . . . sometimes I feel like this God's way of punishing me for all the wrong I done to you, Ms. Geraldine and Momma."
J.R. kissed her softly on the forehead.

"You know Effie Mae—" She looked in his peaceful eyes. "—the one thing about life we ain't ever gon be able to change is it can only end in death." Effie Mae laid her head on his chest finding comfort in J.R.'s sensible words. "Blue like the rest of us—time was preset by God even before he was born." Effie Mae listened to his words with her heart. "And his dying ain't got nothing to do with you or anything you done to anybody." He said, gently wiping away her tears with his hand. "I think if Blue could add days to his life in place of having you in it—" J.R.

smiled. "—I'm certain he would leave things just as they are." A peaceful smile showed on Effie Mae's face as J.R.'s heartfelt words lifted the heavy burden off her shoulders.

"You know what J.R.?"

"What's that?"

"I'm glad I married you." His jaw dropped.

"But you uh—"

"Getting ready to marry Blue?" She said giggling.

"Yeah."

"If I had married Anthony—Blue wouldn't be getting ready to marry me." Effie Mae said chuckling as she tried to rationalize her own puzzling words.

"I guess I'll uh see you uh—"

"Thank you J.R." She kissed him quickly on the lips then picked up the wedding gown and turned to leave.

"Uh, Effie Mae." She again turned.

"Yeah J.R.?"

"If uh, you need somebody to give the bride away—" Effie Mae's widened eyes watered with tears, humbled by her husband's unimaginable offer. "—I'd uh, I'd be honored."

"You trying to get rid of me J.R.?" She teased.
"Never." J.R. quietly chuckled then kissed Effie Mae softly on the cheek. "You gon always be my wife Effie Mae Smith." A boyish smile displayed on J.R.'s face. "And I'm gon be here for you no matter what." She stared into his eyes.

"Thanks for saying that J.R." She placed a light kiss on his lips. "I needed to know that." J.R. watched as his wife hurried out the door on her way to marry the man she loved.

# Chapter Eleven

"Blue man, you look like king of the Player's!" Melvin said as he assisted Blue in getting dressed in his black collared, light grey tuxedo jacket complimented by a white ruffled shirt and the black pants he wore.

"You think so Melvin?"

"Yeah man, Effie Mae's gon fall in love with you all over again when she how good you look!"

"Melvin man, I feel like the luckiest man in the world." Blue suddenly silenced. "If having this day meant I had to die to get it—" His eyes moistened with tears. "I just love Baby girl so much—"

"I know you do man." Melvin said placing a comforting pat on his cousin's back. "You think you gon be able to make it through the ceremony without crying yourself silly man?" Melvin said chuckling.

"Naw cousin, but for every tear I shed that's how much I love Baby girl so I'm gon cry my eyes out." They both laughed.

"Well in that case Blue, go right ahead man and cry me a river man."

• • • •

Huck and Buckeye entered the jazz club exquisitely dressed for the occasion. They looked around the beautifully decorated club as they walked in the direction of the bar in search of Melvin. Huck smiled as he noted the white paper wedding bells hung throughout the establishment; the burgundy and white, double-layered tablecloths on each of the many tables, accented with white vases with pink and white artificial flowers, seemingly blooming.

"Huck man did Melvin do all this?" Buckeye asked, impressed by the stunning decor.

"I don't know who did it Buckeye, but I know Effie Mae and Blue gon love it." Huck continued scrutinizing the room. His visual inspection ended when seeing his father seated alone at a table to the far left of the club. "I see Mr. White's already arrived." Huck said looking his father in the eyes. Mr. White stared back and smirked. "Keep an eye on him Buckeye, this Blue and Effie Mae's day and I ain't gon let Mr. White ruin it." Buckeye shifted his eyes over at Mr. White, obtaining eye contact. The two men stared one to the other then simultaneously turned away. Buckeye again glanced around at the room's décor.

"You know Huck—" He said as his eyes moistened. "Tyrell's been like a little brother to me and it hurts like hell knowing that man ain't gon be here in six months." He again looked over at Mr. White. "Huck man I would die before I let your daddy ruin this day for Tyrell and Effie Mae." Huck looked in Buckeye's tearful eyes.

"We ain't gon let that happen Buckeye." He said touched by his old friend's emotional display over Blue. Mr. White watched from across the room looking intently at Buckeye as if reading his thoughts. He then shifted his cautious eyes to Huck.

"Man if you got any second thoughts about your daddy getting hurt—" Buckeye again glanced over at Mr. White. "—you might want to leave here now . . . because if he do anything to hurt Tyrell—" He abruptly silenced and awaited Huck's reply. Huck looked at him without speaking as he contemplated on his fatal words—and his father's fate.

"Do what you have to do Buckeye."

"Where's Tyrell!" A woman shouted as she entered the jazz club. Huck turned in the direction of the female's intrusive voice seeing Daphne—Blue's ex-wife. "Where's my husband?" She asked, loudly. "I heard he was getting married today!" Huck shifted his eyes over to his father.

"Keep your eyes on Mr. White, I know he had something to do with this." He again looked at Daphne shaking his head in response to her trying to ruin Blue's big day. "And if he try anything—shoot him." Buckeye nodded. "Let me go get Daphne's ass out here."

Mr. White watched as Huck walked in the direction of the club's front entrance. He took note of the three men entering, each exchanging a head nod with Huck before joining Buckeye over at the bar. They simultaneously turned and glared at Mr. White after briefly speaking with Buckeye, then positioned themselves in various locations throughout the club.

"What you doing here Daphne?" Huck asked as he approached her.

"Henry Lee . . . boy is that you?" She said wrapping her arms around his neck then quickly kissing him on the lips. "Boy you look better and better every time I see you!" Huck subtly removed her arms from around his neck then retrieved a white silk handkerchief from the left pocket of his silk, silver gray suit.

"I asked you what you doing here?" Daphne watched with insult as he used the handkerchief to wipe her red lipstick from his mouth. "You and Blue ain't been married in fifteen years—how the hell you gon bring your ass up in here claiming him as your husband?"

"Henry Lee you know Tyrell still love me."

"Who told you that Daphne?"

"Didn't nobody have to tell me, I know my husband."

"You're husband?" Huck shook his head and sarcastically chuckled. "Damn shame . . . when did you ever treat Blue like he was your husband?"

"What?"

"You know what." Huck tilted his head. "Every member in his band had you girl." Daphne seductively smiled.

"And what instrument did you play Henry Lee?" Her smile widened.

"Biggest mistake I ever made."

"You wasn't saying that when you were slapping them sheets in me and Tyrell's bed now were you?"

"I didn't want to hurt your feelings Daphne, bad enough I hurt Blue's."

"You say that now Henry Lee."

"Daphne I'm gon be saying that until the day I die. Every man makes what he considers to be the worst mistake in his life." Huck shook his head with regret. "Messing with you was mines."

"Forget you Henry Lee." She said rolling her eyes.

"Yeah you do that Daphne."

"Where's Tyrell?" She glanced around the club.

"Look here Daphne, let me tell you what you getting ready to do." Huck shifted his eyes briefly over at his father then turned back to Daphne. "You gon turn your ass around and go crawl back under whatever rock Mr. White got you from." She laughed.

"I ain't trying to hear what you talking about Henry Lee." She again rolled her eyes. Huck's agitation increased.

"Then hear this Daphne . . . if you think I'm about to let you bring your ass in here and ruin the best day of my brother's life—" She interjected.

"The best day of Tyrell's life was when he married me." Huck tilted his head.

"Is that right?" He quietly chuckled. "Thing is Daphne, Ol' Blue found his self a real woman and that man's in love."

"You let him tell me that Henry Lee."

"Effie Mae's the best thing that could've ever happened to Ol' Blue." Daphne laughed.

"Effie Mae? What the hell is a Effie Mae?"

"A hundred times more woman than you could ever hope to be Daphne." She rolled her eyes.

"Excuse you!"

"And I ain't gon let you spoil her day . . . Blue's day." Huck again shifted his eyes over at his father then again to Daphne. "Before I let you do that I'll drop you where you stand girl, you understand what I'm saying?"

"I ain't scared of you Henry Lee!"

"Well you should be Daphne—." Huck abruptly silenced when the club's front door opened and Effie Mae entered. A huge smile displayed on Huck's handsome face. Daphne turned in the direction of his gaze, watching as he and the unfamiliar female, carrying a wedding gown, exchanged an intimate smile. "You ready Effie Mae?" He asked ignoring Daphne's presence. Effie Mae looked at the female looking at her with envious eyes. She wondered who she might be, but surmised her to be just another one of Huck's many female friends.

"I guess I'm as ready as I'm gon be Huck."

"That's her?" Daphne said looking Effie Mae from head to toe. "That's Effie Mae?"

"Yeah I'm Effie Mae—you know me?"

"Naw I don't know you, and you don't know me!" Daphne stated stepping in front of Effie Mae. "So let me introduce myself." Mr. White's excitement heightened as he watched the impending altercation. "I'm Tyrell's wife Daphne." She smirked. Effie Mae looked at Huck, confused.

"Daphne's, Blue's trifling ex-wife . . . he divorced her ass fifteen years ago." He looked at her and shook his head with displeasure. "Seems Ol' Daphne couldn't stay off her back."

"What?" Effie Mae said unfamiliar with the saying.

"It ain't important." Huck again turned to Daphne. "What is important is Daphne was getting ready to walk her ass out here, ain't that right Daphne?"

"I ain't going nowhere Henry Lee!" She shouted. Mr. White slightly rose from his chair, but again lowered himself when he noted Buckeye reach inside the pocket of his navy blue, silk suit jacket—placing his hand on the holstered pistol strapped at his side. "Mr. White invited me and I ain't leaving here until he tells me to." Daphne said looking over at Mr. White then back to Huck.

"I tell you what Daphne . . . if you think for one second you gon change Blue's mind about marrying the love of his life I'll give you one chance to try." He turned to Effie Mae and winked. "Get on girl." He noted the wedding gown she carried. "Go get ready so you can marry my brother." Daphne looked at Effie Mae with disdain as she walked away carrying her wedding gown. Effie Mae looked around the club with excited eyes as she admired the exquisite wedding décor then hurried up the stairs.

"Go sit your ass down Daphne while I go and tell Blue his worst nightmare is here." Huck shifted his eyes to Buckeye as he walked away from Daphne and headed in the direction of the stairs. Buckeye nodded ensuring him surveillance of Mr. White would continue. Huck hurried up the steps.

• • • •

"You look so handsome Blue." Effie Mae said as she entered the apartment. He quidkly turned in response to her voice.

"Hey Baby girl." He said embracing Effie Mae in his arms. They passionately kissed.

"Blue?" She said as the kiss ended.

"Yeah Baby girl." He said applying smooches to her lips.

"Who's Daphne?" Melvin's eyes widened when he heard Daphne's name.

"She was once my wife." Blue said shaking his head. "I couldn't trust her as far as I could throw a steel building." He chuckled. "How you find out about Daphne . . . Daddy or Momma?"

"Her."

"What?" Blue's forehead wrinkled with frowns.

"Yeah Blue she downstairs."

"She's what!" He yelled. "I ain't seen that woman in fifteen years why she showing up here now?"

"I think Daphne realize she about to lose the best man this world's ever seen." Blue blushed. Melvin watched as they romantically kissed. kiss.

"So what you gon do about Daphne Blue?"

"Let me go downstairs and get this woman out of here before she get some mess started." Blue said shaking his head with aggravation. "I know they say it's bad luck for the groom to see the bride on her wedding day—" He placed a light kiss on Effie Mae's lips. "—but seeing your ex-wife is even worse!" Blue laughed.

"Blue?"

"Yeah Baby girl." They exchanged a smooch.

"J.R. want to give me away." Blue's jaw dropped.

"He what?" Blue said agitated. "Give you away . . . to me?" Effie Mae giggled.

"Naw Blue give me away to Huck." She teased. "Yeah Blue give me away to you." She again giggled. Blue remained speechless as he considered J.R.'s awkward request. Effie Mae's eyes subtly pleaded. "It's important to me baby." A look of surrender showed on Blue's face.

"Okay Baby girl, if your sure that's what you want."

"It is Blue." She said kissing him gently on the lips. "Thank you baby."

"As long as that man don't try to change his mind at the last minute Baby girl!" She giggled.

"He won't Blue—I hope." She teased. Blue's mouth slightly opened."

"Baby girl!"

"He won't Blue." She stated applying a quick kiss to his lips.

"I can't believe Daphne had the nerves to show up here." Blue said thinking out loud.

"I envy you Blue." Huck said entering the apartment. He looked at Effie Mae and seductively smiled. She blushed. "Yeah Blue, I wish I had never introduced you to Effie Mae, but I guess ain't no point in worrying about that now." He looked at her and winked. She again blushed. "I guess I owe you that one after Daphne." Effie Mae's eyes widened.

"Huck! You messed with Blue's wife?" She asked, not surprised by his intimate history with Daphne.

"Yeah he did." Blue answered. "But so did every member in my band—Melvin even had her!" Blue said half-heartedly laughing. Melvin shifted his guilt-ridden eyes over at Blue then looked at Huck and again to Blue. He believed his sexual indiscretion with Daphne back in the day had gone undiscovered.

"Blue man, I—" Huck interrupted his impending excuse then tilted his head and quietly chuckled, humored by Melvin's apparent weakness.

"Is that right?"

"Blue man how you find out about that?" Melvin asked, embarrassed.

"Daphne." Blue said shaking his head. "That woman was dirty Melvin! How you think I found out about Huck and the rest of my band?"

"You mean to tell me, Daphne told you she messed around with Huck?" Melvin said shifting the focus from himself.

"Yeah, she thought it would make me quit the band and stop hanging with my friends if I knew they messed around with her."

"You should've listened to me Blue." Huck stated. "I tried to tell you about Daphne didn't I?"

"Yeah Huck you did." Huck glanced over at Melvin and titled his head.

"Melvin?"

"Man I was young and dumb!" He stated in his defense. The room silenced as all eyes focused on Melvin. The room suddenly filled with laughter.

"Baby girl told me she was downstairs."

"Yeah Blue she got her ass down there."

"Man what she want?" Blue asked, upset.

"You Blue." Huck teased. "She say she want her husband back."

"Her husband?"

"Yeah Blue . . . she say you still love her." Huck said amused.

"Love her!" Blue scowled. "Man, Daphne know I don't love her no more." He placed a kiss on Effie Mae's lips. "The only woman I love is this woman right here." He said kissing her lightly on the lips. Huck watched with envy as his thoughts wandered back to the day he asked Effie Mae to marry him—many years ago.

"For some reason Blue your daddy seem to think she needed to be here."

"Daddy?" Blue said astonished. "Daddy never even liked Daphne!" He turned to Effie Mae, his eyes apologizing. "Let me go down here Baby girl and stop whatever it is her and Daddy's up to."

"You need help getting downstairs Blue?" Huck asked extending his arm.

"Maybe a little." Effie Mae looked at him with doubt.

"Blue baby I think you gon need more than a little help." She giggled.

"Yeah Baby girl you right." He said applying a smooch to her lips. "I love you Baby girl."

"I love you back Blue." They lovingly smiled at each other then intimately kissed. Melvin noted the resentment evident in Huck's eyes as he watched Blue and what he considered to be his soul mate express their mutual love.

"I'll get him Huck I'm heading that way." Melvin said hurrying over to assist Blue, sympathizing with Huck's uncomfortable position.

"Naw Melvin I got him."

"You sure man?" The two men briefly shared an eye exchange as Huck took hold of Blue's left arm. "I guess I'll see you downstairs then Blue."

"Okay cousin." Blue replied as Huck escorted him from the apartment and over to the stairs. Effie Mae turned to Melvin, still in the apartment. She looked at her wedding gown draped over her arm again looked at Melvin.

"I guess if I'm gon get married in a few hours Melvin, I'm need to get this dress on."

"Oh!" He chuckled, realizing she wanted him to leave. "I guess that means you need me to get out of here?"

"Yeah Melvin I need you to get out of here." She giggled. "I don't think Blue want me getting undressed in front of his cousin, especially after what happened between you and Daphne." Melvin's mouth quickly opened. Effie Mae again giggled.

"Okay Effie Mae." He said grinning. "I see you ain't gon let that go." She laughed. "I told y'all I was young and dumb!"

"Bye Melvin."

"Okay Effie Mae I'm leaving." He said feeling awkward by the compromising situation. "I guess I do need to get downstairs and finish cooking for this reception or y'all ain't gon have nothing to feed them folks that's expecting to eat." Melvin grinned then suddenly silenced. He looked at Effie Mae. She smiled.

"What?"

"Congratulations sweetie."

"Thank you Melvin." He walked over and kissed her softly on the cheek. "I guess I'll see you downstairs.

"Yep."

"Blue's a lucky man." He said placing another kiss to her cheek. Effie Mae blushed then watched as Melvin exited the apartment, returning downstairs to complete the meal he'd began preparing that morning.

---

J.R. attention drew to Huck assisting Blue downstairs as he entered the jazz club and stood at the entrance, visually searching through the crowded establishment for Effie Mae..

"Hey Blue." Huck said alarmed when seeing J.R. "It's starting to look like all hell's getting ready to break loose in here . . . look over at the door." Blue looked in the direction of the front entrance seeing J.R. watching as he and Huck came down the stairs.

"Naw man, Baby girl said he was coming." Blue half-heartedly chuckled. "Believe it or not Huck that man came here to give the bride away." Huck tilted his head.

"Is that right?"

"Yeah—he love Baby girl so much he'd do just about anything she asked, including giving her to me." Blue said humored. Huck quietly grinned, amused by Effie Mae's manipulation of both men.

"That girl know she something else." He said continuing to grin. "Got her husband in here getting ready to give her away to her second fiancé." Blue shook his head in agitation when seeing Daphne seated at a table with his father.

"I'm gon go talk to Daddy, Huck . . . you can go deal with J.R." He said when reaching the bottom step.

"Yeah Blue, you go do that." Huck looked at his father. The two men exchanged a cold stare before Huck turned to J.R. Mr. White watched as he walked over to the door.

"You feeling alright today boy?" Mr. White said turning to Blue as he approached him and Daphne . . . sharing a bottle of gin.

"There's my husband!" Daphne said getting up from the table. "Hey Tyrell." He ignored her greeting, blocking her reaching arms as she tried to wrap them around his neck.

"What you doing here Daphne?" Blue said looking at his father with disappointed eyes.

"I know you didn't think I was just gon sit back and let some Ol' heifer marry my husband!"

"Daddy why you bring Daphne here? You know I'm getting married today." Blue said as tears filled his eyes. "This is me and Effie Mae's day!" He yelled looking into his father's remoreseless eyes. "You dislike Effie Mae so much that you would ruin our wedding day?"

"What you marrying that girl for anyway Tyrell?" Mr. White said seeing him as a fool. "You know your brother already had her." Daphne's mouth slightly opened.

"What?" She shifted her eyes to Huck then again looked at Blue. "Ain't that why you divorced me Tyrell?" He continued to ignore her.

"You divorced Daphne for the exact same thing!"

"Daddy that ain't got nothing to do with you."

"It has everything to do with me if you think I'm gon sit back and let that golddigger have this jazz club once you gone!"

"Daddy I love Effie Mae and she love me!"

"That damn golddigger don't love you Tyrell!" Mr. White yelled. "You marry that tramp and I tell you . . . she won't treat you any better than Daphne done."

"Stay out of this Daddy!" Blue shouted.

"Only this time it'll hurt a hell of a lot worse."

"Daddy why you doing this . . . you know I'm dying!"

Daphne's jaw dropped.

"Dying?" She said looking at Mr. White. "You didn't say nothing about Tyrell dying."

"What you think I brought you here for?" Mr. White stated without conscious. "I figured you could stop him from making the worse mistake in his life—marrying that tramp."

"Daddy if you love me you'll take Daphne and leave!" Blue said pleading through tearful eyes. "Let me marry the woman that gives me a reason for wanting to live another day."

• • • •

"How you doing J.R.?" Huck said extending his hand. The two men shook.

"Uh, I'm not really sure." He stated seeing Blue seemingly arguing with two people, his face wet with tears. J.R. turned to the front door when seeing Ms. Jones entered.

"I hope they haven't started without me." She said thinking out loud, excited about Blue and Effie Mae's wedding. "Hello Henry Lee." She shifted her eyes briefly to J.R. standing near the entrance.

"How you doing Ms. Jones?"

"Oh, I'm doing just fine Henry Lee." She again looked at J.R. "And who's this gentleman right here?" Huck silently grinned, electing not to do the introductions. A disturbed look displayed on Ms. Jones' face when seeing Daphne.

"Is that Daphne?"

"Yeah Ms. Jones that's her." Huck said, instigating.

"What on earth is she doing here?" Ms. Jones said before notiing the distressed look on the her beloved son's face. She again turned to Huck. "Henry Lee do you know what's going on?"

"Naw Ms. Jones, you gon have to ask Mr. White about that?" He said holding back his laughter as she walked away, hurrying to her weeping son.

"Is uh, everything alright?" J.R. asked.

"Yeah." Huck quietly laughed. "And it's about to get even better."

• • • •

"Momma!" Blue cried out as she approached. She embraced him in her arms, laying his head on her shoulder as he wept.

"What's going on Henry?" Ms. Jones asked, enraged. Mr. White shifted his eyes over at Huck then turned back to Ms. Jones—loss for words. She stared angrily at Daphne. "Daphne why are you here?" Ms. Jones yelled. "Haven't you hurt my son enough?"

"I'm here because Mr. White invited me here to keep my husband from marrying some Ol' Jezebel."

"Your husband?" Ms. Jones yelled. "You and Tyrell haven't been married in fifteen years!" She again turned to Mr. White. "Henry you get Daphne out of here right now! And if you don't, when you leave here you'll be going home alone." He again shifted his eyes to Huck seeing the humored look on his face. "And I mean that Henry!"

"Come on now Rosalyn you know that trampl ain't doing nothing but playing Tyrell for a fool." Mr. White said trying to justify his underhandedness.

"No she ain't Daddy!" Blue cried out. "Effie Mae loves me!" He shouted.

"That tramp don't love you Tyrell, she just want to get her hands on this club . . . can't you see that?" He yelled.

"Stop it Henry!" Ms. Jones said infuriated. She quickly turned to Daphne. "And you get this tramp out of here right now!" Daphne's jaw dropped.

"Ms. Jones you don't have to talk about me like that."

"I'll talk about you anyway I damn well please Daphne." She stated, looking her in the eyes. "You have no business being here in the first place."

"Get her out of here Daddy!" Blue yelled as he continued sobbing, his mother gently rubbing his back.

"And if you don't Henry, I won't be going back home with you at all."

"Come on now Rosalyn you don't mean that, you're just upset right now—"

"Yes Henry I am upset—" She again looked at Daphne. "—but I mean exactly what I said." She placed a comforting kiss on Blue's cheek. "And if you ever hurt my baby like that again—" She momentarily looked at Daphne then turned back to Mr. White "—I'll give Henry Lee's friend my permission to put that *hole* in you." He watched as his mistress stormed away, her only child's head still resting on her shoulder as she assisted him over to a table directly in front of the stage. "It's alright sweetheart." Ms. Jones stated rubbing Blue's head, shifting her irate eyes periodically over at Mr. White. "Don't you let any of that mess ruin you and Effie Mae's day . . . you're about to marry a beautiful woman that loves you very much." She said removing a handkerchief from her purse drying Blue's wet face as he gradually calmed down.

"Thank you Momma." Ms. Jones placed a loving kiss on his forehead.

"You're welcome sweetheart." He smiled. She ignored Mr. White as he continuously looked at her from across the room.

"Let's go Daphne." Mr. White said standing to his feet taking hold of Daphne's arm as he prepared to leave—not wanting to lose the only woman he'd ever loved. Huck watched with satisfaction as the duo walked past him and J.R. and exited the club.

"Damn shame." Huck shook his head then turned back to J.R. "Blue told me Effie Mae talked you into giving her away to Ol' Blue."

"I uh, actually offered."

"Offered?" Huck tilted his head. "Is that right?"

"I uh, love Effie Mae and uh, I understand what she's feeling right now even though I uh, son't agree with it." He half-heartedly chuckled. "Legally . . . Effie Mae's still my wife." Huck titled his head but held his tongue. "When she uh, asked me for my support I uh, chose to do it by giving the bride away." Huck quietly grinned. "What?" J.R. said in embarrassed by Huck's laughter.

"I don't know if you know this J.R., but I once asked Effie Mae to marry me."

"She uh, told me about that." Huck again tilted his head, surprised by J.R.'s knowledge of his proposal.

"Is that right?" He chuckled.

"Effie Mae's quite a unique woman so I uh, can understand why you, Blue and Anthony would want to marry her."

"And Gus." Huck said laughing.

"Who?"

"It ain't important . . . Effie Mae's upstairs, I'm sure she'll be glad you came." He again extended his hand to J.R. They shook. "Just walk straight ahead and go right up those stairs."

"Uh, thank you Huck?" J.R. said as he walked away, headed in the direction of the stairs—honored to be giving the bride away to the groom.

# *Chapter Twelve*

J.R. stood quietly outside the opened door once arriving upstairs. He watched as Deborah Ann tied the laces on the back of Effie Mae's wedding gown.

"Effie Mae girl I'm so glad my cousin found you." She said tying the last of the many laces. "I ain't seen Tyrell this happy since—" Deborah Ann thought for a moment. "—ever!" She burst into laughter then noticed J.R. standing outside the door. "Excuse me sir . . . this part of the club is off limits to customers." Effie Mae looked in the direction of the door seeing J.R. A large smiled formed on her face.

"It's okay Deborah Ann that's my special guest." She said approaching J.R. in the hallway hugging him. "Thank you for doing this for me J.R."

"I love you Effie Mae so uh, doing this is a honor." Deborah Ann silently listened, peering at J.R. from the corner of her eye, curious of his intimate words. Effie Mae looked at her, lightly giggling in response to her apparent confusion.

"J.R., this is Blue's cousin Deborah Ann."

"It's uh, nice to meet you Deborah Ann." J.R. said shifting his eyes to Effie Mae as Deborah Ann walked over and shook his extended hand, her mind wandering as she thought of his words of love. Effie Mae quietly laughed when thinking of how Deborah Ann would react when learning of her and J.R.'s relationship.

"Come on Effie Mae so I can do your hair girl." Deborah Ann said, again entering the apartment, suspicious of J.R. Effie Mae went back in the apartment being seated at the kitchen table.

"You can come in J.R." Effie Mae said smiling as Deborah Ann began pinning her hair up in a bun-style hairdo using bobby pins. He walked inside and stood just inside the doorway.

"Effie Mae you never did say who your J.R. was." Deborah Ann said eyeing him. Effie Mae smiled, amused.

"J.R.'s my husband." Deborah Ann's eyes widened as she looked at J.R. and again to Effie Mae.

"Your what girl?" She said believing she'd misunderstood Effie Mae.

"My husband." Effie Mae shifted her eyes to J.R. quietly giggling in response to Deborah Ann's reaction.

"You mean your ex-husband right?"

"Nope . . . J.R.'s my husband."

"As in still married?"

"Yep."

"I don't mean to get in your business Effie Mae, but does Tyrell know about—your husband?" Effie Mae laughed.

"Yeah Deborah Ann he know." Deborah Ann shifted her eyes to J.R., bewildered by the situation. "Blue wanted us to get married, but he knew by the time me and J.R. got divorced—" Effie Mae's eyes slightly moistened. "—he wasn't gon be here." Deborah Ann noted the saddened look on Effie Mae's face.

"You alright Effie Mae?" She asked, glancing over at J.R. "Girl I didn't mean to upset you."

"I'm fine Deborah Ann—" J.R. intervened.

"You uh, sure Effie Mae?"

"Yeah J.R. I'm sure."

"Effie Mae I hope it don't seem like I'm being nosey but—" Deborah Ann again shifted her eyes again to J.R. then turned to Effie Mae. "—if J.R.'s your husband . . . how can you and Tyrell be—"

"Getting married?" She said completing Deborah Ann's thought. An odd look appeared on Deborah Ann's face.

"Don't they have laws against stuff like that Effie Mae?" J.R. quietly laughed as Deborah Ann tried to understand the legality of Effie Mae and Blue's marital arrangement.

"Me and Blue ain't getting legally married." Deborah Ann's mouth slightly opened.

"Huh?" Her confusion increased. J.R. smiled as he humorously waited to hear Effie Mae explain the details of her and Blue's impending nuptial exchange.

"We getting married in spirit Deborah Ann."

"In what girl?" Deborah Ann asked astonished.

"Since me and Blue can't get married legally, we gon have a ceremony pledging our love for one another." Deborah Ann again shifted her eyes to J.R.

"You know what Effie Mae . . . I think I'm gon let you and Tyrell and your husband figure all that out." She said again looking at J.R. as she continued pinning Effie Mae's hair. "All I know is my cousin love you girl and I wouldn't mess that up for nothing in the world!" An adoring smile formed on Effie Mae's face as she thought of becoming Blue's *spiritual* wife.

"Thank you Deborah Ann."

"You're welcome—cousin." They hugged.

"Well Effie Mae I guess I'll let you and—" She glanced over at J.R. "—your husband talk, while I go downstairs and see how much longer it's gon be before they start this—"

"Ceremony." Effie Mae said giggling.

"Anyway—" Deborah Ann again embraced her. "Congratulations girl!"

"Thank you Deborah Ann." J.R. watched with awkwardness as Deborah Ann prepared to leave the apartment. She shifted her eyes over at him as she passed him on her way out. He silently laughed as she walked downstairs then headed over to Effie Mae.

"You sure you want to do this J.R.?" Effie Mae asked, nervous.

"If I uh, wasn't sure Effie Mae I wouldn't be here." She smiled then placed a kiss on his cheek. "I guess I've uh, been kind of hoping—" J.R. hesitated.

"Hoping what J.R.?" Effie Mae asked as she reinforced the bun hairstyle on her head with additional hair pins.

"That uh, after uh, Blue—" She interjected.

"After Blue what J.R.?" Effie Mae said giggling, aware of what his intentions were. He temporarily remained silent as she continued giggling in response to the look of hope beaming in his eyes. J.R. opened his mouth to speak, but nothing came out. "What J.R. . . . . you was hoping me and you could get back together?" Effie Mae blushed. "I guess you ain't giving up are you J.R.?"

"Nope." He said taking hold of her hands, assisting her to her feet. "From the first time I saw you Effie Mae I knew you were the perfect woman for me." J.R.'s eyes slightly moistened. "How can I give up on that?" He gazed in her eyes then raised her hands to his lips and gently kissed them.

"Well J.R. like I told you before . . . you gon have to get in line this time cause Anthony hoping the same thing." She giggled.
J.R.'s mouth slightly dried.

"Anthony." He coughed. "I uh, had forgotten about him." A clever smile displayed on his face. Effie Mae blushed.

"What J.R.?"

"Well uh—" J.R. stuck his chest slightly out. "—may the best man win." Effie Mae's jaw dropped. She laughed. He briefly chuckled then stopped, gazing at Effie Mae, smiling. She again blushed.

"What?"

"Seeing you in your wedding gown reminds me of the day we got married." His smile widened. "You were beautiful then and you just as beautiful now." Effie Mae's blushing smile widened.

"Thank you J.R." She looked in his eyes seeing his unspoken request for a kiss. She slid his hands around her waist, wrapping her arms around his neck. They romantically kissed.

"Is the wedding still on?" Huck asked when arriving at the top of the stairs witnessing the husband and wife's intimate moment. Their kiss ended. Huck tilted his head. Effie Mae giggled.

"Blue's ready for you girl" He said looking momentarily at J.R. then again to Effie Mae. "What you want me to tell him . . . J.R. changed his mind?" Huck teased.

"Stop Huck!" Effie Mae said amused. "You tell my baby whenever he ready for me, I'm ready for him." Huck shifted his eyes to J.R.

"You gon be alright with that J.R.?"

"I uh, I'm not sure."

"Stop Huck!"

"What I do?" He said humored by J.R.'s response then turned to Effie Mae and smiled.

"It's your time girl." She beamed. Huck looked at J.R. "You can bring her down when you hear the saxophone start playing." A surprised look showed on J.R. face.

"Uh, saxophone?" Effie Mae giggled.

"Yeah J.R.—Blue's a saxophonist."

"Oh! Okay." J.R. said, a confused look his face. Huck silently grinned then placed a light kiss on Effie Mae's forehead before exiting the apartment, headed back downstairs.

———————————

J.R. took hold of Effie Mae's arm and prepared to escort her down the stairs when hearing the soothing sound of the saxophone began to play, *Here Comes the Bride.* Slightly supported by his mother standing to his right, Blue waited in anticipation for Effie Mae to make her grand entrance. An enormous smile stretched across his face when seeing Effie Mae emerge from the stairs—her well preserved, white wedding gown flowed as the bun hairstyle on her head complimented her hazel brown eyes. Tears slowly trickled down Blue's face as he watched J.R. guiding the love of his life, down the stairs and over to where he awaited. Ms. Jones removed a handkerchief from her purse and gently dabbed her beloved son's tear soaked face as he extended his hand and awaited J.R. to place Effie Mae's hand in his.

J.R. silently stared at Effie Mae, ambiguous about her decision to marry Blue. On the one hand he knew she longed for this moment. On the other, he hoped by some miracle she would change her mind and come back home with him. An enormous smile appeared on Effie Mae's face as she looked into Blue's love-filled eyes and waited for J.R. to officially give her away to the groom. Continuing his gaze at the woman he loved, Blue looked nervously at J.R. in response to his delay in joining Effie Mae's hand with his.

"J.R." Blue whispered. J.R.'s eyes remained fixated on Effie Mae as he had second thoughts about giving his wife to Blue. He hoped she would turn away from her lover and resume her role as his wife. "J.R." Blue repeated. The sound of muttering filled the room as guest watched and wondered of the questionable delay. Mr. White observed the peculiar encounter, hoping the delay meant his *favorite son* had seen the light. "Baby girl." Blue said pleading with his eyes that she not change her mind. Effie Mae turned to J.R., visually requesting he allow her to unite with Blue.

Ahem!" J.R. cleared his throat as he broke his unrelenting gawk at his wife then turned to Blue.

The two men looked one to the other as J.R. slowly placed Effie Mae's hand into Blue's then kissed her lightly on the cheek before walking away being seated at the table with Ms. Jones. The Bride and Groom locked arms as the saxophone played a final verse of the wedding hymn. A Pastor well aware of the circumstances surrounding their unusual matrimony, stood before the couple and prepared to preside over their nuptials.

"Brothers and Sisters we're here today to join Effie Mae Smith and Tyrell Lee Jones together in spirit." He raised an eyebrow then proceeded. "They have written their own vows and will pledge their love to each other as part of their ceremony. The saxophone quietly began playing one of Blue's favorite musical jazz pieces as he released Effie Mae's arm and took hold of both her hands. His smile seemingly grew as he faced her, gazing helplessly into her eyes. She blushed.

*"Baby girl, my life was without meaning until I met you. You're like the blood that flows warm in my veins; the rhythm by which my heart beats; the air that fills my lungs every time I breathe; the beautiful sound of sweetness every time you speak; My one wish in life is to wake up to your beautiful, smiling face every morning until I wake up no more. You hold my heart in the palms of your hands and Baby girl you have made me the happiest man in this world."* Blue's

eyes erupted with tears. *"So today I pledge my love and my life to you . . . Effie Mae Smith."* Effie Mae smiled then leaned forward and kissed him gently on the lips.

*"Blue, Tyrell Lee Jones—I love you Baby. If I could give you days from my own life so yours could be longer I would. You are my reason for waking up each and every morning. You put the smile in my heart that gave my life new meaning, and I wouldn't change that for nothing in the world. And I promise that I will be the best wife ever to you baby. You hold my heart in the palms of your hands Blue; And you have made me the happiest woman in the world."* Effie Mae's eyes filled with tears. *"So today I pledge my love baby and my life to you—Tyrell Lee Jones."* They gazed into each other's tear filled eyes.

"Now that you have completed your vows and pledged your love to one another . . . Tyrell Lee Jones you may kiss your bride Effie Mae Smith." The pastor announced. Blue embraced Effie Mae in his arms, inhaling then exhaling through his nose as their guest vigorously applauded the newlyweds—watching as the bride and groom locked lips and shared a passionate kiss.

Mr. White scowled as he watched the kiss with disgust—his only thought being how to prevent Effie Mae from taking possession of his son's Jazz Club upon his demise. The bride and groom simultaneously opened their eyes and looked around at the room of applauding onlooker's as their kiss ended. There attention being drawn to the front door of the jazz club as it suddenly opened. All eyes stared in the direction of the bright light beaming in through the opened door seeing Anthony standing stationary in the doorway, Effie Mae's many children acconpanying him—there from Mississippi. J.R. quickly stood.

"Momma!" Lil' J.R. called out scurrying in and rushing over to Effie Mae.

"Daddy!" Sarah said running over to J.R. Anthony's widened eyes locked onto Effie Mae as she stood coddled in Blue's arms, both dressed in wedding apparel appearing to have just gotten married. J.R. quickly gathered the children, escorting them and Anthony from the club.

# *Chapter Thirteen*

"What the hell's going on J. R.?"Anthony said pacing back and forth on the sidewalk, infuriated.

"Daddy I want Momma." Lil' J.R. whined. J.R. opened the front and back doors of his car parked out front.

"Come on children get in the car."

"Daddy I want Momma." Lil' J.R. stated continuing to whine as he and his siblings climbed inside the car. J.R. quickly closed the doors then turned his attention to Anthony.

"I uh, guess Effie Mae never called you back?"

"No, she didn't!" Anthony yelled. "Did she just marry Blue?" He asked bewildered.

"It's not what uh, you think Anthony." J.R. saidm nervously trying to explain.

"I wasn't aware you and she had gotten divorced yet, so how in the hell could she be marrying Blue?" Anthony shouted as he continued pacing.

"If you uh, calm down Anthony, I can explain—"

"I'll do it J.R." Effie Mae said stepping outside of the club, adorned in her wedding dress. Anthony glared at her with fury.

"I'll uh, go ahead and uh, take the children home."

"Okay J.R." Effie Mae stated as she tried to think of what she would say to Anthony. J.R. shifted his eyes to Anthony sympathizing with his emotional upset.

"I want you Momma." Lil' J.R. whimpered reaching his hands outside the car window.

"I'll be over to see y'all in the morning Lil' J.R., okay baby?"

"Okay." A sad look formed on his small face. She kissed him on the forehead through the open window.

"Momma you look pretty . . . did you get married?" Sarah asked. Effie Mae shifted her eyes quickly to Anthony then turned her back to her children.

"I'll talk to y'all in the morning Sarah baby okay?"

"Okay Momma." Sarah's eyes lit up as she admired her momma's beautiful dress.

"Bye babies." Effie Mae said looking at J.R.—her eyes pleaded with him to leave quickly so she could talk to Anthony. "

"I uh, guess I'll see you in the morning?"

"Okay J.R." She said looking briefly at Anthony then turning to J.R. seeing the worried look eyes in his eyes. He watched with sympathetic eyes as Anthony continued pacing—his eyes fixated on the concrete sidewalk. J.R. turned to his newly married wife, wanting desperately to rescue her. She subtly sook her head no, her eyes begging him to go ahead and leave. He stared momentarily at Effie Mae, distressed by her self-inflicted dilemma then got in the car.

"You uh, alright?" J.R. asked trying not to alarm the children.

"Just leave J.R., let me talk to Anthony."

"You uh, sure?" Effie Mae ignored his concern, forcing a smile as she waved goodbye to her children.

"Bye babies."

"Bye Momma." The children said as J.R. reluctantly drove off. Effie Mae heart pounded in her ears as she prepared to face Anthony. She turned to him and momentarily watched as he angrily paced, devastated by the belief that she'd just married Blue. "Come here Anthony." She said with an apologetic look in her eyes. He stopped and stared at her with enaged eyes.

"So I guess you finally chose Blue?" Anthony yelled, refusing to approach her. "So tell me Effie Mae when exactly did you and J.R. get divorced?"

"We ain't Anthony—" He cut her off.

"Then how in the hell could you marry Blue if you're still married to J.R.?"

"I didn't." A look of confusion displayed on Anthony's face.

"What!" He shouted. "You're not making sense Effie Mae!"

"I told you Anthony . . . Blue is dying—"

"Okay—and?"

"He wanted me to marry him before—"

"He what!" Anthony bellowed.

"He wanted us to get married and live together as husband and wife before he died." He looked at Effie Mae with fury then took a deep angry breath.

"And you said yes!" He screamed. Effie Mae's fright heightened as she looked into  Anthony's fuming eyes.

"Yeah Anthony—" She said lowering her eyes. "—I did."

"So exactly when were you going to tell me Effie Mae? Or did you ever plan on telling me?" He said gawking at her with rage-filled eyes.

She gave no reply. "Don't you think that I had a right to know my fiancée was marrying another man?" He shouted. "So what the hell does that mean for us?"

"Right now Anthony it means as long as Blue is alive I'm his wife." Anthony's mouth abruptly opened. "And if you can't understand that then—"

"Understand!" He yelled as his eyes seeming looking right through her. "So I guess that mean our engagement is off? Is that what that means Effie Mae?" He looked her angrily in the eyes. "So I guess our plans to get married are off!"

"I don't know Anthony." Effie Mae said becoming upset by Anthony's growing anger.

"So just what in the hell do you know Effie Mae?" He shouted. Tears erupted from her eyes.

"All I know is I'm hurting so bad right now, I don't know if I'm coming or going." Anthony's anger subsided in response to Effie Mae's weeping. He rushed over and embraced her in his arms, retrieving a handkerchief from his shirt pocket gently dabbing her wet face—careful not to remove her make-up. "I just know one day I'm gon wake up and Blue ain't gon be there."

"I'm sorry Baby." Anthony said kissing her on the cheek. "I was so angry I guess I never thought how all of this was affecting you." He placed a light kiss on her forehead. "Forgive me Baby." Her ears deafened to his repentant words as she looked into nothingness.

"Everybody want to tell me how to live my life just like they know what's best for me, but nobody ain't once thought about how bad I'm hurting."

"Baby I'm sorry, I didn't mean to—" She cut him off.
"You know what it's like to wake up in the morning with a pain so deep in your stomach you can't hardly stand it—" A helpless look showed in Effie Mae's eyes as tears ran down her cheeks. "—cause you know it's gon come a day when the person laying next to you gon close they eyes and ain't ever gon open them again?"

"No Baby I don't." He said continuing to wipe her flowing tears with his handkerchief. "I guess I didn't realize how how devastating all this was for you . . . and Blue."

"Blue?" Effie Mae half-heartedly chuckled. Anthony looked at her with peculiarity, puzzled by her out of place laughter. "Blue taking this better than me!" Effie Mae said giggling through her tears. "And he the one that's dying."

"I'm not giving up on you Baby—on us." Anthony said sympathizing with her circumstances. "Do what you have to do for now and when all this is over, I'll be right here waiting for you Baby." She suddenly chuckled.

"What Baby?"

"I might as well warn you Anthony."

"Of?"

"J. R. ain't giving up either!" Effie Mae giggled.

"J. R.?"A confused look formed on Anthony's face. "When did he come back into the picture?"

"Anthony . . . J.R.'s still my husband!"

"Baby I thought he sent you divorce papers?"

"He did Anthony, but it looks like J.R. ain't giving up that easy."

"Is that what you want Baby—" She looked in Anthony's apprehensive eyes. "—to go back to J.R.?"

"All I want Anthony is to enjoy my life with Blue." He swallowed the enormous lump forming in his throat.

"Okay I think I understand what you're saying . . . I think." He kissed Effie Mae gently on the lips.

"Right now Anthony, I don't want to think about nothing else except Blue."

"Baby you know I'll wait as long as I have too." Anthony stated. "And when you're ready, please call me."

"Anthony—" He interrupted.

"Baby please don't give up on us."

"Anthony—"

"Baby please!" He pleaded. "And remember, I'm only a phone call away okay Baby?" She humorously smiled.

"Yeah Anthony I know." They gazed in each others eyes then romantically kissed.

"You alright Effie Mae?" Huck asked exiting the club startling her and Anthony, ending their intimate kiss. She looked into his inquisitive eyes and giggled in response to him once again witnessing her in an intimate encounter with one of the many men in her life.

"Yeah Huck everything's fine, I was just explaining to my fiancé—" Huck quietly chuckled, shaking his head. "—how I just married Blue." Effie Mae said laughing to herself. "And I ain't even told him yet, how my husband was the one who gave me away to the groom." Huck tilted his head and smiled.

"Girl you something else." He looked briefly to Anthony then back to Effie Mae. "Well your new husband's asking for you girl." Huck stated. Anthony looked at Huck with unfamiliarity, bothered by him interrupting his personal time with Effie Mae.

"Do I know you?" Anthony asked. Huck looked at him and quietly chuckled then turned to Effie Mae amused by Anthony's bold question. She giggled.

"Anthony that's Huck." A perplexed look showed on his face.

"Huck? That's him?" Huck shifted his eyes to Effie Mae then again to Anthony in response to his remark.

"Anthony you don't remember Huck?"

"No, I don't."

"You remember he came to see me before I moved back home with you to Mississippi." Anthony continued his bazzled gaze.

"I remember a man coming over to say goodbye, but I only saw him from inside the car so I didn't really get a good look at him." He extended his hand to Huck. "How are you Huck?" Huck shifted his eyes to Effie Mae before approaching Anthony's.

"It's good to see Effie Mae got people looking out for her." He said as he and Anthony shook. "She gon need it." He nodded, glad to know Effie Mae had support. "You ready girl?" Effie Mae looked in Anthony's frantic eyes.

"I got to go Anthony."

"I love you Baby." He said kissing her lightly on the lips.

"I love you too Anthony."

"I'll be waiting for your call Baby okay?" He said pleading." Huck watched, humored by Anthony's desperation.

"I got to go Anthony."

"Baby promise me you'll call."

"I will Anthony." Huck patiently watched as they intimately kissed, sympathetic to Anthony's position.

"Effie Mae come on girl!" Huck said in response to her prolonged kiss with Anthony. She shifted her eyes over at him then turned to Anthony, looking at him with ambiguity. On the one hand, she looked forward to starting her new life with Blue. On the other—she truly did miss her old life with Anthony.

"Bye Anthony."

"Call me Baby—please!" He applied one last kiss to Effie Mae's lips then released her.

"Bye Anthony." Huck said mocking Effie Mae. "Come on here girl." He chuckled then took hold of Effie Mae's arm, escorting her back inside the jazz club. Anthony walked over to the closed door and opened it to a crack then peeped inside. His heart raced as he watched his fiancée celebrating her wedding day with her new *spiritual* husband.

––––––––––––––

"Good morning beautiful." Blue stated with a huge smile on his face, watching as Effie Mae slowly awakened.

"Good morning love of my life." She said smiling as he enveloped her in his arms, passionately kissing her.

"I can't believe you finally my wife." Blue said placing another kiss on her lips.

"In spirit Blue." Effie Mae said unable to deny her legal marriage to J.R. She noted the look of hurt that flashed briefly in Blue's eyes in response to her truthful words.

"Blue I'm sor—"

"How you want to start our first day off as husband and wife Baby girl?" He asked diverting from the reality of their relationship. A seductively smile formed on his face. They romantically kissed.

"Blue!" Effie Mae blushed. "We did that last night baby . . . a lot." A worried look showed in her eyes. "Baby did your doctor say it was okay for you to do that so often?" Blue again kissed her, trying to minimize her reasonable concerns.

"My doctor ain't seen my beautiful wife." Blue teased. "Maybe the next time I go see him I'll take you with me." He applied a smooch to Effie Mae's lips then gazed in her eyes." She smiled.

"What Blue?"

"Baby girl I want to enjoy you as much as I can for as long as I can." They passionately kissed. Effie Mae's worry progressed into panic. She gently subtly pushed Blue away to avoid intimacy.

"Maybe we should cut back just a little Blue."

"Baby girl!" H said raising his voice, feeling rejected. "I ain't gon die until it's time—I'm a man and I want to enjoy my wife as a man!"

"Okay Baby." Effie Mae said masking her apprehension behind a smile. He pulled her over on him and lovingly kissed her then prepared to engage in intimacy.

"Tyrell are you and Effie Mae woke?" Ms. Jones asked speaking through the closed door. Blue abruptly stopped, frowning as he looked at Effie Mae shaking his head in disbelief.

"Yeah Momma, but we're still on our honeymoon!" He said kissing Effie Mae on the lips and neck. She giggled.

"Can I come in Tyrell . . . I need to talk to you?"

"Momma! Can you come back in about thirty minutes?" He asked, aggravated. Effie Mae quietly laughed.

"This won't take very long Tyrell then you and Effie Mae go back to whatever it was you were doing."

"You may as well talk to her Blue." Effie Mae said relieved by Ms. Jones unexpected interruption. "She ain't gon leave until you do."

"Tyrell!" Ms. Jones persisted.

"Okay Momma!" Blue shook his head with agitation. "Just let us get dressed."

"Alright . . . thank you Tyrell."

"I know you wanted to go see your kids today Baby girl." Blue said slightly winded as he struggled to put his pajamas shirt on. Effie Mae hid her fear when observing his semi-labored breathing—the after effects of their active honeymoon night.

"Let me do that baby." Effie Mae said sliding his arms inside the sleeves of his pajamas shirt. He grasped hold of her right hand and softly kissed it. Effie Mae smiled as she began buttoning his shirt. He again took hold of her hand and again kissed it.

"I can button my own shirt Baby girl."

"You sure Blue?"

"Baby girl I ain't helpless—not yet." He guided her mouth towards his lips and kissed her. "Now get dressed so you can go see your kids."

"Okay Blue." Effie Mae climbed out of bed and walked over to the closet, removing a shirt and pair of pants from the closet then entered the bathroom to wash and dress, leaving the door open to continue her conversation with Blue.

"Baby girl I'm sorry about Momma." Blue apologized as he slid his legs in his pajama pants.

"That's okay Blue . . . this time." She giggled.

"Tyrell it's been ten minutes." Ms. Jones said calling through the door. Blue shook his head in response to her perseverance.

"Momma . . . Effie Mae's getting dressed!" He looked at Effie Mae and again shook his head. "Baby girl if you want, I can tell her to come back later."

"Naw Blue don't do that." Effie Mae stated. "I don't want your momma hating me too." Blue gave no reply as he thought of his father's loathing for the woman he loved. "I need to go see my babies and J.R. anyway—what happened yesterday should've never happen Blue." Effie Mae said as she turned on the water, running it over a towel wrapped around a bar of soap.

"But it did happen Baby girl and now you and J.R. need to figure out how to explain that to y'all kids."

"I don't know why Anthony brought my babies up here the this jazz club Blue!"

"Baby girl it's done . . . now just go work that out with J.R." He glanced over at the apartment door. "I know Momma, and she gon be in here all morning talking about Daddy."

"Your daddy?" Effie Mae chuckled, amused by his foregone conclusion. "How you know that's what your momma gon talk about Blue? All she said was she wanted to talk to you."

"Yeah Baby girl, but I know from experience whenever Momma say she want to talk it's gon be about Daddy." Effie Mae's excitement suddenly heightened.

"You want to meet my babies Blue?"

"Baby girl I think you need talk to J.R. about that first."

"Why Blue? J. R. won't mind." She said buttoning the yellow polka dotted blouse, accenting the yellow straight legged pants she wore.

"You don't know that Baby girl." He stated with concern. "That man may not want me involved in his kid's life . . . remember he is still your husband." Blue looked into Effie Mae's naïve eyes as she exited the bathroom. "Baby girl those kids may not understand our relationship."

"Okay baby, if you want me to talk to J.R. first then I guess I can speak to him when I go over there this morning." An enormous smile suddenly formed on Blue's face. Effie Mae blushed. "What Blue?"

"I still can't believe you back here with me." Her blushing smile widened. "I love you Baby girl, you know that?"

"Yeah I know that Blue." He opened his extended arms.

"Come here." Effie Mae blushed as she strolled over to him. He reached up and pulled her in his arms then intimately kissed her.

"Don't forget I'm still out here Tyrell!" Ms. Jones said yelling through the door.

"I ain't forgot Momma." The newlyweds quietly laughed.

———————————————

Effie Mae stood at J.R.'s back door and knocked, nervous about requesting Blue's involvement in their children's lives. Butterflies fluttered in her stomach when he appeared at the door and silently stared at her.

"Hey J.R." She said looking at him through the screened door.

"Effie Mae." J.R. looked at her, hesitating before he opened the door, allowing her to enter. "Is uh, everything alright?" He asked sensing her nervousness as he closed the door. She looked around not seeing her children.

"Where's my babies at J.R.?" Effie Mae asked, upset by their absence. J.R. stared at her but gave no reply. "Are they here J.R.?" He continued his silence. "J.R., you knew I was coming this morning to talk to my babies!" She said raising her voice, annoyed by his silence.

"Uh, no they're not here Effie Mae."

"I can see that J.R.!" She yelled. "Where they at?"

"They uh, rode the church bus this morning." He said with vagueness. "I uh, didn't want them to be late for Sunday school, so I uh—" Effie Mae glared angrily at him, agitated by him *beating around the bush.*

"So you what J.R.!" She shouted.

"And I know how much Millie Ann hates being late." He half-heartedly chuckled, ignoring her explosive temper as he rambled on. "And you know uh, children . . . if you let one do something they uh, all want to do it." J.R. grinned as he emotionally prepared himself for the altercation he sensed brewing. "So they all went . . . and uh, after yesterday I thought it best we spoke without them being here." Effie Mae accepted his reasoning.

"You probably right J.R." She said trying to think of how to make her request for Blue's involvement in their children's lives known. "How Ms. Geraldine doing?" Effie Mae asked building up her nerves.

"Cousin Daniel and I uh, don't exactly talk to these days." Her ears deafened to his voice as she continued trying to build up her nerves. "Most information I get these days comes from uh, Millie Ann—" J.R. stated then abruptly silenced, looking at Effie Mae without speaking.

"What?" She said irritated. A sympathetic look appeared in his eyes. "Anthony?"

"What about Anthony?" Effie Mae yelled. "And why you worried about him anyway . . . he gon be alright."

"Is he?" J.R. asked, surprised by her callous reply.

"Don't you worry about what's going on with me and Anthony!"

"Uh, okay—"

"Okay what J.R.?" She shouted, aggravated by his continuous gaze.

"Can we talk about what happened yesterday?"

"Ain't that why I'm here?"

"I uh, don't think the children would uh, understand you and Blue's arrangement, so I think it's best if they not—"

"You speaking for my babies J.R. or you?"

"Both."

"You let me talk to my babies!" Effie Mae bellowed. "And I want Blue to be in my babies lives too . . . just like Anthony was!" J.R.'s jaw dropped. His anger soared.

"No!" He yelled. "If you want to play house with Blue, Effie Mae I can't stop you, but I can stop my children from being a part of that, that—" J.R. searched for a word to describe the confusing commitment.

"J.R. you know I'm living with Blue!" She yelled. "How am I gon see my babies if—" He quickly interjected.

"That's something you need to figure out Effie Mae . . . without Blue!" She looked at him with fury in her eyes.

"What J.R.? You jealous . . . is that what it is?" His mouth dried. He coughed. "Jealous because I pledged my love to Blue and not you!" She said lashing out, trying to hurt him.

"How you think I'm suppose to feel Effie Mae? You my wife!" J.R. shouted, anger by her selfishness.

"I'm gon have Anthony send me them divorce papers so I won't have to be your wife no more J.R. Smith!"

"Do you ever think about anybody besides you Effie Mae?"

"You go to hell J.R.!" She screamed then stormed in the direction of the back door preparing to leave.

"Is that really what you want Effie Mae . . . to divorce me?"

"This ain't about you J.R.!" Effie Mae yelled as she again turned to him, her eyes filled with rage. "It's about Blue—the man I love!" He momentarily stared at her fuming from her hurtful words.

"If you want a divorce Effie Mae, Anthony won't have to send then papers I'll have my attorney write up some new ones and deliver them to you myself at your home with Blue." J.R. said trembling as his anger amplified. "But my children gon be staying right here with me since you ain't got a decent place for them to live!" Effie Mae's mouth abruptly opened.

"What you mean I ain't got no descent place for my babies to live J.R.? You know I'm living with Blue."

"Upstairs inside of a jazz club?" He shouted. "Lets see what the judge gon say about that!" Effie Mae looked at him with frightened eyes as he silently stared at her, infuriated. "Do you really think I would let my children to live in a jazz club Effie Mae?"

"Why you doing this J.R.?" She yelled, frightened by his threat to take the children.

"My children deserved better than to see their momma once again living with a man other than their daddy . . . and your husband!"

"I hate you J.R. Smith!"

"You my wife Effie Mae not Blue's—and that comes before any pledge or commitment you made with Blue!"

"You just mad because I'm in Blue's bed and not yours?" He looked at her, bothered by her out of the blue, hurtful words. "Is that what you want J.R.?" Effie Mae said rebelliously looking at him. "Okay J.R. you want me to be your wife—come on." She walked over to him and wrapped her arms around his neck then seductively kissed him. He subtly pushed her away, resisting her unexpected advances.

"Stop Effie Mae."

"Stop what J.R. . . . being your wife? I thought that's what you wanted." She said lowering his lips onto hers, forcing him to kiss her.

"What you doing Effie Mae?"

"You want me to be your wife J.R. then I'll be your wife." She looked into J.R.'s confused eyes then kissed him intimately on the lips and neck.

"Effie Mae—" J.R. said weakening to her enticement.

"What J.R.?" He embraced Effie Mae in his arms, allowing her to passionately kiss him.

"What about Blue?"

"You let me worry about Blue." She said continuing her irresistible seduction. "Like you said—I'm your wife not Blue's." J.R. gazed in Effie Mae's alluring eyes as he made a final attempt at opposing her inducement. She slid his hands around her waist then intimately wrapped her arms around his neck, romantically kissing him. J.R. stared helplessly in her eyes as she led him in the direction of the bedroom. Once inside, J.R. picked Effie Mae up and laid her on his bed then husband and wife engaged in overdue marital intimacy.

# *Chapter Fourteen*

"Where's Effie Mae this evening Tyrell?" Ms. Jones asked as he joined his parents at a table downstairs in the customer filled jazz club, listening to the members of his band playing his favorite jazz pieces.

"She had some business to take care of Momma."

"That man who gave her away who was he?"

"That was J.R."

"J.R.? Who is he?" Ms. Jones asked probing.

"What's with all the questions Momma?" Blue asked becoming agitated.

"You're not hiding anything from me are you Tyrell?" She said shifting her eyes briefly to his father. Mr. White observed Blue's responses to his mother's question, noting how he avoided direct eye contact with her.

"Your mother asked you a question Tyrell." Blue's anxiety heightened as he prepared to tell his parent's the truth.

"You know what Momma . . . I am hiding something." Mr. White shifted his eyes to Ms. Jones then again looked at Blue as he awaited to hear his truth. "To answer your question about the man who gave Effie Mae away—" Blue took a deep breath. "—that's her husband."

"You mean her ex-husband don't you Tyrell?" She said correcting him.

"Naw Momma—J.R. is Effie Mae's husband . . . he's the man she's legally married to." Ms. Jones gasped.

"Oh my goodness!"

"And those children you saw, those are theirs." Mr. White maintained his silence, feeling vindicated in his mistrust of Effie Mae.

"How can you marry a woman that's already married Tyrell?"

"Because I love her Momma, and she loves me!" Blue said raising his voice. "And by the time her and J.R. could get divorce I'd be dead!"

"I knew it!" Mr. White said no longer able to hold his tongue. "I knew it was something about that lowdown tramp." He looked at Ms. Jones then turned to Bliue, staring at him. "What she after Tyrell—this club?"

"Naw Daddy you wrong." A distressed look appeared on Blue's face. "Effie Mae don't have no interest in this club."

"Then why in the hell would she want to marry a dying man?"

"Henry!" Ms. Jones said disturbed by his thoughtless words.

"What Rosalyn?" He stated without apology. "You got gold diggers all over the damn place."

"Now Henry you don't know that Effie Mae's a gold digger—"

"And you don't know that she's not!" He yelled. "You tell me then Rosalyn, why in hell would a woman with a husband marry a man don't have but six months to live?" He looked at Blue as if waiting for him to answer his insulting question. "I'll tell you why Tyrell." His father said staring him in the eyes. "She want to get her greedy hands on what our boy work so hard to get!" He said looking around the club. "All this." Blue's anxiety heightened upset by his father's insensitive words. "And I tell you what else—" Mr. White stated with certainty. "—I bet you her husband's in on it with her."

"You wrong Daddy." Blue said turning to his mother, his eyes pleading for her to stop help. He hoped she'd run interference, stopping his father as she'd done many times before. "Effie Mae love me Momma!" He cried out when Ms. Jones said nothing in his defense. "And besides that . . . J.R.'s a preacher."

"What the hell is that supposed to mean Tyrell?" Mr. White yelled, unimpressed. "You got greedy preachers all over the damn place too!" He shook his head at what he deemed to be Blue's weakness as a man. "What's wrong with you boy?"

"Daddy you don't know Effie Mae . . . that woman would die for me."

"Would she Tyrell?" He said looking at him as a fool. "Then you tell me why she didn't divorce her husband and marry you before you got sick? Huh? Tell me that Tyrell?"

"That's enough Henry!" Ms. Jones said when noticing the distraught look on Blue's face.

"It's a reason for that Daddy, but I ain't telling you or Momma so don't ask!" Blue shouted then began coughing.

"Are you alright Tyrell?" Ms. Jones asked.

"Naw Momma I ain't." Blue's coughing intensified.

"You need some water boy?" Mr. White asked in response to Blue's continuous coughing. His attention suddenly drew to Effie Mae as she entered the club. She quickly noticed Blue violently coughing then headed in the direction of him and his parents.

"Here comes that gold digger now." Mr. White said shifting his eyes briefly to Ms. Jones then back to Effie Mae.

"Now Henry—"

"Look at her." He said with contempt. Ms. Jones looked at Effie Mae as she drew near their table then turned her attention to Blue. "Keep her away from here Rosalyn." Mr. White demanded.

"Noooooo!" Blue cried out. "That's my wife—" His coughing progressed to a noticeable wheeze.

"You alright baby?" Effie Mae asked as she approached. "Blue baby where's your inhaler? Did you take your medicine this morning?"

"Get—me upstairs—Baby girl."

"I'm coming too Tyrell." Ms. Jones said standing.

"No Momma!" Blue said struggling to breathe.

"Listen to your mother Tyrell!" Mr. White shouted in opposition to his request.

"Naw Daddy—Effie Mae's—gon take care—of me." Blue said forcing out the words. Mr. White stared at Effie Mae with disdain, watching as she placed Blue's right arm around her neck, balancing his weight with her left arm as she supported him at the waist. Her fear growing as she felt him gradually weakening as he continued uncontrollably coughing.

"Are you sure you can get him up those stairs Effie Mae?" Ms. Jones called out, nervously looking at the numerous amount of steps. Blue suddenly collapsed.

"Blue!" Effie Mae screamed. "Somebody help!" The band abruptly stopped—observing the incident from the stage. Melvin hurried from the kitchen when hearing Effie Mae's call for help.

"Tyrell!" Ms. Jones said rushing over to him. Mr. White remained seated as he kept a sharp-eye on Effie Mae as customers slowly gathered around, looking on as Effie Mae knelt at Blue's sid, holding his upper body in her arms. Melvin rushed over to the phone in the bar area, his stomach filled with knots, and called for an ambulance.

"We need an ambulance down here at Blue Jazz Club!" Melvin's mouth dried as he spoke. "My cousin, the owner just passed out—he got lung cancer . . . hurry!" He hung up the phone then rushed over to Blue, knealing down at his cousin's side, uncertain of what would happen next.

Mr. White continued his observation of Effie Mae's every move as she wept and looked down on Blue's limp body in horror.

---

"I thought Blue's doctor said he had six months to live." Melvin said in anger as he and Mr. White sat at a table in the jazz club and waited to receive word from Effie Mae or Ms. Jones on Blue's condition that morning. "When they took my poor cousin out of here last night he didn't look like he had six minutes left to—" Mr. White interjected.

"You can't trust nothing them doctors say . . . all they doing is guessing, so I don't trust none of them." Their attention drew to a knock at the door. "Maybe that's Rosalyn now."

"Effie Mae's got a key so she wouldn't need to knock." Melvin said shifting his eyes over at the door. "Besides . . . she said she would call as soon as they knew something."

"Then I guess you better go see who that is." Mr. White said flashing Melvin a common sense look. Melvin rose from the table and prepared to greet the early morning visitor.

"I wonder who that is—we closed." He said thinking out loud. "People know we don't open this place until six o'clock at night." An aggravated look displayed on his face as he walked over to the door, curious of who might possibly be on the other side. He looked through the peep hole and saw a man from the neck down waiting anxiously to enter. Melvin unlocked the door and opened it to a crack, looking out.

"You out kind of early ain't you Gus?" He said stepping aside allowing him to enter then quickly closing and locking the door behind him.

"Melvin man, I know me and Blue had our differences, but that man's like family to me!" Gus stated glancing over at the unfamiliar gentleman seated inside. "In fact me and Blue we're cool until our little misunderstanding over Effie Mae." Melvin shifted his eyes to Mr. White then tried to signal Gus with his eyes not to speak on the subject.

"Did you want something Gus?" He asked redirecting the conversation, trying for a second time to signal Gus with his eyes.

"Yeah you can give me a shot of gin, scotch, something." Gus said grinning.

"Yeah man I can do that—" Melvin paused. "Tonight after six."

"That's cold man, but you know I was only teasing with you about that right?" Gus said laughing as he licked his lips in anticipation of some liquor. "What about that customer over there?" Gus looked at the coffee cup in front of Mr. White with skepticism. "I know he got something stronger than coffee in that cup."

"Gus you know we don't start serving liquor until we open." Melvin stated as his anxiety grew in response to Gus's prolonged visit. He knew for certain Gus would ultimately say something that would prove to be damaging. "Well Gus—me and Mr. White was just sitting here waiting to hear something about Blue, so if you—" Gus interrupted.

"Oh, I didn't mean to disturb y'all—" Mr. White interceded.

"Did I hear Melvin say your name was Gus?" He asked in response to hearing him mention Effie Mae's name.

"That's right Mr. White." Melvin said as his heart began pounding his chest.

"White?" Gus said in recognition of the name. "You any kin to Huck, Mr. White?" He asked. "I mean Henry Lee White, but everybody around here call him Huck."

"Yeah." Mr. White stated with fatherly pride. "Henry Lee's my oldest boy." Gus quickly turned to Melvin, amazed by the discovery then turned back to Mr. White. "I'm also Tyrell's father." Gus' eyes widened and his jaw dropped.

"Man you telling me that—"

"That's right . . . Henry Lee and Tyrell are brothers."

"Brothers?" Gus looked at Melvin and laughed. "Man no wonder Huck was so damn mad when Blue stole Effie Mae from him!" He continued laughing. Melvin panicked.

"Look here Gus I got a lot of work to do before I open tonight, but if you come back after we open I'll give you a shot of liquor on the house, maybe two." Mr. White quickly intervened.

"You go ahead Melvin do what it is you need to do, I'd like to talk to Gus for a few minutes . . . if he don't mind." Melvin again tried to signal Gus with his eyes not to talk to Mr. White. Gus ignored his repeated eye gestures then headed over to joined Mr. White at his table.

"Did I hear you say something about Effie Mae, Gus?" Mr. White asked shifting his eyes to Melvin then back to Gus. Melvin shook his head with disappointment, certain Gus' inability to hold his tongue would result in consequences—for Gus.

"You sure did." Gus said looking briefly over at Melvin as he prepared to *spill his guts*, but only after Melvin had returned to the kitchen—or so Gus thought. "Yeah Mr. White—" An enormous smile stretched across Gus' face. "—me and Effie Mae, we had a thing once upon a time."

"You don't say." Mr. White stated with intrigue. "And just what do you mean Gus when you say y'all had a thing?"

"You didn't hear this from me—" Gus lowered his voice. "—but back in the day Effie Mae was one of Huck's whores." He said grinning through his dingy teeth.

"You don't say." Mr. White listened calmly and carefully.

"Yeah Mr. White." Gus' smile widened. "And let me tell you—Effie Mae turned out to be one of the best whores Ms. Norma had in the house!" Gus burst into laughter.

"Ms. Norma?"

"Yeah, she ran one of the best parlors—" Gus corrected himself. "—I mean whorehouses here in the city."

"You don't say."

"Yeah . . . Effie Mae had men lined up at the front door!" Gus said, his excitement magnifying. "Girl damn near put me in the poorhouse." He stated with a massive smile on his face. "I must've been at Ms. Norma's—" He combed through his memory bank. "—twice, maybe three times a week . . . if I had the extra money." Gus said grinning through his teeth. Mr. White re-adjusted himself in his chair.

"Well tell me this Gus, did Tyrell know about Effie Mae working in Ms. Norma's whorehouse?"

"Know about it!" Gus again burst into laughter. "Hell, Huck made sure Ol' Blue was one of the first to know when he started pimping that girl!" Gus abruptly silenced then shifted his eyes in the direction of the kitchen, his eyes searching for Melvin. "You didn't hear this from me Mr. White, but the only reason Huck pimped that girl was to spite Blue." Mr. White's tilted his head.

"You don't say."

"Then he wouldn't let Tyrell get near that girl!" He again looked in the direction of the kitchen then turned back to Mr. White. Had me and Buckeye watching her trying to see if—" Mr. White interrupted.

"Buckeye?"

"Yeah that's Huck's right hand man." Gus' eyes gave warning. "Between me and you Mr. White—" Gus again glanced around to see if Melvin's ears were within *ear shot.* "—you didn't hear this from me, but I believe Melvin spent a few dollars on Effie Mae his self." Gus winked then grinned. "I didn't say nothing to Huck though because I couldn't prove it."

"You don't say."

"Yeah Ol' Huck kept a real close eye on Effie Mae that's for sure." Gus said cunningly laughed. "But one night when I was out there watching her, I saw Ol' Blue sneak inside her apartment." He again leaned in towards Mr. White. "I bet you a shot of gin Mr. White, Blue got his at a discount." He hesitated. "Or got it free!" Gus ruptured into laughter.

"You don't say." Mr. White deviously grinned. His thoughts now consumed with lust—for Effie Mae.

"I had to report that to Huck." Gus said with a sense if loyalty.

"Yeah I understand, you was doing your job."

"That's right." Gus said feeling justified. "Let me tell you Mr. White, your son was mad as hell . . . for a minute there we thought he was gon kill Blue!" Gus' eyes widened. "But if you ask me—" He again leaned in towards Mr. White. "—it didn't have nothing to do with Blue getting his free." Gus nodded with confirmation. "Naw Mr. White if you ask me, the rift between Huck and Blue went a whole lot deeper than Effie Mae." He said shifing his eyes in the direction of the kitchen, ensuring Melvin hadn't heard his damaging words. "You didn't hear this from me Mr. White, but if you ask me . . . it was just plain old jealousy!" Gus nodded. "Everybody knew Blue was in trouble when Effie Mae chose him over pretty boy Huck." Gus half-heartedly laughed, hoping Melvin hadn't heard him speaking words he knew could cost him his life if they ever reached Huck's ears.

"You don't say."

"Me and Huck go way back Mr. White—always had each other's backs, it was a time when I would've died for that man!" Gus stated with conviction. "But after he damn near beat Effie Mae half to death—" He shook his head in disapproval. "—I had to walk away from my friend . . . that was just plain Ol' evil." He again leaned in. "Between me and you Mr. White, I damn near married Effie Mae." Gus said cunningly grinning. "Yep, I sure did." Mr. White's eyes widened as the lustful smile on his face grew.

"You don't say."

"It was only one thing kept me from marrying Effie Mae." Mr. White tilted his head.

"And what was that Gus?"

"My wife!" The two men burst into laughter. Gus abruptly silenced then looked Mr. White in the eyes. "My momma always taught me and my brothers a man ain't got no business putting his hands on a woman, hitting her." Mr. White nodded in agreement.

"It sounds like your momma was a wise woman Gus."

"Yeah, when she wasn't letting her old man go upside her head when his beer wasn't cold enough!" Mr. White's eyes again widened.

"Well Mr. White it's been a pleasure talking to you about your sons." Gus said chuckling. "But I don't want to take up anymore of your time than I already have talking about all that old stuff." Gus rose from the table, conducting a visual search around the club to ensure Melvin hadn't heard his taboo conversation.

"Well I sure appreciated you conversing with me Gus." Mr. White said standing to his feet. "You be sure to stay in touch Gus, I might have a few more questions about my sons since it seems I'll be sticking around here a little longer than anticipated." He extended his hand to Gus. The two men shook before Gus began his journey to the front door.

"It was good meeting you Mr. White." He said unlocking and opening the door.

"You too Gus."

Melvin remained in hiding as Gus prepared to exit the club, unaware Melvin had heard every word of the damaging report he provided to Mr. White. Gus took a final look around, convinced his words of betrayal hadn't been heard. He walked out then quietly closed the door as he departed. Melvin stared briefly at the closed door and shook his head. He knew Gus' whispering lips were about to bring unimaginable chaos to the lives of those he'd discussed.

Mr. White lowered himself back in his chair, lapsing deep in thought as he wondered how he'd use the information Gus so eagerly shared to his advantage.

---

Ms. Jones gradually awakened from her overnight stay in Blue's hospital room where she slept in a corner chair just left of Blue's bed. She smiled when seeing Effie Mae lying next to him on the bed sleep.

"Effie Mae." She whispered trying to awaken her. "Effie Mae." Ms. Jones repeated. Effie Mae's eyes slowly opened. She quickly looked over at Blue as he lay sleeping then kissed him lightly on the back of his head. Ms. Jones smiled.

"You called me Ms. Jones?" Effie Mae asked turning towards her.

"Yes, I was just wondering if you wanted to go downstairs to the cafeteria and eat some breakfast."

"Ms. Jones I don't want to leave Blue here by his self . . . you go head on I'm gon stay here."

"Oh no you aren't Effie Mae." Ms. Jones politely scolded. "You've been here all night and you need to eat something." She said insisting. "Tyrell will be okay, we aren't going to be gone that long."

"Ms. Jones me and Blue made a commitment to each other—" She cut Effie Mae off.

"Commitment?" She looked at Effie Mae with rational eyes. "Does that commitment include you starving to death?" Ms. Jones lightly laughed. Effie Mae's eyes displayed worry. "Oh come on Effie Mae I don't think Tyrell will be waking up anytime soon, besides he's always a late sleeper—has that changed?" Effie Mae blushed. "Tyrell will be just fine." Effie Mae hesitated.

"I guess I am a little hungry." She said looking over at Blue, kissing him lightly on the cheek. "I love you baby." Effie Mae rose from the bed, masking her fear as she prepared to join Ms. Jones for breakfast.

• • • •

"This seems like a good place for us to sit." Ms. Jones said as her and Effie Mae walked through the semi-filled cafeteria in search of a table to sit. "What do you think Effie Mae?" She said walking over to a table to the far left of the room, isolated from other occupied tables.

"That's fine Ms. Jones."

"Is that all you're eating Effie Mae . . . two slices of toast and two boiled eggs. Ms. Jones asked as she searched for a way to initiated a conversation regarding Blue's confession before his health scare.

"I'll do good if I can eat this." Effie Mae half-heartedly chuckled. "I ain't got much of a appetite.

"Well I guess that's understandable." Ms. Jones said preparing to ease into the conversation of Effie Mae's marital status. "Tyrell spoke to me and his father yesterday just before he got sick." Effie Mae gave no reply as her mind remained focused on Blue—alone in his room. "He told us that you and he weren't really married." Effie Mae sat the piece of toast in her hand back onto her plate and looked at her.

"Ms. Jones I know them words ain't come from Blue cause—" Ms. Jones interrupted.

"Well . . . Tyrell didn't exactly use those words Effie Mae, but he did tell me and his father that you were married to the gentleman that gave you away—I believe Tyrell said his name was J.R.?" Effie Mae briefly lowered her head then looked Ms. Jones in the eyes trying to read her thoughts.

"Ms. Jones me and Blue love one another—"

"Well anyone with eyes can see that Effie Mae!" Ms. Jones said chuckling. "But it concerns me to know why Tyrell would wants to spend his life—" She silenced when seeing the emotional hurt in Effie Mae's eyes.

"Ms. Jones when me and Blue pledged our love to each other we knew we wasn't taking marriage vows, but that was what we both wanted."

"I can certainly understand why Tyrell would want to marry you Effie Mae you're a beautiful woman!"

"Ms. Jones Blue would marry me if I had two heads." Effie Mae laughed.

"Oh my!"

"Ms. Jones . . . Blue the only man I ever loved, but by the time I realized it—" Effie Mae paused. "—it was too late."

"I didn't mean to interrupt your breakfast Effie Mae—" Ms. Jones stated when noticing Effie Mae no longer eating. "—go ahead and finish your breakfast." Effie Mae picked up her toast and resumed eating.

"The first time Blue asked me to marry him Ms. Jones—"

"The first time?"

"Yeah Ms. Jones, the first time." Effie Mae quietly giggled. "I had just put another man's engagement ring on my finger."

"J. R.?" Ms. Jones said guessing.

"Naw Ms. Jones it wasn't J.R." Her eyes widened.

"Oh my, it wasn't."

"I married J.R. when I was seventeen."

"I guess you were pregnant."

"Naw Ms. Jones I wasn't pregnant." Effie Mae giggled.

"In love?"

"Nope, I wasn't in love either." Ms. Jones' eyes again widened.

"Then why on earth would you marry at such a young age Effie Mae, and to a man you weren't in love with?" Effie Mae hesitated before answering.

"Ms. Jones I was trying to please my momma." Ms. Jones' mouth abruptly opened.

"My goodness that's an awfully extreme way of pleasing your mother."

"In a way Ms. Jones I owed it to her." She looked at Effie Mae with oddity.

"Owed it to her?"

"It's a long story Ms. Jones." Effie Mae quietly chuckled. "Me and J.R. got married and had six babies before our marriage went bad—that was when me and Blue got together." A huge smile formed on Effie

Mae's face as she recalled their budding romance. "And for the first time in my life Ms. Jones fell in love."

"With Tyrell?" Ms. Jones asked, apprehensive about Effie Mae's impending reply. Effie Mae giggled.

"Yeah Ms. Jones with Tyrell." Ms. Jones breathed a sigh of relief.

"For a moment there I was almost afraid to ask."

"The only thing is Ms. Jones, I didn't realize I loved Blue until after I had told Anthony I was gon marry him."

"Now who's Anthony?"

"Anthony's my fiancé Ms. Jones."

"You mean your ex-fiancé right?"

"Naw Ms. Jones . . . Anthony still my fiancé." Ms. Jones' mouth slightly opened.

"Oh my! Does he know about you and Tyrell?"

"Yeah Ms. Jones he know." Effie Mae saddened when remembering the hurt on Anthony's face when witnessing her and Blue's *spiritual* commitment.

"Are you alright Effie Mae?" Ms. Jones asked, noticing her abrupt distressed mood.

"Yeah Ms. Jones I'm alright."

"When Tyrell's father and I spoke with him the day we arrived, he told us you were living in Mississippi?"

"That's where I'm from Ms. Jones."

"You are?"

"Yeah, I met Blue after I moved here to New York with my husband."

"Anthony right?" Ms. Jones stated, confused. Effie Mae giggled.

"Naw Ms. Jones . . . J. R."

"Oh, that's right he's the gentleman that gave you away at you and Tyrell's—"

"Commitment." Effie Mae said completing the sentence.

"So if you were living in Mississippi with Anthony, your fiancé—" Ms. Jones paused to ensure she'd named the right man. "—how did you hear about Tyrell being sick?" A loving smile displayed on Effie Mae's face.

"Him."

"Oh, so Tyrell called you?"

"Naw Ms. Jones—Blue didn't call me." Effie Mae blushed. "He sent Huck to Mississippi to get me." Ms. Jones' jaw dropped, astonished by Blue's apparent love for Effie Mae.

"Oh my, now that is true love." Ms. Jones eyes slowly moistened. "It just touches my heart knowing that my baby finally found true love before he—" She abruptly stopped and looked at Effie Mae with acceptance. Effie Mae smiled. "So it looks like Henry was wrong after all."

"Huh?"

"Oh never mind . . . so it was after you came back that Tyrell asked you to make the commitment with him?"

"Blue didn't ask me to make a commitment Ms. Jones."

"He didn't? Oh, so then you asked him?" A puzzled look formed on Ms. Jones' face. "Wait—I'm confused." Effie Mae giggled.

"Ms. Jones, Blue asked me to marry him."

"Marry him?" She said surprised. "My goodness what on earth was Tyrell thinking knowing you were already married?" Ms. Jones hesitated. "And engaged!"

"Ms. Jones if it had been okay with Blue, I would've married him and just had two husbands!" Effie Mae lightly laughed.

"Oh my!" Ms. Jones briefly chuckled then reached over and took hold of Effie Mae's hands. "I'm glad you and Tyrell got together Effie Mae . . . however you did it!" A perplexed look showed on Ms. Jones' face. "I haven't seen my baby this happy in years." She shook her head. "After Daphne . . . it looked like my baby had given up on ever finding his Ms. Right, but when he speaks about you Effie Mae, Tyrell's face just seems to light up and I can hear his love for you in his voice." Ms. Jones gently squeezed Effie Mae's hands. "Thank you Effie Mae for making my baby so happy, I couldn't have found a better wife for Tyrell if I tried." Effie Mae's eyes dampened—she smiled.

"Thank you Ms. Jones, but I hope you feel that way after I tell you what my life been like since I was sixteen." Ms. Jones' mouth slightly opened. "And what I done after my husband walked out on me."

"Walked out on you?" A disappointed look showed on Ms. Jones' face. "Didn't you say you and your husband had six children?"

"Yeah Ms. Jones we do, but that didn't stop J.R. from leaving."

"What on earth would make a man walk out on his wife and six children? Was it another woman?"

"Naw Ms. Jones it wasn't another woman—"

"Then what?"

"Truth is Ms. Jones . . . J.R. had every right to leave." Effie Mae stated with honesty. Ms. Jones looked at her with peculiarity in response to her unusual statement. "Once I tell you my story Ms. Jones all I ask is you remember that the one real thing in my life is my love for my seven babies and Blue."

"Seven!" Ms. Jones blurted out. "Goodness! I thought you said you and J.R. had six children Effie Mae?"

"Me and J.R. got five babies Ms. Jones."

"I don't quite understand what am I missing?"

"Ms. Jones I got two babies that don't even belong to my husband." Ms. Jones gasped.

"My goodness!" She looked around the cafeteria then turned back to Effie Mae. "You've been quite a busy lady haven't you?" Effie Mae giggled.

"My first son belongs to Anthony."

"Your fiancé right?"

"Yeah Ms. Jones . . . my fiancé. " Effie Mae said grinning. "And my baby boy belongs to J.R.'s cousin." Ms. Jones' jaw dropped. She again gasped, shocked by Effie Mae's disclosure.

"Oh my Goodness!" Effie Mae humorously smiled then looked in Ms. Jones' non-judgmental eyes and prepared to share her entire blemished past—minus her employment at Ms. Norma's whorehouse.

# *Chapter Fifteen*

"Hey Baby." Effie Mae said as she and Ms. Jones returned to Blue's room seeing him awake. A large smile formed on his weakened face.

"Hey Baby girl." Effie Mae walked over and prepared to kiss him. He quickly pulled her in his arms.

"Blue!" She said surprised, but delighted by his sudden action. He intimately kissed her.

"Good morning Tyrell." Ms. Jones said interrupting their affectionate moment.

"Hey Momma, I didn't see you come in."

"I guess not, you were so busy kissing your wife." A huge smile formed on Blue's face, pleased by her acceptance of Effie Mae as his wife. His eyes watered.

"Thank you Momma — having you accept Effie Mae as my wife after what I told you and Daddy yesterday means a lot." He place a light kiss on Effie Mae's lips. "I love this woman Momma and I know with all my heart she loves me too." He looked at Effie Mae and smiled. She blushed.

"Well don't expect your father to ever accept Effie Mae as your wife Tyrell."

"As long as you accept her Momma —" Blue placed another kiss on Effie Mae's lips. "—that's all I need.

"Now I don't want you worrying about how your father feels." Ms. Jones stated. "You and your beautiful wife just enjoy each other for as long as you can."

"That's what we plan on doing Momma." Blue said as tears again filled his eyes as he held Effie Mae in his arms. "Thank you Baby girl." He again kissed her.

"For what Blue?"

"For making me the happiest man in the world." Thoughts of his limited life span momentarily flashed through his mind. "Even though I ain't gon be in it much longer." Effie Mae's stomach filled with knots.

"Don't be saying that Blue." She said dismissing his fatal words. Ms. Jones swallowed the enormous lump forming in her throat as the reality of her only son's impending death became reality. Effie Mae's eyes drew to Blue's untouched breakfast tray sitting on the table across his lower legs. "Blue baby?"

"Yes wife." He said applying a smooch to her lips. Effie Mae forced a smile as she masked her fears.

"I know hospital food don't taste as good as your momma's—" She teased. "—but baby you gon have to eat or you gon get so little we ain't gon be able to tell you from a crack in the wall." Blue chuckled.

"Oh my!" Ms. Jones said visualizing Effie Mae's humorous words. "Now that's little Tyrell." She said laughing. "So if you want to come home to that beautiful woman who loves you with all her heart—" Effie Mae intervened.

"Listen to your momma Blue." She teased.

"You're going to have to eat something Tyrell!"

"I am Momma . . . I just woke up!"

"Baby I miss you so much. "Effie Mae said holding back her tears. "And your wife want you back home with her just as soon as them doctors say you can." He beamed. Effie Mae shifted her worried eyes over to Ms. Jones then pulled the table containing Blue's breakfast up to his waist and prepared to feed him.

"You see Momma I told you this woman loves me!" Blue said guiding Effie Mae's head towards him, kissing her on the lips.

"Yes Tyrell, she sure does." Ms. Jones mouth eyes slightly watered as she struggled to contain her fading emotions.

"What you want to eat first Blue?" Effie Mae asked adding salt and pepper to the scrambled eggs next to the pork sausage patties and toast on his plate.

"I'll just drink some coffee for now."

Ms. Jones watched through tearful eyes as Effie Mae assisted him in drinking the cup of black coffee.

———————————

Melvin hurried to the club's front entrance when seeing Huck and Buckeye enter the jazz club.

"Hey Melvin." Huck said shifting his eyes routinely up at the band as if expecting to see Blue standing on stage—blowing his saxophone.

"What's up Huck?" Melvin said trying to mask his anxiety as he prepared to enlightened him of Gus' conversation with his father.

"I see y'all got a full house tonight." Huck said as Melvin alerted him with his eyes to Mr. White seated at a table to the far left of the club. Huck looked over at him then turned back to Melvin. "Blue and Effie Mae upstairs?"

"You didn't hear Huck?"

"Hear what Melvin?" Huck's anxiety heightened from the troubled look on Melvin's face.

"About Blue!" Huck shifted his eyes to Buckeye then again to Melvin.

"What about Blue, Melvin?"

"Man he passed out in here yesterday!" Huck's heart pounded in his ears as he prepared himself for Melvin's report. Buckeye swallowed the lump forming in his throat—he too becoming nervous as they waited to hear Melvin's alarming news.

"Where he at Melvin?"

"Ambulance came and got him man!" Melvin said looking at Buckeye with worried eyes before turning back to Huck. "I thought for sure my cousin was gone." Huck shifted his eyes to Buckeye, hesitant to ask if his half brother had passed away. A baffled look formed on Melvin's face. "I'm surprised you hadn't heard Huck."

"Naw I hadn't . . . me and Buckeye had some business to take care of out of town." Huck's stomach rumbled with butterflies.

"Effie Mae and Auntie Roz been out at that hospital all night and—" Huck interjected.

"How Blue doing?" He asked shifting his eyes to Buckeye. The two men momentarily looked one to the other and awaited Melvin's report, certain the news would be disturbing.

"Effie Mae said his doctor's talking about letting him come home tomorrow." A look of relief displayed on Huck's face.

"That's good to hear."

"Look over to your left Huck." Buckeye said seeing Mr. White flirting with the barmaid standing at his table.

"Yeah Buckeye I saw him." He said looking at his father, shaking his head. "When the cats away—" Melvin intervened.

"And he been sitting there all day man!" He said staring angrily over at him. "That man ain't been out to that hospital once!" Melvin stated, upset. "But he sat his ass in here listening to Gus telling him—" Melvin quickly looked at Huck.

"Telling him what Melvin?"

"Huck man . . . Gus showed up in here—" Melvin shook his head, briefly lookin at Buckeye.

"He finally brought his ass out of hiding huh?" Huck quietly grinned.

"After what I tell you Huck . . . Gus gon wish he'd stayed in hiding." Huck shifted his eyes to Buckeye, troubled by Melvin's mysterious words. He tilted his head.

"Is that right?" He shifted his eyes over at his father, certain of his involvement in whatever Melvin was about to say.

"Yeah Huck . . . he brought his ass in here this morning—" Huck cut him off.

"This morning? You opening up in the morning now Melvin?"

"Naw, I ain't!" Melvin frowned. "That's why I was so surprised when Gus showed up knocking on the door."

"What he want?"

"Claimed he was checking up on Blue." Huck looked at Buckeye and shook his head, amused.

"Checking up on Blue, huh?" Huck quietly laughed. "Gus couldn't stand Blue and Blue couldn't stand him."

"Man . . . Gus hated Blue!" Buckeye said. "He ain't spoke to Blue since that time Effie Mae went into hiding and—"

"Buckeye." Huck said looking at his old friend with reprimanding eyes in response to him speaking on taboo incidents occurring—back in the day.

"Gus don't know it but—" Melvin leaned over towards him. "—I heard him take your father on a trip down memory lane." Huck looked Melvin in the eyes.

"About?"

"Effie Mae." Melvin said shifting his eyes to Buckeye. Huck also turned to Buckeye, an infuriated look in his eyes. He titled his head, stroking his chin hairs.

"Is that right?"

"Took him all the way back to the day when Effie Mae worked at Ms. Norma's." Huck gave no reply.

"What you want me to do Huck?" Buckeye asked awaiting Huck's instruction on what actions he wanted him to take—against Gus. Huck gave a single nod of the head instructing him to find and bring Gus to him.

"I'll get right on it man."

"I owe you Buckeye." Huck again looked over at his father.

"I figured you'd want to know." Melvin said convinced he'd done the right thing given the bad blood between Huck and his father.

"I just wonder now how Mr. White plan on using what Gus told him against Effie Mae." He looked at Melvin. "He sure as hell ain't gon want her with Blue, that's for damn sure."

Mr. White ended his flirtatious moment with the barmaid then noticed Huck unrelenting gawk at him. He looked back then cleverly smiled, alerting Huck that he had the *dirt* on Effie Mae. Both father and son continued their mutual gaze as Mr. White mouthed the words:

"*Lowdown dirty hustler.*" He smirked. Huck ignored his vindictive words as he thought only of Gus' betrayal. He wondered what could've made his long time friend betray him.

"Look here Buckeye, when you find Gus let my old friend know that unless he dead he better—"

"He'll be there . . . you can count on it."

"And pick up number man Curtis and his crew along the way, let him know—" Huck lowered his eyes, upset by Gus forcing him to destroy him. "—Gus ain't under my protection no more." Buckeye turned to leave. "Hold on Buckeye." He stopped. "It can wait until tomorrow."

"You sure man?"

"Come on sit down, have a drink with me."

Mr. White observed with suspicious eyes as the two men walked through the club being seated at a table to his far right. Huck looked over at him with contempt. He stared back at his eldest son and again smirked before looking away.

"How bad you want it to be Huck? I can—" Buckeye silenced when Deborah Ann approached. His smile widened as he watched her place a bottle of scotch and two shot glasses on the table, ignoring his stationary smile. Huck quietly grinned, humored by her obvious rejection of his old friend's advances.

"I think I'll let you decide that Buckeye." Huck said knowing it would be fatal. A disturbed look appeared on Buskeye's face.

"You sure man?"

"What you been up to Deborah Ann?" Huck said electing not to discuss the matter in her presence.

"Working and no . . . I don't have any interest in being one of your whores Henry Lee." Deborah Ann said filling his glass with scotch. "And yes I like my job here at Blue's—" She stated responding to Huck's often proposed offer, before he could ask. Buckeye grinned. Huck cunningly smiled.

"Damn shame . . . because girl as fine as you are you'd have the men eating out of your hands." He shifted his eyes briefly to Buckeye then looked at Deborah Ann seductively smiling. She glanced briefly at him as she filled Buckeye's glass then sat the bottle on the table. Buckeye continued his gawk then reached inside his shirt pocket and took out a ten dollar bill tossing it on the table.

"Keep the change sweetheart." She looked at him and rolled her eyes then reached for the money. Huck quickly placed his hand on top of hers before she could pick it up. Deborah Ann looked at his alluring eyes and attractive smile and awaited his usual pick-up line.

"Blue still paying you that cigarette and beer money?" He asked, playfully flirting.

"That cigarette and beer money pays the bills Henry Lee." She said looking down at his hand still laying on top of hers and tried to resist his irresistible magnetism.

"Girl you come work for me you can pay off old bills and make new ones." Deborah Ann gave no reply as Huck continued to work his charm. "You play your cards right . . . Ol' Huck just might come pay you a visit myself—free of charge of course." He shifted his eyes to Buckeye and silently grinned before turning his attention again to Deborah Ann. He winked. She blushed. His eyes diverted from Deborah Ann, fixating on Effie Mae when seeing her and Ms. Jones enter the club. Buckeye looked around in response to his old friend's lustful gaze seeing Effie Mae. He immediately seized the opportunity to step in where Huck left off—with Deborah Ann.

"Now see Deborah Ann if you were my woman I'd treat you no less than like the queen you are." Buckeye said making a play for her given Huck's preoccupation with Effie Mae.

"Is that so?" She replied. Buckeye cunningly grinned.

"Rightfully so . . . because to me all women are queens and should be treated as such." Deborah Ann rolled her eyes.

"If that weak ass line is the best you got Lawrence—" She said challenging his ineffective pick-up as she slid her hand from underneath Huck, snatching the ten dollar bill off the table. "—I think I like Henry Lee's game better and he trying to turn me into a whore." Buckeye glanced quickly over at Huck, embarrassed by Deborah Ann's emasculating words. Huck looked at him and quietly laughed.

"Buckeye! I know you smoother than that man." Buckeye shifted his eyes to Deborah Ann, loss for words.

"What?" Deborah Ann said challenging him. "You ain't got nothing else to say Lawrence?" She looked at him with contempt. Buckeye maintained his silence, intimidated by her powerful gawk. "That's what I thought!" She said, again rolling her eyes. "Oh, and Lawrence . . . tell

Libby I said hi." Buckeye's jaw dropped and his eyes widened. He passively watched as Deborah Ann walked away.

"Man how she find out about Libby?" Huck's ears deafened to his old friend's question as his eyes followed Effie Mae up the stairs. He poured himself another shot and hurled it in his mouth.

"Look here Buckeye, I'm gon run up here and talk to Effie Mae—see how Blue doing." A mischievous smile formed on his handsome face.

"Huck man, don't mess with that girl in that man's house!" Buckeye said scowling. "Especially while he laid up out there in the hospital sick!" Huck poured himself another shot and tossed it in his mouth then stood.

"That's Effie Mae's call Buckeye . . . you just keep your eyes on Mr. White." He said glancing briefly over at his father now joined by Ms. Jones. Huck turned to Buckeye and winked before walking away. Mr. White's eyes followed Huck, watching as he hurried up the stairs. His gaze abruptly ended when sensing Buckeye's threatening gawk.

• • • •

Effie Mae dropped a folded yellow sheet on the bed in preparation of Blue's return home. She thought of Blue's weakened state as she began unfolding and stretching the fitted sheet over the mattress. Effie Mae stopped and looked over at the door when hearing a knock. Believing it to be Ms. Jones, she hurried over and opened the door seeing the smiling face of Huck.

"Hey Effie Mae." He said entering the apartment closing the door behind him. Effie Mae walked back over to the bed and resumed making the bed.

"Hey Huck."

"Melvin told me they took Blue back to the hospital." He said watching her every move. "He gon be alright?"

"His doctor say as long as he don't have no more setbacks he can come home tomorrow." Huck tilted his head as his lustful smile grew.

"Is that right? I know you glad to hear that?" Effie Mae looked up when sensing his gaze.

"What Huck?" She said unfolding the matching flat sheet, spreading it across the bed.

"What?"

"You know what?" She said retrieving a flowered bedspread from a nearby chair, tossing it on the bed covering up the sheets.

"Ain't too much Ol' Blue can do while he laid up in that hospital." He walked over and wrapped his arms around Effie Mae from behind. "Now is it?" He kissed her seductively on the neck.

"What you doing Huck?"

"What you want me to do Effie Mae?" He gently kissed her on opposite sides of the neck.

"Let me go!"

"That ain't what you want me to do Effie Mae . . . I know you girl." Effie Mae's frustration grew as Huck again kissed her on the neck.

"Huck you saw me and Blue pledge our love to each other . . . that don't mean nothing to you?" He humorously grinned.

"Should it?" His kissing progressed to her shoulders. "I also saw your husband up there giving you away to Ol' Blue, so what would make your pledge to Blue anymore binding than your marriage vows to J.R.?" Effie Mae pulled away out of his hold then angrily faced him.

"Because I love Blue!" She yelled. "And I meant that pledge." He looked at her with doubtful eyes then tilted his head.

"Is that right?" He chuckled. "Didn't you love Ol' Blue the night you laid down with me?" He pulled Effie Mae in his arms and kissed her on the lips. "What's different?" He asked kissing her the lips. She turned away. Huck cunningly grinned, amused by her resistance. "Why you playing hard to get girl? Is it because Ms. Jones and Mr. White's downstairs? Is that it Effie Mae?" He intimately embraced Effie Mae from behind and began kissing her upper back and neck. "Come on—we can go to my place if you scared Blue gon find out." He grinned. "I ain't gon tell."

"Let me go Huck!"

"You know I can't do that Effie Mae."

"First J.R., now you." Effie Mae shouted, upset by the many men in her life expecting her to fulfill their intimate desires. Huck abruptly released her.

"J. R.?" He humorous smiled. "I thought he gave you to Ol' Blue?" Huck said laughing. "I guess J.R. changed his mind" Effie Mae gave no reply as her back remained turned to him. He kissed "Is that what happened Effie Mae?" Huck asked kissing her on the back of the neck. "I'd hate for Ol' Blue to hear that." He hesitated. "If just might kill him." He burst into laughter.

"Leave me alone Huck I'm tired . . . I been at the hospital all night and most of the day, I just need to get some rest."

"Yeah you do that Effie Mae." He turned her around and raised her hands to his lips then softly kissed them. "You get your rest." He gazed in her eyes. "But the next time I want you . . . you being tired ain't gon matter." He said applying a romantic kiss to her lips. "And if I get to thinking about you through the night—I'm coming back." Effie Mae's fear heightened as she heard the persistence in Huck's voice. Huck looked at the freshly made bed and smiled. "I'll see you in the morning." He again kissed her. "And I don't want you tired." She looked at him but gave no reply. "What time that doctor say he was letting Blue go anyway?" Effie Mae maintained her silence. "Don't rest too long." He seductively smiled and winked then released her. She watched in agitation as Huck walked away, exiting the apartment with the promise to return in the morning.

---

Effie Mae awakened from the vigorous shaking of her bed that following morning.

"Leave me alone Huck." She said still half asleep. The shaking continued. "Leave me alone Huck." She stated, raising her voice. Again the bed shook. Effie Mae turned over on her back and looked up at the figure standing to the right of the bed. She quickly sat up. "Mr. White?" She said alarmed by his presence. "Did something happen to Blue?"A look of panic displayed on Effie Mae's face.

"Tyrell's fine." Mr. White stated with a suggestive smile on his face. Effie Mae's anxiety grew in response to the lust beaming in his eyes. She slowly pulled up the sheet, covering her exposed neck and shoulders from underneath the thin red straps of the negligee she wore. She trembled as thoughts of her assault by her two cousins at age sixteen, resurfaced.

"Did you need something Mr. White?" She asked trying to mask her fear.

"Yeah I need something Effie Mae." He said easing himself down on the bed.

"Melvin can get you what—" He cut her off.

"What I need right now . . . Melvin can't give me." His smile widened. "I need you to give me the same thing you been giving my sons."

"I don't know what you talking about Mr. White?"

"Yeah Effie Mae you know exactly what I'm talking about." His eyes locked onto her body hidden underneath the yellow sheet. "So whatever it is you think I'm talking about—" He reached over and snatched the sheet from her upper body. "—that's exactly what I'm talking about." He stated as he tenderly massaged her shoulder then slid his hand down onto her breast. She swiftly pushed it away. Mr. Whitee cunningly snickered. "I had a little talk with Gus." Effie Mae looked in his shameless eyes and tried to anticipate his next move. "You know Gus don't you Effie Mae? Because he sure seems to know you—and know you well girl!" He again moved his hand towards her breast. She again pushed it away. "Yeah, Gus' description of your services peaked this old man's interest and I'm willing to pay whatever price you ask." He ran his hand up Effie Mae's arm, stopping at the red strap on her shoulder. "That's how convinced I am you'll be everything Gus said you were."

"I don't do that no more Mr. White."

"Yeah Effie Mae you do . . . I've seen how you and Henry Lee—"

"Blue your son Mr. White I don't think he would want me being with his daddy even if I was in the business."

"What Tyrell do or don't want right now—" Mr. White's desire for her escalated. "—don't mean a damn thing to me!" He continued grinning. "Hell from what I heard, Tyrell was paying for it himself!" A lustful gaze showed in Mr. White's eyes. "Or was he getting his for free? Gus seemed to think he was." He again clasped the strap of Effie Mae's negligee, twisting it between his thumb and index finger then rolling it down her shoulder. "Gus said you had my boys damn near about to kill one another over you girl!" Mr. White said as his excitement soared. She remained frozen as his roaming hand again moved towards her breast.

"Leave me alone Mr. White!" She yelled. "Don't make me have to scream." Effie Mae said pushing his hand away. Mr. White cleverly grinned as he removed the large knife he'd pulled on Huck, from its leather holster.

"Go ahead Effie Mae—scream!" He said taunting her. "But by the time Melvin hear you—" A slick smile stretched across his face. "—he's the only one downstairs you know, and he somewhere in the back sleep." He again fixated his eyes on Effie Mae's semi-bare upper body and smiled with delight. "And Rosalyn's at the hotel sleep . . . hell she don't even know I'm gone." Effie Mae's heart pounded as her feelings of helplessness to Blue's father's impending assault terrified her. "So you go ahead Effie Mae—" Mr. White's calm demeanor abruptly changed to aggression. "Scream . . . and girl I'll cut you from one ear to the other!" He stated with viciousness. "Then I'll wipe your blood off my knife and use it to cut up that T-bone steak I plan on eating for dinner tonight."

Effie Mae's nervous eyes glanced over at the closed door. She now hoped Huck would make good on his promise to return that morning.

"Why you doing this Mr. White?" She asked trying to reason with him. "I thought you loved Blue." He again twisted the negligee strap arouns his index finger, his hand again moving towards her breast. Effie Mae pushed it away and tried to cover herself with the sheet.

"I do love Tyrell." Mr. White said as his lustful smile widened. "But I love being with a woman like you a whole lot more." He snatched the sheet away, gawking at the clingy red silk negligee highlighting her feminine attributes. Effie Mae's fear soared as she thought of what his next move would be. "So now Effie Mae . . . are you going to do this willingly and take this two hundred dollars I got—" He held up the knife. "—or am I going to have to take it and possibly hurt you in the process?" He put the knife up against her throat, kissing her gently on the shoulder. "Either way I'm getting what I came here for." He said growing impatient. "You understand me girl?" He said raising his voice.

Effie Mae looked in Mr. White's enraged eyes, too terrified to speak as he placed an intimate kiss her on the shoulder then looked at her with eagerness. "Only thing is . . . the price goes down by a hundred dollars if I have to take it." Effie Mae's stomach bundled with nerves as she awaited her fate. "You didn't answer my question Effie Mae." Her eyes deflected to the apartment door when seeing it begin to open.

"You all rested Effie Mae?" Huck asked as he entered. Mr. White swiftly turned, startled by Huck's unexpected arrival. Huck mouth flung open when seeing his father seated on the bed—Effie Mae's eyes filled with fear. "Daddy?" Huck said tilting his head in response to the large knife held in his father's right hand, drawn on Effie Mae. "What the hell you doing man?" He yelled.

"Daddy?" Mr. White glared at him. "That's Mr. White to you boy." He shifted his eyes briefly to Effie Mae then back to Huck. "Stay where you at Henry Lee!" He shouted. "If you even look like you trying to stop me I'll jam this knife clean through your whore!"

"Stop you from what Daddy?" Huck said trying to remain calm as his anger accelerated, seeing the fear in Effie Mae's eyes increasing. "What . . . you gon take Blue's woman while he sick in the hospital?" Huck asked as his mind searched for a way to stop him from hurting Effie Mae. "It would kill Ol' Blue if he even thought his own daddy— the man who said he loved him, would be in here trying to take his woman at knife point." Mr. White gave no reply—his only thought being to have his son's *spiritual* wife—by any means necessary. Huck continued his face-off with his father, ambiguous about what action he should take. On the one hand he knew taking him down wouldn't take much even with the large knife he held. On the other, he knew hurting him would have regrettable consequences.

"I'll give you two hundred dollars for your whore Henry Lee!" Mr. White said bargaining. "That's a lot of money for a man to pay for one whore." He shifted his eyes again at Effie Mae and lustfully smiled. "But according to Gus she's damn well worth it!" His excitement surged at the thought of intimacy with Effie Mae. "And the way I've seen you around here sniffing up behind her—" Mr. White again ran his hand up Effie Mae's right arm as he kept a watchful eye on Huck. "—leads me to believe Ol' Gus was right on the money."

"I can't let you do that Daddy."

"Tell me something Henry Lee—"

"What's that?"

"What brought you here in the wee hours of the morning?" Huck looked at him but gave no reply. "You a betting man Henry Lee?" Mr. White asked as he kept his knife drawn on Effie Mae. "Well if you are I'd be willing to bet you this entire two hundred dollars you're here for the very same reason I am!"

"What if I am Daddy?" Huck looked over at Effie Mae. "It ain't the same." Mr. White laughed.

"Ain't the same? Is that how you justify being with your brother's woman Henry Lee—by convincing yourself because it's you it ain't the same?" He continued laughing.

"Me and Effie Mae got a special connection . . . soul mates, ain't that right Effie Mae?" She looked in Huck's eyes seeing his assurance that he would never allow his father to hurt her, even if it meant taking his own father's life.

"Yeah Huck." She said shifting her eyes to Mr. White's large knife pointed at her.

"Blue already know me and Effie Mae sometimes get together—" Mr. White quickly interjected.

"Your brother's weak!" He shouted. "Always have been." He shook his head in disappointment. "I told Rosalyn about always babying that boy—turned into a cry baby! Damn shame too." Mr. White again shifted his lustful eyes at Effie Mae then resumed his visual stand-off with Huck. "So you think because you say—you and your whore got a special connection that gives you the right to have her anytime you want her Henry Lee?" Huck looked at Effie Mae, his eyes apologizing for his father's biting words.

"I didn't say that Daddy."

"Good because it don't!"

"Blue looking the other way with me and Effie Mae is a hell of a lot different than his own daddy being with the woman he—"

"Shut up Henry Lee!" Mr. White shouted. "I've heard just about enough of your hypocrisy. Huck's fury heightened in response to his father's challenging words, and the growing fear in Effie Mae's eyes.

"What about Blue, Daddy? I don't think he'd—" Mr. White again cut him off.

"Right now Henry Lee, I don't give a damn about what you, Tyrell or anybody else thinks! I got my mind on one thing—"

"And what's that Daddy?" Blue asked interrupting him. Mr. White quickly turned in the direction of the doorway when hearing Blue's winded voice. "What you doing Daddy?" Blue asked standing at the top of the stairs assisted by Melvin. He noted the large knife clutched in his father's hand drawn on the woman he love. "Momma's downstairs wondering where you at."

"You leave your mother out of this Tyrell!" Mr. White stated. Blue's eyes looked pass his father and directly into the frightened eyes of Effie Mae. He took several small breaths, overcome by fury. Melvin subtly turned, his plan being to sneak back downstairs to alert Ms. Jones of the crime being committed by Mr. White—and to call the police.

"Stay where are Melvin!" Mr. White yelled pressing the knife against Effie Mae's throat when seeing his subtle movement from the corner of his eyes. "You take one more step—" He grabbed Effie Mae's arm, pulling her closer. "—and you gon need a bucket to catch the blood she gon bleed!" Blue ruptured in fury.

"You gon kill my wife Daddy?" He said raising his voice as his eyes dampened with tears.

"Wife?" Mr. White said bursting into a quiet laughter. He looked at Effie Mae and scowled. "This whore ain't none of your wife Tyrell!" He looked over at Blue. "What's wrong with you boy? Can't you see this tramp ain't doing nothing but playing you for a damn fool?"

"You wrong Daddy." Blue said looking affectionately at Effie Mae. "That woman loves me." Mr. White half-heartedly laughed.

"Love?" He shifted his eyes to Effie Mae then to Huck and again to Blue. "Women like this don't love nobody but themselves Tyrell, and this whore right here . . . she ain't no different." He glanced angrily over at Effie Mae. "This tramp would say and do anything to get her hands on this jazz club and over your dead body!" Mr. White looked Blue in the eyes. "And I'll be damn if I let her do that Tyrell." He shifted his eyes quickly to Huck then back to Blue. "And I bet you your no good brother's in on it with her . . . in one way or another." Huck stared at his father without speaking as he fought back the growing urge to rip him apart for his mistreatment and harsh words, spoken about Effie Mae.

Mr. White looked at Huck with resentment then turned briefly to Blue without remorse as he continued holding this knife against Effie Mae's throat.

"You wrong Daddy." Blue said becoming weaker from his prolonged standing.

"Listen to me Tyrell!" Mr. White raised his voice with aggravation. "That whore don't love you boy!" He shouted trying to convince Blue of his sincere belief. "Sleeping with your brother, Gus, and ain't no telling who else." He looked over at Melvin. "Gus even tells me your own cousin had her." Melvin shifted his eyes over to Blue, guilt-ridden by the lust he often felt for Effie Mae. Blue ignored his father's vindictive words. Huck looked over at Melvin and tilted his head—his eyes saying, *Is that right?"* Melvin said nothing in his defense.
"How the hell you gon fall in love with a whore anyway boy?" Mr. White said looking at Blue as a fool. "Didn't you learn anything from being married to Daphne? Don't you know once a whore always a whore?" He shifted his eyes to Huck. "Ain't that right Henry Lee?" Huck's contempt for his father erupted as he prepared to take action.

"Mr. White—"

"Oh, so it's Mr. White again." He said looking at Huck, chuckling.

"You got one more time to call Effie Mae a whore." Huck said shifting his eyes over at Blue then back to his father. "Then you gon see how easy it's gon be for me to make you to eat that blade."

"You take one step towards me Henry Lee and I guarantee you I'll—"

"Henry!" Ms. Jones called out. "Are you up there?" She asked from downstairs when hearing his voice.

"Yeah Ms. Jones he up here come on up." Huck said.

"Stay where you at Rosalyn!" Mr. White yelled.

"Yeah Momma you don't need to come up here—" Blue said looking his father in the eyes. "—Daddy's gon be down in just a few minutes, ain't that right Daddy?" Blue said looking over at Effie Mae then again to his father. "Daddy if you kill Baby girl you may as well kill me too because I won't live without her." Tears streamed down Blue's face. "Now I'm coming over there and I'm taking my wife in my arms and she's gon welcome her husband back home—" Blue said sounding like Effie Mae's *knight in shining armor about to rescue the damsel in distress.* "—then we gon lay here and tell each other how much we love one another and we gon forget any of this ever happened." Effie Mae's fear grew when seeing the determined look in Blue's eyes. Mr. White gave no reply as he shifted his eyes quickly to Huck then back to Blue.

"So if you gon kill me Daddy you better do it now because I ain't gon let you just keep holding that knife up to my wife's throat." Blue took a step forward.

"I can't let you do that Blue." Huck said looking him in the eyes. "I'm walking over there to our daddy—" Huck shifted his eyes to Mr. White. "—and he gon kill me or I'm gon kill him." He glanced over at Effie Mae then back to his father. "Or he gon do the right thing and put that blade down and walk away so we both leave here breathing air." Huck looked at Effie Mae and winked. "So what's it gon be Daddy?" Mr. White shifted his eyes quickly to Blue when seeing him take another step forward.

"I'm warning you boy!" Mr. White yelled. "You better stay your ass where you at Tyrell." He turned his knife on Blue.

"You just gon have to kill me Daddy because—"

"Henry!" Ms. Jones again called out. "What's taking you so long?" She asked standing at the bottom of the stairs.

"He coming Momma, just give us a few more minutes."

"Okay Tyrell, but if he's not down here in the next three minutes I'm coming up there!" Mr. White looked in the faces of both his sons then reluctantly laid the knife down on the bed and raised both his hands in surrender. Huck moved quickly towards him and retrieved the knife.

Mr. White's eyes widened when seeing the holstered gun attached at Huck's side. Blue hurried over to Effie Mae taking her in his arms as Melvin blocked the doorway.

"You alright Baby girl?" Blue asked kissing her repeatedly on the lips and face.

"Yeah Blue I'm alright." He looked at his father with disillusioned eyes.

"I always loved you Daddy, but today I saw a man I didn't know, a man that if I let myself I could easily hate." He looked briefly over at Huck and nodded—thanking him for his bravery then turned his attention again to his father. "Daddy I want you to go downstairs and get Momma and take her back home to Buffalo today." Mr. White shifted his eyes to Huck, confused as to why he didn't shoot him and end his impending assault on Effie Mae before Blue witnessed his irreparable behavior. "I don't care what you have to tell her but whatever it is, it's gon be a whole lot better than what really happened."

"Let's go Mr. White." Melvin said glaring at him. Mr. White rose from the bed and stood to his feet then looked at Blue without speaking. He glanced over at Huck—no words being spoken between father and son as Mr. White slowly walked in the direction of the door.

"And Daddy—" Mr. White stopped when hearing the sound of Blue's voice. He turned and looked into the infuriated eyes of his favorite son. "—the next time you see me." Blue briefly paused. "—it's gon be at my funeral." Mr. White gave no reply. He took a final gawk at Effie Mae sending a bone chilling fright up her spine then continued walking away. He again stopped, flashing Huck an eery stare then snickered before exiting the apartment to join Ms. Jones downstairs.

# Chapter Sixteen

Effie Mae entered J.R.'s church as his Sunday morning service concluded. She waited quietly in the foyer until she could speak with him in private. Exiting the pulpit J.R. walked down the center aisle of the sanctuary on his way to the church's front door where he ritualistically stood and said his farewells to members and guest as they departed the church. His eyes brightened when seeing her. Effie Mae smiled. He blushed as he entered the foyer, stationing himself in front of the glass doors at the church's entrance.

"Momma!" Lil' J.R. called out when seeing her. He hurried over.

"Hey baby." She said leaning down and kissing him on top of the head.

"Momma I want to go with you." He whined.

"I'm getting ready to come over to your daddy's house and see y'all Lil' J.R., okay?" He nodded. "But I need to talk to your daddy after he get through saying bye to all the people."

"Momma!" Sarah said exiting the sanctuary.

"Hey my sweet Sarah." Effie Mae kissed her on the forehead.

"Momma you coming over to our house?"

"I sure am baby." Sarah smiled.

"Hey Momma." Millie Ann said walking over and hugging her.

"Hey Millie Ann baby."

"Momma I'm gon have D. J. today!" Effie Mae's eyes lit up. "You want to come see him?"

"Millie Ann baby, I would love to see my—" She abruptly stopped not wanting the other children to know their cousin Daniel's son was their baby brother. "Thank you baby."

"Hi Momma!" Mahalia, Lena and Billie said as they walked out of the sanctuary.

"Hey babies." Effie Mae hugged them each. "I love y'all."

"Momma you coming over to our house?" Billie asked, excited.

"Yeah Billie baby just as soon as we leave here."

"Momma can you come and live with us like you did with Anthony?" Mahalia asked. Effie Mae shifted her eyes to J.R., uncomfortable by her young daughter's choice of words.

"Not yet baby—"

"Why Momma?" She asked disappointed. J.R. looked briefly over at Effie Mae noting the challenged look on her face.as he spoke with an elderly female member accompanied by her thirtyish daughter.

"There's uh, somebody waiting to see me so I guess I'll uh, see you ladies at Wednesday night Bible study?"

"Okay Rev. Smith—" The elderly woman said shifting her eyes over at Effie Mae with curiosity. "We'll see you on Wednesday night."

"Rev. Smith—" The elderly woman's daughter said disturbed by Effie Mae's presence. "—that woman over there with your children, is she a new member here at the church?" She asked having set her sights on J.R. as a possible husband.

"Make sure you uh, bring your Bibles for Wednesday night Bible study." J.R. said guiding them out the door as their eyes remained focused on Effie Mae.

"Uh, Effie Mae." He said somewhat giddy as he approached her. "If uh, you were coming for Sunday morning service you missed it by—" J.R. looked at his watch. "—two hours." He chuckled.

"I need to talk to you J.R." His humorous moment ended when seeing the serious look on Effie Mae's face.

"Uh, Okay."

"I need you to send my babies out to the car." His curiosity peaked.

"Uh, Okay."

"Uh, children go ahead and get in the car . . . me and uh, your momma need to talk." J.R. said trying to read the look in Effie Mae's eyes. "I'll uh, be out shortly." He removed his keys from his pocker and handed them to Millie Ann.

"I want to stay with you Momma." Lil' J.R. said taking hold of her hand.

"I'm gon be coming with y'all Lil' J.R., just let me and your daddy talk for a minute okay baby?" He lowered his head.

"Okay." Effie Mae raised his head and kissed him on the forehead. He smiled then scurried out the door to join his siblings. Effie Mae turned to J.R.

"Is uh, everything alright? Blue okay?" He asked unable to block his thoughts of the intimacy they'd recently shared.

"Yeah J.R." He noted the worried look in her eyes.

"So uh, what's with the long face?" Effie Mae's eyes moistened with tears.

"They had to take Blue back to the hospital."

"Is he uh, alright?"

"He back home now." She said feeling responsible. "I should've been there for himJ.R"

"Where uh—"

"I was with you J.R."

"With me . . . oh!" He said realizing Blue's health scare occurred during they're time of intimacy. J.R. looked at Effie Mae with intimate eyes as he recalled their rendezvous on that day.

"Don't be looking at me like that."

"You uh, said Blue went back to the hospital? Is he okay? Are you okay?" J.R. asked trying to organize his thoughts.

"Naw J.R. I ain't."

"Is it uh, anything I can do to help?"

"J.R. what happened the other day—" He smiled. "—should've never happened."

"Why?" He said surprised by her words. "I had every right to be with my wife." He gently took hold of Effie Mae hands and gazed into her eyes. "Effie Mae you didn't make me do anything I didn't want to do or that I'm ashamed of doing." She turned away when J.R. tried to kiss her. "Do you regret what happened between us Effie Mae?"

"Yeah J.R. I do." He looked at Effie Mae with disbelief.

"But you don't regret marrying another man while being legally married to me?" She lowered her head then looked at him without apology.

"J.R. we ain't been together in that way in a long time . . . us being together like that made me feel like I wasn't being true to Blue." J.R. mouth opened, stunned by her rationale.

"True to Blue?" He starred into her eyes.

"J.R. I know I wasn't the wife I should've been to you—" He sarcastically chuckled.

"Wasn't the wife . . . Effie Mae you have two sons and neither one belongs to me!" J.R. took a deep breath and tried to calm himself down. "And you standing there telling me, your husband . . . how you want to be true to Blue?"

"I know you still my husband J.R., but—"

"But what Effie Mae?" He said raising his voice. "You think being true to Blue makes up for you being unfaithful to me?"

"That ain't what I said J.R."

"Then what you saying Effie Mae?"He yelled.

"Until what happened the other day J.R. we been married in name only—you know that." He looked at her, temporarily loss for words.

"Okay so what now?"

"I know you said Blue couldn't be in our babies lives, but—" He interjected.

"Is that what this is about Effie Mae?" J.R. asked disappointed by her hidden agenda. Effie Mae watched as he turned away, walking over to the church's entrance, standing in front of the glass door looking out. "Okay." Effie Mae's mouth abruptly opened, surprised by her response.

"What?"

"I said okay." J.R. turned and faced her. "I uh, guess it wouldn't be fair for the children not to see their mother because she chooses to live her life with another man other than their father." Effie Mae dismissed his bitter words as she delighted in Blue being in her children's lives.

"You saying you gon let my babies be with me and—"

"Blue?" He said completing her sentence. "Yeah Effie Mae that what I'm saying." Her eyes displayed gratitude. "You can uh, spend time with your children and uh, Blue—" J.R. hesitated. "But not at the jazz club."

"So where am I supposed to see my babies at J.R.?" She asked in protest to his demand.

"No jazz club Effie Mae—take it or leave it." She looked in J.R.'s stern eyes loss for words.

"Why don't you uh, bring him over—" J.R.'s mouth dried. He coughed. "—Blue . . . over to the house this Saturday and uh, let's see what happens."

"Thank you J.R." Effie Mae said believing she would eventually convince him to change his mind about her children visiting her at the jazz club.

"But—" J.R. said. "—if I see for one minute Blue's presence is causing my children the least bit of upset it ends!" He looked in Effie Mae's distressed eyes. "No more Blue—you got that Effie Mae?" She silently looked at him, trying to hold back her tears.

"Yeah J.R. I got it." He momentarily stared at her—his thoughts again drifting to the intimacy they shared.

"Thank you."

"Thank you?" A puzzled look appeared on her face. "What you thanking me for J.R."

"For making me realize I'm still a man." Effie Mae blushed.

"Momma said you was."

"Huh?"

"Never mind J.R." She giggled. "Let me remember to call Momma when I get home."

--------------------

Blue gazed at Effie Mae, following the mouth watering kiss they'd just shared as they lay in bed that morning. He wondered of the unusually wide smile on her face.

"Do my kisses always put a smile that big on your face Baby girl?"

"Always Blue, you know that baby."

"Naw . . . not like that Baby girl." His curiosity grew. "What's got you so happy?"

"You Blue—you what's got me so happy."

"Naw Baby girl, I see something in those beautiful eyes that say different." He stared in her excited eyes.

"Okay Blue I'll tell you—" She placed a quick kiss on his lips. "—J.R. said you can be in my babies lives Blue!" Effie Mae blurted out. A troubled look showed on Blue's face. "Ain't you happy baby?"

"Yeah Baby girl I am, but—"

"But what Blue?"

"Baby girl that man ain't just said I could be in his kid's lives without putting a stipulation in there somewhere!"

"J.R. know how much I love you Blue, and how much I want you in my babies lives—"

"Yeah Baby girl he do . . . that's what's bothering me."

"What you mean Blue?"

"It's something you ain't telling me Baby girl?" Blue stated waiting to hear her omitted information. "I need you to be honest with me Baby girl." She intimately kissed him.

"I see what you trying to do Baby girl." He said as she continued placing kisses on his lips. "Go ahead and tell me." A troubled looked displayed on Effie Mae's face.

"J.R. said if my babies don't like you being around you can't be around them no more." Blue remained momentarily silent then laughed out loud.

"What Blue?" Effie Mae said confused by his laughter. "Why you laughing?"

"Baby girl that man know he loves you!" He said applying a smooch to her lips. "First he give you away to me . . . now he letting me play daddy to his kids." Blue continued chuckling. "And all the while Baby girl you still that man's wife."

"My babies gon love you Blue just like I do!" Effie Mae said refusing to believe anything to the contrary. His eyes moistened.

"What's wrong baby?" She asked not understanding his tears. "I thought you was happy."

"I am Baby girl." Tears ran down Blue's face. "I ain't ever had children before—having you and your kids in my life, finally makes it feel complete." Effie Mae kissed his tear soaked lips.

"I love you Tyrell Lee Jones."

"I love you too Baby girl." A huge smile formed on her face as she looked in his eyes and smiled.

"What you smiling about now?"

"I'm off the pill Blue!" She stated with excitement. "Now we can have our own baby." He shook his head, frustrated.

"Baby girl I told you now, I can't have kids!"

"I know you said that Blue, but just in case—" She kissed him, excited at the thought. "—I don't want them pills blocking nothing." Blue noted the sparkle of optimism in Effie Mae's eyes as she applied a light kiss to his chest.

"Even if by some miracle I did get you pregnant Baby girl, I wouldn't be here to help you raise our child." She ignored his truthful words.

"What you think we should name our baby boy, Blue?"

"Baby girl—"

"What Blue?"

"I told you I can't have kids!"

"Miracles can happen Blue." Effie Mae said determined to have a child with the man she loved.

"Baby girl—" She cut him off.

"The next son I have Blue, I don't care who the daddy is I'm naming my baby boy after you Blue."

"Baby girl what if that man don't want his son named after me?"

"What man wouldn't want his son's name to be Tyrell Lee Jones Jr.?" Effie Mae teased. Blue boyishly smiled.

"A man who's name ain't Tyrell Lee Jones." He said chuckling.

"Well that's just gon be too bad Blue now ain't it?" She stated selfishly. "Besides Blue, any man I have a child with gon know just how much I love you, and if that man love me . . . Lil' Tyrell Lee Jones is gon come in this world knowing the man he named after meant the world to his momma." New tears formed in Blue's eyes. Effie Mae wiped them with her hand.

"Okay Baby girl." He said relenting to her hope. They romantically kissed. "I love you Tyrell Lee Jones." He blushed.

"Baby girl I need to talk to you about something." Effie Mae's nerves rumbled in her stomach, frightened by what Blue might say.

"I don't want to talk about nothing else right now Blue."

"Baby girl—"

"What Blue?"

"I think we need to talk about your next husband."

"You my husband Blue."

"Baby girl I got less than six months left on this earth . . . if that long."

"I don't want to talk about that Blue."

"Yeah Baby girl we need too." She turned away—her back now facing him. Blue embraced her from behind. "When I leave here—" Effie Mae cut him off.

"You ain't going nowhere Blue!"

"Yeah Baby girl I am." He kissed the back of her head. "And I don't want you wasting your life crying over me."

"I don't want to talk about it Blue."

"I want you to move on with your life and be happy."

"Can't nobody make me happy like you Blue." Her eyes erupted with tears.

"Yeah Baby girl it is."

"Then you tell me who Blue?"

"You already married to him."

"Who? J.R.?"

"Yeah Baby girl, J.R."

"I don't want J.R.!" Effie Mae yelled. "I want you Blue." She turned and faced him—kissing him repeatedly on the face and lips.

"Baby girl—"

"What Blue?" She continued kissing him.

"Baby girl stop!" Blue said raising his voice. "I need you to listen to me girl!"

"I don't want to listen to you Blue!" She yelled, again turning her back to him.

"Baby girl look at me!" Effie Mae slowly rolled over and looked in his peaceful face. "Just listen okay?"

"Okay." She stated reluctantly agreeing.

"I think if you let him, J.R. can make you every bit as happy as me." She threw the covers over her head.

"You don't know that Blue."

"I know Anthony won't." Blue stated. Effie Mae giggled from underneath the covers, amused by Blue's thoughts on Anthony.

"That boy at home right now waiting on you—" She silenced.

"On what Baby girl . . . me to die?"

"Don't say that Blue."

"Baby girl you been calling me ever since you left here with that man." He chuckled. "But when you with J.R., you seem to be right where you belong." Effie Mae remained under the cover as she listened. " Do you love J.R., Baby girl?" She hesitated before answering.

"I do Blue, but not like I love you."

"Do you love Anthony?" Effie Mae chuckled.

"What?" Blue said in response to her laughter.

"Blue that boy done changed so much it's just like I don't even know him no more!"

"Changed?"

"He different Blue." He looked at her silhouette underneath the covers.

"Baby girl?"

"What Blue?"

"Take that cover off your head and talk to me." She slowly removed the covers from over her head and again faced him. He applied a quick kiss to her lips. "Can you see how marrying Anthony ain't right for you?"

"Yeah, I guess." Effie Mae stated, unconvinced. "But I still ain't sure about being with J.R., Blue."

"Will you just think about it Baby girl?"

"Okay Blue." She said hoping he's put the matter to rest.

"You know what else I want you to do Baby girl?" Effie Mae giggled, humored by Blue's plans for her life.

"What Blue?"

"I want you to start spending time with J.R., you know—dating him." Effie Mae's jaw dropped.

"Uh-uh Blue . . . I ain't trying to date J.R."

"Baby girl just think about it."

"Only man I want to date is you Blue."

"Baby girl."

"What?"

"Date me?" He chuckled. "Then don't expect to do much dancing unless you plan on holding me up the whole time we out on the dance floor." Blue laughed.

"Stop it Blue." Effie Mae said pouting.

"I remember you telling me that when you married J.R. you didn't know him or love him."

"That's Momma's husband, Blue." He quietly grinned.

"Naw Baby girl . . . that's your husband."

"Momma was the one who wanted me to marry J.R., not me."

"Just give that man a chance Baby girl."

"Naw Blue, right now I don't even think I like J.R. Smith." Effie Mae said thinking of his recent threat to take away her children.

"Do you love me Baby girl?" A huge smiled formed on her face.

"Baby you the only man I ever loved." He blushed. She placed a kiss on Blue's waiting lips.

"Then as the only man you ever loved —" He placed a loving kiss on her lips. "—I'm asking you to do this as my last wish."

"Uh-uh Blue don't ask me to do that."

"All I'm asking Baby girl is for the woman I love to be with the man I know will make her happy." Effie Mae gave no reply. "At least try and get to know him Baby girl!" Blue urged. "See if you hadn't married him trying to please your momma, you could've loved J.R. for yourself." Blue noted the unenthusiastic look in her eyes. "Baby girl."

"What Blue?"

"Just promise me okay?"

"Promise you what Blue?" Effie Mae said raising her voice.

"That you'll think about what I said." He again kissed her. She forced an apathetic smile.

"Okay Blue . . . if that's what you want."

"And Baby girl—"

"What Blue?" She said, annoyed. "You gon tell me to think about dating Huck too!" He looked at Effie Mae with angry eyes.

"You stay away from my brother!" Blue said raising his voice. "Now he definitely ain't no good for you."

"I was just teasing Blue." They exchanged an intimate kiss. She looked at him and humorously smiled. "What else you want me to do Blue?"

"Baby girl give that man some loving!" Effie Mae's mouth flung open.

"Who Huck?" She teased. Blue turned away in agitation. "I'm just teasing you baby." Effie Mae said turning him over, kissing him.

"You know who I'm talking about Baby girl—your husband."

"I don't want to do that Blue."

"Baby girl that man's still your husband."

"You my husband Blue." He smiled pleased to hear her words, but understood the necessity in helping Effie Mae to move forward with her life.

"Baby girl listen to me."

"I am listening Blue."

"I'd rather you be with J.R. than with Anthony or Daniel!" Effie Mae's mouth opened, surprised to hear him speak of Daniel.

"Daniel?"

"Baby girl that man ain't going nowhere!" Blue said amused. "He's in love with you."

"I can't help how he feel."

"And now that his wife's sick, he's gon use y'all son any way he can to get to you."

"I got something to tell you Blue." An apprehensive look entered his eyes, alarmed by her impending message.

"You remember the day I went over to J.R.'s house to see my babies—" Blue noted guilt the guilt beaming in Effie Mae's eyes.

"Yeah . . . the day Momma kept knocking at the door and wouldn't leave." Effie Mae giggled.

"Me and J.R.—" His eyes widened.

"With your kids there!"

"Naw Blue—" She chuckled. "—my babies was at church."

"Then what was J.R. doing at home—" A baffled look appeared on Blue's face. "—ain't he the preacher?" Effie Mae giggled.

"He sent my babies to church on the bus so we could talk."

"Talk?" He grinned. "Baby girl it sounds like that man planned on doing more than just talk." Effie Mae again giggled.

"Ain't that what you said you wanted me to do Blue?" He suddenly felt insecure by his own decision. "Why you think J.R. changed his mind about you being in my babies lives?"

"What!" Blue frowned. "Baby girl what did you do?" He looked at her seeing actions as being little different than when she worked at Ms. Norma's whorehouse.

"He was talking 'bout taking my babies from me Blue . . . I didn't know what else to do." Effie Mae saw the hurt look in his eyes. "But I told J.R. we couldn't do that no more."

"Baby girl I told you now, I'm a dying man."

"Don't talk like that Blue."

"And if I keep messing with you—" He grinned. "—it's gon kill me!"

"I don't want to hear that Blue." Effie Mae stated, unamused.

"I'm costing on fumes Baby girl, so you got my permission to be with your husband—he got more energy than I do." Blue continued laughing.

"I thought you loved me Blue?" Effie Mae said feeling rejected.

"More than anything Baby girl." He intimately kissed her.

"How am I gon explain to J.R. it's okay for me to be with him after I just told him he couldn't?" Blue cunningly grinned.

"Baby girl I don't think that man's gon ask for an explanation." He said laughing. She blushed. "Now let me see what my fume level is this morning." Effie Mae giggled as Blue pulled her over on him and prepared to engage in intimacy.

———————————

Effie Mae sat on Blue's lap downstairs in the club as they listened to his band rehearsing before the club's opened for the evening.

"Hey Blue!" The bass guitarist called out from the stage after the band finished playing one of Blue's favorite pieces. "How'd that sound man?"

"Sounded good, but it's missing something." Blue said with a serious look on his face.

"You think so man?" He said looking at Blue with concern. "Something like what?" Blue hesitated as if thinking.

"Me!" He said laughing.

"Then get on up here man!" The tenor saxophonist said laughing. Blue looked at Effie Mae, his eyes requesting permission to join his band. She shifted her eyes over at Melvin, stocking the bar. He looked at Blue seeing his eagerness to join his band on stage then shifted his eyes to Effie Mae and humped his shoulders. Blue guided her lips towards his and kissed her.

"Help me up Baby girl." He stated with a enormous smile on his face. Her heart seemingly dropped in her stomach.

"Blue baby did your doctor say it was okay for you to be blowing—" He placed a quick kiss on her lips.

"Help me up." Effie Mae again looked at Melvin as she rose from Blue's lap—she hoped he'd intervene. "Hey y'all the king of the saxophone getting ready to come up here and show us how it's done!" The bass guitarist said grinning.

"Come on up here Blue!" The trumpet player urged. An enormous smile displayed on Blue's face.

"I'll get him." The drummer said when seeing Effie Mae assisting him towards the stage. She nervously watched as the drummer hurried from the stage, taking hold of Blue's arm helping him up on stage.

"Thanks man." Blue said, hyped. Effie Mae's worried eyes met with Melvin's. Their visual exchange ended at the sound of the ringing phone.

"It's for you Effie Mae . . . it's your momma."

"Tell her I'll call her back Melvin." He nodded then relayed the message.

"Come here Baby girl." Blue said as the drummer lowered him onto the chair brought up on stage. He smiled as Effie Mae approached then pulled her gently on his lap.

"Blue!" She giggled.

"I love you Baby girl." The band members watched as he enveloped Effie Mae in his arms then passionately kissed her.

"Come on Blue man!" The pianist said grinning. "You got all night to do that."

"Ain't nothing wrong with getting started early, I may not be here after I get through blowing this horn!" Blue teased. Effie Mae's stomach bundled with nerves.

"Don't be saying that Blue." He placed a quick kiss on her lips, ignoring her concern. "Blue baby you think you ought to be blowing that horn?"

"Somebody get me my horn!" He shouted. Effie Mae rose from his lap refusing to watch him play.

"Tell your momma I said hi Effie Mae." Melvin said. She glanced over at him hoping he'd talk Blue out of his decision to play with his band. He looked back at her with ambiguity. On the one hand, he understood her fears. On the other he empathized with his cousin's desire to play.

"That's what I'm talking about!" Blue yelled out as the guitar player handed him his saxophone. He shifted his eyes to Effie Mae as she headed up the stairs. Rationalizing within himself that he'd make it up to her later, Blue raised his saxophone up to his mouth accepting the reality this would be the last time he'd ever play his beloved horn with his much loved band. He shifted his eyes to Melvin—he nodded, unable to forbid his cousin to play one last time.

Effie Mae entered the apartment, her eyes wet with tears. She picked up the phone and called her momma.

"Hello."

"Hey Momma."

"You alright child? How Blue doing?" Millie asked when hearing the sorrow in her eldest daughter's voice.

"Blue still alive Momma if that's what you asking."

"That's good to hear."

"Momma . . . Blue's doctor only giving him six months to live."

"J.R. told me—I sure was sorry to hear that Effie Mae.

"And you know what's funny Momma?"

"Funny?"

Effie Mae chuckled through her fears.

"Blue seem to be taking it better than me." Her eyes erupted with tears.

"I know you hurting child."

"Yeah Momma I am, bad!"

"All I know to tell you Effie Mae is to love that man like you ain't ever loved him before." Millie stated sympathetically. "So when he leaves this old world it's gon be a smile so big on his face everybody gon know he truly was loved."

"Thank you for saying that Momma."

"You welcome child."

"Momma you gon come to New York when—" Effie Mae silenced, unable to speak on Blue's denise.

"If this body of mines let me travel that far."

"You alright Momma?" Effie Mae asked, alarmed from the evasiveness in Millie's voice.

"I'm fine child, just a few aches and pains is all."

"You sure Momma?"

"Yeah I'm sure." Millie dismissed any seriousness that might be related to her discomfort. "I can't imagine where it could possibly be anything else."

"Well Momma driving ain't the only way to travel you know—you can always fly." Millie's eyes widened.

"Fly?"

"Yeah Momma fly." Effie Mae giggled in response to her momma's fear of flying.

"Until the good Lord gives me wings these feet of mines staying flat on the ground." Millie sad chuckling. "I may not get there in the time a plane could fly me there, but I won't be far behind."

"How's things going with you and J.R.?" Effie Mae burst into laughter.

"I found out Momma!"

"Found out what child?"

"J.R. ain't no difference than Anthony or Blue!" Millie gasped.

"Bye Effie Mae."

"Bye Momma." Effie Mae hung up. Her attention quickly drew to Melvin rushing into the apartment, a frantic look on his face.

"What wrong Melvin?"

"It's Tyrell!"

"What about?" Her heart pounded with fear. "What's going on Melvin?"

"You need to come downstairs—now!" He shouted, hurrying from the apartment. Effie Mae followed. She stopped when arriving at the bottom of the stairs. Her mouth slightly opened as she walked slowly in the direction of the stage—her hand clasped over her mouth as tears streamed down her face in response to seeing him. Standing center stage, his saxophone perched in his lips, Blue smiled as he prepared to play. He inhaled then exhaled and began blowing his horn, Effie Mae watched in awe as the soothing sound of Blue's horn filled the acoustics of the club. He suddenly stopped and smiled a gloating smile.

"That was beautiful baby." Effie Mae said walking up on stage entering into Blue's loving arms—his saxophone still held in his hand. They romantically kissed. Melvin hurried on stage and removed the horn from Blue's hand.

"You ready Blue?" The guitarist asked interrupting his passionate kiss with Effie Mae.

"All I need is my horn!" Blue said excited. He placed a quick kiss on Effie Mae's lips then reached for his saxophone. Melvin shifted his tear filled eyes to Effie Mae before giving Blue his horn. She nodded. He apprehensively handed his beloved cousin his saxophone, knowing this would be the last time he would ever hear him play. Effie Mae walked off the stage being seated directly in front of the stage, watching without fear as Blue again raised the saxophone to his mouth and began blowing—his band joining in.

———————————————

"Daddy how much sugar do I need to put in these greens?" Mahalia asked holding a half cup of sugar over the pot. J.R.'s eyes widened as ge removed a large pan of baked pork chops from the oven, placing it on a towel lying on the counter.

"That's too much Mahalia, a couple of tablespoons should be fine." He said opening the refrigerator retrieving a carton of milk and butter, sitting it on the table. "You only need enough sugar to give them a little taste of sweetness, not to candy them." He chuckled.

"Okay Daddy." She dumped half cup of sugar in the simmering pot of greens and stirred.

"Daddy can I mashed the potatoes?" Lena asked removing the potato masher from a drawer over by the sink.

"Okay Lena but uh, wash your hands first.

"Okay Daddy." She hurried to the sink to wash her hands.

"Daddy can I make the cornbread too?" Mahalia asked removing a bag of cornmeal from the cupboard.

"That's fine Mahalia, but put just a tablespoon of sugar in the mix." J.R. looked in the living room for his overactive son when realizing he'd not heard his voice for nearly twenty minutes. He noticed Millie Ann in there sitting on the floor helping Sarah with her homework.

"You listening to me little girl?" Millie Ann said scolding her baby sister.

"Yeah . . . but you going too fast."

"Okay—let's start over."

"No!" Sarah yelled. "I'm hungry."

"I'm hungry too Daddy." Lil' J.R. said entering the kitchen from his bedroom.

"Come here Lil' J.R." Billie said sitting on the living room floor in front of the television. "Come watch cartoons with me."

"Noooo!" He shouted.

"Calm down Lil' J.R." J.R. said as his anxiety increased in response to Effie Mae and Blue's expected visit with the children.

"I'm hungry Daddy."

"Supper's almost ready Lil' J.R., now go sit down with your sister like she asked!"

"Come on Lil' J.R." Billie stated. "I'll give you a nickel." His eyes lit up. He scurried in the living room, plopping down in front of the television next to her. J.R.'s attention diverted from his children when hearing knocking at the back door.

"I'll get it!" Lil' J.R. yelled leaping up from the floor, running in the kitchen." J.R. stepped in front of his eager son, blocking him.

"No Lil' J.R. I'll get it, now uh . . . go sit down." Lil' J.R. lowered his head then returned to the living room. J.R.'s anxiety grew as he neared the back door. He peeped through the back door curtain seeing his estranged wife and her *spirit* husband patiently waiting. He took a deep breath and opened the door.

"Hey J.R." Effie Mae said walking pass him as she entered the house. Blue followed.

"How you doing J.R.?" The two men shook.

"Uh, Blue . . . you feeling okay?"

"I'm feeling alright—just taking it one day at a time." Blue said trying to mask his nervous tension.

"Momma!" Lil' J.R. said hurrying in the kitchen.

"Slow down Lil' J.R." J.R. said shifting his eyes to Effie Mae as their young son rushed over and hugged her around the hips.

"Hey baby!" She kissed him on top of the head. He looked curiously over at Blue then again to his momma.

"Who is that Momma?" Lil' J.R. asked, again looking at Blue. J.R. shifted his eyes to Effie Mae and waited to hear her introduction of Blue to their son.

"Lil' J.R. this is my special friend Tyrell." She said, nervous. Mahalia and Lena looked at their daddy then stared at Blue. Millie Ann rose from the living room floor and looked in the kitchen at Blue. He looked back, uneasy by her unrelenting stare. Millie Ann shifted her eyes to her momma then turned to her daddy then again looked at Blue. She suddenly darted from the living room, running down the hall, entering her bedroom then slamming the door. Effie Mae glanced over at J.R. He showed no reaction to his eldest daughter's unexpected response to Blue's presence, but continued observing his other children and their reaction to their momma's special friend—Tyrell.

Effie Mae's eyes drew to Sarah as she entered the kitchen from the living room and walked over to her then stopped in front of her.

"Hi Momma."

"Hey my sweet Sarah." She said leaning down, kissing her on the forehead. "I love you baby."

"I love you too Momma." Effie Mae shifted her eyes briefly to J.R., troubled by Millie Ann's reaction to Blue. Her attention drew to Billie as she entered the room walking over to her daddy taking hold of his hand. She looked at Blue with questioning eyes.

"Come on Billie . . . give Momma a hug." Effie Mae said trying to maintain control of her emotions. Billie strolled over to her momma then reached up and hugged her. She looked at Blue seeing the nervous, but friendly look in his eyes. Effie Mae kissed her on the forehead. "I love you baby."

"I love you too Momma." Billie again looked at Blue then walked away, strolling back over to her daddy, taking hold of his hand then resumed her gaze at Blue.

"Tyrell why don't you go in the living room and sit down—" Effie Mae said shifing her eyes briefly to J.R. "—I want to go talk to my baby." He nodded. J.R. watched with envious eyes as Blue walked unassisted in the living room being seated on the sofa. Effie Mae hurried down the hallway, stopping in front of Millie Ann's bedroom.

"Millie Ann baby I'm coming in okay?"

"Okay Momma." Effie Mae opened the door and entered, closing it behind her. She looked at her teenage daughter hoping to explain to her the necessity for having Blue in her life.

"What wrong baby?"

"Momma is that Blue?"

"Yeah Millie Ann that's him." A frightened look displayed in Millie Ann's eyes. "Why you ask baby?"

"Is that your new husband?"

"Millie Ann baby—"

"Sarah said you and Blue got married and Anthony was crying." Effie Mae's stomach bundled with nerves as she thought of how to explain what Sarah believed to be true.

"Millie Ann . . . me and your daddy still married baby so all me and Blue can be is special friends.

"Lena said she saw you and Blue getting married too Momma." Effie Mae's mind raced, uncertain how to clarify Millie Ann's correct, yet incorrect information received from her sisters. "You don't love Daddy no more?"

"Millie Ann baby I still love your daddy, but different than how I love Blue." Millie Ann saddened.

"You and Daddy getting a divorce?" Effie Mae's anxiety accelerated in response to Millie Ann's unexpected question.

"Naw baby I wouldn't do that without talking to my babies first." She looked into her young daughter's worried eyes. "Millie Ann do it bother you seeing me and Blue together?" Millie Ann nodded.

"Why you gotta be with him Momma?"

"Millie Ann baby, I love Blue—" Effie Mae said trying to read her facial expression on her young daughter's. "And he love me too baby, but me loving Blue don't mean I don't love your daddy . . . you understand what I'm saying baby?" Millie Ann shook her head no. "Come here baby." Effie Mae took Millie Ann's hands and placed them inside her own and gently held them. "You always liked candy right baby?" Millie Ann nodded yes. "What's your favorite kind of candy Millie Ann?"

"Chocolate."

"Is all chocolate the same Millie Ann?"

"Huh?"

"Just listen to me baby." Effie Mae said trying to sugar coat her relationship with Blue. "Since it's different kinds of chocolate . . . some with peanuts, pecans and some even got coconut—" Millie Ann listened trying to understand her momma's puzzling words. "So which one do you like best baby?"

"Chocolate with peanuts." Millie Ann said trying to understand how chocolate candy, her daddy and Blue all related. "I don't understand Momma?"

"Just let me finish baby okay."

"Okay."

"Because chocolate is your favorite candy Millie Ann, do you think you would like chocolate with pecans?" She shook her head yes. "So let's just say your daddy is chocolate with pecans and Blue is chocolate with peanuts and you like them both because they both chocolate . . . but since you got a choice you choose the chocolate with peanuts because you like it best." Millie Ann listened to the unusual analogy. "Do you understand now what I'm trying to say Millie Ann?" She shook her head yes, still slightly confused.

"I think so." Millie Ann took a minute to think. "You love Daddy and Blue—both." She said attempting to make the connection between her daddy, Blue and the chocolate candy with pecans or peanuts. "But you love Blue better because he's the chocolate candy you like the best." Effie Mae blushed.

"I guess you could say that Millie Ann." She said humored by the comparison. "I guess I ain't look at it that way." Effie Mae giggled. "Millie Ann if me being with Blue make you unhappy then I won't bring him over no more okay baby?"

"Okay Momma." Millie Ann looked in her momma's distressed eyes. "If you love Blue Momma, he must really be a nice man." Effie Mae's eyes moistened in response to Millie Ann's welcoming words.

"Millie Ann baby he's a wonderful man." Effie Mae delighted in knowing Blue would now be in her children's lives.

"If you want to bring Blue over here Momma it's okay." Millie Ann said hugging her. "As long as it don't upset Daddy."

"Okay Millie Ann, I'm gon make sure we don't do nothing to upset your daddy."

"Okay Momma."

"You want to meet him baby?" Effie Mae asked hoping she'd say yes.

"Yeah."

"Thank you baby." Tears slowly emerged from Effie Mae's eyes. "I love you Millie Ann."

"I love you too Momma." She said looking in her momma's tearful eyes. She removed a tissue from the box of Kleenex on the dresser and handed it to her momma. "Here Momma . . . I don't' want Daddy or Blue to see you crying Momma." Effie Mae humorously smiled as she wiped away her tears.

"Thank you Millie Ann." She looked her oldest daughter in the eyes, her anxiety lessening. "You ready baby?" Millie Ann nodded. Effie Mae opened the door then she and Millie Ann exited the room. Blue looked up when seeing them walking down the hall headed in his direction.

J.R.'s attention quickly drew to his estranged and teenage daughter as they entered the living room. He hoped Millie Ann had been able *talked some sense* into her momma, and that Blue's visit today would be his first and last with his children. His mouth dried when seeing Millie Ann walk over to Blue and smile. J.R. coughed.

"Tyrell baby this is my big girl Millie Ann." He looked at Millie Ann and smiled.

"How you doing Millie Ann?"

"Fine." She looked at her momma and smiled then turned back to Blue. "Can I call you Blue?" She asked out of the blue. J.R. again coughed. Blue's eyes widened as he looked quickly to Effie Mae, surprised by Millie Ann's startling, but welcoming request. Effie Mae's eyes moistened with tears.

"If you want to call me Blue, Millie Ann I'd like that since that's what all my friends call me." Millie Ann leaned down and hugged him. Effie Mae looked in the kitchen at J.R seeing the disappointed look on his face.

"Uh, children . . . go wash up for dinner." He turned to Effie Mae feeling defeated. "The uh, girl's have cooked plenty enough food if you and uh, Blue would like to join us for supper." Effie Mae ignored the hurt displayed in his eyes. Her only thought being Blue's happiness.

"We would love to eat supper with my babies J.R." She said looking at Millie Ann and smiling.

# Chapter Seventeen

Huck indulged in a bottle of scotch in the back room of the Envoy Bar & Grill as he waited for Buckeye to arrive with Gus.

"Where you find him Buckeye?" He asked when seeing his old friend escorting a badly beaten and bloody Gus in the room.

"He had his ass down at the train station hiding in the women's restroom." Huck chuckled then tossed back a shot of scotch before looking a orrified Gus in the eyes.

"What you planned on doing Gus?" Huck refilled his glass. "Swimming out through the toilet?"

"He gon wish he had!" Buckeye said looking at Gus with contempt.

"Did you tell Curtis what I said Buckeye?"

"Yeah Huck I told him." Gus tried to widened his swollen, black eyes. "He was glad to hear it too man." Huck titled his head.

"Is that right?"

"Yeah . . . number man Curtis said he found out Gus was the one that ratted him out three years ago, causing his number house to be busted—setting him back by five grand!" Huck again tilted his head.

"Is that right?" He shifted his eyes over to Gus. "Sit your ass down." Gus looked at him with defiance and continued standing. Huck glanced at Buckeye and nodded. Buckeye drew back his fist and forcefully hit Gus in the stomach. He clutched his abdomen as he doubled over.

"Now sit your ass down like Huck told you too!" Buckeye shouted. Gus slowly lowered himself in the chair across the table from Huck, looking him in the eyes. Huck looked briefly up at Buckeye then turned his attention back to Gus. He cunningly smiled.

"Tell me Gus . . . when did we stop being friends? Did I do something to you Gus that I don't remember doing?" Huck asked, shifting his eyes briefly at his empty shot glass, waiting for Gus to answer. Gus continued his silence. Buckeye stared at him and awaited Huck's instruction on what action he wanted him to take in response to

Gus' stubborn silence. "Look like Gus still mad at me Buckeye, what you think?" Huck said refilling his glass then tossing its contents in his mouth before again turning to Buckeye. "But he won't tell me what I done."

"What you want me to do Huck?"

"You hear that Gus?" Huck said taunting him. "Buckeye want to know what I want him to do to you." Gus shifted his frightened eyes to Buckeye then back to Huck. "What you think I should tell him?"

"Maaalrrannn." Gus garbled attempting to speak through his swollen, bloody lips.

"Speak up Gus I can't hear you." Huck said holding back his fury.

"Maaalrrannn."

"You know what he saying Buckeye?"

"Yeah I know what he saying—put a hole in my two-faced ass." Huck hurled the shot of scotch in his mouth then poured himself another drink.

"Is that it Gus? Is that what you saying?" Gus frantically shook his head no. "Because that's what Buckeye said he heard." Huck deviously smiled. "Do you know why Buckeye, Curtis and his crew pulled you out of toilet Gus?" Gus nodded yes. "Naw Gus you don't know." Huck stated before hurling the shot in his mouth. "Thanks to somebody's big mouth Gus . . . I almost had to kill my own daddy." Gus' eyes widened with fear. "For some reason he seemed to think Effie Mae was still in the business, tried to force himself on her." Gus again tried to speak.

"Maaalrrannn."

"You wouldn't happen to know where he got that misinformation from would you Gus?" Huck lightly stroked his chin hairs. "You know what I think Gus?" He shifted his eyes to Buckeye then again to Gus. "I think he got that from you Gus." Gus abruptly stood and tried to get away. Buckeye quickly seized him.

"Bring your ass back here snitch!" Huck cunningly grinned.

"Now why would you want to tell my daddy something like that Gue?"

"Iwwwaass—slaayymaa." Gus shook his head, babbling.

"Speak up Gus I can't hear you."

"Sounds to me Huck like Gus said he wanted me to go ahead and put that hole in ass." Gus briskly shook his head no, horrified by Buckeye deadly words.

"I tell you what I'm gon do Gus." Huck said looking briefly to Buckeye, cleverly grinning. "I ain't gon hurt you Gus—nope I ain't gon lay one hand on you." Gus gave a sigh of relief.

"Thaaaaa—yooooo."

"Naw Gus don't thank me." Huck stared at him with disdain. "I'm gon leave that up to Curtis and his crew." Gus' eyes filled with tears when hearing Huck's fatal words. "Let them decide what they think would be just punishment for a man who betrays a trusted friend and won't tell him why." Tears streamed down Gus' face. "Oh, so you want to cry now huh?" Huck said unsympathetic to Gus' tears. "Well you keep on crying Gus and hope Curtis can find it in his heart to pity your tears in exchange for the five grand your big mouth cost him . . . and if he don't—" Huck shifted his eyes briefly to Buckeye. "—I guess he gon put a hole in your ass like Buckeye's been aching to do."

"Pleeeeeeez" Gus yelled out. Huck looked at his one time friend with curiosity, still clueless of the reason for his betrayal. Huck shook his head.

"Damn shame." He knew this would be the last time he'd see his one time friend—dead or alive. "Get his ass out of my face Buckeye before I forget this man was once somebody I trusted as my friend." Huck refilled his glass then tossed back the shot. "And look here Buckeye, if he try anything go ahead and put that hole in ass—two if it'll make you feel better." Buckeye forcefully grabbed Gus' arm, yanking him out of the chair. Gus vigorously struggled, trying to free himself from Buckeye's grasp. He abruptly stopped when hearing the sound of a gun cocking. He quickly turned seeing Huck's thirty eight caliber drawn on him.

"Since you was once my friend Gus you know damn well I won't hesitate to use this?" Gus' eyes shifted to Huck's finger positioned on the trigger. "Now get your ass out here before you cause me to have to mess up Boney-nee's half-cleaned floor with your blood. Buckeye hit Gus in the mouth.

"Man you try that again—" He shoved Gus. "I'm gon drop your ass where you stand!" Tears dripped from Gus' wet face, forming a trail of blood tinged teardrops on the floor as Buckeye lead him from the back room of closed establishment at gunpoint. Boney-nee watched with nonchalant eyes as Buckeye escorted Gus out the front door and over to Curtis' awaiting car parked out front.

———————————

"Rev. Smith?" Blue called out as he entered J.R.s church early Wednesday morning.

"I'm here!" J.R. hollered out from his office located in the front of the sanctuary. He opened the door and peeped out. His eyes widened when identifying his visitor as Blue.

"Uh, Blue?" He said hurrying to greet him, puzzled by his unexpected visit. "Uh, good morning."

"How you doing J.R.?"

"I'm uh, I'm good." J.R. glanced at his watch. "If uh, you're here for Wednesday evening service you're about eight hours too early." He said amused. J.R.'s humorous moment ended when seeing the serious look on Blue's face.

"Uh, you okay Blue?" J.R. asked, concerned.

"Yeah J.R. everything's fine . . . you got a minute?"

"Uh, yeah." J.R. looked in the direction of the church's entrance. "Did uh, Effie Mae come with you?"

"Naw Baby girl ain't been feeling too well, so I just let her sleep."

"It's uh, not serious is it?"

"Not too serious J.R." A smile formed on Blue's face. "I don't think Baby girl even know it yet J.R. —" He lightly grinned. "—but she's pregnant." J.R.'s mouth slightly opened.

"Uh, pregnant?" He extended his hand to Blue. "Well uh, congratulations." The two men shook. "I'm sure Effie Mae's pretty excited about having a little Blue." J.R. said forcing a chuckled as he masked what felt like the proverbial *kick in the chest*.

"The reason I'm here J.R. is because I think it's time we talked."

"About you and uh, Effie Mae spending time with the children?"

"Naw—" Blue said slightly balancing himself on a cane. "—about how Baby girl's gon make it after I'm gone." J.R.'s mouth dried. He coughed.

"Are you uh, sure it's me you should be discussing this with?" J.R. said uneasy talking about his wife with her current lover. "I'm uh, pretty sure Effie Mae plans to go back to her life with Anthony." Blue shook his head as his unsteady gait weakened.

"J.R., Effie Mae's your wife man—not Anthony's!" Blue said raising his voice. J.R.'s eyes widened when hearing Blue's acknowledgment of Effie Mae as his wife. "So that mean she still have a life with you—one that carries a whole lot more weight than an engagement to Anthony!" J.R. noticed Blue's feebleness.

"Uh, did you need some help sitting down Blue?"

"Yeah J.R. I do, unless you plan on picking me up off the floor." Blue said laughing." J.R. took hold of Blue's left arm and escorted him to a pew, assisting him down on the bench being seated next to him.

"I do want to thank you though J.R. for letting me be a part of your kid's lives these past few months. Blue's eyes moistened. "You don't know how much that meant to Baby girl."

"You alright?" J.R. asked in response to Blue's dampening eyes.

"Yeah J.R. I'm fine." He quietly chuckled. "I guess I always been a cry-baby, at least that's what the kids use to call me back in school." A boyish look showed on Blue's face. "J.R., Anthony don't have no more right to Baby girl than I do." J.R.'s eyes slightly widened, surprised by Blue's admission. "I know you and Effie Mae was split up when we got together, but Baby girl was still your wife and I apologize for that man."

"Effie Mae's a big girl and uh, it was her choice." Blue smiled as he recalled Effie Mae's words indicating that she *chose* him.

"Well J.R., I'm passing Baby girl's heart on to you." J.R.'s mouth dried, surprised by Blue's bold statement. He coughed. "What you do with it that's for you to decide." He looked at J.R. with hopeful eyes. "If you want to let Anthony or even worse, my big brother—" J.R. interjected.

"Big brother?" A confused look formed on J.R.'s face. "Who uh, is uh—"

"Huck." Blue stated. J.R."s eyes widened, shocked to hear that the two men were brothers.

"Uh, Huck's your—"

"Brother?" Blue said completing J.R.'s question. "Yeah we have the same daddy . . . Henry Lee White Sr."

"That's uh, interesting."

"What I'm trying to say J.R. is if you don't hold on to what's rightfully yours, you gon wake up one day man and find yourself regretting the day you let the woman you love get away." J.R. listened to Blue's unexpected words. "My time is almost up and the last thing I want is Baby girl dying with me from grief." Blue's eyes filled with tears. "That's where you need to come in."

"Uh, Effie Mae knows I'm here for—"

"Naw J.R., you need to be here for Baby girl now . . . or Anthony, Daniel and Huck gon step in and claim your wife as their woman."

"It's uh, not much I can do when my wife's in love with you, engaged to Anthony, spending time with Huck—" J.R. silenced when seeing the uncomfortable look in Blue's eyes when hearing him speak on Effie Mae's intimacy with Huck. "—I uh, shouldn't have said—"

"Don't worry about me man, I'm leaving all that for you to figure out." He looked J.R. in the eyes. "But if you don't step in there now, Huck's gon make his move on Baby girl before she can even think about putting Anthony's ring back on her finger." Blue hesitated. "But the man you really need to watch out for is your Daniel." J.R. eyes widened stunned by Blue's truthful allegation.

"I don't think uh, Effie Mae would uh—" Blue grinned. "J.R. your cousin's in love with your wife man . . . you can't see that!" Blue said chuckling. "In fact, he so in love with Baby girl he'd walk through hell's fire and swim the Red Sea to get to her!" Blue burst into laughter. J.R. reluctantly chuckled. "I already told Baby girl he gon use their son to get to her now that his wife's sick." J.R. hid his frustration as Blue spoke on his cousin's continued betrayal. Blue suddenly began vigorously coughing. He retrieved an inhaler from his shirt pocket and raised it to his mouth, administering two puffs.

"You uh, you okay Blue?" J.R. asked watching with worry.

"Yeah—just—give me—a minute." Blue said inhaling and exhaling attempting to normalize his breathing.

"Do I uh, need to call for an—" Blue shook his head no.

"My time—is almost—up—" J.R. looked at Blue with alarm as he continued trying to stabilize his breathing, again taking two quick puffs from the inhaler. "So it's time—for you—to start being—Baby girl's husband." Blue paused. "In every way." J.R. lowered his eyes, uncomfortable with Blue's forwardness.

"We uh . . . me and uh, Effie Mae spoke and she wants—" Blue interrupted.

"To be true to me?" He quietly chuckled. "Yeah she told me about that J.R."

"She uh, told you about—" Blue noted the embarrassed look on J.R.'s face.

"J.R. you ain't got no reason to feel ashamed about making love to your wife!"

"I uh—" Blue cut him off.

"You got every right to be loving on Baby girl and you should!"

"I uh, don't think Effie Mae would uh, agree with—"

"Yeah J.R. she would." Blue cunningly grinned. "You may not believe this J.R. but Baby girl do love you."

"I uh, don't think she uh—"

"Yeah J.R. she do." Blue nodded. "Before I met Baby girl—" A huge smile stretched across Blue's face. "—I was a real lady's man." He cunningly grinned. "So I kind of know a little something about women." Blue began coughing. J.R. watched, uncertain if he needed to call for an ambulance.

"You uh, alright Blue?" He nodded as he removed the inhaler as his cough persisted then repeating the administration process, inhaling and exhaling until his cough gradually subsided.

"You let me—handle Baby—girl." A big smile displayed on Blue's face. "You just be ready." He grinned. J.R. blushed. Blue looked around the sanctuary. "You know J.R., I ain't been to church in years, but I never stopped believing in the Lord." He peacefully stated. "If it's alright with you J.R.—" He looked J.R. in the eyes. "—I'd like to have my funeral here at your church."

"Uh, here?" J.R.'s mouth dried. He coughed.

"I was also hoping you'd give my eulogy." J.R.'s mouth again dried. He coughed a second time, hesitating before answering Blue's surprising request, feeling slightly uncomfortable.

"I'd uh, I'd be uh . . . honored to deliver your eulogy Blue."

"I'm taking Baby girl with me tomorrow to pick out my casket and make all the funeral arrangements." Blue shook his head as his eyes began to water. "I know that's gon kill by baby." J.R.'s mouth quickly dried. He coughed a third time. "Give her a few days J.R. then take Baby girl out on the town." J.R.'s eyes widened.

"Out on uh, the town?"

"You ever take Baby girl out on a date before J.R.?"

"After the uh, children started coming—" Blue intervened. "

"What about before y'all started having kids?"

"Effie Mae and I uh, we didn't exactly date."

"But you have dated other women before haven't you J.R.?" An uncomfortable look showed on J.R.'s face.

"With uh, seminary I uh, didn't have much time do to all the studying required—" J.R. rambled. "I uh, did invite a few ladies to church on some Sundays." Blue quietly laughed.

"I'm sorry for laughing J.R., but that ain't what I meant man." He looked at J.R., humored by his inexperience with women. "You ever took a woman out—besides to church on Sunday J.R.?" J.R.'s discomfort increased.

"I uh—"

"What about dinner, or maybe a movie . . . you know just show a lady to a good time?"

"I guess I'd uh, have to say no." Blue humorously smiled.

"J.R. take your wife out on the town man!" He said with insistence. "Take her shopping, to a nice dinner, maybe even a jazz club—" J.R.'s mouth slightly opened.

"Jazz club?"

"J.R., you ain't got to drink man, and Baby girl definitely don't need to be drinking! All you doing is relaxing and listening to the sweet sound of jazz, letting it set the evening for a night of loving." Blue smiled as he envisioned the evening being for him and Effie Mae. "You understand what I'm saying don't you J.R.?" Blue asked noticing the look of reluctance on his face. "You know J.R., what one man won't do another man will."

"I uh, guess taking my wife to dinner won't hurt."

"Good . . . because I definitely don't want to see Baby girl with Anthony." Blue frowned. "That man ain't right for Baby girl." J.R.'s curiosity heightened.

"Did uh, something happen between you and uh, Anthony that Effie Mae uh, hasn't told me?"

"You can start by taking Baby girl to Jersey City." Blue said electing not to discuss his thoughts on Anthony with him. "Baby girl loves it there." A huge smile stretched across Blue's face as he recalled their first trip there and Effie Mae's excitement. "Then J.R. you can take her shopping—buy her a nice dress, anything with polka-dots—" J.R. cut him off.

"Can we uh, slow down a minute?" Blue noted the apprehensive look in his eyes. "What if uh, my wife won't—"

"She will J.R." Blue nodded. "And J.R. make a night of it man." J.R.'s mouth abruptly opened.

"Huh?"

"Man enjoy your wife!" An encouraging smile displayed on Blue's face. "Well J.R.—" He said lightly coughing. "—I've said all I came here to say . . . it's up to you what you do with it." Blue grabbed hold of the pew in front of him and tried to lift himself. He turned to J.R. "You think you can help me up man? "Apparently I don't have the strength to do it." J.R. quickly stood, taking hold of Blue's left arm.

"Uh, yeah." He said assisting Blue to his feet.

"I guess when I get back home I'll prepare Baby girl for tomorrow." He shook his head knowing Effie Mae's response would be explosive.

"Uh, was it something special you wanted me to say Blue?"

"To Baby girl?"

"For your uh, eulogy."

"Give me a few days J.R., let me think of something flattering I can say about myself." The two men laughed as J.R. guided him from the pew into the center aisle of the church. "I'll bring it back when I'm done."

"Uh, okay."

"I want Baby girl there with me when I write it."

"You uh, think Effie Mae can uh, handle that?"

"Naw J.R. she can't." He looked in J.R.'s worried eyes then glanced around the sanctuary. "I guess it won't be long now." J.R. looked at him with empathetic eyes. "Thank you J.R."

"Can you uh, make it out?" J.R. asked watching as Blue walked slowly through the sanctuary on his way to the front door with the assistance of a cane. Blue stopped and turned. "Uh, did you forget something Blue?" Blue quietly chuckled.

"J.R. don't let that girl put that horn in my casket—I can't blow it!" They briefly laughed. Blue resumed his journey to the church doors. He again stopped and faced J.R.

"You uh, okay Blue?"

"I thought I'd let you know J.R."

"Uh, know?"

"I can't have kids." Blue shook his head. "Nope, never could so as much as I would love for Baby girl to be carrying myt child—it's not mines." J.R.'s heart raced as he watched Blue turn and walk away, exiting the church. His mouth dried as he wondered if history had repeated itself and Effie Mae had once again become pregnant with the potential of three fathers to her unborn child. He coughed.

———————————————

Huck stood at the entrance of the jazz club seeing Blue seated at a table in the center of room, accompanied by a few of his band members appearing to be celebrating.

"What you think that's all about Buckeye?" A clueless look showed on Buckeye's face. He humped his shoulders. "Let's go see." Huck stated. They walked through the club, headed in the direction of Blue and his companions. "You celebrating something Blue?" Blue abruptly looked up when hearing Huck's voice. "I see you got a packed house in here tonight."

"Yeah my band surprised me with a party tonight." Blue said appreciatively. Huck tilted his head.

"Is that right?" He shiftyed his eyest at the three men seated at the table then turned back to Blue. The men looked one to the other, ill at ease by Huck's presence.

"Alright then Blue—" The bass guitarist said shifting his eyes to Huck. "—I guess we gon get back up here on this stage start entertaining your customers."

"Thank y'all man for giving me this going away party." Blue said as his eyes filled with tears. "And look here . . . when I'm gon I need y'all to look out for my wife." Huck stared at him bothered by him referencing to Effie Mae as his wife.

"Blue man you already know we gon do that." The drummer said getting up from the table, preparing to return to the stage. "We gon dedicate this next set to you Blue—play some of your favorite tunes man." The pianist said, also getting up.

"I appreciate that man." Blue said wiping his tear-filled eyes with a paper napkin as the men walked away returning to the stage being joined by the additional band member that were seated at the bar. Huck stared angrily up on stage at Blue's band then turned his attention to back to Blue.

"Did I hear you say something about a going away party Blue? You going somewhere?"

"Yeah to the funeral home tomorrow so I can make these arrangements!" Blue said irritated by Huck's insensitivity.

"You in a hurry to leave here Blue?" He ignored Huck's question, looking over at Buckeye.

"How you doing Lawrence man?"

"Jjust been taking it one day at a—"

"Whose idea was this anyway Blue?" Huck asked, interrupting.

"In case you ain't noticed Huck I'm already down three and a half months and I figure my doctor was being generous when he said six." He said raising his voice. Huck titled his head.

"Is that right?"

"Man I don't won't Baby girl trying to do all that stuff after I'm gone, she gon have enough to worry about as it is!" Huck shifted his eyes to Buckeye. He humped his shoulders indicating he agreed with Blue. A huge smile suddenly formed on Blue's face. Huck looked in the direction of his brother's gaze seeing Effie Mae standing at the bottom of the stairs. He watched with envy as she looked at Blue and smiled. "Hey Baby girl." Blue said as she approached. Effie Mae leaned down and kissed him gently on the lips. "What you doing up?"

"I was feeling better so I thought I'd come downstairs and spend some time with my baby." She applied another kiss to Blue's lips then looked around the club. "Blue baby you having a party in here tonight?" Huck looked at him and waited to hear his reply.

"Come on Baby girl sit down." Blue said, gently pulling Effie Mae onto his lap, lovingly kissing her as he avoided answering her question.

"How you doing Effie Mae?" Huck asked looking at her with lust-filled eyes.

"I been a little sick, but other than that I'm fine Huck."

"Sick?" Huck tilted his head. "You pregnant again Effie Mae?" He asked turning to Buckeye and quietly laughing. "Is that it Blue? You and Effie Mae trying to have a little Blue before you—" He stopped.

"I told Baby girl about always worrying about me, she just sick from worry." Blue said forcing a chuckle. "But she gon be alright, ain't that right Baby girl?" Huck watched with resentment as Blue raised Effie Mae's hands to his lips and lightly kissed them.

"That's right baby." She said giggling. They smooched.

"I guess me and Baby girl gon head on back upstairs." Blue said sensing Huck's jealousy and impending verbal attack. He also wanted to distance Effie Mae from Huck's seductive gawk. "I don't want my wife spending too much time downstairs—"

"Wife?" Huck said shifting his eyes to Buckeye, offended by Blue referring to Effie Mae his wife.

"I ain't even thinking about drinking Blue—" She giggled. "—I want Tyrell Lee Jones Jr.—" Effie Mae placed an intimate kiss on Blue's lips. "— to come in this world healthy." Blue beamed. Huck's jealousy magnified as he watched his *soul mate* coddled with his half-brother— and rival. He stroked his chin hairs and gazed at Effie Mae.

"Well I tell you what Effie Mae—" He shifted his eyes briefly to Blue. "—if Ol' Blue can't get the job done—" He winked. "—you know Ol' Huck can." Blue tried to ignore Huck's insult. "Maybe if you can't have a Blue Jr., you'll settle for a Henry Lee White—the third." He grinned and again winked.

"Let's go Baby girl!" Blue said infuriated. Effie Mae rose from his lap. Huck watched in amusement as she placed Blue's arm around her neck and assisted him to his feet. "It was good seeing you again Buckeye." Blue stated ignoring Huck's presence.

"You too Tyrell." Buckeye's eyes moistened. "You take care man." Blue stared momentarily at Huck then embraced Effie Mae in his arms and romantically kissed her. Huck laughed, humored by Blue's response to his belittling words.

"That all you got Blue?" Huck hollered out, watching as Effie Mae assisted him up the stairs.

"That's all this woman right here needs!"

"You need a real man to help you up those stairs Blue?" Huck said laughing.

"Why you do that man like that Huck?" Buckeye said sympathetic to Blue's fatal condition.

"Like what Buckeye?"

"You know you hurt that man's ego."

"Blue ain't got no more right to Effie Mae than me Buckeye." Huck said as he continued watching Blue holding helplessly onto Effie Mae as they progressed up the stairs. "Only man do is her husband—her real husband." Buckeye listened but gave no reply. "Not Blue, Anthony or old Daniel." Huck said angry with envy. "And as long as she playing wife to Blue, whenever I want her I'm gon have her." He again looked over at the stairs. "Now let's get out of here."

# *Chapter Eighteen*

"Stop crying Baby girl." Blue said as she hysterically wept as they sat in his car parked out front of the jazz club after returning home from the funeral palor.

"I can't Blue!" Effie Mae yelled, her face saturated with tears.

"You gon have to . . . it's only a matter of time before I'm gone Baby girl!"

"I can't live without you Blue!" She shouted, wrapping her arms desperately around Blue's neck, holding him tightly.

"Effie Mae stop girl!" He said removing her arms from around his neck. "Look at me Baby girl." Effie Mae laid her head on his chest refusing to look at him. "I don't want you dying with me!" Blue said placing a kiss her on the forehead. "Will you look at me Baby girl?" She slowly raised her head and looked into his calming eyes. "I need you to be strong!"

"What am I gon do without you Blue?" Effie Mae cried out.

"I tell you what you gon do—" Blue looked at her with determined eyes. "—you gon keep living your life." He placed another kiss onto forehead. "Baby gil you got all them beautiful kids and they need you girl!" He said kissing her lightly on the lips. "I want you to stay sober, go back to your husband and you and J.R. raised them kids!"

"I don't want to go back to J.R., Blue." She said hysterically sobbing. "I want you Blue!" He looked in her tear drenched eyes as his own flooded with tears.

"I know you do Baby girl and if it was up to me—"

"Don't leave me Blue!" Effie Mae pleaded, her hope dwindling.

"I love you Baby girl!" He cried out kissing her repeatedly on the face and lips.

"I can't' live without you Blue." Effie Mae stated desperately.

"Naw Baby girl don't talk like that." Blue said looking in her tear filled eyes. "This my destiny not yours Baby girl." He applied a gentle kiss to her lips. "I know it don't seem like it now, but you gon be alright—" She cut him off.

"It ain't Blue!" Effie Mae shouted. "It ain't ever gon be alright ever again Blue!"

"Don't say that Baby girl." He said kissing her continually on the lips.

"Don't leave me Blue." Effie Mae stated, crying.

"I know you don't want to hear this Baby girl—" Blue again kissed her. "It's gon hurt like hell when I'm gone but—"

"Ahhhhhhh . . . don't leave me Blue!" She said crying hysterically.

"You gon get through this Baby girl you hear me? I need you to be strong okay?" Blue kissed her wet lips, his own face soaked with tears. "Promise me you won't forget me Baby girl."

"I ain't ever gon forget you Blue!" She shouted. They passionately kissed. "I love you Tyrell Lee Jones."

"That's all I need to hear Baby girl." He said laying Effie Mae's head on his chest—repeatedly kissing her on the forehead as they both wept.

---

Blue lay in bed growing weaker. He smiled and admired Effie Mae as she modeled a white dress highlighted with red polka-dots, accented with a red patent leather belt fastened around her waist.

"How I look Blue?" She asked spinning around in her red high heel shoes as if a model, flaunting the red button style earrings complimenting the bun hairstyle adorned on her head.

"You look beautiful Baby girl." Blue said envious of the impending date Effie Mae prepared to spend with her husband. "J.R.'s gon fall in love with you all over again." He said trying not to show his insecurity. "And don't be worrying about me—"

"You know I ain't gon do nothing but worry about you Blue." He fought back his tears the thought of her being intimate with J.R., now bothered him.

"Baby girl you just enjoy your husband and if that man want to love on you—" She cut him off.

"I ain't doing that Blue."

"Just see how the night goes Baby girl okay?"

"I'm only doing this Blue because you want me to."

"I told you Baby girl—" His frustration grew. "—I don't want you sitting around here watching me die girl!"

"I ain't gon be gone too long Blue." She said ignoring his upsetting words. He stared at her.

"Baby girl did you hear what I just said?"

"I want to get back in time to give you your medicine and—" He interjected.

"Baby girl!"

"What Blue?" Effie Mae yelled.

"Listen to me girl . . . I want you to go and have a good time with your husband—"

"You my husband Blue." Effie Mae kicked off her shoes and climbed in bed, laying down next to him. Blue embraced her in his arms and passionately kissed her then gazed into her hazel brown eyes. He smiled. She blushed.

"I love you Baby girl."

"I'm so glad I met you Blue."

"You know Baby girl . . . I was just thinking the other day." He kissed Effie Mae on the lips. "You the only good thing Huck ever done for me in my whole life." Her blushing smile widened.

"You bet not let Huck hear you saying that Blue." Effie Mae said giggling. He looked at her, ambiguous about her date with J.R. On the one hand, he knew it was what she needed to begin moving on with her life. On the other, he wanted desperately to have her all to himself. "J.R. better get here soon Blue or I'm gon take these clothes off and lay right here with you baby." Blue intimately kissed her, wishing things could have been different.

"Just give him a little more time Baby girl he'll be here."

"I ain't gon be waiting around here all night for J.R." She said trying to find an excuse not to go.

"Baby girl . . . I'm sure any minute now Melvin's gon call up here and say J.R.'s downstairs waiting."

"He better be Blue or I'm just gon keep laying right here with my husband." He smiled, delighted to hear Effie Mae refer to him as her husband.

"Say that again—I don't think I heard you the first time." Blue teased. She giggled.

"I said I'm gon lay right here with you Blue—my husband." A huge smile formed on his face.

"That's what I thought I heard." They kissed. "I just wish I had more time—"

"Don't be talking like that Blue." Effis Mae said in denial of his approaching death.

"I wish I had married you when we first talked about us leaving here—" Blue stated, abruptly silencing when hearing a knock at the door. "It's open man." His eyes quickly moistened with tears. Melvin slowly opened the door and peeped in. His eyes widened when seeing Effie Mae lying in bed intimately embraced in Blue's arms.

"J.R.'s downstairs Effie Mae." A huge lump formed in Blue's throat.

"Let him know Baby girl's gon be down in just a minute." Melvin looked in his cousin's dampened eyes seeing his emotional hurt.

"You gon be able to let that beautiful woman go cousin?" Melvin asked, chuckling.

"I hope not Melvin." Effie Mae said wiping Blue's tears away with his sheet."

"J.R.'s lucky he got here when he did Melvin." Blue said trying not to cry. "One more minute and I was gon keep my wife right here with me." Melvin forced a chuckle as he sympathized with the hurt he knew his cousin felt. He closed the door and returned downstairs to deliver the message.

"Don't you go nowhere while I'm gon Blue." Effie Mae teased trying to hide her fear of the possibility.

"I ain't going nowhere Baby girl." He said placing a quick kiss to her lips. "I'll be right here waiting, when you get back home." He hesitated. "Dead or alive." He laughed. Effie Mae panicked.

"Don't be saying that Blue."

"I'm just teasing with you Baby girl." He again kissed her. "Now go be with your husband." Blue said gazing into her eyes. "And don't be worrying about me you just enjoy yourself." He applied a final kiss to Effie Mae's lips. She climbed out of the bed and put on her shoes, adjusting her dress and hair before walking over to the door.

"Hey." Blue said smiling.

"Huh?" Effie Mae blushed.

"I love you Baby girl."

"I know." She turned and looked at him then smiled. "I love you back Blue."

"Bye Effie Mae."

"Bye Tyrell." He watched as she walked away, exiting the apartment. He stared at the closed door then burst into tears and quietly wept.

---

"Did I tell you how beautiful you look?" J.R. asked as he drove down the highway on their way to Jersey City.

"Yeah J.R. you did." Effie Mae giggled. "I think that make about the tenth time."

"Uh, okay." His mouth dried. He coughed.

"So what you got planned for us J.R.?" Effie Mae asked, amused.

"There's uh, a jazz club Blue recommended." Effie Mae's mouth opened.

"A jazz club J.R.?"

"Just to listen—not to drink." He stated in his defense. She again giggled. "But first there's a restaurant Blue said I should take you to." She smiled, trying not to laugh.

"What?" J.R. said in response to the enormous smile on her face.

"I ain't gon say nothing, I'm just gon enjoy the night." Effie Mae said, silently chuckling. "Then I'm gon thank Blue when I get back home."

"I'm uh, not real familiar with that side of life."

"I know J.R." She said humored. "So what else did Blue say you should do?"

"Well he uh, he told me uh . . . about a nice motel." Effie Mae's jaw dropped.

"A motel? I'm definitely gon be talking to Blue when I get back home." She girlishly grinned.

"If you don't uh, want to uh, go we don't have to but—"

"But what J.R.?" She blushed.

"I was uh, hoping we could uh—"

"Hoping we could what J.R.?"

"That we'd uh, but only if you want to and not because it's uh, what Blue wants—"

"Okay."

"Huh?" He looked over at Effie Mae, stunned by her unexpected response.

"I said okay J.R., we can go to the motel." She said believing it would please Blue. J.R. smiled.

"Uh, thank you."

"You welcome J.R."

———————————

"Good morning Baby girl." Blue said startling Effie Mae as she entered through the front door of the jazz club—the following morning.

"Blue baby you feeling alright?" She asked when seeing him sitting on the edge of the stage. She also noted his out of character early morning rising.

"I'm fine Baby girl." He said, appearing progressively weaker. "Come sit with me." Effie Mae walked over and sat next to him on the stage. He put his arm around her and placed a loving kiss on her lips. "How was your date with J.R.?"

"It was wonderful Blue!" Effie Mae said beaming. "But I guess I can thank you for J.R. showing me such a good time." She giggled. Blue slightly lowered head.

"What's wrong baby?"

"I was just thinking . . . since you didn't come home last night I guess you and J.R. —"

"Let's not talk about that part of the date Blue."

"Baby girl I don't want you to be afraid of hurting me."

"Well I am Blue." Effie Mae said laying her head against his chest. "I don't ever want to hurt you baby." He placed a light kiss on her forehead.

"Funny thing is—all this time we been together you being with J.R. never bothered me." He lightly chuckled. "Now it's bothering the hell out of me!" Blue lowered his head. "I guess I'm feeling a little insecure."

"Baby you ain't got nothing to be worried about, it's you I love Blue not J.R." Effie Mae stated gently raising his head, kissing him on the lips. "Blue you know the only reason I went on a date with J.R. was because you wanted me to baby, you know that."

"I know Baby girl." Blue said disappointed with himself. "I guess since I ain't been able to love on you lately, I'm feeling like I'm less of a man." Effie Mae wrapped her arms around his neck and intimately kissed him.

"Baby you know that ain't the reason why I love you!" She grasped hold of his right hand and held it against her cheek. "I love you baby because you the best thing I ever had in my life." Effie Mae said rubbing Blue's hand softly against her face, moving it to her lips then kissing it. He smiled. "I don't want you to ever think us not being together in that way would ever change what I feel for you Blue." His eyes dampened as Effie Mae placed a loving kiss on his lips.

"Thank you for saying that Baby girl." They smooched. "Help me upstairs so I can go lay down."

"So we can go lay down Blue." She looked into Blue's brightened eyes and smiled. He beamed.

---

J.R. walked through the sanctuary replacing Bibles and hymn books missing from the back pocket of each of the wooden pews in preparation for Wednesday evening Bible study. His attention drew to the foyer when hearing the church's front door open and close. He patiently waited for his unseen visitor to appear. J.R's eyes widened when seeing Blue's emaciated face as he slowly made his way through the foyer into the sanctuary, greatly dependent on a cane.

"Good afternoon Blue." J.R. said hurrying over to his aid in response to his diminished physical appearance. "Uh, how are you?"

"For a dying man J.R.—" Blue half-heartedly chuckled. "—I'm doing as well as I can." A weakened smile formed on Blue's frail face. "I woke up this morning with the woman that gives my heart a reason to keep beating." He said elated. "What more could a man ask for?" His affectionate words reminded J.R. that his legal wife continued to live her life as Blue's *spiritual* wife.

"I guess you uh, finished your eulogy?" J.R. asked bothered by Blue's romantic words.

"Well J.R., after two weeks of trying . . . I couldn't think of a single thing to say about myself that would tell Baby girl how much I love her." Blue's eyes filled with tears. "So instead, I wrote her a love letter if that's alright with you?" J.R.'s mouth dried. He coughed.

"Uh, love letter?"

"I know what I'm asking is wrong J.R. since you still Baby girl's husband—" J.R. again coughed, challenged by Blue's acknowledgment of Effie Mae as his legal wife.

"If uh, that's what you want Blue uh, a love letter's fine." J.R. stated, agreeing with ambiguity. On the one hand, he knew Effie Mae hearing Blue's last words in a love letter would give her the comfort he could never provide. On the other, he felt his wife being serenaded in a love letter from her deceased lover dishonored him as her husband. "I'm uh, sure a love letter from you would uh, mean more to Effie Mae than anything you could've said about yourself." The two men briefly laughed.

"Thank you J.R."

"You're uh, welcome Blue." J.R.'s eyes drew to the large white envelope Blue held in his right hand. "Is that uh—"

"You think you could help me sit down first J.R.?" Blue asked, notably feeble.

"Oh, okay." J.R. quickly placed the books in his hands on one of the pews then grasped hold of Blue's arm gradually lowering him down on the nearest bench being seated next to him.

"Thank you J.R." Blue said through repeated inhales and exhales as he tried to catch his breath from his walk through the sanctuary. He handed J.R. the envelope.

"This uh, looks like a pretty big letter." J.R. said humorously as he looked at the sizeable envelope with peculiarity.

"Oh . . . naw J.R. my letter to Baby girl's inside—let me take it out." J.R. handed him back the envelop. Blue reached inside and removed the letter. "I got some—other stuff—in there too." He began coughing. "I—need you to hold—onto it for Baby girl." J.R. watched with concern as Blue's removed an inhaler from his shirt pocket and held it to his mouth.

"You uh, okay Blue?" He asked observing as Blue took two quick puffs.

"This just—part of my—sickness J.R." Blue said reaching inside his pants pocket retrieving a bottle. He opened it then tossed a couple pills in his mouth then returned both the inhaler and pill bottle to his pockets.

"Uh, Blue . . . you need some water?"

"I got it J.R." Blue said moistening his mouth with saliva then swallowing. "Thanks for asking man, I take these pills to stop all that coughing." He looked into J.R.'s worried eyes. "It won't be long now." J.R. nodded with understanding. "About a month—after I'm gone—I want you—to give this—to Baby girl." Blue stated speaking through sporadic breaths as he handed the envelop back to J.R.

"You mind if I uh, ask what's in here." J.R. asked, visually exploring the large envelop. A loving smile showed on Blue's face.

"It's a—picture of me—and Baby—girl's wedding." J.R. looked quickly over at him, shocked by his unanticipated words. Blue again removed the inhaler and put it to his mouth taking two puffs then inhaling and exhaling. "A picture of me—with my horn and—some other stuff." He continued inhaling and exhaling with noticeable difficulty. "I figure—after about a month, Baby girl—should be ready—for it."

"I'll uh, make sure she gets it." Blue noticed the sympathetic look in J.R.'s eyes. The two men remained momentarily silent.

"Well J.R., I guess I'll be—seeing you soon." Blue said grabbing hold of the pew in front of him, attempting to lift himself. J.R. quickly stood assisting Blue to his feet.

"I uh, guess you will—m" J.R. coughed. "—in a way." He watched with compassion as Blue again held the inhaler to his mouth repeating the administration of the medication. "I uh, just hope I can read your love letter to Effie Mae to your satisfaction.

"I guess—I'll—never know." Blue quietly laughed as he inhaled and exhaled. "As long as it tells—Baby girl—just how much I—love her." He looked J.R. in the eyes. "That's all that matters."

"God Bless you Blue." J.R. said embracing him.

"Remember J.R." Blue said as J.R. assisted him into the center aisle of the sanctuary. "Effie Mae's your wife." Blue's eyes filled with tears.

"You uh, didn't drive here did you Blue?" J.R. asked, alarmed. Blue chuckled.

"Naw J.R., I couldn't—if I wanted too." He said amused. "I just hate having—to leave—Baby girl." J.R. watched with sympathetic eyes as tears rolled down Blue's face. He looked J.R. in the eyes. "I'm leaving her—in your hands." Blue suddenly chuckled. A curious looked formed on J.R.'s face in response to Blue's sudden laughter. "I was—just thinking J.R., if I wasn't dying—would you have ever—divorced Baby girl?"

"No . . . I wouldn't have." He stated without hesitation. "I guess uh, Effie Mae will always be my wife." Blue quietly grinned then confirmed J.R.'s statement with a nod of the head.

"You remember—that J.R." Blue turned and slowly walked away. J.R. watched with sorrowful eyes as Blue walked away making his final exit from the church.

# *Chapter Nineteen*

"Good morning Blue, how you feeling baby?" Effie Mae asked as he awakened. He reached over and pulled her in his arms and passionately kissed her.

"Baby girl I feel better than I have in months."

"Maybe those doctors was wrong Blue." She said hopeful. "It's been four months and it seems like you getting better baby!" Effie Mae stated, closing a blind eye to Blue's debilitated state. He repeatedly kissed her on the lips and face. She giggled.

"You know what?"

"What Blue?"

"I feel well enough to love on you this morning." Effie Mae's heart seemingly sank into her stomach as she looked in his excited eyes—horrified by his request.

"You sure Blue?"

A huge smile formed on his face.

"I'm positive Baby girl!"

"As long as you sure."

"I can show you better than I can tell you." He stated seductively then kissed her. Effie Mae masked her fear behind a giggle as she and Blue looked lovingly into one another's eyes and prepared to engaged in intimacy for the first time in weeks.

• • • •

Blue lay in bed after he and Effie Mae's brief intimate encounter, watching as she dressed in preparation to visit with her children.

"I wish you could come with me to see my babies, Blue." Effie Mae said fastening the buttons on her navy blue polka-dotted blouse complementing the straight-legged navy blue pants she wore.

"I wish I could too, Baby girl."

"Lil' J.R.'s been asking for me to come eat dinner with them again." Blue silently chuckled.

"He ain't spoiled is he?" He said teasing. Effie Mae giggled as she stood in front of the mirror brushing her hair. She looked over at him and smiled. He winked.

"Yeah Blue he is but that's my baby."

"Come here Baby girl."

"Blue . . . I'm trying to get ready." Effie Mae blushed, believing him to again be requesting intimacy.

"Come here." She giggled then walked over to the bed in response of his beckoning. He pulled Effie Mae towards him, enveloping her in his arms. She continued giggling. They romantically kissed. Blue suddenly stopped.

"You alright baby?" Effie Mae asked, frightened by the unusual gaze in his eyes.

"I just wanted—to hold you—in my arms one last time." He said becoming winded. Effie Mae's heart pounded in her ears when hearing his devastating words.

"Don't be saying that Blue." He looked in her hazel brown eyes and winked.

"I won't be here—when—you get back—Baby girl." A peaceful smile formed on his face. Effie Mae burst into tears as she looked in Blue's weakening eyes.

"Then I ain't going Blue!" She yelled.

"Baby girl—go see—your kids." He said as his breathing gradually diminished. "I don't—want you—to lay here—and watch—me die."

"I'm calling the ambulance Blue—" Effie Mae shouted, rising from the bed. Blue caught hold of her arm pulling her back.

"Uh-uh." He said shaking his head no. "I'm dying—Baby girl."
"You ain't gon die Blue!" She bellowed. "You getting better baby!" Blue shook his head no, then looked up at the ceiling.

"I've asked—the Lord—for His—forgiveness—and I'm ready—to go."

"Stop it Blue!" Effie Mae shouted.

"Uh-uh—Baby girl—that ain't—how—I'm leaving—this world." He again embraced her. "Now—kiss me—goodbye—go see—your babies."

"I ain't leaving you Blue!" Effie Mae frantically yelled.

"Baby girl—" His breaths deepened. "—you want—lay here— watch—me die?" He said trying to raise his voice.

"I want to stay here with you baby." Effie Mae stated lifting Blue's upper body up from the bed, holding him in her arms, kissing him repeatedly on the lips and face. A slight smile formed on Blue's face as his chest displayed labored respirations.

"Hey." He said breathing deeply.

"Huh?" Effie Mae replied as tears saturated her face.

"I love—you—Baby—girl."

"Don't leave me Blue!" She pleaded.

"Tell—me—you—love me." He stated as his breathing gradually slowed.

"You ain't going nowhere Blue!" Effie Mae cried out, refusing to accept the truth. Tears ran down her cheeks dripping onto Blue's face as she cradled him in her arms.

"Tell—me!"

"I love you Tyrell Lee Jones." She stated weeping. A weakened smile stretched briefly across his thin face as Effie Mae kissed him on the lips then watched him inhaled and exhaled one last time, peacefully dying. She looked into Blue's lifeless eyes then placed her hand over his eyelids and gently closed them, rocking him in her arms as she wept.

---

Three days after Blue's death, Effie Mae intermittently cried, refusing to get out of bed despite Deborah Ann and Melvin's continuous urging her to come downstairs and join Blue's patrons and friends who'd come to give their heartfelt condolences.

"Effie Mae?" Deborah Ann said calling through the locked apartment door. Effie Mae gave no reply. "Effie Mae girl I know you hurting, but being locked up here in this apartment ain't good for you sweetie." Deborah Ann said continuing to knock. "Effie Mae you know this ain't what Tyrell wanted for you girl." The silence inside the apartment continued. "Effie Mae girl before Tyrell passed he made me promise I wouldn't let you die with him—" Deborah Ann abruptly silenced when hearing the door unlock and began slowly opening. Her mouth slightly opened as an emotionally drained Effie Mae stood on the other side. Deborah Ann rushed in and embraced her.

"Effie Mae you alright girl?"

"I want Blue!" Effie Mae cried out, weeping.

"I know you do Effie Mae but Blue's gone baby." Tears erupted from Effie Mae's swollen red eyes.

"I don't want him to be gone Deborah Ann, I want him here with me."

"We all want him here baby but—" Deborah Ann's eyes filled with tears as she too began crying.

"Y'all gon be alright?" Melvin asked, standing outside the open door. He looked at Deborah Ann and gestured her with his head to leave, allowing him to speak to Effie Mae alone. She ended their embrace.

"Effie Mae I'm going downstairs so I can get back to work." She shifted her teary eyes briefly to Melvin in response to Effie Mae's deteriorated state. "If you need anything girl just pick up the phone and call me, okay baby?" An empty stare displayed in Effie Mae's eyes. She gave no reply. Melvin looked at Deborah Ann as she walked past him on her way out of the apartment. He noted the uneasy look on her face as he entered taking Effie Mae in his arms.

"Effie Mae don't you think you would feel better if you came downstairs sweetie?" Melvin asked, softly. "You have people down there who want to give Tyrell's wife their condolences." She looked in his gentle eyes, but maintained her silence. "Don't you want to come down and represent your man Effie Mae?" She silently gazed at Melvin then laid her head on his warm chest. "Sweetie you know the last thing Tyrell would want is you up here in this apartment isolating yourself from the people who loved him and you." Effie Mae slowly raised her head, looking in Melvin's sensitive eyes then again rested her head on his chest and wept.

"It hurts Melvin!" She cried out.

"I know sweetie." He said as his eyes moistened. "I know it don't seem like it now Effie Mae but it's gon get better."

"It ain't gon get better Melvin!" She shouted. "Blue gone and he ain't coming back." Tears continued emerging from Effie Mae's eyes, soaking into Melvin white shirt. "How it's gon get better Melvin? Blue ain't here!" He remained silent, struggling to hold back his own emotional pain as he searched for words that would penetrate the excruciating pain he knew ached inside Effie Mae's heart. He suddenly chuckled.

"I can hear Ol' Blue now—" Melvin said humorously. "Baby girl I want you to miss me, but don't stop living!" Effie Mae's sobbing increased.

"Blue! Come back Blue—I need you baby!" She hollered out, dwindling from Melvin's hold, dropping to her knees.

"Effie Mae!" Melvin said raising her from the floor, again laying her head on his chest as she continued crying. "Effie Mae calm down sweetie."

"I can't calm down Melvin!" She yelled. "I want Blue!"

"I know you do sweetie I want him back too, but we both know it don't work that way."

"Why did he have to die Melvin?" She asked in desperation. "He told me he loved me Melvin, so why he leave me?"

"Effie Mae . . . you know Tyrell loved you more than anything in this world."

"Come back Blue!" Effie Mae cried out as she continued weeping. Melvin listened with helplessness, trying to think of what he could say to calm her down.

"Did you hear that Effie Mae?" He said looking around the apartment. She looked at him with tear filled eyes but gave no reply.

"There it go again . . . I know you heard it that time."

"Heard what Melvin?" She asked through her weeping.

"You know if I didn't know better I'd swear I heard Tyrell." Effie Mae's crying lessened as she looked up at Melvin.

"What?"

Melvin looked up at the ceiling.

"There it goes again." He gazed in Effie Mae's eyes and wiped her tears. "What was that you said cousin?" Effie Mae looked at him with wonder. "Okay, I'll let her know." Melvin said nodding his head. "Tyrell Lee Jones told me to tell you . . . I love you Baby girl." Effie Mae's eyes lit up. "You know what else I heard my cousin say?" She listened as if Blue were actually speaking to Melvin. "He said Baby girl I want you to live your life and take care of them babies." A smile gradually formed on Effie Mae's face. "Don't you hear him Effie Mae?" Melvin asked holding his hand up to his ear as if listening. "Because I hear him as clear as day." Effie Mae found comfort in Melvin's *make believe*. "What's that you said Tyrell?" Melvin said looking in Effie Mae's attentive eyes as he continued pretending to be communicating with Blue. "Okay man, I'll tell her." Effie Mae giggled in response to his imaginary conversation. "Tyrell told me to tell you just like this . . . Baby girl I want you to clean yourself up, go downstairs and let everybody know how wonderful your husband was." She continued giggling through her emotional pain. Melvin grinned.

"I guess I never knew until now Melvin how much you sound like Blue." Effie Mae looked at him with peace in her eyes. Melvin cunningly laughed. "Back in the day, me and Tyrell use to play tricks on everybody especially the ladies." He continued grinning. "We got in a lot of trouble behind that too." Effie Mae smiled then placed a kiss on his cheek.

"Thank you Melvin."

"You welcome—Baby girl." He teased. They laughed. "Now will you come downstairs and represent your man Effie Mae?" She nodded. He gazed at her. "When was the last time you ate? You need me to fix you something?"

"I am kind of hungry Melvin, but I don't know if I'm ready to—" He interjected.

"Don't let me have to tell Tyrell on you." Melvin joked. Effie Mae giggled.

"Okay Melvin, you can go ahead and fix me something." He momentarily looked in her hazel brown eyes. She smiled.

"What Melvin?"

"My cousin was a lucky man." Her blushing smile widened. "You know Effie Mae it was times when I would've loved to have walked in my cousin's shoes." Her mouth slightly opened, surprised by his admission. "But I loved my cousin and I would've never done anything to hurt that man." He slowly moved his lips towards Effie Mae's mouth. She showed no resistance as Melvin gently kissed her on the lips. "If things don't work out with J.R., Anthony or Huck—" Effie Mae's mouth abruptly opened.

"Huck?" Effie Mae laughed. "Blue told me to stay away from him." Melvin's mouth opemed in response to Blue's request. He laughed out loud.

"What I'm saying Effie Mae . . . is if things don't work with all those dudes—" He again placed a kiss on Effie Mae's lips. "—remember I'm here sweetie." She gazed in Melvin's eyes as he passionately kissed her then abruptly pulled away.

"I think you need to go back downstairs Melvin."

"I think you right Effie Mae." He looked her seductively in the eyes then placed a final kiss on her lips as he prepared to leave. She watched as he walked away, exiting the apartment. Effie Mae blushed as she thought about what had just taken place between her and Blue's favorite cousin.

---

"We gon play this next number in remembrance of our band leader and friend Tyrell "Blue" Jones." The saxophonist said as Melvin escorted Effie Mae to a table in front of the stage as she came downstairs. Tears quickly erupted from her eyes as she looked up seeing the band—absent Blue.

"And we want to say to his wife Effie Mae on behalf of Blue—" The bass guitarist stated. "—we love you Baby girl!" The band said in unison. Effie Mae looked up on stage, her eyes flooded with tears as the band began playing Blue's favorite jazz piece. A smile formed on her tear soaked face as she envisioned Blue standing on stage playing his saxophone.

"Hey Effie Mae." She looked up when hearing the sound of Huck's voice. "You doing alright girl?" He noted the blank stare in her eyes and the flowing tears running down her cheeks. "Naw, you ain't alright." He seated himself in the chair next to her and removed a handkerchief from the pocket of the burgundy vest, complimenting his matching burgundy suit. He dabbed Effie Mae's tears then laid her head on his chest, gently stroking her hair as she silently wept.

"I'm sorry about Tyrell, Effie Mae." Buckeye said sitting in a chair across the table from her. "I just want you to know I loved that man like he was my brother." He looked in her pained eyes, sympathizing with her hurt. "And I'm gon miss the hell out of him!" Effie Mae looked over at him and smiled. Buckeye shifted his eyes to the band. "I can still see Tyrell standing up on that stage blowing his saxophone!" He lightly chuckled. "That boy knew he could play that horn!" Buckeye's eyes dampened as he lowered his head and silently wept. "Damn, I sure am gon miss that boy."

"Ol' Blue knew he loved him some Effie Mae too Buckeye." Huck said reminiscing on happier times. "I remember the first time I introduced him to her." Effie Mae looked up at him and listened as he recalled the day. "They act like it was love at first sight or something." Huck said looking over at his old friend, grinning. Effie Mae quietly giggled. "Was it?" He asked teasing her. She blushed. "I'm here for you girl." Huck said placing a kiss on her forehead. "Just let me know what you need and you got it." He held Effie Mae in his arms, watching as she silently wept. "I loved him too." His attention drew to the club's front entrance when the glare from the city's street lights beamed in through the open door as patrons entered the club. Huck looked with familiarity at the female entering then quietly laughed to himself when recognizing the female as Effie Mae's younger sister. He also took note of the unfamiliar male standing to her right.

"Here come them eyeballs Effie Mae." She slowly raised her head from Huck's chest.

"What?"

"Look over at the door." Effie Mae glanced in the direction of the front entrance. A huge smile stretched across her face when seeing Annie Mae and Pete as they visually searched the crowded club.

"Annie Mae!" She called out pulling away from Huck's intimate hold. He watched as she hurried towards the front entrance to greet her baby sister and brother-n-law. The two sisters affectionately hugged.

"Effie Mae you alright?" Annie Mae asked, worried about her big sister's emotional well-being.

"When did y'all get here Annie Mae?" Effie Mae asked avoiding her baby sister's question.

"J.R. called Momma and told her about Blue." Pete intervened when seeing the emotional hurt Effie Mae tried to mask.

"Hey Sister-in-law." Effie Mae looked over at him then ended her embrace with her baby sister. She walked over to her brother-in-law, melting in his arms—Pete's firm hold comforting her.

"Hey Pete." He kissed her on the cheek.

"How you doing Ol' crazy girl?"

"I'm hurting real bad Pete." She said, her eyes becoming wet with tears.

"I know that pain . . . and I know it ain't easy." Pete laid Effie Mae's head on his chest as she wept. "I only met Blue once, but he seemed to be a good man."

"He was Pete—"

"And he loved your crazy behind." Pete teased. Effie Mae looked up at him and giggled in response to his playful words. "You a strong woman Sister-in-law . . . you gon make it through this." He said looking in her tearful eyes. "Once all that hurting stop you gon be just fine."

"Thank you for saying that Pete."

"Now stop all that crying girl before you get me started." He said as his eyes slightly moistened. Effie Mae giggled through her sniffles. Pete wiped her tears with his hand then released her.

"Y'all come sit down with me and Huck." Effie Mae said leading them in the direction of her table. "And Buckeye."

"Buckeye?" A puzzled look formed on Pete's face. "That a friend of yours Sister-in-law?" She giggled.

"I don't know how I should answer that." She thought back to the day Buckeye delivered her into the brutal hands of Huck, and how it nearly ended her life. Effie Mae smiled. "Let's just say he more of a friend to Huck than to me." She quieted when noticing the blushing smile on her baby sister's face at the mention of Huck's name. She discreetly shifted her eyes to Pete then back to Annie Mae.

"Annie Mae—" Effie Mae said startling her.

"Huh?"

"You got something on your face—wipe that off." She said subtly alerting her baby sister to the blushing smile she apparently hadn't realized displayed on her face at the mention of Huck's name. Annie Mae quickly shifted her eyes to her husband then again to Effie Mae. The two sisters silently giggled. Huck and Buckeye watched as Effie Mae approached the table with her guests.

"You remember my baby sister don't you Huck?" He shifted his eyes to Effie Mae trying to keep a straight face.

"Yeah I remember your sister . . . Annie Mae right?" She stared at Huck unable to avoid gawking. He briefly lowered his head and blushed then looked over at Pete as Annie Mae continued her unrelenting gaze. "You doing alright Annie Mae?" Buckeye silently grinned as he observed their awkward exchange.

"I'm doing fine Huck . . . how you doing?" She asked being seated across the table to the left of Buckeye. Huck noted the lustful smile on his old friend's face as he looked at Annie Mae with interest and cunningly grinned.

"And that's Pete . . . my baby sister's husband."

"What's going on man?" Huck said. The two men shook.

"Just taking care of the family—working hard." Pete said being seated to the left of Annie Mae. A bothered look formed on Buckeye's face after Effie Mae's introduction ended without including him.

"Alright Effie Mae I see—so you just ain't gon introduce me to nobody huh?" He said focused solely on Annie Mae. Huck continued silently grinning. Effie Mae ignored Buckeye's words. "Yeah, well everybody I'm Buckeye—how y'all doing?"

"How's it going Buckeye?" Pete said shifting his eyes to Effie Mae.

"I can't complain man." Buckeye turned his attention to Annie Mae, a huge smile on his face as he extended his hand to her. "Buckeye's my nickname." He said flirting. "But my real name is Lawrence." He gently took hold of Annie Mae's hand as she reached to shake and raised it to his lips lightly kissing it. Pete's jaw dropped. He gazed angrily at Buckeye, upset by his inappropriate greeting with his wife. Huck watched, amused by Buckeye's obvious attraction to Effie Mae's— married baby sister. Pete rose to his feet.

"Get up Annie Mae!" He said looking Buckeye in the eyes as he guided Annie Mae away from him and exchanged seats with her. "This woman right here—" Pete stated continuing his angry gawk at Buckeye. "—that's my heart." He put his arm around Annie Mae then placed a kiss on her lips. "—and I can't live without my heart." Huck laughed out loud.

"I understand brother." Buckeye stated apologetically. "I didn't mean you no disrespect." He shifted his eyes to Huck amused then back to Pete. "I hope you don't mind me saying it but I think your wife is one fine sister!" He peeked around Pete's head and looked at Annie Mae then smiled. He winked. She blushed. Huck continued laughing.

"Don't be trying to hit on my baby sister Buckeye." Effie Mae said protective of Annie Mae. "My baby sister and Pete been married since they was kids and they got six babies back home." Huck looked at his old friend, humored by his flirtatious behavior with Annie Mae. "Sounds liked you better stay away from Effie Mae's baby sister Buckeye." He said continuing to laugh. "I don't think she's like Effie Mae." Pete quickly turned to him insulted by the comparison.

"Naw man my wife ain't nothing like Effie Mae!" He said offended by Huck biting words. Pete looked at Effie Mae, his eyes apologizing for his abrupt words. "I'm sorry Sister-in-law I didn't mean to—"

"That's okay Pete." Effie Mae said half-heartedly chuckling. "Ain't nobody like Effie Mae Reed." An abrupt silence fell over the group as Huck glanced around the table at his peculiar companions as an abrupt silence fell over the group. He quietly grinned sensing the knife-cutting tension amongst the five.

"What y'all drinking?" He asked.

# *Chapter Twenty*

"Where's she at?" Huck asked Melvin as he rushed through the front door of the jazz club.

"She upstairs Huck." Melvin said shaking his head. "We can't get her to come out the apartment and she won't open the door." An uneasy look showed on Melvin's face. "The family car from the funeral home's been waiting out there now for thirty minutes!"

"You and Deborah Ann go ahead on Melvin . . . I'll bring Effie Mae." Huck hurried up the stairs. "Open this door Effie Mae!" He hollered, forcefully pounding on the locked door. "Come on now girl open this door." He said waiting for Effie Mae to answer. "Don't make me break this door down Effie Mae!" Huck stopped when hearing Effie Mae unlock the door—seconds before opening it. He rushed in and embraced her seeing the vacant gaze in her eyes. "What's going on Effie Mae?"

"I can't do it Huck!" She cried out as tears flowed from her eyes.

"Yeah you can." He kissed her lightly on the forehead. "I got you Effie Mae, come on so you can say goodbye to your man—you know Blue wouldn't want you acting like this girl."

"I don't want to say goodbye Huck!" She shouted.

"Effie Mae!" Huck yelled, growing impatient.

"What Huck?"

"Girl you stronger than that and Blue knew you were!" He looked in Effie Mae's tear-filled eyes. "So come on say goodbye to my brother before they put him in that ground." Effie Mae's crying progressed into sobbing.

"Nooooooo, I don't want them to put him in the ground Huck!" She stated becoming hysterical.

"Effie Mae!" Huck yelled.

"What Huck!" He looked in her pained eyes.

"Come on girl . . . Blue waiting on you—" He paused. "—Baby girl." She stared in Huck's eyes as if Blue himself were speaking to her then gradually calmed. He took hold of Effie Mae's arm and escorted her from the apartment, down the stairs and walked through the empty jazz club, outside to his late model candy-apple red Cadillac. Huck assisted her inside his car then hurried to the other side and got in speeding away—on his way to J.R.'s church.

—————————————

All heads turned when seeing Effie Mae enter the church shrouded in black, her face buried in Huck's embrace as he guided her down the center aisle of the sanctuary filled with family, friends and patrons of Blue's Jazz Club—all there to say their goodbye's to Tyrell "Blue" Jones.

Huck swallowed the enormous lump in his throat as he looked upon the body of his beloved half brother as he journeyed towards the front pew designated for the grieving *widow*, immediate family and the jazz club's employees. Included amongst the many gawking eyes were Daphne, Mr. White and Ms. Jones tearfully sobbing as she stared upon the body of her only son.

Seated midcenter of the sanctuary sat Daniel holding he and Effie Mae's sleeping toddler son. He watched with sympathetic eyes as Huck escorted a brokenhearted Effie Mae to the front of the church, her face still hidden inside Huck's comforting embrace as she sat on the front pew directly in front of Blue's open casket.

Sitting a row behind, Mr. White scrutinized the two—his mind occupied with thoughts of taking ownership of Blue's Jazz Club—soon. His attention drew to the pulpit when seeing J.R. entered, standing before the many bereaved as he prepared to deliver Blue's eulogy, momentarily looking around the sanctuary with ambiguity. On the one hand, J.R. genuinely sympathized with Effie Mae's grieving. On the other, he found it hurtful to watch his wife weeping over her *spiritual* husband as his widow. Adding to his awkward position, he now had to eulogize Blue by reading his love letter written to Effie Mae.

"My uh, sincere condolences go out to uh, Effie Mae for the loss of uh—" J.R. paused when seeing her look up at him before again burying her face in Huck's embrace. "—a man I know she loved with all her heart and uh, I know without doubt he felt the very same way about her." Mr. White glared angrily at J.R.—infuriated by the words he'd just spoken. "Before his passing, Blue—" J.R. corrected himself. "—Tyrell came to me and uh, we talked." Effie Mae raised her head. "He uh, asked me if I would eulogize his funeral . . . given our uh, *odd* relationship." He shifted his eyes to Effie Mae seeing her face again hidden. "And uh, surprisingly I felt honored." J.R. let out a nervous chuckled. "So uh, I stand here today truly honored to be speaking on behalf of Tyrell Lee Jones." Effie Mae again looked up at him, her eyes flooded with tears. She smiled. J.R. continued.

"Tyrell's initial plan was for him to write his own eulogy, but uh, after being unable to find the words to uh, flatter himself—" He half-heartedly chuckled. "—those were Tyrell's words not mines." Effie Mae giggled silently through her tears. "He decided instead—" J.R. took a deep breath and looked at Effie Mae. "—to write a love letter to the woman he loved." She began weeping. "So uh, I've been instructed by Tyrell to read the letter on his behalf." J.R.'s mouth dried. He coughed. "And uh, afterwards his uh, jazz band will play Blue's favorite piece— with his cousin Melvin Jones playing Blue's saxophone." He again paused. "Ahem!" He cleared his throat then took a swallow of water from the glass sitting on the podium as he prepared himself for the reaction he knew Effie Mae would have in response to hearing Blue's love-filled words. J.R. took another deep breath and began reading:

*"Effie Mae was the name I heard when I looked up and saw the face of the woman who would redefine me from a man who was looking for love; to a man who found the love of his life. Before you Baby girl, life was something I lived. After you, life became something I loved living."*

"Ahhhhhhhh! Effie Mae cried out. J.R. looked briefly at her then continued.

*"Having you in my life made everyday feel like Christmas and you were the best present under my tree. If I'd lived to be a hundred those years would never be equivalent to one day spent with you. If I had the choice to live twenty more years of my life without you or die after spending the time with you I was blessed to have—I would choose to die.* Effie Mae's cries echoed throughout the sanctuary. *"We pledged our love when we chose to be married in spirit, and it's with love that I pledge my love to you again."* A lump formed in J.R.'s throat as he continued reading. *"Baby girl, my life was without meaning until I met you. You're like the blood that flows warm in my veins; the rhythm by which my heart beats; the air that fills my lungs every time I breath; the beautiful sound of sweetness every time you speak; My one wish in life is to wake up to your beautiful, smiling face every morning until I wake up no more. You hold my heart in the palms of your hands and Baby girl, you have made me the happiest man in this world. So today, I pledge my love and my life to you Effie Mae Smith."* J.R. swallowed the seemingly growing lump in his throat as his eyes moistened and he fought back his tears after concluding Blue's heart-wrenching letter to the woman he loved—*Effie Mae Reed-Smith.*

Effie Mae slowly pulled away from Huck's hold, her eyes fixated on Blue's peaceful face as she walked towards the bronze colored casket surrounded by blue flowers of various sorts, accented with an array of white flowers. She lovingly smiled when seeing him adorned in the clothing he'd worn the day of their *spiritual commitment*.

All eyes watched as she leaned over and kissed Blue lightly on the lips then gazed upon the man she deeply loved through tear filled eyes. She applied a second kiss to his lips before speaking.

*"Blue, Tyrell Lee Jones I love you baby. If I could give you days from my own life so yours could be longer I would. You are my reason for waking up each and every morning. You put the smile in my heart that gave my life new meaning, and I wouldn't change that for nothing in the world,and I promised you that I would be the best wife ever to you baby. You hold my heart in the palms of your hands Blue, and you made me the happiest woman in the world. So baby I will always pledge my love and my life to you — Tyrell Lee Jones."*

Effie Mae looked silently upon her *spiritual* husband as emotional pain ripped through her heart, rendering her unable to remove her eyes from Blue's face.

"Blue!" She cried out. "Come back Blue . . . I need you baby! Blue! Come back!" Effie Mae screamed out. "Noooooooo!" Huck quickly stood, moving towards her—catching her seconds after she collapsed, falling in his arms. J.R. hurried from the pulpit in response to Effie Mae's expected response. Pete and Annie Mae also rushed to her aid.

"I got her." Huck said as tears rolled down his handsome face. Melvin watched with concern then removed Blue's shiny brass saxophone from its case. He gestured to the band making their way to the front of the church—the pianist being seated at the piano. The band watched as Melvin nervously raised Blue's horn to his lips and began playing. They joined in.

Mr. White smirked as he inwardly rejoiced, watching as Huck moved hastily through the sanctuary carrying Effie Mae in his arm as the soothing sound of the jazz filled the church's acoustics, silencing the chaotic chatter in the sanctuary. He knew for certain the jazz club now belonged to him.

Huck quickly exited through the front doors of the church as he headed out to his car parked midway down the block. J.R. hurried ahead and opened the car door. Annie Mae and Pete followed. They watched as Huck lowered Effie Mae's limp body onto the front seat then rushed around to the drivers side and got in and sped away.

———————————

Seated on the side of the bed, Huck watched with worried eyes as Effie Mae lay sleeping in the upstairs apartment at the jazz club, still wearing her black dress. Annie Mae and Pete—also present in that apartment, watched as Huck sat guard over Effie Mae.

"Blue!" Effie Mae called out as she began to awaken.

"Effie Mae!"

"Huck?" She said in response to hearing his voice. "What you doing in my bed? You can't be in here trying to love on me—" Annie Mae's mouth quickly opened. Pete grinned.

"Effie Mae . . . ain't nobody trying to love on you girl!" Huck stated, humor. "Wake up!"

"Where's my baby sister and Pete?"

"We over here!" Annie Mae said. "You alright Effie Mae?"

"I don't know Annie Mae—what happen?" Huck intervened.

"You passed out at the church . . . I brought you home so you could lay down get some rest." Effie Mae smiled.

"Thank you Huck."

"Love on you." He said silently chuckling. "You ain't ever had no problem with me loving on you before." Annie Mae's jaw dropped.

"Huck . . . ain't my family in here?"

"Look here Sister-in-law." Pete said grinning. "You want me and Annie Mae to come back later, give you Huck some time alone?" He teased.

"Pete!" Annie Mae yelled.

"What? I ain't doing nothing but playing with your sister, Annie Mae."

"Sometimes I have to watch Huck." Effie Mae said blushing. Huck looked at her with objective eyes.

"Effie Mae . . . you got to watch me?" He cunningly grinned. "Girl you something else." Effie Mae heard the many of voices downstairs.

"What's going on Huck?"

"You got a whole lot of people downstairs waiting to see you girl, give you their condolences for Ol' Blue. What you want to do?" She slowly sat up.

"I guess I'm gon have to go down there and see them." She looked down at her black dress. "I guess I need to wash up and get out of this dress first." Pete stood.

"Well Sister-in-law now that we know you alright me and Annie Mae gon head on downstairs." He shifted his eyes to Annie Mae. "Melvin? Is that what he said his name was Annie Mae?"

"Yeah that's what he said Pete."

"Melvin's Blue's cousin." Effie Mae said shifting her eyes briefly to Huck.

"I thought he put me in the mind of somebody." Pete said nodding hiw heda. "Anyway, Melvin said something about bringing out some food—said he was getting ready to start feeding folks." Pete rubbed his stomach. "That sound like music to my ears cause I'm hungry!" He took hold of Annie Mae's hand and assisted her to her feet. "We gon head on downstairs Sister-in-law—"

"You gon be alright Effie Mae?" Annie Mae asked, worried.

"I don't know what I'm gon be Annie Mae." Effie Mae said laying back down.

"You need me to stay up here with you Effie Mae?" Annie Mae asked shifting her eyes to Huck, looking at him with suspicion. Huck chuckled, humored by her protectiveness of her big sister.

"You and Pete go head on so y'all can eat." Effie Mae in response to her baby sister's concern. Annie Mae again shifted her eyes to Huck.

"You sure Effie Mae?"

"Yeah little girl I'm gon be alright."

"Yeah she gon be alright." Huck said mocking her. "You go on downstairs with Pete so y'all can eat." He shifted his eyes to Effie Mae and silently chuckled. "That man said he was hungry."

"Stop Huck." Effie Mae said in response to him teasing her baby sister.

"What?" Huck said amused. "Pete said he was hungry you heard him." He half heartedly grinned then looked at Pete with seriousness. "Y'all go ahead on and eat." Pete shifted his eyes to Effie Mae then again to Huck. "I'll have your sister-in-law downstairs in fifteen minutes, she know I ain't gon leave her up here by herself." He looked at Effie Mae. "Ain't that right?" She smiled. "Get up."

"I ain't ready to get up Huck."

"Come on now Effie Mae, get up girl!" She looked at him then slowly sat up, positioning herself on the side of the bed next to him. She looked over at Annie Mae and Pete still waiting at the door.

"I'll be down in fifteen minutes—" Effie Mae said shifted her eyes to Huck. "—like Huck said." Pete glanced briefly at Huck.

"Alright then Sister-in-law—" Pete glanced briefly to Huck. "—we gon be downstairs eating."

"Alright Pete." Effie Mae stated.

"Yeah . . . alright Pete." Huck mocked. Pete stared at him, offended by the humorous smile on his face.

"Fifteen minutes right?" Pete said looking into Huck's amused eyes.

"Give or take." Huck replied slightly grinning. Annie Mae shifted her worried eyes over to her big sister as Pete opened the door.

"I'm gon be down there Annie Mae—you and Pete go on." Effie Mae said humored by her baby sister's protectiveness.

"Effie Mae a grown woman . . . she gon be alright." Pete said giving Huck a final stare before he and Annie Mae exited the apartment closing the door behind them.

• • • •

Tears erupted from Effie Mae's eyes as she arrived downstairs fifteen minutes later escorted by Huck—seeing the enormous crowd of Blue's patrons, friends and family standing to their feet and applauding. Effie Mae looked up at the band and recalled the day of Blue's final performance—her crying intensified.

"I'm glad to see you alright sweetie." Melvin said applying a kiss to Effie Mae's cheek as he led her and Huck to a table in front of the stage where Annie Mae, Pete and Buckeye were already seated. "What y'all drinking tonight?" Melvin asked then swiftly turned to Effie Mae. "You know I wasn't talking to you right?" She giggled.

"Yeah Melvin I know that."

"I don't know what they drinking Melvin—" Huck said glancing over at Buckeye, seated next to Pete. "—but you can bring me and Buckeye a bottle of scotch." Pete abruptly turned to Effie Mae.

"You gon be alright with that Sister-in-law? I know you and that scotch don't get along—"

"Yeah she gon be alright." Huck said looking Pete in the eyes. "I ain't gon let her—" Pete cut him off.

"You ain't gon let her?" He looked at Huck with doubt. Huck shifted his eyes to Buckeyes than again to Pete offended by him minimizing his importance in Effie Mae's life. He cunningly grinned then embraced Effie Mae in his arms and romantically kissed her. Annie Mae's eyes widened and her mouth flung open as she witnessed the intimate exchange. Pete gave no reaction to Huck's intentional taunting— ignoring the gloating smile on Huck's handsome face as the kiss ended.

"You see Pete—" Huck slightly chuckled. "—the scotch is for me and Buckeye." He shifted his eyes to Buckeye and cunningly grinned. "Unless you ready to grow some hair on your chest." Pete glanced over at Buckeye, uneasy by Huck's emasculating words.

"Naw man I don't need it." Pete again shifted his eyes to Buckeye then back to Huck in rebuttal to his offensive statement. "You see Huck—my chest already look like a bear's." Huck tilted his head.

"Is that right?" Melvin quickly intervened seeing tempers about to spiral out of control.

"How about I just bring a bottle of scotch and three glasses?" He stated nervously.

"Yeah Melvin you do that." Huck said glaring at Pete.

"Oh uh, Effie Mae I meant to tell you—"

"Tell me what Melvin?" He leaned down and whispered in her ear. She looked up and in the direction of the front entrance seeing Daniel standing there. She nodded, giving Melvin permission to let him come over to the table.

"You sure?"

"Yeah Melvin it's okay." He waved his hand beckoning Daniel over then walked away headed for the bar to retrieve the bottle of scotch—and three shot glasses. Huck watched through envious eyes as Daniel approached.

"You doing alright Effie Mae?" Daniel asked, his eyes displaying concern. He momentarily shifted his eyes over at Huck, uneasy by his presence. "I'm sorry about Blue, I know how much he meant to you, if you need anything . . . a shoulder to cry on—" Daniel teased. "—all you got to do is ask." He silently gazed at Effie Mae, his lingering love still evident. "I mean it Effie Mae . . . if you need me I'm here." She looked at him and smiled. Huck stared at Daniel as he listened to his subtle pleading.

"Thank you Mr. Daniel . . . how Ms. Geraldine doing?"

"Better, but she got a long ways to go before she can even think about coming home!" He stated looking around the table at Effie Mae's companions—stopping short of Huck. "I got D.J. out in the car with Millie Ann . . . is it alright if I bring him in so you can see him?" Effie Mae's eyes lit up.

"I can go out there and see my baby Mr. Daniel that way I can see my baby Millie Ann too."

"Naw you go ahead and stay right where you at Effie Mae, I'll bring that boy in here to you." Daniel said glancing around the club at the many patrons indulging in various types of alcoholic beverages. "I wouldn't even think about bringing Millie Ann in this place." He scowled. "But I'll tell her you said hi."

"Thank you Mr. Daniel and tell my baby Millie Ann I said as soon as I'm feeling better I gon come to the house and see all my babies."

"Alright Effie Mae I sure will do that."

"Yeah you do that Daniel." Huck stated sarcastically. "And tell Effie Mae's babies Huck said hi too." Daniel ignored his bothersome words.

"Let me just run out here and get this boy so I can get him—in and out because I know Melvin don't want me to have him in here for too long, not with them selling liquor in this place."

"That's right!" Melvin said as he returned to the table curious of Daniel's visit. "Our customers come here to enjoy the sweet sound of jazz, and to enjoy a shot or two of something that's gon make that music sound even sweeter." He smiled. "So if we gon keep packing the house, having that liquor license is a must! So Daniel you make that visit sweet and short—real short." He turned to Effie Mae. "You understand what I'm saying don't you Effie Mae?"

"Yeah Melvin I understand." She smiled as Melvin again walked away.

"I'll be right back then Effie Mae." Huck watched as Daniel hurried away, exiting the club—returning minutes later carrying the toddler in his arms. A huge smile stretched across Effie Mae's face as Daniel handed her the smiling toddler. Melvin observed from the bar where he held a bottle of scotch waiting for Daniel to leave, refusing to bring the liquor over in the presence of the child.

"Look at my baby." Effie Mae said kissing him on the cheek. D.J. looked at her and giggled then cooed. "You see my baby Annie Mae?" Annie Mae's jaw dropped.

"Effie Mae that's your baby? By who?" She looked at Huck. Pete shifted his eyes to Daniel then back to Effie Mae's secret child.

"I love you D.J. baby." Effie Mae said kissing him on his forehead. He reached his chubby hands towards her mouth and tried to grabbed her lips then giggled. Effie Mae smiled and looked up at Daniel.

"Mr. Daniel this my baby sister Annie Mae and my brother-in-law Pete." They looked at Daniel but gave no reply.

"It's nice to finally meet some of Effie Mae's family." Daniel said delighted to meet them. "I've known Effie Mae all these years and I ain't ever met any of her people." A huge smile hightlighted his face as he gazed into Effie Mae's hazel brown eyes. Huck looked at him and titled his head.

"Is that right?" He said bothered by Daniel's inclusion in Effie Mae's family. Daniel shifted his eyes briefly over at him then turned to Pete and Annie Mae.

"You got something to tell us Sister-in-law?" Pete asked recalling the conversation they'd had the previous year regarding D.J. being Effie Mae's son. He also remembered her denial. Huck looked at Pete and quietly chuckled then waited to hear Effie Mae's explanation of her mysterious son.

"Mr. Daniel is my baby boy's Daddy." Annie Mae gasped. Huck laughed out loud.

"Okay Sister-in-law tell me this." Pete looked at Daniel with curiosity. "Just who is Mr. Daniel? We ain't never heard you make mention of that man." Huck again looked at her and humorously waited for her response.

"Mr. Daniel's . . . J.R.'s cousin." Annie Mae gasped a second time.

"Effie Mae!" She scowled. "J.R.'s cousin?" Effie Mae disregarded her young sister's objection. Huck silently laughed as he observed the amusing fiasco.

"Sister-in-law—" Pete looked at her with judgmental eyes. "—you know I ain't ever judged you before." He shifted his displeased eyes to Daniel then again to Effie Mae. "Now I know the Parker family ain't ever believed in divorce." He turned at Annie Mae. "But as much as I love this girl right here, if she ever dishonored me like you done J.R.—" Pete stared Effie Mae in the eyes. "—I'd divorce her faster than a tornado can run through Kansas."

"Effie Mae—" Annie Mae said shocked. "—what was you thinking?" She looked at Daniel and thought how much older he was than her big sister. Pete noticed the embarrassed look on Daniel's face.

"That's enough Annie Mae." Pete said when seeing the embarrassing look on Daniel's face.

"No wonder you didn't want Momma to know who D.J. was!"

"Momma know all about D.J., Annie Mae and Mr. Daniel." Annie Mae again gasped.

"What?" She said raising her voice. "Momma know . . . and she didn't say nothing about it to me!" She turned at Pete. "Wait 'til we get back home Pete—I can't believe Momma knew about this and didn't say nothing to me!" Huck watched in silence, humored by Annie Mae's animated responses. He looked up at Daniel standing slightly over him and titled his head. Effie Mae noticed Melvin watching in the distance holding up the bottle of scotch and three glasses.

"I see Melvin looking over this way, so you gon have take my baby out of here."

"Yeah Daniel get y'all baby out of here." Huck said looking at him with threatening eyes. "I'm thirsty." He shifted his eyes to Pete and awaited his reply. Pete ignored him.

"I can't wait 'til I see Momma—"

"Annie Mae!"

"What Pete?"

"You want to leave here tonight girl?"

"No!" She pouted. "I want to stay here with my big sister."

"Then stop all that noise or we gon be pulling out of here heading back home real quick!" Annie Mae glanced briefly at D.J. then to Daniel and again to Effie Mae but said nothing further. Effie Mae kissed her baby boy on the cheek. He giggled then looked at her with unfamiliarity. "I love you D.J." She said placing another kiss on his soft cheek before handing him back to Daniel.

"Let me know when you ready to talk Effie Mae." Daniel said unable to resist staring at the woman who held his heart.

"Give me a few weeks Mr. Daniel if that's okay."

"Yeah Effie Mae that fine, whenever you ready just let me know." He continued his gaze. "You take care Effie Mae and I'll be waiting to hear from you." Daniel leaned over and kissed her lightly on the cheek ignoring Huck's intimidating stare. "Say bye to your Momma, D.J." Daniel said holding his son's chubby hand, waving goodbye.

"Bye my sweet baby." Effie Mae said as he smiled then giggled. An affectionate smile formed on Daniel face as he observed Effie Mae's loving exchange with their son. His attention drew to Melvin walking towards the table with the bottle of scotch and glasses.

"Well, it was good meeting some of Effie Mae's family." Daniel said to turning to Pete and Annie Mae.

"Same here." Pete replied, shifting his eyes to Effie Mae. Annie Mae remained silent. She watched with disapproval as Daniel departed from the club, her newly discovered nephew in his arms.

"Effie Mae how old is that man?" She asked troubled by the age difference. Huck turned to Effie Mae and waited to hear her reply. Buckeye remained mute, strangely amused by the entire awkward event. "And how come that old man got your baby?" Huck quietly chuckled.

Effie Mae ignored her baby sister's probing questions as friends of Blue's and patrons of the jazz club approached to express their deepest condolences.

# Chapter Twenty-One

Melvin rushed from the kitchen on his way to the club's front entrance in response to the continued pounding on the door. He peeped through the peephole seeing Mr. White standing on the other side accompanied by an unfamiliar White gentleman wearing an expensive suit and carrying a black brief case. He unlocked and opened the door allowing them to enter.

"Good morning Mr. White." Melvin said curious of his reason for being there given his last reprehensible encounter with both sons, over Effie Mae. Melvin also wondered of the gentleman accompanying him. "Can I help you with something Mr. White?"

"Morning Melvin . . . this here's Mr. Garrett my attorney."

"How you doing Mr. Garrett?" Melvin said awaiting further explanation from Mr. White for his early morning visit.

"I'm well and how are you this morning Mr. uh—"

"Jones—Melvin Jones."

"Please to meet you Mr. Jones." The two men shook. Melvin again turned to Mr. White.

"Did you need something Mr. White?"

"Yeah Melvin I do." He said shifting his eyes to his attorney then again to Melvin. "Since Tyrell wasn't legally married to that woman and there's no will . . . that I know of—" Mr. White again glanced over at Mr. Garrett. "—it looks like this jazz club is mines and Tyrell's mother of course." He looked in the direction of the stairs. "Where's Henry Lee? I don't want him giving me any trouble about this either!"

"I think he might be upstairs if you want to speak to him." Melvin shifted his eyes over to Mr. Garrett as he awaited Mr. White's reply.

"Why would I need to speak to that no good hustler?" He stated. "I don't have to speak to Henry Lee about a damn thing—what for he ain't nobody!" Mr. White yelled. "And as soon as Mr. Garrett here gets all the legal documents in order I'll be taking this place over." Melvin's jaw dropped, shocked by Mr. White's unforseen announcement.

"Now what you can tell Henry Lee is that apartment upstairs he got that woman living in—that's mines too." Melvin looked briefly over at Mr. Garrett, stunned my Mr. White's bold statement. "Tell him me and Rosalyn's coming back here in about a week or two and we're moving in—" A callous look displayed on Mr. White's face. "—and I want that gold digger out of there before we get here."

"Hold on Mr. White." Melvin said no longer able to hold his piece. "Blue loved Effie Mae and it ain't no way he would've ever left this world without making a way for her to keep this jazz club and that apartment." Mr. White looked at Mr. Garrett and smirked.

"Well Tyrell's not here to substantiate that—now is he?" Mr. Garrett nodded confirming his client's statement. "And until somebody show me papers proving otherwise I want that whore—" Melvin cut him off.

"Whore?" He said frowning, infuriated by Mr. White's biting words.

"That's what I said ain't it?" He said looking Melvin squarely in the eyes daring him to continue defending Effie Mae's honor. Melvin's fury magnified.

"Like I said—" Mr. White continued his face off with Melvin. "—until anybody can show me papers saying this place belongs to that whore—" He daringly emphasized. "—this club belongs to me and I'm prepared to do whatever it takes to keep it!" Melvin gave no reply. He walked quietly over to the bar, a deadly gaze beaming from his eyes as Mr. White took a visual inventory of the club. "I can see a lot of changes need to be made in this place too." He stated continuing to look around. "Kind of tacky for my taste."

"Mr. White?" Mr. Garrett said interrupting his triumphed moment when seeing Melvin reach underneath the counter retrieving what looked like a .22 caliber pistol. "Perhaps we should leave here now." Mr. Garrett's eyes remained on Melvin. "I think it would be to our benefit if we wait until we hear back from Mrs. Smith after she's obtained the appropriate documents, if indeed they do exist?" Mr. White turned to his attorney hearing the sound of fear in his voice. He shifted his eyes quickly to Melvin when seeing fear in Mr. Garrett's eyes fixated on the cocked pistol gripped in Melvin's right hand aimed in the direction of both men.

"Now Melvin—" Mr. White said looking down the barrel of the gun. "—you work with me on this and I'll let you keep your job, might even cut you in on this place." He looked up the stairs hoping his offer of betrayal hadn't been heard by Huck. Melvin ignored his unscrupulous offer as he angrily glared at the two men.

"Mr. White?" Mr. Garret stated nervously. "I do believe it would be in both our best interest if we vacated the premises now."

"Think about what I said Melvin." Mr. White said as he and Mr. Garrett walked swiftly in the direction of the front door. Melvin slowly followed—his gun still drawn.

"Uh, Mr. Jones—" Mr. Garret stated. "—we'll await Mrs. Smith's call whenever she's—" He hurried out the door, accompanied by Mr. White when hearing the gun cock. Melvin watched as they climbed in Mr. Garrett's silver Mercedes Benz parked out front and sped away.

"Bastard!" Melvin shouted thinking out loud. He closed and locked the door then un-cocked is pistol and as he walked back over to the bar, returning the pistol back underneath the counter. His mind raced as he hurried up the stairs to deliver Mr. White's message to take over the jazz club, to Effie Mae. "Effie Mae!" Melvin shouted pounding frantically on the locked door, unsure if Huck might possibly be inside. "Effie Mae wake up!" The door abruptly opened. Huck stood on the other side wearing a black, ribbed tank top and navy blue pin-striped pants.

"What's going on Melvin?" He asked awakened by the disruptive banging. A uneasy look formed on his face when seeing rage burning in Melvin's eyes.

"Huck man, your father just left here . . . him and his attorney." Huck tilted his head.

"Is that right?"

"Talking about this club belongs to him and my Auntie Rosalyn now!"

"He said what?" Huck said stunned by his father's unthinkable words.

"Man he said he owns this place Huck!" Melvin's breaths deepened as his anger grew. "Told me to let you know he was moving in that apartment in a couple weeks . . . said he wanted Effie Mae out!" Huck again tilted his head.

"Is that right?" He looked briefly inside at Effie Mae and shook his head in disbelief. "That girl's got enough to worry about."

"Who is that Huck?" Effie Mae asked still half asleep.

"It's Melvin."

"Melvin? Is something wrong?"

"Nothing I can't handle—go back to sleep." Huck said masking his anger not wanting to upset her. He again turned to Melvin. "Thanks Melvin."

"What you gon do Huck?" Melvin asked speaking just above a whisper.

"I'm gon call Mr. White on his bluff." Huck said clueless on how exactly he planned on doing it. Melvin saw fury growing in Huck's eyes. "I'll bring Mr. White to his knees before I let him hurt that girl Melvin, believe that.

---

"Huck man, I can't believe Tyrell would put Effie Mae in a position where your father or anybody else could throw that girl out on the streets!" Buckeye said as he shared a bottle of scotch with his old friend at the jazz club as the band continued hornoring Blue by playing his favorite jazz tunes—three weeks after his passing away. "Man I know Blue and he loved that girl too much to let that happen." Huck looked his old friend in the eyes as he listened to his logic.

"You think I'd let that happen Buckeye?" Huck said filling his glass with scotch. "You know me better than that." He tossed back the shot. "And I know my brother—and I know he did something to make sure Effie Mae got everything he owned."

"You think maybe he got too sick to do anything Huck?" Buckeye asked as he refilled his empty glass.

"Naw Buckeye it's like you said . . . Blue loved Effie Mae too much to let that happen." Huck remained deep in thought as he stared at his empty glass. "If it took Blue his last breath, he was gon make sure Effie Mae got whatever was his." Huck said continuing his gazed at the unfilled glass. "He wouldn't just leave that girl with nothing, especially knowing Mr. White's been waiting on him to die so he could get his greedy hands on this club." He picked up the bottle of scotch, his thoughts being occupied with genuine concern over his father actually stealing Blue's assets that were rightfully meant for Effie Mae's.

"Huck man—" Buckeye's eyes widened as he watched Huck overfilling the shot glass spilling good scotch on the table—unnoticed by Huck. "–you spilling that man!" Buckeye said raising his voice, yanking the bottle from his hand. Huck's eyes shifted to his overfilled glass. He quickly gathered a stack of cocktail napkins off the table and began soaking up the wasted beverage.

"It would hurt Blue's heart Buckeye if he knew his daddy would even think of doing something to hurt that girl." Buckeye closely watched as Huck absorbed good scotch into paper napkins. He hurriedly gulped down the contents of his glass then quickly poured himself another shot minutes before Huck hurled his scotch into his mouth and again reached for the bottle, still deep in thought.

"Let me get that for you man." Buckeye stated, quickly grabbing the bottle, refilling his old friend's glass trying to avoid another spill and waste of good scotch. Huck vaguely noticed.

"I know Blue—" Huck said as his mind searched hard for answers. "—and I know he had to have told somebody something." He tossed back the shot poured by Buckeye then rolled his glass between his fingers. "Melvin—" Huck stated. "—if Blue told anybody anything it would be him."

"You think so Huck?" Buckeye asked pouring himself another shot. "Well I sure hope you find out something soon because man it looks like your father plan on taking this club and everything else Tyrell owned." Buckeye's eyes widened with concern.

"Damn if I let that happen Buckeye."

"Hey Huck." Melvin said as he approached. "It's a lady over at the bar say she know you."

"A lady?" Huck blushed then cleverly smiled. "Ol' Huck know a whole lot of ladies Melvin." He said shifting his eyes over to Buckeye. The two men cunningly grinned.

"Well this ain't the type of woman I've ever seen you with Huck." A mysteriously look appeared on Huck's face. He again shifted his eyes to Buckeye. Buckeye humped his shoulders.

"What type of lady is that Melvin?" Huck asked with interest.

"This lady looks like she been around the block a few times—quite a few times." Melvin chuckled.

"Did she give you her name Melvin?"

"Yeah she gave it to me." Melvin tried to remember. "Let's see—I think she said her name was uh, Rita?"

"Rita?" Huck again shifted his eyes to Buckeye. "How old do you think Rita is Melvin?"

"I don't know . . . maybe in her mid to late fifties."

"Where she at?"

"She sitting down on the far end of the bar near the stage." Huck looked in the direction of the bar, identifying the woman as his mother. He shook his head, agitated.

"Damn shame."

"Do you know her Huck?"

"Yeah Melvin I know her." Melvin's eyes widened.

"You do?" He said shocked. "What you want me to tell her?"

"Is she drunk?"

"Not yet, but she definitely working on it."

"Go ahead bring her on over Melvin." Buckeye hesitated, hoping Huck's acquaintance with the woman wouldn't bring troubled.

"You sure man?"

"Yeah Melvin I'm sure."

"Then I'll be right back with her." Melvin shifted his worried eyes to Buckeye then walked away.

"You said you know who she is Huck?" Buckeye asked eager to know who the woman could be.

"Yeah Buckeye . . . you know her too."

"I do?" He said watching in anticipation as Melvin waved his hand gaining the woman's attention then beckoning her over. She stood and began her journey over to Huck's table. Buckeye's jaw dropped when laying eyes on the mysterious female.

"Huck man, ain't that your momma?" He said surprised by her presence. Huck looked briefly at her as she approached.

"Yeah Buckeye, that's her."

"Hey Henry Lee!" She said staggering over to the table. "Boy where your Ol' hateful ass been hiding?" Huck shifted his eyes to Buckeye. "I ain't seen your sorry ass in must be over two years." She stared at him. "Ol Bastard."

"Sit down Momma." Huck said annoyed. Buckeye stood and pulled out a chair.

"Here you go Ms. Rita . . . go ahead and have a seat." She glared at him with unfamiliarity as she sat across the table from Huck. Buckeye being seated to her right.

"Ms. Rita?" She said gawking at him. "Do I know you?"

"Yeah Momma you know him." She scowled.

"I do?"

"That's Lawrence, Momma."

"Lawrence? You mean that little boy had those big pop eyes—that's him?" She looked at Buckeye with mistrust. Huck silently chuckled. "How you been doing Lawrence?" She asked frowning. "I see you still got them big ass eyes."

"Momma!"

"What little boy?"

"Leave that man alone Momma."

"I'm doing good Ms. Rita."

"What you doing here Momma?"

"What you mean what I'm doing here?" She looked at the bottle of scotch sitting in the center of the table. "What's that y'all drinking Henry Lee?" Ms. Rita asked fixating her eyes on Buckeye's shot glass filled to the rim seconds before reaching over and snatching it up then hurling the brown liquid into her mouth, sitting the glass back on the table. Buckeye looked swiftly to Huck—aggravated by his mother's unanticipated move. Huck silently chuckled.

"You didn't answer me Momma, I asked what you was doing here?"

"I heard about your brother . . . Rosalyn's boy, what was his name again?" Ms. Rita asked refilling Buckeye's glass as she spoke then tossing it into her mouth. "Taiwan? Tynell? Toenail—" Huck intervened.

"Tyrell Momma, but what's that got to do with you?"

"What you mean what's that got to do with me? That was my husband's son wasn't it?" Huck tilted his head and stared at her. "What the hell you looking at me like that for Henry Lee?"

"Your husband?" Huck poured himself a drink. "When was the last time Mr. White was your husband Momma?"

"I came here so I could go to that boy's funeral and give my condolences." She ignored Huck's question.

"Condolences?" Huck shifted his eyes to Buckeye then again turned to his mother. "Give your condolences to who Momma . . . Daddy and his woman?" She again ignored Huck's question.

"When is the funeral anyway?"

"Momma they buried Ol' Blue a few weeks ago."

"They did!" She said surprised, again shifting her eyes to the bottle of scotch. "I sure wish somebody had called and told me."

"Since you missed the funeral Momma ain't no reason for you to stay."

"I'll stay here if I want to Henry Lee, you don't own this damn city!" Huck shifted his eyes over at Buckeye then back to his mother.

"How long you think it's gon be before you run into Daddy and Ms. Jones, Momma?"

"The talk around Buffalo is that your daddy inherited this jazz club." Ms. Rita said picking up the bottle of scotch and pouring herself another shot in Buckeye's glass. He shifted his widened eyes to Huck in response to her drinking up their scotch. Huck signaled him with a nod to let her have it. "And whatever your daddy owns, as his wife—" She swallowed the strong liquid without hesitation. "—I own." Huck titled his head.

"Is that right?"

"What you mean is that right? You know damn well it's right!" Huck looked in his mother's glassy red eyes. "He never did divorce me you know.

"Divorce you?" He looked at her with skepticism. "Divorce works both ways Momma." She stared at him.

"So legally—" Ms. Rita said dismissing Huck's common sense suggestion. "—Henry Lee White Sr. is still my husband." Huck shifted his eyes to Buckeye. He humped his shoulders in response to Ms. Rita's truth.

"Last I heard Momma—" Huck shifted his eyes briefly to his old friend then again looked at his mother. "—your husband was still looking for papers proving he owned anything, so before you start drinking up the inventory make sure your Mr. White got proof he's the rightful owner." Ms. Rita looked at him with inquisitive eyes.

"You know something I don't know Henry Lee?" He stared momentarily at her, but gave no reply. She turned to Buckeye and tried to read the tell-tale look on his face. He looked away not wanting to get involved. "Anyway—" She turned her attention back to Huck. "I also think it's time you to started being a father to those kids you and Benita brought in this world . . . my grandchildren." She shifted her eyes to the bottle of scotch. Huck looked at his old friend and nodded, giving his okay for his mother have another shot. Buckeye reluctantly picked up the bottle and filled his glass, Ms. Rita now used as her own.

"What you talking about Momma?"

"I saw Benita before I left town." She guzzled down the shot. "Those kids sure have grown." She said shifting her eyes to the bottle of scotch then to Buckeye. He hesitated then looked at Huck before pouring her another drink per Huck's subtle nod. Buckeye watched unenthusiastically as his favorite beverage again filled Ms. Rita's glass. "I think Benita said James was nineteen and Marcia—I believe is twenty, if I'm remembering it right."

"Was you sober Momma?" Buckeye grinned in response to Huck's blunt question. She looked briefly at Huck, but disregarded his question. "You know Benita ain't ever wanted them kids to have nothing to do with me Momma—what's changed?"

"The talk around town is that her and that boy she left you for and married, got divorced last year." Buckeye observed the emotionless gaze in Huck's eyes as he tried to mask the hurt from being deprived a relationship with his children.

"Let me get that for you man." Buckeye said quickly retrieving the bottle of scotch when seeing Huck reach for it. He poured his old friend another shot, paranoid of another possible spill.

"I guess she must be thinking since you and her have those kids—" Ms. Rita licked her lips as she intently focused on the scotch. "—it's your turn to be husband and daddy."

"When you leaving Momma?"

"You trying to get rid of me Henry Lee—" She asked snatching the bottle of out of Buckeye's hand, raising it to her mouth. Buckeye's jaw dropped as he watched her guzzled down about an ounce of the powerful liquid then refilled her glass. Buckeye looked quickly to Huck, his eyes requesting he intervene.

"I ain't trying to get rid of you Momma." Huck said please to see her. "I'm just trying to save you from being hurt." Frowns of defiance formed on her forehead.

"Hurt by who?"

"Now you know if Mr. White's here . . . so is Ms. Jones, you gon be able to handle that Momma?"

"What the hell you mean am I gon be able to handle that?" Ms. Rita said raising her voice. "I been handling it all these years ain't I?" She again reached for the bottle of scotch. Huck slid it away.

"Is that how you gon handle it Momma?" He held up the bottle. "With this stuff right here?"

"Don't you worry about how the hell I'm gon handle it little boy!" She yelled. "And you put that damn bottle back on this table before I jump across this table and knock the hell out of you little boy!" Buckeye's jaw dropped, alarmed by what Huck's response would be to his mother's threatening words.

"I ain't no little boy Momma." Huck said staring at her as he recalled the physical abuse she inflicted on him as a child. "I'm a grown man."

"I don't give a damn how grown you are Henry Lee, I'm still your momma!"

"I ain't gon let you hit me Momma."

"How in the hell you gon stop me little boy?"

"I ain't gon hit you—" He shifted his eyes to Buckeye then again looked at his mother. "—but I'm sure as hell gon stop you from hitting me." Buckeye watched the verbal altercation with concern.

"Ms. Rita can I drop you somewhere?" He asked trying to run interference.

"You can't drop me no damn place you Ol' popeyed bastard!" A look of warning beamed from her eyes. "You better talk to your little friend Henry Lee!" She shouted. "Over here disrespecting me talking about can he drop me someplace—hell no!" She stared angrily at Buckeye. "You can't drop me no damn place!" He looked at Huck and waited for instruction on how to diffuse the explosive situation.

"Buckeye can't disrespect you no more than you already disrespecting yourself Momma." Ms. Rita swiftly rose from the table, unbalanced.

"Don't let me have to come over there little boy!" She shouted. "I'll hit you so damn hard you gon think you been run over by a bus!" Huck abruptly stood. He looked at his mother with pity then turned to Buckeye.

"Let's go."

Huck walked away.

"Come back here Henry Lee!" His mother yelled. "Don't you walk away from me little boy!"

"It was good seeing you again Ms. Rita." Buckeye said snatching the bottle of scotch off the table before hurrying away to catch up with his old friend. Ms. Rita watched with infuriated eyes as the two men departed from the club taking with them—the bottle of scotch.

# Chapter Twenty-Two

Effie Mae ignored the ringing phone as she lay cradled in bed inside the darkened apartment, quietly weeping over the loss of Blue.

"Effie Mae!" Deborah Ann said calling through the locked door. "Effie Mae it's Deborah Ann . . . a lady called on the downstairs phone and said she's been trying to reach you for the last three days but you ain't been answering baby." Effie Mae listened, but gave no reply. "I think she said her name was Millie?" Deborah Ann continued knocking. "Effie Mae!"

"Okay." Effie Mae said in response to her persistent knocking. "Give me a minute Deborah Ann." She said rolling over on her back then sitting up in bed. Effie Mae turned on the light and tried to wipe away her tears. She looked at the clock on the nightstand, uncertain if the two o'clock time displayed—was morning or afternoon. She climbed out of bed and covered herself with the pink satin robe she picked up off the floor, continuing to wipe her reddened eyes before unlocking and opening the door.

Deborah Ann's mouth quickly opened when seeing an unkempt, disheveled, mentally drained Effie Mae standing on the other side. She also noted her red, puffy, tear-filled eyes. She hurried in the apartment preparing to console Effie Mae with a hug. Deborah Ann abruptly stopped. She covered her nose with her hand in response to the days old smell of body odor radiating from Effie Mae.

"Effie Mae girl you don't look too good." Deborah Ann said keeping her distance—grimacing as she looked around the junky, disorganized, odorous apartment.

"I'm alright Deborah Ann." Effie Mae said as Deborah Ann continued her visual inspection of the apartment, her attention being drawn to the kitchen and the multitude of dirty dishes and plates of uneaten, molded food on the table and counters. Deborah Ann's eyes widened when seeing the multitude of clothing scattered about the apartments—clean and unclean. She gasped when seeing the black dress Effie Mae wore to Blue's funeral tossed inside the trash can.

"Baby look at this place." Deborah Ann said disturbed by the abundance of filth.

"You said I had a call downstairs Deborah Ann?"

"Yeah you do." Deborah Ann sporadically held her breath trying to avoid inhaling the putrid aroma flowing throughout the apartment. "The woman on the phone said she's been calling—" Deborah Ann paused when seeing unopened mail strewn about the dirty apartment. "Effie Mae why don't you let me help you clean this place up sweetie?" She stated, sympathetically. "Should you be up here in this apartment all by yourself? Don't you have a husband somewhere in town you can go spend some time with? And where's Huck?"

"I'm okay Deborah Ann." Effie Mae said going in the kitchen, turning on the faucet and splashing cold water over her face using the kitchen towel to dry it. Deborah Ann watched in awe as Effie Mae tried to comb through her entangled hair with her finger.

"Baby you don't look maybe you should—"

"That's my momma Deborah Ann."

"Huh?" Deborah Ann said as her concern grew over Effie Mae's fragile state. "What did you say?"

"Millie Reed, that's my momma."

"Good . . . because you definitely need to talk to somebody." Deborah Ann's eyes moistened as she empathized with Effie Mae's unhealthy grieving. "Effie Mae I know Tyrell would be heartbroken if he saw how you were handling his death." Effie Mae looked at her, but said nothing. "Well I'm gon go ahead and get back downstairs—help Melvin get things ready for tonight." Deborah Ann said as she prepared to leave. She suddenly stopped and turned to Effie Mae, troubled by her deteriorating status.

"Effie Mae anytime you want to talk I'm here for you . . . girl don't shut everybody out.".

"Thank you Deborah Ann."

"Girl you know this ain't what Tyrell wanted for you."

"Tell my momma to call me up here Deborah Ann I'll answer it."

"I sure hope talking to your momma helps you Effie Mae." Deborah Ann said walking away.

"Deborah Ann—" Effie Mae called out. Deborah Ann stopped and again turned to her. "—don't uh—"

"Don't uh, what?"

"Don't tell my momma how you found me."

"Girl I wouldn't scare your momma like that!" Deborah Ann laughed out loud. "But if you keep on like this Effie Mae, I'm gon have to tell somebody, Melvin, Huck, Mr. Daniel . . . what's your husband's name?" Effie Mae giggled.

"Thank you Deborah Ann."

"You're welcome cousin." She walked over to Effie Mae and hugged her. "It's gon be alright baby." Deborah Ann again looked around the apartment. "But after you get off that phone with your momma, you get your butt in that bathtub and soak for about an hour—two!" Effie Mae's mouth flung open. "Cause baby you ain't smelling right!" Deborah Ann covered her nose and hurried from the apartment.

———————————————

Huck lay cuddled in bed with Effie Mae, asleep. Awakened by the sound of the ringing phone, he glanced quickly to Effie Mae hoping she'd not been disturbed by the sound.

"I'll get it." She said still half asleep.

"Naw I got it—go back to sleep." He said picking up the phone. "Yeah."

"Huck man it's Melvin . . . your father's down here again with his attorney." Huck tilted his head.

"Is that right?"

"What you want me to do?"

"I'll be down Melvin."

"Alright man . . . I'll let them know." Huck hung up and looked at Effie Mae seeing her eyes partially opened.

"Is something wrong Huck?"

"Don't worry about it—I'll handle it." He kissed her lightly on the cheek then climbed out of bed wearing only his black silk boxers. He retrieved his brown pinstriped pants, gold shirt and matching vest, thrown over the back of a chair and put them on before stepping into a pair of chocolate brown alligator shoes. He removed his holstered pistol from underneath the mattress and strapped it on, shifting his eyes over to Effie Mae, now asleep. Huck exited the apartment, angered at what his father was trying to do—hurrying down the stairs prepared to do battle with his awaiting opponents.

• • • •

"I don't want any trouble out of you Henry Lee!" Mr. White yelled as Huck reached the bottom step. Huck glanced briefly at Mr. Garrett standing to the left of Mr. White.

"What you doing here Mr. White?" Mr. Garrett quickly intervened.

"Mr. White Junior—I'm uh, Mr. Garrett your father's attorney." He switched his brief case from his right hand to his left and extended his hand to shake.

"You didn't answer me Mr. White." Huck said ignoring his attorney's greeting. He glared at his father who stared furiously back. Mr. Garrett's anxiety heightened when seeing the pistol holstered at Huck's side.

"I'm uh, assisting your father in—" Huck cut him off.

"In what? Trying to take what don't belong to him and throwing his son's wife out on the streets!"

"Wife!" Mr. White shouted. "That tramp ain't none of Tyrell's wife." Melvin looked at Huck with nervous eyes. He wondered if he needed to call Buckeye, knowing without doubt words like that would result in a violent altercation.

"Look here old man." Huck said exhaling through his nose. "You got one more time to let that word slip off your tongue when talking about Effie Mae!" He gazed deep into his father's eyes. "Then you gon be giving Ol' Blue my best in person." He looked over at his father's attorney. "Mr. Garrett you don't know me so I'm giving you warning—" A large lump formed in Mr. Garrett's throat. "—I want you and your client to get y'all asses out of here while you still breathing in air." Mr. Garrett shifted his eyes to Mr. White frightened by Huck's bone-chilling threat he felt certain Huck would make good on.

"I ain't afraid of you Henry Lee!" Mr. White shouted.

"Well you should be Mr. White." Huck said as his fury soared. "I don't just have my momma's good looks—" Melvin looked at him and chuckled, humored by Huck's lack of vanity. "—but I got that same rage she had in her the night she took a switchblade to your ass—damn near killed you too!" He gazed at his father without blinking. "You remember that night don't you Mr. White? It was the same night you told her you didn't give a damn about her no more."

"I'm not leaving here Henry Lee until I get what's rightfully mines!" Huck shifted his eyes to Melvin, visually instructing him to leave the room to avoid witnessing his next anticipated move. Melvin's eyes pleaded with him not to do it.

"What's it gon be Mr. Garrett?" Huck said diverting his rage to him. "You gon get your client and leave or am I gon have to forget this man is the father of my dead brother?"

"That's right Henry Lee I am!" Mr. White stated with confidence. "That's why I know this club belongs to me."

"Let me put it to you this way Mr. White—" Huck looked briefly to Melvin then turned back to his father. "—If you don't get your old ass out of here now . . . one of us gon leave here walking and the other's gon need to be carried out." Huck removed his pistol from its holster. "And I like walking." Mr. Garrett nervously intervened.

"Mr. White . . . I think perhaps we should take this gentleman's advice and leave here before something happens that neither one of us will recover from."

"Listen to your attorney Mr. White." Huck threatened. "And once you leave don't you or your attorney bring y'all asses back in here talking about taking over nothing unless you got papers proving you got the right to."

"Mr. White—" Mr. Garrett said shifting his eyes to Melvin then again to Huck. "I recommend we vacate the premises now." He grabbed hold of Mr. White's right arm. "Something tells me Mr. White Junior's bite is far worse than his bark." Mr. Garrett cautiously backed away, headed in the direction of the club's front entrance. Huck continued his visual standoff with his father Mr. Garrett approached the front door then reached behind and opened it, aggressively pulling Mr. White outside with him then promptly closing the door behind.

"Look here Melvin if they come back, unless they holding papers up to the window proving Mr. White owns this place . . . leave their asses outside." Melvin watched as Huck headed back upstairs. He breathed a sigh of relief—grateful that the altercation hadn't ended in bloodshed.

• • • •

Ten minutes after Huck returned upstairs the phone again rang. He quickly picked it up to avoid awakening Effie Mae.

"Yeah."

"Huck man it looks like it's gon be a busy morning."

"They back?" He asked reaching for his pistol.

"Naw, but your mother's down here and she brought friends."

"I'll be there in a minute Melvin."

"Alright man." Melvin hung up. Huck looked at Effie Mae still asleep and quietly climbed out of bed. He removed his gun from its holster and slid it back underneath the mattress then walked over to the door, shifting his eyes briefly at Effie Mae before exiting the apartment. He shook his head with agitation then headed downstairs to meet with his mother—and friends. Huck looked over at the bar when arriving downstairs, seeing his mother seated then shifted his eyes to the young male and female sitting at a table.

"You just miss your husband and his attorney by about ten minutes Momma." Her eyes widened.

"His attorney? What the hell he need with an attorney?"

"Naw Momma . . . Mr. Garrett ain't no divorce attorney." Huck quietly laughed. He again glanced over at the unfamiliar young adults staring at him then turned to Melvin. Melvin humped his shoulders indicating he had no idea who they were.

"What you doing here Momma? I thought you was going back home to Buffalo." She ignored him.

"James, Marcia . . . come say hi to your father." Ms. Rita stated. Huck looked at the children he'd not seen since they were toddlers. His attention diverted to the female retuning from the restroom. A large smile formed on her face when seeing him.

"Long time no see Henry Lee . . . you remember me don't you?" The female asked.

"Don't look like it's been long enough Benita." Huck said shifting his eyes to his mother. "What you doing Momma? What you bring Benita and those kids out here for?"

"Those kids have a right to know their father."

"Who said it was your place to make that happen?" He said, again looking at Benita. "I think that was decided over twenty years ago—ain't that right Benita?" James and Marcia stood as they continued their gawked at the father they never knew. Huck stared back—apprehensive about what they were about to say.

"Man I look just like you!" James said frowning. "Thing is—that until I ran into that old woman over there coming out of the liquor store claiming to be my grandmother, I never even knew you existed man!" Huck shifted his eyes to Benita then looked at his daughter who bore a striking resemblance to Mr. White.

"So I guess that means you must be my daddy too." Marcia stated, sarcastically. She looked at her mother and again to Huck then slightly tilted her head. "Damn shame." Huck laughed on the inside when seeing his mannerism in his daughter, continuing his gaze at his children—speechless.

Melvin observed the awkward reunion as he stocked the bar with various types and brands of bottled liquor. A puzzled look showed on his face as he witnessed yet another altercation centered around Huck and his family.

"Is something wrong Huck?" Effie Mae asked standing at the bottom of the stairs wearing Blue's oversized baby blue pajama pants and shirt. He abruptly turned when hearing her voice. She looked around the club at the unfamiliar individuals present. "Is those friends of Blue's?" Effie Mae asked, semi-awakened. Huck hurried over to her, troubled by her peculiar behavior and the oversized men's pajamas she wore.

"You alright Effie Mae?"

"You didn't come back Blue."

"Blue?" He shifted his eyes to Melvin then again to Effie Mae. "Come on girl let me take you back upstairs." He put his arm around her—worried about her current state of mind. He looked briefly at his children the turned and walked away.

"Now who in the hell was that heifer?" Ms. Rita asked Melvin as Huck escorting Effie Mae back upstairs.

"That was Effie Mae—Tyrell's wife." Ms. Rita frowned.

"Wife!" She yelled. "I didn't hear nothing about Rosalyn's boy being married not since that last tramp, what was her name?" She looked at Melvin then turned to Benita.

"Daphne." Melvin stated.

"Yeah that was it." Ms. Rita again looked at Melvin and the bottles of liquor. "I guess Henry Lee Sr. didn't know about Tynell's new wife since he seems to think this club belong to him . . . I mean us." She said correcting herself.

• • • •

"What's that you wearing Effie Mae?" Huck asked looking at the oversized pajamas. She looked down at her clothing.

"These was Blue's."

"Take them off!" Huck stated.

"What? Why?" A puzzled looked formed on her face.

"Do you know a minute ago you called me Blue?"

"Huh? When?"

"Take them things off?" Huck said uneasy by her odd behavior. Effie Mae looked him in the eyes, uncertain what to do. "I ain't gon tell you no more Effie Mae." She again looked down at the pajamas, but made no effort to take them off. "Effie Mae you got five seconds to take them pajamas off before I tear them off!" She gave no reply. "I mean it Effie Mae." Huck said reaching over, grabbing hold of the pajamas shirt preparing to forcefully remove it.

"Okay!" Effie Mae blurted out. She gazed into Huck's angry eyes then pulled the buttoned pajama shirt over her head—taking it off exposing her pink brassiere underneath. A dazed look remained in her eyes as she untied the string holding up the pajamas pants allowing them to drop to the floor. Huck looked at her with worry as she stepped out of the pants and stood wearing only her brassiere and matching panties.

"Go wash up, get dressed . . . I'm getting you out of here today." He said frightened by her bizarre actions. "I'm taking you there to see your kids." Effie Mae walked pass him, her eyes showing no emotion as she entered the bathroom, closing the door behind her.

––––––––––––––––––

"Uh, Effie Mae?" J.R. said startled when seeing her standing on the porch when he opened the back door on his way to the church. "How uh, how long you been standing there?" Effie Mae gave no reply. J.R.'s concern grew in response to her silence. "Did uh, somebody bring you here?" He asked noticing the blank stare in her eyes. "Why uh, don't you come inside the house." He said assisting her in the house.

"Huck." Effie Mae blurted out answeriang J.R.'s question.

"Huht?"

"Huck brought me over here."

"Oh uh, okay." J.R. said disappointed to hear of Huck's continued involvement in his wife's life. He gazed at Effie Mae, pleased by her unexpected visit. "You uh, doing alright Effie Mae?" J.R. asked as she sat on the sofa—her eyes filling with tears. J.R. sat down next to her in response to seeing her emerging tears.

"It hurts J.R.!" Effie Mae cried out, weeping. He embraced her in his arms, laying her head on his chest as thoughts of her again taking her place as his wife.

"Effie Mae I'm here . . . let me help you through this." J.R. said subtly pleading. She gave no reply. "Me and uh, Blue talked before he uh—" Effie Mae looked up at him when hearing Blue's name. "—we uh, talked and uh—"

"I wake up every morning J.R. hoping when I open my eyes the man I love gon be laying beside me." J.R.'s mouth dried. He coughed. "And when he ain't . . . I feel a pain so deep in my heart—" She looked in J.R.'s attentive eyes. "—make me wish I was dead with Blue." A frightened look emtered J.R.'s eyes.

"Effie Mae—" He said disturbed by her troubling words.

"What J.R.?"

"Your children need you!"

"My babies don't need me they got you." She stated speaking from hurt. J.R.'s mouth dried as he tried to think of what to say next. He coughed.

"Blue uh, thanked me for letting him spend time with the children." A smile slowly formed on Effie Mae's wet face.

"Blue loved my babies J.R., and my babies loved him."

"And that's why he uh, would never want you to leave them because he's no longer here." A bewildered look showed on Effie Mae's face.

"But uh, even though Blue's gone, in a way he's still here." J.R. said trying desperately to comfort his grieving wife.

"What?"

"The way you loved Blue—" J.R. carefully chose his words. "—he's gon always be with you in your heart, your memories, and—"

"That ain't the same J.R.!" Effie Mae yelled.

"Effie Mae I uh—"

"I want to hear my baby telling me he love me—" J.R. interjected.

"I uh, know that's what you want Effie Mae . . . but he can't—"

"I know that J.R.!" Effie Mae began sobbing.

"I'm here Effie Mae." J.R. said kissing her softly on the forehead.

"J.R. you know I'm engaged to Anthony?"

"Uh, Blue said you might be pregnant?" He said redirecting the conversation from Anthony. A surprised look showed on Effie Mae's face.

"Blue told you that J.R."

"Uh, yeah he did." He said electing not to tell her of Blue's admission that he couldn't father children. "Was he right?" Effie Mae smiled through her tears.

"Yeah J.R." She girlishly smiled. "I been so busy crying and missing Blue, I ain't gave no thought to me being pregnant."

"Is it ours?" He asked nervous as he waited to hear her answer. Effie Mae giggled.

"Yeah J.R. it's ours." J.R.'s face lit up, delighted by the thought of them having another child. Effie Mae recalled the talk she had with Blue about naming her baby after him—if it were a boy. "J.R. if we have us a baby boy can we name him after Blue?" J.R.'s mouth dried. He coughed.

"Uh, after Blue?"

"Please J.R."

"You uh, want us to name our son after Blue?"

"Yeah J.R." He took a deep breath as he considered Effie Mae's request with ambiguity. On the one hand, he truly understood how much it meant to her. On the other—he felt that in naming his son after Blue it could create a situation in the future he'd rather not deal with.

"Tyrell Lee Jones—Smith." J.R. said thinking out loud. He chuckled.

"What J.R.?"

"I guess if uh, we can call Anthony's son Lil' J.R.—" Effie Mae giggled. "—we can certainly name our son after Blue." An odd look showed on J.R.'s face. "Tyrell Lee Jones—Smith?" He repeated seeing the excited look in Effie Mae's eyes. "That uh, sounds like a perfect name for our son." Effie Mae's face lit up.

"Thank you J.R." She kissed him lightly on the lips. He smiled feeling victorious.

"Oh that's right, I almost forgot."

"What?"

"I uh, need to get up for a minute." He said placing a quick kiss on Effie Mae forehead before she raised her head from his chest. "I'll be right back."

"What is it J.R.?" Effie Mae said curious. J.R. hurried from the living room and headed down the hall then entered his bedroom. Seconds later he rushed out of his room carrying the large white envelope.

"This was uh, one of the last things Blue gave me before he uh—" Effie Mae's eyes dampened. "He uh, asked me to hold on to it for at least a month then give it to you, but I guess three and a half weeks is close enough." J.R. chuckled then handed her the envelope.

"Did Blue tell you what he put in here J.R.?" Effie Mae asked looking at the large envelope.

"It uh, did once contain the love letter Blue wrote." J.R. hesitated when seeing tears in Effie Mae's eyes. He again sat down, taking her in his arms. "You uh, alright?" She nodded.

"Blue really did love me J.R."

"Yeah Effie Mae he really did."

"What else did my baby put in this big Ol' envelope?" She giggled.

"Well uh, let's see." J.R. tried to remember. "There's a wedding picture of you and him." Effie Mae smiled. J.R. continued. "A picture of Blue and his horn—" She again giggled. "—and some other stuff he wanted you to have, but didn't say what it was."

"Thank you J.R." Effie Mae said kissing him on the cheek. "I ain't ready to look at it yet."

"Maybe I uh, should've waited the four weeks like Blue suggested."

"It ain't that J.R., I want to wait til I get home."

"Oh!" J.R. said surprised by her unexpected reply. "If uh, it's anything I can do to make this time easier for you uh, please let me help you." Effie Mae listened to his comforting words and for the first time appreciated them—and him.

"Hold me J.R."

"Huh?"

"Hold me."

"Uh, okay." J.R. enveloped Effie Mae in his arms and intimately held her. She laid her head on his chest and allowed him to love her. A triumphant smile highlighted J.R.'s face as he kissed his wife softly on the lips.

———————————————

"Huck man . . . how's Effie Mae doing?" Buckeye asked bothered by his old friend unusual quietness as they sat in the backroom of the Envoy Bar & Grill sharing a bottle of scotch. Huck hurled a shot of scotch in his mouth.

"You tell me Buckeye—" He refilled his glass. "—this morning she called me Blue." An odd look appeared on Buckeye's face.

"Blue . . . that don't sound good Huck." Buckeye said guzzling down his scotch and refilling his glass.

"Naw Buckeye it don't." Huck resumed his silenced as he thought of his children. Buckeye noted his old friend's glass still empty.

"Something bothering you Huck?"

"Yeah Buckeye . . . everything."

"You heard anymore from Ms. Rita?" Huck's broke his stare at the empty shot glass, looking into Buckeye's inquisitive eyes.

"Yeah, she one of them things that's bothering me." Buckeye chuckled. "She showed her ass up at the club this morning with Benita and my kids." Buckeye's jaw dropped.

"Benita? Man where your momma get Benita from?"

"I don't know where she got from Buckeye, but she need to take her back." Buckeye laughed. "And get this Buckeye, my son—"

"How old is that boy now Huck?"

"I don't know . . . eighteen, nineteen." Huck said shifting his eyes again to his empty glass. "All I know Buckeye is that my son looked at me—" He looked across the table at Buckeye. "—and told me he never knew I existed." Buckeye's eyes widened.

"What!" He shouted. "Man I always said Benita was dirty, especially after how she done you with uh, what was his name Huck?"

"Tommy."

"Yeah, Ol' pigeon-toed Tommy!" Buckeye noted the hurt look in Huck's eyes. He picked up the bottle of scotch and filled his old friend's glass before pouring himself another shot. "You know what Huck—I bet you Benita told those kids Tommy was their daddy!"

"I don't know what she told them Buckeye, but I know what she didn't." Huck said picking up the bottle preparing to pour himself another drink. He shifted his eyes to Buckeye when seeing his glass already full. He thanked him with an appreciative nod. "My son looked at me like I was stranger." Huck said flinging the scotch inside his mouth. Buckeye shook his head, sympathizing with his old friend's awkward moment.

"Man that's cold—I know that had to hurt!" Huck refilled his glass.

"What you think Buckeye?"

"Man I'm sorry."

"What you sorry for Buckeye? You didn't have nothing to do with it." He looked at Buckeye. "Did you?" The two friends laughed then turned their glasses up, guzzling down the strong alcoholic beverage.

"What you gon do Huck?"

"Ain't no point in worrying about that right now Buckeye." A worried look appeared in Huck's eyes. "Right now I need to make sure Effie Mae's gon be alright . . . Mr. White's still hell bent on taking that club and putting that girl out on the streets." A deadly gaze showed in Huck's eyes. "I can't let him do that." Buckeye's uneasiness increased seeing the look in his old friend's eyes.

"What you gon do man?"

"Blue had to have done something to make sure Effie Mae would be alright, Buckeye." Huck said convinced. "He knew how dirty Mr. White was—" Huck silenced when seeing the cunning look on Buckeye's face. He tilted his head.

"You with Effie Mae now Huck?" Buckeye asked grinning. Huck looked momentarily at him, but gave no reply. "I hope this don't sound cold Huck, but now that Blue's gone it ain't nothing really stopping you from getting with Effie Mae."

"It ain't nothing I'd love more Buckeye than to step into Ol' Blue's shoes with Effie Mae, but it seems my brother told her before he left here to stay away from me."

"What?" Buckeye laughed. "Man that cold Huck!"

"And since she still crazy in love with Ol' Blue—" Huck gulped down another shot. "—she listening to him Buckeye from the grave. Huck quietly grinned, shaking his head.

"I guess you can't blame Tyrell for looking out for his woman—" A mystified looked displayed in Buckeye's eyes. "—even from beyond the grave." He laughed out loud.

"Yeah I guess Ol' Blue thought Effie Mae and her husband needed to give it another try especially now that she pregnant."

"Pregnant?" Buckeye's eyes widened. "Is it Tyrell's?"

"Naw Buckeye . . . Blue couldn't have kids." Buckeye's eyes again widened.

"I didn't know that man!" Buckeye thought for a moment. "I always wondered why Effie Mae hadn't had any kids by him."

"I may not be able to have Effie Mae, Buckeye . . . but she gon always be my friend and she gon always be in my life—believe that."

"I believe it Huck." Buckeye poured the last of the scotch in his glass.

"So her kids better get use to calling me Uncle Huck." Buckeye chuckled. "I'm serious Buckeye, I love that girl too much for her not to be in my life."

"Okay man, I believe you—Uncle Huck." Buckeye's chuckle progressed into laughter.

# Chapter Twenty-Three

Melvin watched Effie Mae as she entered the jazz club, returning from her visit J.R.—and her children. She glanced over at him in the bar as she headed in the direction of the stairs.

"You doing alright Effie Mae?" He asked, worried after receiving Deborah Ann's report on Effie Mae's diminished emotional state only a few days ago. She stopped.

"Yeah Melvin I'm fine." Effie Mae smiled.

"Everything alright with your kids?"

"Yeah Melvin they fine."

"If you need anything just let me know." Melvin smiled.

"I will Melvin." Effie Mae said blushing in response to his silent gaze. "What Melvin?"

"I'm just thinking that's all." His smile grew.

"Thinking?" She continued blushing.

"I was just thinking about us and what could've been once upon a time." A serious look showed on Melvin's face.

"That was a long time ago Melvin."

"I understand that but—"

"But what?"

"Feelings don't just go away, especially if you don't want them to." Effie Mae's mouth slightly opened.

"Feelings?"

"For a minute . . . I had real feelings for you Effie Mae, but like I said, I could never have done Tyrell like that, I know how much that man loved you."

"Losing Blue broke my heart in so many pieces Melvin, right now I can't even think about loving another man."

"I understand." He stated. "Well sweetie when your heart's whole again and you ready to share it with somebody I'm here—that is if you think I'm that somebody you want to share it with." Effie Mae blushed.

"Thank you Melvin." They shared an affectionate smile then Effie Mae continued up the stairs to the apartment. Her eyes moistened with tears as she stood outside the door. She thought how Blue wouldn't be waiting for inside as he'd done so many times before when she'd returned home after visiting with her children. Tears erupted from her eyes as she unlocked the door and went inside. Effie Mae tossed the large white envelope on the bed then walked over to the dresser and removed Blue's red plaid pajama pants and shirt. She entered the bathroom to wash and dress for bed, exiting minutes later wearing the pajamas.

She pulled back the covers on the bed then sat down—picking up the large envelope, preparing to explore the contents of the mysterious envelope. She reached inside and taking hold of the first paper item her fingers touched, removing a photo blank side up. Effie Mae turned it over discovering it to be the picture of her and Blue on their wedding day.

"I miss you so much baby." She said talking to his picture. "Why you have to leave me baby?" She laid the picture on the bed and again inserted her hand inside the envelope, removing a picture of Blue. Effie Mae pressed the picture against her heart and wept as she imagined hearing his voice:

*"Hey."*

"Huh?" She stated out loud.

*"I love you Baby girl."*

"I love you back Blue." Effie Mae said raising the photo to her lips, softly kissing it. "Blue, Tyrell Lee Jones . . . I love baby." She placed a second kiss on the photo then laid it on top of the pillow—where Blue last laid his head. She elected not to removed anything further from the envelope, deciding to simply put it away for another day. Effie Mae slid the large envelope underneath Blue's pillow.

"Effie Mae!" Deborah Ann called through the closed door.

"Yeah Deborah Ann?"

"Can I come in?"

Effie Mae used the sleeve of the pajama shirt to quickly wipe away her tears.

"Yeah Deborah Ann—it's open." Deborah Ann entered seeing Effie Mae's reddened eyes.

"Effie Mae you alright girl?"

"Yeah Deborah Ann I'm alright."

"Girl I see those tears in your eyes!" Effie Mae looked at her, but remained speechless. Deborah Ann's eyes drew to the photo of Blue lying on the pillow. A perplexed look formed on her face. "Effie Mae why you got that picture of Tyrell laying on that pillow?" Effie Mae looked at her but gave no reply. "Baby is it good for you to be doing something like that? And where you get that from anyway?"

"Blue." Effie Mae stated. A peculiar look appeared on Deborah Ann's face.

"What?"

"Blue gave it to me."

"He did what girl?" Effie Mae giggled. "Effie Mae girl you feeling alright?"

"Yeah Deborah Ann I'm fine—"

"Then what you mean Tyrell gave it to you?"

"Blue gave it to J.R. to give to me." She said amused.

"J.R.?" Deborah Ann said trying to remember. "That's your ex-husband right?"

"Nope—"

"He ain't, I thought—"

" J.R.'s my husband Deborah Ann." Effie Mae giggled then turned her attention to Blue's photo. "But this my real husband right here." Deborah Ann looked at her with worried eyes, uncertain how to respond. "Having Blue's picture is like having my baby right here with me." Effie Mae said placing a kiss on the photo. Deborah Ann's eyes widened.

"That's good Effie Mae—I think." She said uneasy by Effie Mae's affection with the photo. "If it makes you happy." She momentarily stared at Effie Mae. "I just know Tyrell would be glad to see you happy again." Deborah Ann picked up the wedding picture lying on the bed. "The one thing I know for sure Effie Mae . . . my cousin know he loved you!"

"And Effie Mae loved your cousin!"

"Effie Mae girl you so silly." The two women laughed. Deborah Ann suddenly remembered her reason for being there. "Oh, you almost made me forget the reason I came up here."

"If you came to see if I cleaned the place up—" Deborah Ann interjected.

"No, that wasn't it." She looked around the apartment. "But I'm sure glad to see you didr." She sniffed. "Smells a lot better too!" They laughed. "What I came up here for was to tell you that a man called for you while you were gone.

"Was it Mr. Daniel?"

"Who?" Deborah Ann said unfamiliar with the name.

"He told me to tell you to call Anthony?" Effie Mae's mouth abruptly opened.

"I forgot to call that boy."

"I know it ain't none of my business Effie Mae, but girl who is Anthony?" Deborah Ann asked, preparing herself for one of Effie Mae's eye opening answers. "Not another husband is he?" Effie Mae giggled.

"Close." Deborah Ann's eyes widened.

"Huh?"

"Anthony's my fiancé."

"Your what girl?" She said shaking her head in response to Effie Mae's complicated life. "Girl your life is too complicated for me." Deborah Ann shook her head as she turned to leave. "I'll talk to you later girl." She stopped and looked at the picture of Blue lying on the pillow. "Bye Blue!" Effie Mae giggled as Deborah Ann exited the apartment then hurried over to the phone to call Anthony.

• • • •

"Hey Anthony."

"Baby!" He said thrilled to hear her voice. "It's so good to hear your voice—how have you been?"

"Not too good Anthony, Blue passed away last month. His mouth slightly opened, surprised by the news.

"Last month? Baby why didn't you call me? Do you need me to come up there—"

"Slow down Anthony."

"Baby what have you been doing? Who's been helping you through this? Baby you promised you would call me when—"

"I love you Anthony." He abruptly silenced.

"Huh?"

"I said I love you."

"That's really good to hear Baby." Anthony said finding hope for their future together in those words. "I love you too Baby." He swallowed the lump forming in his throat. "Baby . . . I hope this doesn't sound selfish, but does this mean we can move forward with our plans to get married now?" Effie Mae gave no reply. "Baby?"

"What Anthony?"

"You didn't answer me."

"Anthony before Blue passed we talked."

"Talked?" A new lump formed in his throat. "That doesn't sound good Baby."

"He asked me if I loved you Anthony."

"Of course you do Baby you just said you did."

"Listen to me Anthony!" Effie Mae said. "I do love you Anthony but—"

"But? But what Baby?"

"We've changed so much Anthony—" He cut her off.

"Baby, we discussed that already and we both agreed we just needed to get to know each other as adults, remember?"

"I remember Anthony but—"

"Baby don't do this."

"Anthony I still see you as that curly haired boy with the bow tie." She said giggling.

"Well, I don't wear my hair quite as curly anymore but I'm still me."

"That's just it Anthony—it's that curly haired boy I thought I was getting back with, but when we got back together you wasn't him."

"Baby you're not making sense."

"What if it don't work Anthony?"

"Baby all you need to know is that I love you and you love me—" She interjected.

"Anthony, Blue didn't think you was good for me." Effie Mae blurted.

"What? Baby, Blue's no longer here."

"I know that Anthony."

"Okay so what are you saying?"

"What I'm saying Anthony—" She paused. "—I could never love you or any man like I loved Blue."

"Okay, I can accept that—"

"Anthony I am still married to J.R."

"Baby I thought we agreed that was only a technicality." Effie Mae gave no reply. "Baby?"

"Anthony I think I owe it to J.R. to be the wife I never—" He interjected.

"What do mean?" Anthony said agitated. "Baby . . . J.R. walked out on you and the children or have you forgotten?" He asked, his anxiety increasing. "Baby don't do this."

"Anthony—" He cut her off.

"Baby you've never loved J.R. what's changed?"

"Anthony—"

"Baby do you even think you could love J.R.?"

"I don't know Anthony but—"

"But what?" Anthony said frustrated. "Baby will you promise me that before you make any decisions you'll think about it, I think right now you're grieving and—"

"J.R.'s really been here for me Anthony—"

"Baby that's not fair!" He yelled. "I would've been there if you had taken the time to let me know about Blue's passing!" He took a deep breath trying to calm himself. "So what about us Baby and our son?"

"Lil' J.R. gon always be your son Anthony and I'm gon always make sure he know that—and that he know you."

"love you Baby." Anthony said refusing to give up. "And I love the son we created."

"I love you too Anthony."

"Baby will you please call me when you've decided what you want to do.

"I will Anthony."

"Bye Baby."

"Bye Anthony." Effie Mae held the phone momentarily in her hand before hanging up. She wondered if she would one day regret ending her relationship with Anthony.

"Effie Mae it's me again." Deborah Ann stated from outside the door. "Girl it's a man downstairs saying he want to speak to you."

"A man?"

"He said his name is Daniel?"

"Daniel!"

"And he has the cutest little baby with him." Effie Mae eyes lit up as she swiftly rose from the bed and hurried over opening the door seeing the inquisitive look in Deborah Ann's eyes.

"Bring him up Deborah Ann!" She looked at Effie Mae and wondered of her excitement.

"Okay girl I'll be right back with Daniel?" Deborah said as she turned and walked away. Effie Mae quickly pulled the bed covers back up on the bed. Her eyes drew to the photo of Blue lying on the pillow appearing to be looking at her. She picked it up and kissed it.

"I love you Blue." She said before sliding the picture underneath Blue's pillow when hearing footsteps coming up the stairs. Effie Mae rushed into the hallway and waited. Her eyes beamed when Daniel reached the top of the stairs holding D.J. in his right arm—a diaper bag dangling from his left shoulder.

"Look at my baby." She said eagerly removing the toddler from Daniel's hold. "You see my baby Deborah Ann?" Effie Mae said placing a kiss on top of the toddler's head. Deborah Ann shifted her eyes from the toddler to Daniel then back to Effie Mae wondering if the older gentleman carrying Effie Mae's baby could be the father.

"Effie Mae he's gorgeous." She said shifting her eyes again to Daniel.

"Thank you Deborah Ann." Effie Mae giggled seeing the questioning look in Deborah Ann's eyes. "Yeah Deborah Ann—Mr. Daniel's my baby boy's daddy."

"I'm not even gon ask." Deborah Ann said throwing her hands up in surrender. Effie Mae giggled as Deborah Ann headed back downstairs.

• • • •

Effie Mae kissed her toddler son on the cheek. He looked at her with unfamiliarity then grasped hold of her hair and pulled. He giggled.

"Uh-uh baby." Effie Mae said removing his hand from her wavy black hair then lovingly kissed it. Daniel watched with love filled eyes. "I love you D.J." She said kissing his forehead.

"You gon invite me in?" Daniel teased.

"You can come in Mr. Daniel." Effie Mae said giggling as she returned inside the apartment being seated on the sofa. Daniel closed the door then followed her.

"How you been doing Effie Mae?" He asked sitting down next to her. "I didn't know if you felt like talking, since you been dealing with a lot since Blue passed."

"Momma love you D.J." Effie Mae said electing not to discuss Blue with him.

"I also thought you might want to see our boy since you didn't get a chance to celebrate his first birthday." A large smile formed on Effie Mae's face.

"Happy birthday Daniel Lee Jones Jr." Effie Mae said kissing him on the cheek. The toddler giggled. Daniel delighted in hearing her call their son by his birth name given to him by Ms. Geraldine the day she forcefully took the infant from Effie Mae. "I love you Daniel Lee Jones Jr." Effie Mae repeated. He reached for her moving lips and again giggled. Effie Mae looked at Daniel.

"Thank you Mr. Daniel." He stared helplessly at her. She blushed. "What?"

"It sure would be nice if you would thank this old man with a kiss." Her blushing smile widened. "You know I'm still crazy about you." Daniel said moving his lips towards her's. Effie Mae showed no resistance, allowing him to intimately kiss her. "I sure do miss that." Daniel stated with delight. Effie Mae again turned to her baby boy.

"Happy birthday baby." D.J. looked at his daddy then back to Effie Mae and smiled.

"I want you to know Effie Mae even if Geraldine wasn't in the hospital, I still would've brought our boy over here so you could celebrate his birthday.

"How Ms. Geraldine doing?" She asked, unconvinced by his untested words. Daniel sighed.

"Not much better." He shook his head. "Progress seem to be at a standstill, but her doctor thinks she can do more than she doing."

"I'm just glad she still alive." Effie Mae stated. "I love you my sweet D.J." She kissed the toddler's chubby hand. Daniel looked around the apartment seeing a pair of navy blue pinstriped pants and matching vest lying over a chair.

"Huck staying here with you Effie Mae?"

"Nope—why?"

"I know it ain't none of my business—"

"Huck's been looking out for me since Blue passed."

"Looking out for you my foot!" Daniel stated, skeptical. "I know Huck and I know he doing more than just looking out for you." Effie Mae neither denied or confirmed his suspicions. She turned her attention again to her toddler son as he began to squirm and cry.

"What's wrong momma's big boy?" She said bouncing him on her knee. Daniel picked up the diaper bag sitting on the florr and removed an eight ounce bottle of milk.

"Ain't nothing wrong with that boy but hungry." He handed Effie Mae of the bottle of milk. D.J. grabbed it from her hand then shoved it in his mouth.

"I guess he is hungry."

"Yeah . . . he probably sleepy too." Daniel said looking at him. "Ain't you boy?"

"He gon be okay if I lay him on the bed?"

"Yeah, he'll be fine." Effie Mae rose from the sofa carrying her baby boy then taking him over to the bed and laying him down. The toddler continued sucking his bottle as his eyes gradually closed.

"I guess he was hungry and sleepy." Effie Mae said kissing her sleeping son on the cheek. Daniel intently watched as she returned to the sofa and again sat down. "What?" She blushed.

"Girl you just don't know what you do to me."

"Mr. Daniel!"

"Naw, that ain't what I'm talking about." He took hold of her hands and placed them inside his own. "I love you Effie Mae, but not just love you, I'm in love with you girl." He wrapped Effie Mae's arms around his neck and embraced her. "I never knew how good it felt to be in love." He gazed into her hazel brown eyes then intimately kissed her on the lips. "But no matter how much I love you—I know I can't ever have you." Daniel said placing another kiss on her lips. "You still my cousin's wife."

"Mr. Daniel—" He cut her off.

"Call me Daniel." He stated softly. She blushed.

"Daniel—" He smiled. "—you know us being together wasn't right.

"I know that Effie Mae." He said agitated by her words.

"J.R. and Ms. Geraldine got hurt and—"

"Yeah I know." Daniel state with regret. "And I ain't ever gon forgive myself for hurting Geraldine or J.R. like that." He shook his head. "But as wrong as it was Effie Mae—" He again gazed in eyes. "—if I could do it all over again I wouldn't hesitate." She blushed. Daniel looked over at their sleeping son. "And I love you for giving me that little boy right there!" He chuckled. "Even though most folks think I'm his granddaddy." Effie Mae laughed then looked in Daniel's inviting eyes. "What?"

"You gon let me have another one of them kisses?" She giggled.

"Go ahead Daniel." They again kissed. Effie Mae laid her head on his chest following the kiss.

"Being here with you like this reminds me of when we was together—" She looked quickly up at him.

"Do it also remind you of how Ms. Geraldine caught you in my bed?"

"Now there you go things Effie Mae." She looked at him with remorse.

"Ms. Geraldine ain't ever gon forgive me for that either." She looked over at D.J. "I guess I can't blame her though."

"Forgive you?" Daniel said glancing briefly up at the ceiling. He shook his head in frustration. "I ain't had a day's peace Effie Mae—" He continued shaking his head. "—I been listening to that woman day and night talking about how I betrayed her!"

"I guess you did—"

"We betrayed her!" Daniel said making sure he include Effie Mae. "But it wasn't just us being together, what hurt Geraldine most Effie Mae—"

"Was what?"

"Geraldine knowing that I love with you girl." He stated without remorse. "Effie Mae I watched that woman get bitter and bitter by the day!" He looked Effie Mae in the eyes. "I believe that the reason why she had that stroke too!"

"You think so Daniel?"

"It was!" He said convinced. "The day Geraldine had that stroke she just wouldn't let it go Effie Mae . . . kept on until she made me tell her I was in love with you." Effie Mae's mouth abruptly opened, shocked by him professing his love for her to his wife. "I tell you it wasn't long after that Geraldine had that stroke!"

"Daniel you told your wife that?"

"Yeah I told her!" He stated without regret. "Geraldine knew how I felt about you Effie Mae—wasn't no point in trying to hide it." Daniel said without shame. "I couldn't if I tried." He again kissed Effie Mae on the lips. She showed no objection. "I can't help how I feel about you." Daniel said again moving his lips towards Effie Mae's. She turned quickly away. "What's wrong?"

"I know what you trying to do."

"What's wrong with that?" He said placing a light kiss on her lips.

"This Blue's house."

"Okay, I understand." He grinned. "You think maybe you can come by the house one day so we can spend a little time together?"

"I don't know about that Mr. Daniel."

"Daniel."

"Huh?"

"Call me Daniel, I like that." He cunningly grinned. "You can't blame this old man for trying can you?" Effie Mae blushed.

"That depends."

"On what?" Daniel asked kissing her on the cheek, working his lips around to her mouth. "It ain't nothing we ain't done before." He whispered in her ear.

"Me and J.R. talking 'bout getting back together."

"Talking?" He said sporadically smooching Effie Mae on the lips.

"I'm pregnant Daniel." He abruptly released her.

"Pregnant?" Daniel looked at her, agitated by her unexpected news. "By Blue?"

"Naw . . . it's J.R.'s."

"What the hell!" A perplexed look on displayed on his face. "When did you and J.R. start seeing each other in that way?"

"We wasn't." Effie Mae said giggling. "Blue thought—" Daniel cut her off.

"Blue?"

"Yeah, he thought I should give J.R. a chance—"

"A chance to do what?" Daniel scowled.

"Not that Daniel." She again giggled.

"You getting back with J.R. on account of Blue?"

"In a way Daniel."

"Mr. Daniel."

"Huh?"

"Call me Mr. Daniel." He said upset by her decision to reunite with her husband. Effie Mae subtly laughed at his childish behavior.

"Maybe this time me and J.R. can get it right."

"Is that what you want Effie Mae?" Daniel asked hoping he still had a chance—in absence of Blue.

"Maybe this baby I'm carrying . . . Tyrell Lee Jones Smith is the son me and J.R.'s been trying to have." "Tyrell Lee Jones?" Daniel looked at her, confused by her words. "Effie Mae I thought you said that was J.R.'s baby?"

"It is Mr. Daniel." She giggled.

"You teasing me Effie Mae?"

"Nope . . . we talked about it—" Daniel interjected.

"We?"

"Me and Blue." His eyes widened.

"Blue knew you was pregnant Effie Mae?"

"Yeah he knew." She again giggled. "Blue knew before I did!"

"So y'all . . . you and Blue talked about naming J.R.'s son after Blue?"

"Yep."

"And J.R. agreed to that mess?"

"Yep." Effie Mae said amused. "Mr. Daniel it ain't no different than Anthony's son being called Lil' J.R." Daniel briefly ruminated on Effie Mae's words.

"I guess you right." He said looking at her in amazement as he digested the odd news. "Tyrell Lee Jones—Smith?" Daniel repeated.

"I asked Blue and he said yeah—" Effie Mae silenced.

"You alright Effie Mae?"

"I miss him so much Mr. Daniel."

"Call me Daniel."

"Naming my baby boy after Blue gon tell this world how much I loved Tyrell Lee Jones." Her eyes filled with tears. Daniel's filled with envy.

"If you and J.R. do have a boy Effie Mae, don't forget about our boy."

"Daniel if I had a hundred baby boys—" Effie Mae giggled. "—Daniel Lee Jones Jr. ain't gon ever stop being my baby boy, you know that."

"J.R. might not feel that way, especially with me being the daddy of that boy." Daniel said manipulating her. "It sure would be nice if J.R. would let our boy spend time with his momma and the other kids." Effie Mae's eye lit up.

"My babies would love that Daniel!"

"Yeah, but I know right now I'm the last person J.R. won't hanging around."

"You let me talk to J.R., Daniel"

"You sure you want to do that Effie Mae?" Daniel said playing on Effie Mae's love for her children. She smiled.

"I got him to let Blue be in my baby's life." A cunning smiled formed on Daniel's face. Effie Mae blushed.

"What?"

"Girl you keep calling me Daniel like that—" He grinned.

"Mr. Daniel!"

"Alright Effie Mae . . . I was just testing the waters."

"Well from now on Daniel, only man gon be testing these waters is my husband." She giggled. Daniel again kissed her intimately on the lips.

"You might want to lock this door when you got company." Huck said startling them as he stood in the doorway. They looked over at him. Huck said nothing further as he looked at Effie Mae seeing her again wearing Blue's pajamas. He shifted his eyes over at D.J. asleep on the bed, his empty bottle lying next to him. He again turned to Effie Mae, upset by Daniel's being there.

"Well Effie Mae—" Daniel shifted his eyes briefly to Huck. "—I guess I better get this boy on home, feed him and—" Huck interjected.

"Yeah you do that Daniel." He stated with sarcasm. Daniel again shifted his eyes to Huck then turned back to Effie Mae.

"Call me when you ready to talk Effie Mae."

"I will Mr. Daniel." He shifted his eyes to Huck a third time before standing to retrieve his sleeping son from the bed. Huck watched with intimidating eyes as Daniel walked over and picked up his son, taking him over to Effie Mae to say her goodbyes.

"Happy Birthday my sweet baby." She said placing a kiss on the toddler's forehead before retrieving his diaper bag from off the floor, adjusting it on Daniel's shoulder then stuffing the empty bottle inside. Effie Mae ignored Huck's jealous gaze as she escorted Daniel over to the door where Huck stood partially blocking the doorway. The two men looked one to the other before Huck gradually stepped aside, allowing Daniel to exit. "Bye Mr. Daniel." She said exchanging a smile with her former lover.

"Yeah, bye Mr. Daniel." Huck said mocking him. Daniel shifted his eyes briefly over at him.

"Thank you Mr. Daniel for bringing my baby boy over for his birthday."

"I meant what I said Effie Mae okay?"

"Okay Mr. Daniel." Huck observed with angry eyes as Daniel placed a kiss on Effie Mae's cheek before heading down the stairs.

"What was all that about?" Huck asked turning his attention to Effie Mae. She looked at him then walked over and got in the bed, throwing the cover over her head.

# Chapter Twenty-Four

Mr. White—accompanied by his attorney convened at the jazz club with Huck and Buckeye to discuss the circumstances surrounding Blue's estate.

"It's been a few weeks now gentlemen—" Mr. Garrett said shifting his worried eyes to Mr. White, his heart rapidly pounding in his chest as he prepared to delivered adverse information. "Because we've not yet seen any documentation identifying a designated beneficiary of Mr. Jones' estate—" Mr. Garrett nervously swallowed as his mouth dried in anticipation of Huck's expected reaction to his unwelcoming news. "—it looks like Mr. Jones' estate will have to go into probate." Huck shifted his eyes to Buckeye then again turned to Mr. Garrett with mistrust. A huge smile stretched across Mr. White's face.

"And while my attorney's figuring all that out—" He smirked. "—I'll be running this place." Mr. White said looking Huck defiantly in the eyes. "Now get your whore—" He stopped when seeing rage burning in Huck's eyes. "—I'm giving you two weeks to get that woman out of my apartment Henry Lee and it's not a damn thing you can do to stop me!" Buckeye eased his hand onto his pistol and prepared to shoot on Huck's command.

"Mr. White—" Mr. Garrett said when seeing Buckeye's sudden movement. He ignored his attorney's beckoning as he continued his taunting Huck.

"Let's see what that gold digger think about that!"

"Mr. White—" Mr. Garrett repeated, his forehead dampening with beads of sweat. He removed a handkerchief from the upper left pocket of his expensive grey suit and dabbed his face.

"Can he do that?" Huck asked.

"Technically he can." Mr. Garrett said, again shifting his eyes to Buckeye. Huck also looked at his old friend before turning back to Mr. Garrett. "He can't assume ownership, but he can definitely manage the daily operations." Huck tilted his head.

"Is that right?"

"Legally, Mrs. Smith has no right to Mr. Jones' estate—so legally she can be evicted." Mr. Garret stated continuing to dab his forehead.

"And since me and Tyrell's mother are his next of kin that means until all this legal mess is sorted out, this jazz club technically—" Mr. White looked at Huck and cunningly smirked. "—is mines."

Huck shifted his eyes over to Buckeye seeing a look in his eyes requesting he allow him to shoot his father. Huck subtly shook his head no, certain Mr. White would one day eat his words.

"Don't move too quick Mr. White." Huck stated with warning. "I know Blue, and I know how much he loved Effie Mae." Huck turned to Mr. Garrett. "My brother would've gave his life for that woman Mr. Garrett . . . so giving her this club wouldn't have been nothing for him to do." Buckeye nodded in agreement. "As a betting man Mr. Garrett I'd be willing to bet everything I own that Ol Blue left everything he owned to the woman he loved—not Mr. White." Huck stared at his father, watching the prideful look on his face turned to one of concern. "And you can take that to the grave with you Mr. White."

"Well my only advice to you Mr. White Jr.—" Mr. Garrett said beginning to give credence to Huck's convincing words on Blue's wishes. "—is for you to keep looking for a will or any legal documents identifying Mrs. Smith as beneficiary or legal owner of this establishment." Mr. Garrett stood as he concluded the meeting then extended his hand to Huck. "I'll be waiting to hear from you." The two men shook. A victorious look showed on Mr. White face—confident he'd won *round one.*

"This ain't the end Mr. White." Huck stated in response to the sneer on his father's face.

"You just get your whore—" Mr. White abruptly silenced when Buckeye rose from the table. "—two weeks Henry Lee and I want her out!" Mr. Garrett conducted a visual inspection of the club noting the well stocked liquor over in the bar, the quality table and chairs, hardwood floors, and the red carpeted stage containing a large black upright piano. He now wondered if perhaps Huck's words had merit and that Mr. White wouldn't be named as beneficiary as he anticipated.

"Well, Mr. White unless there's a document somewhere to the contrary of what you believe—" Mr. Garrett glanced briefly to Huck then back to Mr. White. "—it looks like you'll be the new owner of this very impressive jazz club." A proud look formed on Mr. White's face.

"A lot can happen in two weeks Mr. Garrett." Huck stated masking his fear—the papers identifying transfer of Blue's assets to Effie Mae might never be found.

"Well, Mr. White Jr., if anything does happen be sure to notify me the minute you think you have something."

"Count on it." Huck said angered by the smug look on his father's face. Mr. Garrett looked apprehensively over at Buckeye still standing at arms. "Good day gentlemen." He said moving swiftly in the direction of the front entrance. Mr. Garrett halted when realizing Mr. White hadn't yet joined him.

"Mr. White are you coming?"

"You go ahead on Mr. Garrett I think I'll stick around for a minute, get settled in my new club." He shifted his spiteful eyes over at Huck.

"Then would you uh, please call me once you've vacated the premises?" Mr. Garrett said, again looking over at Buckeye noting the eager look on his face indicating he wanted to do harm to Mr. White. "Uh, Mr. White perhaps you should return later—give these gentlemen time to digest—" He cut him off.

"I'll be fine Mr. Garrett." Mr. White said walking over to the bar being seated. Mr. Garrett's anxiety amplified when seeing the burning rage in Huck eyes as he looked at his father.

"Mr. White—"

"You go ahead on Mr. Garrett." Mr. White stated dismissing his attorney's worries.

"Are you uh, sure you want me to do that?"

"I'll call you later . . . you have a good day."

"You uh, be sure to—" Mr. Garrett silenced when seeing Melvin glaring at him. "—call me Mr. White please!" He swiftly exited out the front door.

"Hey Melvin." Mr. White said eager to step into the role of proprietor, despite his attorney's legal advice.

"Did you need something Mr. White?"

"Yeah, I need you to bring me something wet to drink?" Melvin shifted his eyes to Huck then turned back to Mr. White.

"Something wet like what?"

"I'll let you decide."

Buckeye walked over to the bar and seated himself at the end of the bar, deciding to take advantage of the situation.

"Hey Melvin bring me something wet too."

"Buckeye man . . . you know I can't do that." Buckeye's eyes widened.

"Why not?"

"Because we ain't open yet that's why!"

"You didn't say that when Mr. White asked for a drink."

"That's because as of now—" Melvin again shifted his eyes to Huck then back to Buckeye. "—Mr. White's my new boss." Huck quickly turned to him.

"Effie Mae own this club Melvin." He said challenging his father. Mr. White looked at Melvin but gave no reply. "You remember that." Huck again turned to his father, preparing for an verbal altercation. The front door of the jazz club swung open and Ms. Rita, accompanied by Benita and Huck's children entered. Huck shook his head then turned to Melvin. "You gon have to start making sure that front door locked Melvin." He said watching as the club's uninvited guest seated themselves at a table mid-center of the room. "I see you got all kinds of creatures crawling up in here." Huck looked at Benita. Buckeye laughed.

"What you doing here Rita?" Mr. White said agitated.

"What you mean what I'm doing here—you here ain't you?" She slurred, slightly intoxicated. "I came here to check on my jazz club that's what the hell I'm doing here!"

"Your jazz Club?"

"Yeah that's righ . . . my jazz club." She scoffed. "The last time I checked I was still your wife that means whatever's yours is mines—"

"That's a lie!" He shouted. "It'll be over my dead body before you get a damn thing from me Rita!" Buckeye looked over at Huck, placing his hand on the pistol strapped at his side when seeing Mr. White stand.

"Be careful what you asked for Mr. White." Huck said in defense of his mother. "I can make that happen if that's what you really want." Mr. White looked into Huck's predictable eyes then sat back down. "I don't want Momma here no more than you do—" She intervened.

"What the hell you mean you don't want me here?" She yelled. Huck shifted his eyes briefly over at her then turned his back to his father.

"But if you put your hands on my momma, Mr. White you ain't gon have to worry about giving her nothing—" Huck looked him defiantly in the eyes. "—she gon inherit it." Mr. White stared briefly at his estranged wife then shifted his eyes to Huck, but maintained his silence. "You understand what I'm saying don't you Mr. White?" Huck's attention drew to Benita when sensing her unrelenting gaze and the look of admiration on her face, impressed by his powerful nature. He slightly lowered his head and blushed then turned to his mother.

"What you doing here Momma?"

"What you mean what I'm doing here little boy?"

"You back—why?"

"You heard what I told your—" Huck cut her off.

"If that's what you came here for Momma you wasting your time." Huck looked at his father—his back now turned as he waited for Melvin to bring him a drink. "Until Mr. White got proof that he owns anything let's get one thing straight—" Mr. White turned around. "—Effie Mae owns this club." Huck said looking at his father in opposition.

"We'll see about that Henry Lee!" Mr. White stated, convinced the jazz club already belonged to him. "I'm ready for that drink now Melvin." He said raising his voice—turning his back to his estranged wife—and Huck.

"Will a shot of gin be okay Mr. White?" Melvin asked.

"Hand it here."

"If you think I'd let you take this club from Effie Mae, you don't know me at all Mr. White." Huck stated as his anger mounted. Mr. White listened to his threatening words, undaunted. "Ol Blue left this place to the woman he loved and I'm gon see to it that she gets it." Mr. White shifted his eyes to Melvin then looked over at Buckeye observing his unseen hand located inside his suit jacket. "And I won't hesitate to hurt anybody that try to keep that from happening."

"I don't want any trouble out of you Henry Lee!" Mr. White shouted.

"Yeah you do Mr. White, because that's what you gon get if you try to take this club from Effie Mae." Ms. Rita intervened.

"Effie Mae?" A puzzled looked appeared on her face. "Who the hell is Effie Mae and what the hell do she have to do with anything? I asked Marvin over there who she was—" Huck interjected. Melvin's eyes widened.

"Who?"

"Marvin . . . that man over there serving the liquor."

"That's Melvin Momma." She ignored his correction.

"All he would say is that she was Tynell's wife?" Huck again interrupted.

"Tyrell, Momma."

"What?"

"Ol' Blue's name was Tyrell—not Tynell." She again ignored Huck's correction.

"If Rosalyn's boy was married to this Effie Mae then why in hell Henry Lee Sr. so sure he gon get this damn place?" Ms. Rita asked, confused. "That don't make no damn sense!"

"That ain't got nothing to do with Momma."

"What you mean it don't have nothing to do with me? It do if it's gon keep me from getting my jazz club!"

"It's hers Momma—no matter what Mr. White thinks." Mr. White's turned his attention to the shot of gin Melvin placed in front of him, unconcerned about Huck's unproven words. "So if that's what you waiting on Momma, you waiting on something you ain't ever gon get." He again noted Benita's gaze. "Momma told me you and Ol' pigeon-toed Tommy got divorced. "Huck shook his head, humored. "Damn shame, so who got tired of who?" Buckeye laughed.

"Why you worried about it Henry Lee, you interested or something?" She asked flirtatiously.

"Naw." Huck quietly chuckled. "Sometimes Benita another man's trash is just that—trash." Buckeye and Melvin bursts into laughter. Huck's son James, quickly stood.

"Hey man, don't be talking to my mother like that!" He yelled. Huck looked at his brave son then shited his eyes over at Buckeye then back to James.

"I know I ain't ever been your father James, so this ain't gon work in your favor." Huck turned to Benita then looked back at his son. "But if you call me man again using that tone, it's gon make me think you grown enough to make a move on me." Mr. White quickly turned in response to Huck's threatening words to his son. "You ain't trying to make a move on me are you James?"

"I'm just telling you Henry Lee—" James stated boldly. "You watch how you talk to my mother." Buckeye's eyes widened with concern. He knew given his old friend current state of mind over Mr. White trying to take what he knew Blue wanted Effie Mae to have, he wouldn't hold his temper much longer.

"You need to talk to your son Benita." Huck said holding back his fury. Buckeye quickly interjected.

"Look here James . . . you don't know my friend he ain't somebody you want to mess with." Buckeye turned to Benita. "You need to get your son Benita if you don't want to see him get hurt—now I'm telling him and you for his own good to chill out." He looked at James. "When you speak to father, you speak to that man with respect!"

"Huck?" Effie Mae quietly called out disrupting the heated altercation. He quickly turned when hearing her voice—seeing her standing at the bottom of the stairs wearing Blue's oversized, plaid green pajamas.

"Come here girl." He said smiling. "I got some people I want you to meet." Ms. Rita watched with contempt as Effie Mae walked over to Huck. He gently pulled her in his arms. Benita watched the intimate interaction with envious eyes.

"I thought you said she was Tynell's wife Henry Lee?"

"I love this woman too Momma, and I ain't gon let you, Mr. White and nobody else do anything to hurt her." Mr. White listened, refusing to acknowledge Effie Mae's presence. Huck looked around at the onlookers then placed two fingers underneath Effie Mae's chin, gently raising her head. He lowered his mouth onto hers and romantically kissed her. His mother's mouth abruptly opened.

"What the hell was that?" She said scowling. "What was you and Tynell doing sharing that hoe?" Melvin's jaw dropped in response to her demeaning words in reference to Effie Mae—in front of Huck. "I guess it wouldn't be the first time." She said looking at Effie Mae with disgust.

"You see that woman over there with all the mouth." Huck said. Effie Mae looked over at Ms. Rita. "That's my momma—Rita."

"I don't know what the hell you introducing her to me for." She said turning up her nose. "I don't want to meet that heifer."

"And that woman over there wishing at this moment she was you, that's Benita." She looked at Effie Mae and rolled her eyes. Buckeye chuckled. "Those kids sitting next to her—those are hers and mines." Effie Mae's mouth slightly opened, surprised to see Huck's children. "But they didn't know I existed." He looked at James before shifted his eyes momentarily to Buckeye. "Ain't that right Buckeye?"

"That's what you said Huck."

"So I'm gon keep on not existing." Huck said applying another kiss to Effie Mae's lips. "Come on let's go back upstairs—" He looked at Benita. "—and go back to bed." He glanced around the room into the many gazing eyes before engaging in a cold hard mutual stare with his father then he and Effie Mae headed back upstairs. Buckeye and Melvin looked one to the other, humored by the awkward dispute. They laughed.

"Melvin man, you can give me that shot of scotch now." Buckeye said declaring Huck the winner of *round two*. "We celebrating man!" Mr. White looked over at him, masking his worry as he tossed back his shot of gin.

# Chapter Twenty-Five

"Look at him Buckeye." Huck said watching his father as he mingled with the patrons of Blue's Jazz Club going from table to table greeting customers, a function usually reserved for Melvin.

"Blue would roll over in his grave Huck if he saw what your father was doing to Effie Mae." Buckeye stated watching with careful eyes as Huck filled his glass with scotch from the bottle they shared. "I'm surprised your father still letting her stay in that apartment considering how bad her wanted her out there."

"It ain't like he didn't try Buckeye." Huck said, his eyes fixated on the scotch in his glass. "Ms. Jones wouldn't let him—talked him out of evicting that girl from where she knew Blue wanted her to be." He looked over at Ms. Jones seated at a table near the stage. "Other than that he'd had out weeks ago." Huck hurled the scotch in his mouth then again looked over at Ms. Jones, this time with suspicious eyes. "Ms Jones knew how much Blue loved Effie Mae." He looked across the table at his old friend. "You know what else Buckeye—"

"What's that Huck?"

"I think Ms. Jones know a whole lot more than that."

"Like what?" Buckeye asked listening as he tossed back a shot.

"Like who the rightful owner of this jazz club is."

"Huck man, you think Tyrell's momma would keep that information from Effie Mae knowing your father trying to take everything Tyrell wanted her to have?"

"Yeah Buckeye, she would." An angry look formed on Buckeye's face.

"What?" He said raising his voice.

"Just like Blue loved Effie Mae—" Huck rolled his empty glass between his fingers. "—Ms. Jones love Mr. White." He looked briefly over at Ms. Jones. "I tell you something else Buckeye . . . Blue also loved his momma, he told her something." Buckeye shifted his eyes over at her and shook his head, frustrated.

"If that's true Huck that woman know she wrong for that!" He said refilling his empty glass. "What you gon do man?" Huck glanced over at his father.

"Before I let Mr. White take this club from Effie Mae, Buckeye—I'll make him wish he never heard of this place." He again turned his attention to Ms. Jones. "But Ms. Jones—" Huck nodded with certainty. "Yeah she know something."

· · · ·

"How's everybody doing tonight?" Mr. White asked as he continued greeting loyal patron and newcomers of the jazz club.

"This my first time coming to Blue's Jazz Club." A gentleman seated at a table accompanied by a male and two females stated. "And I'm really liking it man."

"Then welcome . . . I'm Henry Lee White but all  my friends call me Hank—I'm the new owner here." He shifted his eyes over at Huck then extended his hand to the man. They shook.

"Yeah the is sound pretty smooth." The second man said nodding.

"I've heard a lot of good things about this club." The first man said bobbing his head to the sound of the band. "This place really holds up to its reputation."

"Glad to hear you approve." Mr. White said turning to the band. "You know I hand picked the musicians myself." He stated, boastfully.

"Well you did a good job man!" The second man said shaking his head with approval.

"My son Tyrell—" Mr. White forced a look of grief on his face. "—the original owner, passed away a few months ago and left this place to me."

"I heard something about that." The first man stated. "My condolences for your loss Hank."

"You have my condolences too." The female accompanying him stated with sincerity.

"Thank you darling." Mr. White said giving the appearance of being sorrowed. "Now!" A big smile formed on his face. "What y'all drinking tonight?"

"Whatever you can fill that glass with." The second man said grinning.

"I'm a rum and coke man myself." The first man stated.

"Then how about I have Melvin bring a bottle of rum over here — on the house." Mr. White said beckoning Melvin with his hand. "I'll let y'all pay for the coke." He chuckled.

"You need something Mr. White?" Melvin asked, unable to mask his disappointment in Mr. White's poor management of the jazz club.

"Yeah look here Melvin, get my friends here a bottle of rum on the house . . . the only thing they'll be paying for tonight is the coke." Melvin's mouth slightly opened as he looked at Mr. White in disbelief. He shifted his eyes over at Huck and shook his head as he walked away to retrieve the *free* bottle of rum.

"Y'all enjoy yourselves now." Mr. White said moving on to the next table. "How's everybody doing tonight?"

"That music is slamming!" A female sitting at the table stated."

"Glad to hear you enjoying it!" Mr. White said extending his hand to her. "I'm Henry Lee White Sr., but my friends call me Hank — I'm the new owner of this fine establishment." He said believing it to be true. "What y'all drinking tonight?"

• • • •

Melvin made a detour over to Huck and Buckeye's table before returning with the free bottle of rum, deciding it was time to update Huck on the reckless behavior of his father and give his prediction on the future of Blue's Jazz Club.

"What's up Melvin?" Huck said as he approached.

"Huck man, your father's been giving away bottle after bottle of free liquor every night!" Melvin shook his head, infuriated. "If he keep on doing that the only thing we gon have left to serve customers is water!" He looked over at Mr. White when sensing him watching as he spoke with Huck and Buckeye.

"Don't worry about it Melvin." Huck said looking in his father's vindictive eyes. "Let him enjoy it while he can."

"Hey Hank —" A gentleman seated a few tables from where he stood called out breaking Mr. White's stare. "Don't seem like that one bottle was enough, we still sober!"

"I'll have Melvin bring you another bottle . . . or two. Mr. White said looking briefly over at Melvin. "What y'all drinking?" Melvin shook his head, enraged by Mr. White's recklessness.

"And he been doing that every night since he took this place over." Huck noted the hopeless look on Melvin's face.

"I ain't gon let that happen Melvin —" Melvin interjected.

"I hope not Huck—a few more months of your father running this place like this all that's gon be left of Blue's Jazz Club is a name and a memory."

"Blue worked too hard to get this club where it is." Huck said thinking out loud as he stared at his father.

"I remember . . . my cousin worked late into the night painting, fixing holes in the walls, buying bootlegged whiskey from Boney-knees Ol' jack-legged uncle—" Buckeye intervened.

"I remember at one point Tyrell was even running numbers for number man Curtis!" The three men laughed.

"Man Tyrell was doing whatever it took—"

"And borrowing money from everybody!" Buckeye said chuckling.

"Especially from me." Huck grinned. "I had to put a couple more ladies out on the streets to help Ol' Blue get everything you see in here today."

"I think Tyrell got money from all of us." Melvin stated. "For a minute there I thought I was gon have to start pimping!" He burst into laughter then abruptly stopped. "Me and Tyrell put in a lot of hours making this place what it is today Huck." Melvin's eyes moistened as he thought of the club possibly closing. "And after he opened this place, me and Deborah Ann worked in here for free for Tyrell for the first six months." Buckeye's eyes widened.

"For free?"

"Yeah Buckeye . . . Tyrell didn't have no money to pay nobody!" Melvin said as his eyes watered. "But that was my cousin and I loved him man."

"We all did Melvin." Huck said holding back his own tears. "That's why I can't let Mr. White tear down what my brother worked so hard to build up."

"And get this Huck—" Melvin shifted his angry wet eyes briefly over at Mr. White then back to Huck. "—Deborah Ann said he been taking money right out the cash register like it's his own personal bank account!" Huck's mind raced as he listened to Melvin's disturbing report. He looked over at Mr. White, determined to stop him. "And some of the waitresses said he been taking their tips right off the table!" Huck tilted his head.

"Is that right?"

"I'm just about ready to quit man." Melvin said feeling defeated. "I loved my cousin, but I can't stand y'all father Huck!"

"This place need you Melvin." Huck said understanding his frustration. "Blue counted on you to keep the place running." He shifted his eyes over to Ms. Jones. "I give you my guarantee Melvin—Mr. White's time is about up." Huck again shifted his eyes over to Ms. Jones then stood.

"What you getting ready to do Huck?" Melvin asked concerned it might be bloodshed.

"I think it's time me and Ms. Jones had a talk." He stated. "Keep an eye on Mr. White, Buckeye . . . and if he even look like he coming my way stop him." Buckeye nodded.

"Well I hope she say something that's gon keep me from walking out that door." Melvin said as he prepared to deliver the free bottle of rum per Mr. White's request. Buckeye watched Mr. White as Huck walked across the room to join Ms. Jones.

• • • •

"How you doing Ms. Jones?" Huck asked sitting down at her table.

"I'm doing fine Henry Lee, how are you?"

"Not too good Ms. Jones." She looked in his glaring eyes and tried to mask her guilt.

"I'm sorry to hear that Henry Lee." Ms. Jones said, glancing nervously over at Mr. White observing him as he continued greeting customers and giving away complimentary bottles of liquor. She again turmed to Huck.

"Ms. Jones, Blue worked real hard—spent every penny he had to get this club up and running, this was his dream." An endearing smile formed on her face.

"Yes." She nodded. "Yes Henry Lee it certainly was."

"And from what I can see Ms. Jones, Mr. White tearing it down faster than it took Ol' Blue to build it." Her anxiety increased as she again shifted her eyes to Mr. White. "Ms. Jones I knew my brother and I know it's only been two women in his life he ever loved—his momma and Effie Mae." Huck said trying to hold his temper. "I don't mean you no disrespect Ms. Jones but I think you know Blue gave this place to Effie Mae." She quickly looked over at Mr. White. "And knowing Blue—he probably gave you a little something too." She picked up the glass of cola she'd been sipping on and took a nervous swallow.

"I don't know what you're talking about Henry Lee." Ms. Jones said, again looking in the direction of Mr. White—not seeing him. "Well you're wrong Henry Lee, Tyrell never said anything to me about this club." Huck looked at her with doubtful eyes then titled his head.

"Is that right?"

"Yes Henry Lee it is." Ms. Jones again picked up the glass and took sipped of cola. Huck's impatience increased.

"I don't want to be disrespectful Ms. Jones, even though Momma loved her scotch she taught me to respect the older folks even though she never did herself." He silently chuckled.

"Well that's Rita now isn't it?"

"I think you lying Ms. Jones." Huck stated trying to be respectful. She turned away, uncertain how to respond to Huck's blatant accusation.

"Well I'm sorry you feel that way Henry Lee." She said taking another swallow of the cola. "I have no reason to lie about—" Huck cut her off.

"Yeah Ms. Jones, you do." She looked in his chastising eyes and again turned away. "But I'm gon let your conscious be your judge Ms. Jones, but I want you to think about how Ol' Blue would feel if he knew what you was doing to the woman he loved." Huck stood and prepared to leave, angered by her dishonesty. He stared momentarily at her then began walking away.

"Henry Lee—wait!" He stopped and returned to her table, again being seated. "You were right." Ms. Jones stated shifting her eyes to Mr. White's last known location, seeing him engaged in conversation with customers. She slightly lowered her head, unable to look Huck in the eyes. "Tyrell did tell me that he'd given this place to Effie Mae." An enormous sense of relief entered Huck's heart when hearing Ms. Jones confirmed what he knew were Blue's final wishes. Ms. Jones raised her head and looked Huck in the eyes. "But I have no idea what he did with the papers proving it." She stated sounding truthful. Huck momentarily stared at her trying to read the look in her eyes.

"I believe you Ms. Jones."

"It's just that your father—" Ms. Jones took another sip of the cola. "—he wanted this place so bad and I just didn't have the heart to tell him Tyrell had given it to Effie Mae."

"Thank you Ms. Jones." Huck stated with sincerity. "I knew you would do the right thing." He stood, feeling victorious as he began walking away.

"But—" She hollered out. Huck again turned to her. "—I'll deny every telling you that if anybody ask me." Huck looked at her in disbelief—loss for words as she again raised the half filled glass of cola up to her mouth. He watched enraged as she sat the glass back on the table and glanced over at Mr. White then looked back into his disappointed eyes. Huck shook his head then walked away. Buckeye watched as Huck returned to the table. He noted the disturbed look in his old friend's eyes.

"What she say Huck?" He asked, anxious to hear if Huck's gut feelings were right.

"Just what I thought she would say Buckeye." Huck said filling his glass with scotch before looking over at his father, cleverly smiling. "Blue left this place and everything else he owned to Effie Mae, but Ms. Jones said she don't know what he done with the papers proving it."

"You believe her Huck!" Buckeye asked, unconvinced by Ms. Jones' denial. Huck tossed the shot of scotch in his mouth.

"Yeah Buckeye, I believe her." He noted the blank stare in Huck's eyes.

"Something wrong Huck?"

"Yeah Buckeye—a whole lot's wrong." Huck poured himself another drink then scoffed it down. "Ms. Jones knowing Blue gave this place to Effie Mae is one thing—" He looked Buckeye in the eyes. "—proving it is another."

"What you mean man I thought you said—" Huck interjected.

"She told me she'd deny it if ever anybody asked her." Buckeye's forehead wrinkled with frowns.

"What!" He yelled. "Man what's wrong with that woman? I knew she couldn't be trusted, I wouldn't believe nothing she had to say Huck!" Buckeye looked over at her and angrily stared. "I bet she would say or do anything your father told her to do!"

"Yeah Buckeye she would." Huck said subconsciously gazed at the half-empty bottle of scotch as he reflected on Buckeye's words. "I believe her Buckeye." Buckeye's jaw dropped.

"You do?" Huck looked up from the bottle and into his old friend's widened eyes.

"Yeah Buckeye I do."

"What make you think that?"

"If Ms. Jones had anything in writing she would've gave it to Mr. White and he would've found some crooked attorney to put everything in his name cutting Effie Mae out." Huck said picking up the bottle of scotch filling his glass. "Naw Buckeye, she don't know."

"Huck man your father's crazy!" Buckeye looked over at Ms. Jones. "And so is Tyrell's momma!" Huck quietly chuckled.

"Blue loved his momma Buckeye—but he wasn't no fool, he knew better than to give Ms. Jones them papers." Huck flung the shot of scotch in his mouth. "He knew his momma wouldn't think twice about giving them papers to Mr. White."

"What you gon do Huck?"

"Like I said Buckeye . . . Blue loved Effie Mae with everything he had in him, he wasn't about to leave that girl with nothing." Huck stood. "It's time for me to talk to Effie Mae—see what she remembers." He shifted his eyes briefly to his father then walked away, hurrying up the stairs. Huck knew with certainty Mr. White's reign had reached its end.

• • • •

"Effie Mae!" Huck pounded on the locked apartment door. "Wake up girl!" The door slowly opened. Effie Mae stood on the other side, awakened by his banging.

"Huck." She said wiping her eyes. "What time is it?"

"It's time to celebrate girl!" He said picking Effie Mae up, twirling her around then placing a quick kiss on her lips.

"What's going on Huck?" She asked looking in his excited eyes. He lowered her back down then closed the door.

"Girl this club is yours, just like I been saying all along!" A confused look appeared on Effie Mae's face.

"What?"

"Effie Mae, Blue left this club to you girl!"

"Who told you that Huck?"

"His momma—Ms. Jones."

"Ms. Jones told you that?" Huck's enthusiasm magnified.

"Think Effie Mae, did Blue ever give you papers—anything saying you owned this place?"

"Naw Huck, not that I know of."

"Think hard Effie Mae!"

"I'm trying Huck."

"Here's what I want you to do—I want you to look around this apartment, go through everything Blue owned—closets, boxes, drawers, anything you ever saw him put anything in—" Effie Mae walked away, getting back in bed. "Did you hear me Effie Mae?" She threw the cover over her head.

"Yeah I heard you Huck, I'm gon do it in the morning." He looked at the blanket covered silhouette.

"Effie Mae what you doing?"

"I'm tired Huck!"

"That's right you pregnant." He shook his head. "You go ahead get your rest, but in the morning Effie Mae you do like I said." He said speaking to her through the blanket. "This club is yours girl, but if Mr.

White keep running it the way he doing—won't be nothing left to have." Huck watched as she rolled over. He sat down on the bed and kissed her on the back of her head through the covers. "Bye Effie Mae."

"Bye Huck." He rose from the bed and exited the apartment, returning downstairs.

• • • •

Buckeye's attention drew to the stairs when seeing Huck returning. His gawk continued as he waited for his old friend to join him at the table to report what he'd discovered.

"It's time to celebrate Buckeye!" Huck said, excited. His zest dwindled when seeing the distressed look on Buckeye's face. "What's going on Buckeye?"

"Huck man you got any warrants out on you?"

"Warrants?" Huck looked at him with questioning eyes. "Naw, my attorney cleared all that up a while back—what's going on?"

"Before the night's up man somebody's going to jail!" Huck's curiosity grew as he waited for an explanation.

"Mr. White finally made Melvin shoot him?" Huck said grinning.

"This ain't about Melvin or your father man—look over at the bar." Huck turned in the direction of the bar seeing his mother drunk and mumbling to herself. "Man . . . Ms. Rita been over there tossing back them shots like it's Kool-Aid." Huck's eyes scanned the club in search of his father. "And she's been cutting her eyes over at Ms. Jones for the last fifteen minutes— I'm telling you Huck if looks could kill, Ms. Jones would already be six feet under!" Buckeye burst into laughter.

"Where's Mr. White?" Huck asked looking around the club.

"The last time I saw him, he was whispering in the ear of one of the waitresses." Buckeye cunningly grinned. Huck tilted his head.

"Is that right?"

"I'm telling you Huck your momma so drunk she cussed Melvin out because he wouldn't give her a free bottle of scotch." Buckeye shook his head as his eyes widened. "And you know yourself—Ms. Rita can be hell when she sober and now she drunk!" Huck quietly chuckled.

"You ever seen my momma sober Buckeye? I know I ain't." The two men laughed.

"Man I know it ain't gon be long before Ms. Rita get some mess stated with that woman."

"Yeah you right Buckeye." Huck poured himself another drink. "Mr. White gon need to get in here—get Ms. Jones out of here before Momma let loose." He glanced around at the various tables of customers. "Where you say you last saw him Buckeye?"

"Huck I ain't seen your father since he was all up on that fine butt new waitress he hired whispering in her ear." Buckeye cunningly grinned. "And that was about twenty minutes ago, and I ain't seen either one of them since." He again grinned. Huck shook his head in response to his father's womanizing.

"Damn shame." He tossed back the shot of scotch and again looked over at his mother. "Let me get Momma out of here before all hell break loose." Huck said getting up from the table, hurrying over to the bar. "What you doing here Momma?"

"What the hell you mean what I'm doing here little boy?" She slurred. "I own this damn club."

"Come on now Momma you ain't got nothing saying you or Daddy own this place."

"Get the hell away from me Henry Lee!" She yelled swinging her fist, trying to hit him. Huck intercepted her intended blows. "You don't want to do that Momma."

"What the hell you mean I don't want to do that?" She said struggling to break free from his hold. "Let me go Henry Lee!" She shouted. "Don't make me hurt you little boy."

"I ain't no little boy Momma I told you now—I'm a grown man."

"I don't give a damn how grown you are Henry Lee, I'm gon always be growner than you."

"I know that Momma, but I can't let you hit me." He said continuing to hold her.

"Turn me a loose Henry Lee!" Ms. Rita shouted, trying to removed Huck's arms from around her. Melvin hurried from the kitchen when hearing the mother and son squabble.

"Huck man . . . you gon have to get your momma out of here." He warned. "You know I have to call the police if it looks like somebody might get hurt." Melvin humped his shoulders in a matter of fact gesture. "Insurance company's rules."

"The police?" Ms. Rita slurred. "Call the damn police Marvin you jackass!" She shouted staring Melvin in the eyes. "I don't give a damn! And when you call them—tell them my husband's hoe sitting her ass in here uglying up the place." Ms. Jones turned in response to Ms. Rita's offensive words. "That's right heifer—" She said gawking at her husband's longtime mistress. "—I'm talking about you."

"Come on now Momma—" Huck said pleading with her. "—it's time for you to go." She looked at him, but ignored his words.

"That's my damn husband you been messing with all these damn years wench!" Ms. Rita said yelled before standing up.

"What you doing Momma?"

"Get your ass out of my way Henry Lee." She said yanking her arm from Huck's grasp, shoving him out of the way as she prepared to confront Ms. Jones.

"Come on now Momma." Huck said taking hold of her. "You heard Melvin say he was getting ready to call the police."

"And you heard me say I don't give a damn what Marvin getting ready to do!" She staggered over towards Ms. Jones's a few tables away.

"Hey Handsome." Huck blushed in response to the seductive voice of an unseen female coming up behind him, momentarily distracting him from his mother and Ms. Jones' progressing quarrel. He turned and looked in the flirtatious smile of Benita.

"Why you let my momma come up here Benita?"

"Ms. Rita's a grown ass woman Henry Lee, if she want to come up here and check on her jazz club—"

"Momma don't have no more right to this club than Mr. White."

"You try telling her that Henry Lee." Benita stated. "Right now the only thing I want to do is talk about me and you." She wrapped her arms around Huck's neck and tried to kiss him. "Boy you always were good looking, I don't know what I was thinking when I let you get away." Huck grabbed her gripping arms and tried to unlock her unyielding grasp, continuing to be distracted from his mother as she approached Ms. Jones and stood over her holding a glass of scotch in her right hand.

"Heifer you think I'm just gon let you have my damn husband?" Ms. Rita said slurring her words—trying to maintain her balance. "Well if you do wench you got another thing coming you old ass slut!"

"Rita you better get your drunk ass out of my face!" Ms. Jones stated with warning, still being seated.

"What you say to me wench?"

"You heard me." Ms. Jones rose from her seat. "Rita you have five seconds to get the hell away from me before I whip your old ass like I did last year!"

"You just try and I'll hit you so hard heifer—you gon think you've been struck by lightning!" Ms. Rita yelled before swinging her left hand, missing. Ms. Jones dodged the intended blow then quickly countered, stricking her opponent in the face, knocking Ms. Rita over onto the table directly behind her—sending the customers sitting there screaming and scurrying away. The band ceased playing in response to the violent altercation. Melvin motioned them with his hands to continue playing, hoping to minimize the disruption as he picked up the phone and called the police as the sound of jazz again filled the acoustics of the club.

"Yeah operator—get me the police." He said keeping his eyes on the two middle-aged women engaged in battle. "I need the police down here at Blue's Jazz Club . . . I have two women in here about to tear one another apart."

"Stop now Benita!" Huck said repeatedly removing her gripping arms from around his neck. "Since your little girlfriend's not standing anywhere around in her men's pajamas—" Benita suggestively smiled. "—let's me and you get out of here, go someplace where we can get reacquainted." Huck quickly turned his head when she tried to kiss him—her approaching lips landing on the back of his head. He continued effortlessly trying to pry her arms from around his neck.

"I ain't trying to mess with you Benita."

"Don't be acting like you ain't interested Henry Lee." She said trying to kiss him. "Boy you know you want me."

"Yeah I want you Benita—out of my face." Buckeye watched from across the room hysterically laughing as he observed the ongoing struggle between his old friend and the mother of his children.

"Buckeye!" Huck yelled out irritated. Buckeye laughed as he hurried over to Huck's aid, witnessing for the first time his old friend resisting the intimate embrace of a female.

"You called me Huck?"

"Man get Benita's ass off me!" Huck said entangled in her grip. "Then get her ass out of here Buckeye and don't let her back in." Buckeye grabbed Benita from behind and held her as Huck broke free.

"Let go of me Lawrence!" She shouted. Huck momentarily stared at her as he adjusted his fashionable attire.

"Get your hands off me Lawrence before I—"

"Before you what Benita?" Huck said looking at her with angry eyes. "Only thing you getting ready to do is get your ass out of here—go take care of your kids."

"I ain't leaving here Henry Lee until Ms. Rita say she's ready to go!"

"Yeah you leaving and so is Momma." Huck turned in the direction of Ms. Jones's table, now surrounded by a crowd of on-lookers. He looked over at Melvin.

"Man I already called the police." He stated in a matter-of-fact toner as he continued to monitor the *bar room brawl*.

"Look here Buckeye . . . I'm gon get Momma and take her out the back way." Huck shook his head thinking of the difficulty he would endure in doing so. "You get Benita out of here—" Huck looked momentarily at Benita. "—and look here Buckeye after you do that—lock the door."

"So that's how it's gon be Henry Lee?" Benita stated as Buckeye continue retraining her. Huck ignored her—his only thought being to get his mother out before the police arrived. Buckeye escorted Benita out of the club, locking the door behind her. Huck worked his way through the crowd of onlookers until reaching his mother and Ms. Jones. He laughed out loud when seeing his mother pinned down on a table by Ms. Jones.

"What you doing Momma?"

"Get this heifer off of me Henry Lee!" She shouted. Huck continued laughing, amused by the mutual combat between his father's mistress and estranged wife. He shook his head.

"Come on now Ms. Jones let my momma go."

"You better get her out here Henry Lee before I hurt her!"

"I get up from here wench, we'll see who's gon get hurt!" Ms. Rita shouted, slurring. Huck's chuckling persisted.

"Look like she got you Momma." He stated then turned to Ms. Jones trying to contain his laughter. "Melvin already called the police Ms. Jones, if they get here and you and Momma still in here fighting they gon take both of y'all to jail."

"Ain't nobody taking me no damn place Henry Lee!" Ms. Rita yelled, exhausted. "Get off me heifer!"

"Here's what I'm gon do Ms. Jones—" Huck said preparing himself for his mother's expected resistance. "—I'm gon hold Momma, give you a chance to leave."

"You'd better keep her away from me Henry Lee." Ms. Jones said infuriated. "Or I'm going to hurt her!"

"Naw Ms. Jones don't do that I got her." Huck lessened his laughter as he prepared to intervene. "You go ahead on and leave." Huck seized his mother seconds after Ms. Jones released her.

"Let me go little boy!" Ms. Rita yelled, struggling to break his hold. "I ain't finished with that hoe yet."

"Yeah Momma, you finished." Huck said as he raised her from the table, ushering her out the back when seeing the multitude of police entering through the front door, unlocked by Melvin.

"Police!" An officer shouted.

# *Chapter Twenty-Six*

After three weeks of looking through closets, drawers and multiple boxes in search of documents verifying ownership of Blue's Jazz Club — without results, Effie Mae sat on the bed rummaging through a large black trunk containing more of Blue's belongings being distracted when hearing a knock at the door.

"Yeah Deborah Ann."

"Effie Mae it's J.R."

"It's open J.R." She said continuing to sort through the many items and documents inside the trunk. J.R. opened the door and poked his head in. His eyes slightly widened when seeing the many boxes of clothes, papers and various other items scattered about the apartment.

"You uh, feeling okay?" He asked looking around the cluttered space as he entered — closing the door behind him.

"Yeah, I'm just a little tired." His concern grew when hearing the exhaustion in her voice.

"You sure?"

"Yeah J.R. — I said I was." Effie Mae said slightly agitated. He backed off sensing her frustration.

"I uh, wanted to come by and thank you for having supper with me and the children last week."

"J.R. you don't have to thank me for being with you and my babies."

"I uh, know you probably got other things to do —" He silenced when his attention again drew to the excessive messiness. "—you uh, going somewhere?" He asked, curious of the packed and semi-packed boxes located in various places throughout the apartment.

"Yeah J.R. — I am." Effie Mae looked up at him. "Blue's daddy putting me out of here." J.R.'s mouth flung open.

"What?" He said raising his voice, upset by the news. "Effie Mae why didn't you tell me?"

"I thought Ms. Jones was gon be able to stop him but —"

"Come home Effie Mae with and the —" She cut him off.

"I can't do that J.R."

"So uh, where will you go?"

"Don't worry J.R., I'll find someplace to go." She said dismissing the disappointed look on J.R.'s face. His mouth dried at thought of her returning home to Mississippi to be with Anthony. He coughed.

"A place where Effie Mae?" J.R. said suspicious of her vague response. "Cousin Daniel's?"

"J.R. please!" Effie Mae yelled. "That ain't what I said!"

"Why don't you uh, just come home for a few weeks Effie Mae until you can find somewhere to—"

"I ain't ready for that!" J.R. slowly inhaled, exhaling through his nose as he tried to remain calm.

"I uh, guess if you ain't ready then I uh—I won't push." He said hoping she'd change her mind. "Will you at least let me know where uh, you are when you get there?"

"Yeah J.R. I will." Effie Mae said merely responding to his voice. He again looked around the disorganized apartment.

"So uh, you moving does that mean Blue didn't uh, leave a will?"

"Naw J.R. it don't . . . it just mean we can't find it."

"We?" He asked curious of who *we* consisted of.

"Me and Huck."

"Huck?" J.R.'s mouth again dried. He coughed. "Are you and he uh—"

"Huck's my friend J.R." Effie Mae yelled.

"I was uh, just curious." A lump formed in his throat. He knew for certain Huck being in Effie Mae's life consisted of more than just a friendship.

"Ms. Jones told Huck . . . Blue left this place to me." A baffled look appeared on J.R.'s face. "Then how can uh, Blue's father put you—"

"Ms. Jones told Huck she gon deny it if anybody asked her." J.R.'s mouth quickly opened, surprised by Ms. Jones' dishonorable actions.

"Why would she uh, not want to—"

"Cause Mr. White won't this club and everything else belonging to Blue." J.R.'s mouth dried when noticing the picture of Blue lying on the pillow.

"Uh, did you ever get a chance to look through the stuff Blue left you in uh, that huge white envelope?" He asked feeling insecure by the photo.

"Naw J.R. not yet." She stopped, visually searching for the mysterious envelope. "I ain't even sure I remember what I did with it, I been so busy looking for them papers." J.R.'s attention again drew to Blue's picture.

"I guess uh, Blue's uh, picture lying on this pillow brings you some sort of uh, comfort?" Effie Mae ignored the look of discomfort in his eyes.

"Yeah J.R. it do." Her eyes dampened when looking momentarily at the photo seeing Blue's captivating smile. "It make me feel like my baby still here with me." She said smiling through her tears.

"I guess uh, if it brings you comfort—"

"That's where I put it J.R.!"

"Huh?"

"That's what I did with it."

"Did with what?" J.R. asked watching as she removed Blue's photo off the pillow and kissed it before laying it on the bed. His mouth dried. He coughed. Effie Mae raised the pillow and looked underneath.

"Here it is!" She said excited. J.R. looked at the peculiar envelope with ambiguity. On the one hand he wondered if perhaps it contained the documents validating Effie Mae's ownership of the Jazz Club—and the apartment. On the other hand, somewhere inside himself he hoped it wasn't even though he knew in his heart it was what Effie Mae wanted. She picked up the envelope and handed it to him.

"Yeah—that uh, looks like it."

"Will you look in it for me J.R.?" Effie Mae asked believing it to contain additional photos and maybe even a little cash. "I got to finish packing this stuff—Mr. White want me out this weekend."

"This weekend?" J.R. said raising his voice. He looked up at the ceiling and shook his head, frustrated. He again turned to Effie Mae. "How Effie Mae? You're pregnant!"

"J.R., Mr. White don't care bout that."

"So he uh, still expects you to pack your stuff—and Blues, and be out by this weekend?"

"Yep he do."

"Even though you pregnant?"

"J.R.—" Effie Mae walked over to the closet. "—that man hate me so much, he don't care nothing 'bout that." J.R.'s head lightly pounded.

"Hate you?"

"Yep."

"Why?"

"He think I was trying to trick Blue out of this jazz club." J.R.'s anger heightened in response to Mr. White's rediculous accusation.

"Do I uh, need to talk to Mr. White?"

"Naw J.R. that man ain't trying to hear what you or nobody else got to say." Effie Mae suddenly giggled. A odd look displayed on J.R.'s face, curious of her out of place laughter.

"What?"

"Mr. White think you was in on it with me." J.R.'s jaw dropped.

"He what?" He yelled.

"Don't worry about it J.R., just go ahead and look in that envelope, maybe Blue left me some money." She giggled. J.R. panicked.

"You uh, sure you want me to uh, open it?" He asked, stalling.

"Yeah J.R. I'm sure." She looked over at him and quietly chuckled. "If Blue did put me some money in there I hope it's enough for me to buy this place from his daddy." Effie Mae stated with minimal hope." J.R. continued his curious gaze at the white envelope, apprehensive about opening it. He hoped the documents resolving Effie Mae's dilemma would be inside, but worried if such documents did exist — they might delay or even change Effie Mae's mind about resuming her role as his wife. J.R. nervously gawked at the envelope.

"I don't uh, mind opening it . . . it's just that uh —"

"J.R.!"

"Huh?" He shifted his worried eyes over at her.

"Open that thing!" Effie Mae said giggling as she retrieved her old suitcase from inside the closet.

"Uh, okay." He gazed briefly at the envelope before slowly beginning to open it.

"What is it J.R.?" Effie Mae asked as she yanked clothing from hangers, tossing them on the bed. J.R.'s hand slightly trembled as he reached inside the envelope and pulled out the first document. He turned it over identifying it as the deed to Blue's Jazz Club naming Effie Mae as the owner. J.R,'s jaw dropped.

"What? Did Blue leave me some money?" Effie Mae asked continuing to removing clothes from the closet. He looked over at her, unable to speak as he again reached inside the envelope — this time sliding out a document entitled, *Last Will And Testament*, signed by both Blue and Effie Mae. J.R.'s eyes widened as he removed document after document — all containing both Blue's and Effie Mae's signatures.

"Uh, Effie Mae —"

"Yeah J.R." She said tossing articles of clothing on the bed.

"Do you uh, remember Blue having you sign anything?"

"Anything like what J.R.?"

"Papers?"

"Blue had me sign a lot things before we got married—" Effie Mae quickly looked at him. "—I'm sorry J.R., I shouldn't have said—" He interjected.

"It's okay Effie Mae—I was there remember?" J.R. humorously smiled. "Did Blue ever tell you what it was you were uh, signing?"

"Naw J.R. . . all I remember him saying was it was his wedding gift to me." She said removing some of Blue's clothes from the closet. "Why? Did Blue leave me some money or something that's gon help me keep this place?" Effie Mae said clueless of J.R.'s reason for his specific questions. "I hope so because I'm gon need some money to—" He cut her off.

"Uh, Effie Mae?"

"Yeah J.R."

"Stop packing."

"What?"

"Stop packing." A look of disbelief displayed on his face. "Uh, that wedding gift from Blue—" J.R. paused. "—it was uh, this jazz club, this apartment, Blue's bank accounts, his car and everything else he owned in this world." Effie Mae's mouth abruptly opened. She dropped the clothing held in her hand then slowly turned to J.R.

"You sure J.R.?" She asked frightened by his unbelievable words.

"Yeah, but uh—"

"But what J.R.?"

"I uh, think you should uh, come look at it for yourself?" She noted J.R.'s rapid breathing as she began walking towards him, looking slowly at the documents he held in his hands confirming J.R.'s words.

"I knew my Baby loved me." Effie Mae said lowering herself onto the bed. She picked up Blue's picture and looked at it with tear filled eyes then lovingly kissed. "Tyrell Lee Jones." J.R. mouth dried as he wondered how her new found fortune would affect their future together. He coughed.

———————————

Melvin unlocked and opened the front door of the jazz club allowing Mr. White and Mr. Garrett to enter. Huck and Buckeye waited at a table in the center of the club—the look of victory highlighted on both men's faces.

"I take it Mr. White Jr. you called this meeting because you've found something?" Mr. Garrett asked being seated at Huck's right. Mr. White nervously lowered himself in the chair, right of Mr. Garrett.

"Make sure whatever he gives you Mr. Garrett you look it over with wide eyes." Mr. White stated, shifting his eyes over at Huck. "He's a known hustler." Huck looked his father in the eyes.

"You know Mr. White—it takes one to know one, don't you think?" He titled his head. "But it looks like this time Ol' Blue out hustled you."

"How about I just take a look at what is it you have Mr. White Jr.?" Mr. Garrett said glancing briefly over at Buckeye. Huck handed him the envelope containing copies of all the documents verifying Effie Mae's ownership of Blue's Jazz Club and all of Blue's other assets.

"Those are just copies." Huck stated. "If you want the originals you can get them from Effie Mae's Attorney, Mr. Williamson—David Williamson." Huck shifted his eyes to Buckeye and victoriously winked.

"Well, if these are copies of the originals as you say Mr. White Jr. then it looks like Mrs. Effie Mae Smith is the rightful owner of all the assets belonging to Tyrell Lee Jones, including this jazz club." Mr. Garrett stated, continuing to carefully examine the documents. Huck turned and faced his father.

"Well Mr. White—" A huge smile spread across Huck's handsome face. "—on behalf of Effie Mae, Blue's wife." He emphasized. "I got just one thing to say—" Huck shifted his briefly to Buckeye then back to his father. "—get your ass off this woman's property you ain't welcome here." Huck noting a subtle smile on Mr. Garrett's face. "Now Ms. Jones—" Huck looked over at his old friend noting the sarcastic look on his face. "—she's welcome here anytime she in town . . . Ol' Blue loved his momma, so I wouldn't do nothing he wouldn't want me to."

"Well, Mr. White Jr.—" Mr. Garrett said putting the documents inside his open briefcase. "—it looks like Mrs. Smith has herself a jazz club." He looked in Mr. White's defeated eyes with caution before standing. "Congratulations gentlemen."

"Henry Lee don't you ever in your life call me your daddy boy!" Mr. White shouted. "You ain't no son of mines." Huck laughed out loud

"Well Mr. White looks like we both agree on that." Father and son simultaneously rose from the table. "You ain't got no son and I ain't got no daddy." Huck shook his head. "Damn shame."

Mr. White looked over at Melvin watching from the bar, quietly laughing as he witnessed him being *dethroned* as the owner of Blue's Jazz Club.

"That's right Melvin—laugh!" Mr. White stated with malice. "You be grateful I don't' own this damn club, I was just getting ready to fire your sorry ass!" Melvin's mouth flung open. "I heard how you'd been stealing money from the cash register—damn thief!" Melvin's jaw dropped, shocked by Mr. White's *bold faced* lie. Mr. Garrett's forehead moistened when seeing Buckeye reach inside his suit jacket, placing his hand on his holstered pistol in response to Mr. White's vindictive words.

"Mr. White . . . why don't we uh, leave here now while things are still peaceful?" Mr. Garrett said removing a handkerchief from his shirt pocket, dabbing his wet forehead, shifting his nervous eyes over to Buckeye. "Mr. White can we please leave here now?"

"Give me a minute Mr. Garrett." Mr. White said turning to Huck. "You think you done something don't you Henry Lee?"

"Yeah Mr. White I do." Huck said staring him boldly in the eyes. "I kept a greedy old man from taking what he knew wasn't meant for or didn't belong to him." A vengeful look beamed from Mr. White's eyes.

"You don't say." He said cunningly chuckling, turning to Mr. Garrett. "Let's get out of this dump." Mr. White said downplaying its worth.

"Yeah, you do that Mr. White." Huck stated.  Mr. White shifted his eyes to Buckeye then looked over at Melvin and again back to Huck as he began walking in the direction of the front door joining Mr. Garrett already there and waiting.

"Sorry I wasted your time Mr. Garrett." Mr. White said masking his intent to ultimately one day seize the jazz club from Effie Mae . . . by any means necessary.

"You gentlemen have a nice day." Mr. Garrett said, quickly exiting the establishment. Mr. White joined slowly him, but not before exchanging a cold hard stare with his disavowed eldest son.

"I know one thing." Melvin said hurrying over to the door locking it after they'd departed.

"What's that Melvin?" Huck asked.

"Opening that door before we open for business—is bad business!" Melvin laughed. "Now what y'all drinking?" He asked mocking Mr. White.

"Scotch . . . on the house!" Huck and Buckeye stated in unison. The three men laughed as they prepared to celebrate.

# Chapter Twenty-Seven

"Hello."

"Hey Momma!"

"Effie Mae?"

"He loved me Momma!" Effie Mae stated with excitement.

"Who loved you child?"

"Blue, Momma . . . he loved me!"

"What's going on Effie Mae got you so excited?"

"Momma, Blue gave me his jazz club!" Millie gasped.

"What you say child?"

"He loved me Momma!"

"I heard you say that already—but what's all that talk about him giving you his jazz club?"

"He did Momma . . . Blue signed everything over to me, but I didn't know it—" Millie interjected.

"Effie Mae . . . you sure about that child?"

"Yeah Momma, Blue gave the papers to J.R., and J.R. gave them to me, but we didn't know that's what the papers was when Blue gave them to J.R., then Blue's daddy tried to take everything and—"

"Effie Mae!" Millie cut her off. "Slow down child."

"What Momma?"

"What's all this is talk about J.R., Blue and papers?"

"Momma, Blue signed some papers giving me everything he owned including his jazz club, then his daddy—" Millie again interjected.

"His daddy?"

"Yeah Momma . . . Mr. White, he tried to take everything from me and put me out on the streets, but Huck—"

"Huck?" Millie scowled. "Effie Mae you ain't messing with that man is you?" She dismissed her momma's probing question. "It ain't been that long since Blue passed."

"Momma, Huck's my friend!" Millie raised an eyebrow.

"Your friend huh?"

"Yeah Momma."

"Well before you get yourself caught up in some mess with your friend, don't forget you still got a husband—"

"I know that Momma!" Effie Mae said not wanting to speak on her marriage to J.R. "If it wasn't for Huck I'd be calling you from a payphone and living on the streets Momma."

"You know it ain't no way J.R. gon let you live on the streets child."

"Just be happy for me Momma."

"I am Effie Mae, but—"

"But what Momma?"

"What you know about running a jazz club child?"Millie asked worried. "And don't forgot about that drinking problem got you in trouble with your sister over Pete." Millie chuckled.

"Naw Momma, I ain't forgot." Effie Mae's excitement dwindled. "I'm pregnant Momma!" She said redirecting the conversation. Millie gasped, but gave no reply.

"Did you hear me Momma?"

"Yeah child I heard you—but I'm half scared to ask who the daddy of that child is." Millie said bracing herself for the answer.

"It's J.R.'s Momma!" Millie again gasped.

"J.R.?" She stated, stunned. "You sure 'bout that Effie Mae? I remember you said that once before and the truth just about destroyed your poor husband and you."

"I ain't forgot Momma."

"Sissy Hill ain't stopped talking 'bout that yet—" Millie half-heartedly chuckled. "—to any ears willing to listen to that mess."

"Well Momma . . . Ms. Sissy can stop all her talking now."

"All I got to say Effie Mae is I sure hope you right this time."

"J.R. and Blue was the last men I was with Momma before I got pregnant." Effie Mae quieted. "And Momma—Blue couldn't have babies."

"Did he tell you that Effie Mae?"

"Yeah Momma he did." Effie Mae saddened. "We talked about it and Blue said something about him having the mumps when he was a boy." Millie shook her head with pity.

"I sure am sorry to hear that Effie Mae."

"You know what I'm hoping Momma?"

"If you still hoping for that man to come back from the grave—" Effie Mae interrupted.

"I would love that Momma, but I don't think all the hoping in the world gon make that happen."

"I'm glad you finally realize it."

"I would love it Momma if somehow this baby growing inside me could be Blue's." A loving smile spread across Effie Mae's face. "I wanted so bad for me and Blue to have us a child of our own."

"How was you gon get pregnant Effie Mae when you was taking birth control pills?"

"I got off my pills Momma!"

"Then how do you know you ain't carrying Betsy Lewis' son's baby Effie Mae?"

"Because I wasn't nowhere near Anthony when I got pregnant Momma." Effie Mae giggled.

"Do J.R. know you pregnant Effie Mae?"

"Yeah Momma he know, we talked about it." She paused. "Don't judge me Momma—"

"Judge you about what child?"

"I love you Momma." Effie Mae said electing not to tell her momma of her intent to name her baby after Blue—if it's a boy.
"What is it you ain't telling me Effie Mae?"

"I said I love you Momma." Millie smiled deciding not to pursue it any further.

"I love you too child."

"Now Momma I know you don't fly, but you gon have to grow you some wings or get ready for that long train trip up here from Mississippi— cause I ain't having this baby without you." Effie Mae giggled.

"Fly?"

"Yeah Momma—fly."

"Then I guess I'm just gon have to take up knitting."

"What that got to do with you flying Momma?"

"Not a thing cause I ain't about to get on nobody's plane." Effie Mae's confusion grew. "So I'm gon be knitting all while I'm making that long trip to New York—by train."

"Momma . . . a train?"

"Yeah child, a train."

"Momma!"

"Don't momma me, I ain't doing no flying unless I wake up one morning and find that the good Lord done placed a pair of wings on my back." Millie laughed.

"Okay Momma . . . as long as you get here that's all that matter to me." A warm smile formed on Effie Mae's face. "Thank you Momma."

"You welcome child."

"Bye Momma." Effie Mae hung up then quickly dialed Anthony's number.

• • • •

"Hey Anthony."

"Hey Baby." An enormous smile formed on Anthony's face, delighted to hear her voice. "It feels so good to hear your voice Baby, how have you been?"

"I'm fine Anthony."

"Baby you sound really happy—that's good."

"Anthony, Blue gave me his jazz club."

"He did what?"

"When we got married—" She stopped.

"It's okay Baby, I was there remember?"

"I'm sorry Anthony."

"It's okay Baby, now what were you saying?"

"Anthony, Blue had me sign a bunch of papers but I didn't know he was giving everything to me—"

"Everything?" Anthony said, astonished. "Baby are you sure?"

"Yeah Anthony, but then Blue's daddy tried to take everything from me . . . even this apartment—m" Anthony's eyes widened. "—Anthony that man was getting ready to put me out on the streets—"

"Baby slow down, tell me what's going on." Anthony said trying to digest her multiple words.

"Blue gave me his jazz club Anthony—"

"Okay I heard that . . . I also heard you say Blue's father was trying to do what?"

"He was trying to put me out on the streets Anthony, but Huck talked to her and she said—" He interrupted.

"Baby hold on you said her—who's her?"

"Blue's momma, Anthony . . . she told Huck, Blue left this jazz club to me—"

"Huck?" Anthony said disappointed to hear of Huck's continued presence in Effie Mae's life. "I'm sure he would've found some unsavory place for you to live." He stated underneath his breath.

"Huh?"

"Baby are you and he—"

"What I didn't know Anthony—" Effie Mae said evading his question. "—Blue had gave the papers to J.R. to hold for me."

"To J.R.?"

"Yeah . . . so when I went over to J.R.'s house he gave me the envelope but I never looked inside.

"Envelope?"

"Yeah Anthony that's what Blue put the papers in . . . so a few days ago when J.R. came over—"

"Baby are you and J.R.—"

"Anthony listen!"

"Okay Baby I'm listening, I just don't know if I like what I think I'm about to hear."

"Anyway . . . it turned out Blue gave everything to me."

"That's great Baby but—"

"But what Anthony?"

"So what does that mean for us Baby?"

"It means Anthony since I don't know the first thing about running a jazz club—" Effie Mae giggled. "—I was hoping you would come to New York and run it for me." His mouth abruptly opened.

"Run—Blue's jazz club?"

"Yeah Anthony!" Effie Mae said with enthusiasm. "Boy you got all that education." Anthony remained speechless, overwhelmed by Effie Mae's offer. "Did you hear me Anthony?"

"Yes Baby I heard you." He said trying to digest her news. "And Baby . . . I would be honored to run your jazz club."

"Thank you Anthony." A smile of gratitude displayed on Effie Mae's face. "Now you can spend time with Lil' J.R."

"I would love that Baby, but—"

"But what Anthony?"

"Out of respect to J.R., maybe the three of us should decide how my involvement in Lil' J.R.'s life should be handled."

"Okay Anthony."

"Thank you Baby." He briefly silenced. "I also want to thank you for including me in your new business." Anthony's optimism grew as he thought of how this might also be a new beginning for him and Effie Mae."

"Anthony I need to tell you something before you get here." A lump formed in his throat as he prepared himself for possible heartbreaking news.

"Baby—"

"I'm pregnant Anthony."

"You are!" He stated with excitement. "Finally, we have another baby on the way?"

"Naw Anthony we don't."

"What do mean? You said you were pregnant right?"

"Yeah Anthony I—" He interrupted.

"So what you're telling me is that you're pregnant—" Anthony took a deep breath before swallowing the lump in his throat. "—it's just not mines." Effie Mae heard disappointment in his voice. "So I guess you and Blue made a baby after all."

"Naw Anthony."

"Baby please tell me you're not pregnant with Huck's child." Effie Mae giggled.

"Naw Anthony this ain't none of Huck's baby." She said continuing to giggle. "It's J.R.'s."

"Now that's a surprise." Anthony said oddly relieved. "I wasn't aware you and J.R. were—"

"One time Anthony."

"One time?"

"Yeah and I got pregnant!" Effie Mae giggled.

"So I guess you stopped taking the pill."

"Yeah Anthony I did—I'm sorry." A brief moment of guilt entered Effie Mae's conscience. "I thought maybe me and Blue could have a baby."

"You and Blue." Anthony said hurt. "So why then are you pregnant by J.R.?"

"Blue couldn't have babies Anthony."

"Okay?" Anthony tried to understand how J.R. fit into the equation. "So Baby you're telling me because Blue couldn't have children, you and J.R.—what?" Effie Mae giggled.

"That ain't what happened Anthony!"

"Then I don't understand."

"J.R. was angry at me because I was marrying Blue, so he said he was gon take my babies from me."

"So in exchange you and he—"

"Yeah Anthony, I'm sorry."

"And now you're pregnant, but not with our child . . . but with J.R.'s." Anthony took a deep breath, upset by the news. Effie Mae's excitement suddenly increased.

"But guess what Anthony?"

"I'd rather not."

"Since me and Blue couldn't have a baby—if me and J.R. have a baby boy we gon name him after Blue!" Anthony's eyes widened, shocked by Effie Mae's disturbing announcement.

"Baby did you say you were naming you and J.R.'s child—if it's a boy, after Blue?"

"Yeah Anthony!" Effie Mae stated proudly. "Tyrell Lee Jones Smith."

"Baby does J.R. know that?"

"Yeah Anthony he do—why?"

"So tell me Baby, did you ever really love me?"

"Yeah Anthony I did."

"And now?"

"I still do."

"Are you sure?"

"Yeah Anthony I'm sure." She giggled.

"Well I guess what goes around truly does come back around."

"Huh?"

"Never mind." He said dismissing the thought. "So when do you want me there? I'm sure I'll have to put in at least a three or four week notice with the accounting firm."

"Whenever you can get here Anthony is fine, Melvin can take care of everything until you get here."

"Melvin?" Anthony's insecurity mounted. "Is he someone I should be worried about?" Effie Mae girlishly blushed as she thought of the kiss she and Melvin once shared and his offer to take Blue's place.

"Naw Anthony . . . Melvin ain't nobody you need to be worried about." Her blushing smile widened.

"So Baby I guess I'll see you in a couple of—" Anthony quieted.

"What wrong Anthony?"

"Is there anything else you need to tell me Baby before I get there? I don't think I could handle any more surprises." Effie Mae giggled.

"Nope, that's all."

"Are you sure?"

"Yeah Anthony I'm sure." She continuing to giggling.

"Good." He stated breathing a sigh of relief. "I guess that means I'll have to sell my—our house?"

"Is that good or bad Anthony?"

"It's great." He stated. "I love you Baby." Effie Mae smiled when hearing love in his voice despite her recent disclosure.

"I love you too Anthony."

"Bye Baby."

"Bye, Anthony." She momentarily paused then hung up.

---

J.R. watched as Effie Mae washed dishes after eating dinner with him and the children. She blushed when noticing his gaze.

"What?"

"You always looked so beautiful when you were pregnant." He said smiling. "It seems kind of uh, unreal us with another child on the way." J.R. said trying to work up the nerves to ask Effie Mae when she planned on moving back in. "The uh, children really like when you have supper with us—" J.R. briefly chuckled. "—especially Lil' J.R."

"I love eating supper with my babies J.R."

"You uh, have any idea when you might be moving back in?" Effie Mae's anxiety increased.

"J.R. right now I want to be in the place where me and Blue spent his last days." She said electing not to tell J.R. she didn't plan on coming back. His mouth dried. He coughed. "I ain't ready to move out of there just yet."

"Uh, okay . . . then I uh, I won't pressure you."

"I need a little more time J.R." Effie Mae said electing also not to tell him of Anthony's impending arrival. She instead decided to discuss Daniel's recent request. "I'm glad Daniel took our babies over to his house yesterday to see D.J." A startled look formed on J.R.'s face, astonished by her referring to his cousin as Daniel and not—Mr. Daniel.

"Uh, Daniel?"

"What?"

"When did you uh, start calling Cousin Daniel . . . Daniel?"

"J.R. I think he stopped being Mr. Daniel when we was making D.J." J.R.'s mouth quickly opened in response to Effie Mae's bold statement.

"Uh, okay—"

"What J.R.?" Effie Mae said hearing the accusatory tone in his voice.

"Are you and Cousin Daniel—" J.R.'s his mouth dried.

"Naw J.R. we ain't."

"I was uh, just wondering." He coughed. Effie Mae dismissed the cynical look in J.R.'s eyes.

"Why you ask?"

"It's just that uh . . . I had heard he still had feelings for you—" J.R. briefly paused. "—strong feelings." Effie Mae laughed within herself, amused by her estranged husband's *humble* jealousy.

"That's over J.R."

"Maybe for you . . . I'm not so sure about Cousin Daniel."

"I know what me and Daniel done was wrong J.R., and people got hurt—" He quickly intervened.

"People?" J.R. said slightly raising his voice, looking at her in disbelief. "No—not people Effie Mae . . . me and Geraldine!"

"I know that J.R, but ain't no way me and Daniel can't take it back now." An angry gaze entered his eyes in response to Effie Mae's lack of empathy. "J.R. we all still family—" He cut her off.

"Family?" J.R. raised his voice, given the fact her last child had been fathered by his cousin. Effie Mae looked in the living room hoping the children's attention hadn't been drawn to their daddy's angry outburst.

"J.R. —" She said slightly lowered her voice. "—I want my baby D.J. to grow up with Lil' J.R. and his sisters."

"Ahem!" J.R. cleared his throat then looked in the living room, concerned his children might hear their momma's speaking of her taboo behavior with his cousin. He again turned to Effie Mae and silently stared at her.

"What?"

"Do you really want the children to hear this conversation?"

"What J.R.? All I said is I want D.J. to grow with my babies."

"I don't think they need to know you're the mother of my Cousin Daniel's son." He said speaking slightly above a whisper.

"Naw J.R. they don't—it's bad enough Millie Ann know."

"You give yourself to my cousin then you and he have a child and I'm supposed to do what Effie Mae?" J.R. said trying to contain his hurt and anger.

"Accept it J.R." His jaw quickly dropped, shocked by her blatant disregard for his feelings.

"Is that really what you expect for me to do—accept you and Cousin Daniel's adultery?" J.R.'s agitation soared. "No!" He said increasing his tone. Effie Mae shifting her eyes in the living room at her children seeing them engrossed in watching television.

"I understand you was hurt J.R. but—"

"Do you Effie Mae?" J.R. said looking angrily at her, unconvinced. "Do you really understand the hurt I felt knowing my wife had shared our bed with my cousin?" She stared in his enraged eyes, unable to speak. "No Effie Mae, you don't!"

"J.R., me and you wasn't even together when—" He cut her off.

"Together . . . you was my wife Effie Mae!" J.R. yelled. She looked quickly in the living room, uncertain if the children had heard J.R.'s heated words. Seeing their eyes still glued to the television, Effie Mae turned back to him.

"J.R. my babies love D.J. —"

"I said no!" He shouted not wanting Daniel or the child he fathered with his wife's in his life. J.R.'s eyes met with his children's—their attention drawn to the kitchen in response to his angry outburst. Millie Ann looked at her momma noting the worried look on her face. She shifted her eyes to her daddy seeing his obvious upset.

"Y'all finish watching television Millie Ann."

"Okay Momma." She said turning the channel—increasing the volume. "Y'all let's watch this!" Millie Ann said drawing their attention back to the televion and new cartoon. Effie Mae turned back to J.R. seeing the bitter look in his eyes.

"J.R.—" He interrupted.

"Don't you dare ask me to accept a child you had by my cousin!" Effie Mae's eyes filled with tears.

"Why you doing this J.R., because me and Daniel made a son?" He quickly shifted his eyes in the living room in response to her candid words.

"You proud of that?" J.R. asked looking at her with judgmental eyes. "You think what you and Cousin Daniel done decent—" He abruptly silenced, withholding his harsh words when seeing Millie Ann walking towards the kitchen. She entered looking in both her angry parents faces, each trying to hide their obvious agitation.

"Daddy you want me to take Lil' J.R. them outside?"

"I'm sorry Millie Ann baby." Effie Mae apologized as she wiped her tear filled eyes. "Me and your daddy didn't mean for y'all to hear us arguing."

"Uh, go ahead Millie Ann." J.R. said, anxious to finish he and Effie Mae's bitter discussion. "Me and uh, your momma . . . we uh, need to talk" Millie Ann looked at her momma—her eyes asking if she were okay. Effie Mae subtly nodded.

"Okay Daddy." She again looked at her momma then returned to the living room, frightened by their bickering. "Let's go outside y'all and play tag."

"Ooooh!" Sarah leaped up from the floor. "I'm it!"

"Uh-uh, I'm it!" Lil' J.R. shouted. Millie Ann led her siblings out the front door to avoid their angry parents in the kitchen, waiting to continue their emotional arguing. Their eyes remained on the children exiting the house before they resumed the heated discussion.

"My baby D.J. should be out there playing with Lil' J.R. and his sisters, J.R!" Effie Mae said, upset.

"And I uh, have no problem with that—"

"Then what is it J.R.?" She yelled.

"Seeing a child my wife and my cousin created is a reminder—"

"Of what J.R.?"

"Of you and Cousin Daniel—" He looked her in the eyes. "—being together that's what!" Effie Mae gave no reply. "Do you know how difficult it's been knowing my wife, the woman I love and mother of my children—" J.R. momentarily lowered his head as he envisioned her betrayal. He again looked up at her. "—Effie Mae you laid down with my cousin and—" His agitation magnified. "—no Effie Mae you don't!"

"I thought you was a man of God, J.R.!" Effie Mae shouted. "What happened to forgiveness?" She turned and walked away, looking out at her children as they ran through the yard playing a game of tag. Effie Mae smiled then turned back to J.R. hoping to resume their unresolved dispute as she for the first time truly felt her husband's pain. She walked back over and sat next to J.R. at the kitchen table. "No matter how hard people try to do good J.R., they gon always make mistakes—"

"Mistake!" J.R.'s eyes slightly widened in response to her chosen words to describe her affair with his cousin. "Is that what you call being in bed with my cousin, Effie Mae—a mistake?"

"Ain't nobody perfect J.R. not even you!" Effie Mae shouted.

"I don't see my wife giving birth to my cousin son . . . a mistake Effie Mae?" J.R. said raising his voice, hurt by her lack of compassion for his hurt.

"That ain't what I said J.R."

"As a man of God, my belief about adultery is it's an intentional act, not a mistake." He stated with chastisement.

"And what you call walking out on me and our babies, J.R.—a mistake J.R. or intentional?" He continued his angry gaze, but gave no reply. "I ain't blaming you for what me and Daniel done—"

"Good!"

"If you had been home in your own bed wouldn't been no room for no other man to be laying there." J.R.'s mouth flung open.

"Me leaving didn't give you the right to invite my cousin into your bed Effie Mae!" He shouted.

"I ain't saying it was J.R.!" Effie Mae said accepting minimal blame for her actions. "You ain't the first man to have a family member lay down with his wife, and guess what J.R.—" She yelled. "—you ain't gon be the last!"

"Is that's suppose to make me feel any less hurt Effie Mae?"

"That ain't what I said J.R.!"

"Then tell me Effie Mae—" She cut him off.

"Maybe the next time you stand in the pulpit and preach on forgiveness, you need to ask yourself if you practicing what you preach." J.R. lowered his eyes, humbled by her *sermon worthy* words.

"Maybe uh, I should let you deliver that sermon." He said looking at her with meek eyes. Effie Mae took hold of his hand and placed it on her slightly protruding pregnant belly.

"We got our own baby growing inside of me now—"

"Is that our baby Effie Mae?" She giggled.

"Yeah J.R. it's our baby." She said laying her head on his chest. "You may not be D.J.'s daddy J.R., but I'm his momma and I want my babies to grow up together same as me and Annie Mae, no matter who the daddy is."

"If uh, it means that much for you to have D.J. in the children's lives—" J.R.'s mouth dried. He coughed.

"It do J.R."

"Then I uh . . . I'll try." He placed a gentle kiss on her forehead. "But don't expect it to happen overnight." Effie Mae smiled, humored.

"I won't."

"Good! Because seeing Cousin Daniel and my wife together—"

"This ain't about me and Daniel, J.R.." She stated raising his hand up to her cheek. "It's about our babies and how much they love D.J. and it don't matter to them if he they cousin or baby brother." J.R. lightly chuckled.

"I uh, guess in a way he's both." He stated. Effie Mae giggled. "And uh, maybe one day I might even be able to accept Cousin Daniel betrayal." Effie Mae smiled.

"I think Daniel would love that J.R."

"I uh, said might."

"Thank you J.R."

"It might take a sermon or two on forgiveness before that happens though."

"Naw J.R. it's definitely gon take more than two sermons." Effie Mae teased.

"You think five or six might be enough?" He quietly grinned. J.R.'s humor ended when seeing the serious look on Effie Mae's face.

"What?"

"You was wrong J.R. about me not understanding your hurt." He looked at her, curious of her unclear statement. "I understand good what it mean to be hurt." Effie Mae's eyes moistened with tears. "When I lost Blue I felt a hurt like I ain't ever felt before."

"Effie Mae—" J.R. said kissing her lightly on the forehead. "I uh, should've asked how you were—" She cut him off.

"It look like Blue was right."

"Huh?"

"He thought I should give myself a chance being your wife again." J.R. placed a third kiss on her forehead as he thought of Blue's last word to him. "From now on J.R. you gon be the only man in my life." A cynical look formed on his face.

"From now on Effie Mae?" J.R. said, unconvinced. Effie Mae smiled.

"Yeah J.R."

"Why don't we uh, take it one day at a time?" He gazed in Effie Mae's eyes then placed an intimate kiss on her lips.

# Chapter Twenty-Eight

"Effie Mae! It's Deborah Ann." Effie Mae awakened from Deborah Ann's repeated knocking as she lay in bed asleep.

"It's open Deborah Ann." She said from underneath the covers thrown over her head. Deborah Ann opened the door and stood just outside of it.

"Effie Mae . . . did I wake you up girl?"

"Yep."

"Well it's a man downstairs asking for you."

"A man?"

"Yeah, and girl—" A big smile formed on Deborah Ann's face. "—he is fine!" She stated. "Effie Mae girl he's got a nice beard, some cute glasses and a beautiful smile." Effie Mae threw the covers from over her head.

"Did he say what his name was Deborah Ann?"

"No—yes, girl I don't even remember!" Deborah Ann said confused with excitement. "What I do remember is that he said he wanted to surprise you girl." Effie Mae's eyes lit up.

"Is it Anthony?"

"Anthony?" Deborah Ann thought for a moment. "Girl ain't that the man you said was your fiancé?" Effie Mae's excitement dwindled.

"Yeah Deborah Ann, but that's over."

"Well Effie Mae girl if you don't want him, I'll take him." Deborah Ann teased. "Effie Mae you know you be getting some fine butt men!"

"Deborah Ann . . . Anthony's Lil' J.R.'s daddy." A confused look showed in Deborah Ann's eyes.

"I thought Lil' J.R. was your husband's son." Deborah briefly hesitated. "I don't mean to be getting all up in your business Effie Mae, but have a baby by every man you been with girl?" Effie Mae's mouth abruptly opened. "Tyrell said you had a lot of kids."

"Blue said that?"

"He sure did girl, but he didn't say they were by three four different daddys."

"I know it probably seem that way Deborah Ann—" Effie Mae smiled when she thought of how Deborah Ann would react if she knew of the multitude of men she'd been with. "--Naw Deborah Ann . . . I ain't had babies by every man I been with." Effie Mae thought of the child her and Blue would never have. Her eyes slightly dampened. "I was hoping me and Blue could have our own baby—" Deborah Ann noticed Effie Mae's moistening eyes and diminished bliss.

"Effie Mae girl, I wasn't trying to make you sad."

"I think about this baby growing inside of me and I wish so bad it was Blue's."

"I know my cousin . . . and I know Tyrell would love that baby whether it was his or not."

"And that's just what I'm gon do." Effie Mae said drying her tears with the sheet. Deborah Ann watched as Effie Mae fluffed her hair with her fingers. "How I look?"

"A mess!" The two women laughed.

"Do I?"

"Naw girl I was just messing with you." Deborah Ann said laughing. "But you might want to wash your face, brush your teeth, throw on a little lipstick and brush your hair—" Effie Mae's mouth flung open. "—I'm just saying girl." Effie Mae giggled.

"Well give me a few minutes to get ready Deborah Ann." An odd look formed on Deborah Ann's face.

"Effie Mae—I know it ain't none of my business girl—" She said looking at the oversized men's pajamas Effie Mae wore. "—but what's up with them men's pajama?" Effie Mae smiled.

"These was my baby's pajamas . . . I'm gon take them off Deborah Ann."

"I'm glad to hear that."

"The last thing Anthony want to see is me in here wearing Blue's pajamas."

"Did you want me to bring Anthony up here Effie Mae or were you coming down?"

"First make sure the man downstairs is Anthony." Effie Mae grinned. "Then you can bring him up."

"Okay girl." Deborah Ann turned to leave then stopped. She again faced Effie Mae. "I don't want to sound nosey Effie Mae, but did Tyrell know about Anthony—him being your fiancé and all?" Effie Mae smiled when remembering Blue's first proposal after she'd accepted Anthony's engagement ring.

"Yeah Deborah Ann he knew."

"About y'all being engaged?"

"Blue asked me if things didn't work out with me and Anthony if I would marry him." A puzzled look showed on Deborah Ann's face.

"I don't mean to keep getting in your business Effie Mae, but when you and Tyrell got married were you still engaged to Anthony?" Effie Mae giggled.

"Yeah Deborah Ann I was." Deborah Ann momentarily reflected on Effie Mae's response.

"Girl my cousin know he loved you!"

"And I loved your cousin right back Deborah Ann." Effie Mae giggled as tears rolled down her cheeks. A lump formed in Deborah Ann's throat, her eyes also dampened with tears.

"Well Effie Mae I guess I better go down here and get Anthony." She thought for a moment. "If that is Anthony." Deborah Ann burst into laughter then hurried downstairs. Effie Mae quickly climbed out of bed, rushing in the bathroom then splashing water over her face. She dried it with a towel hanging near the sink then scurried back out and over to the dresser. Effie Mae picked up a bottle of mouthwash and swished it around in her mouth then spit it in the trash can. She pulled open the top dresser drawer and removed a purple silk, floor length night gown with matching robe—slipping into it after slipping out of Blue's olive green pajama shirt and pants. She grabbed a tube of lipstick from her make-up bag brightening her lips with a red lipstick then running her fingers through her wavy black hair as she waited for Deborah Ann to return with Anthony.

"Baby!" Anthony said as he approached the top of the stairs. Effie Mae's eyes lit up when seeing his captivating smile.

"Anthony!" She said hurrying into his open arms as he entered the apartment. His eyes shifted to her slightly protruding belly seconds before they passionately kissed. Deborah Ann watched with widened eyes.

"I've missed you Baby." Anthony said gazing into her hazel brown eyes.

"I've missed you too Anthony." They again kissed. Effie Mae shifted her eyes to Deborah Ann when sensing her stare. She giggled. "Yeah Deborah Ann—this is Anthony."

"Girl I sure hope so the way y'all all over each other." Deborah Ann said shifting her eyes from Anthony to Effie Mae then back to Anthony. "Hi Anthony." He looked at her with questioning eyes.

"Anthony this is Deborah Ann . . . Blue's cousin."

"Blue's cousin?" A surprised looked appeared on his face. He ended their embrace and extended his hand to Deborah Ann. She looked briefly to Effie Mae, her eyes asking permission to shake his hand. Effie Mae giggled. Deborah Ann took hold of Anthony's hand, gazing in his friendly eyes as they shook.

"Deborah Ann, Anthony was the first boy to ask me to marry him when we was just kids—I was seventeen and Anthony was nineteen."

"I guess y'all were kids, so what happened with that Effie Mae?"

"I got married!" Effie Mae laughed.

"To J.R. right?" Deborah Ann said trying to remember the information Effie Mae shared with her previously. Anthony glanced briefly at Effie Mae, surprised by Deborah Ann's knowledge of J.R., given her being Blue's cousin. "Didn't you say he was your son's father? How that happen?" Effie Mae giggled.

"Me and Anthony got together when I went home for a visit—" Effie Mae blushed. "—and we made Lil' J.R." Deborah Ann shifted her eyes over at Anthony then again turned to Effie Mae and back to Anthony— staring at him.

"Girl I can't wait to hear the story behind that!"

"You want me to send him downstairs to you Deborah Ann when I'm done with him?" Effie Mae teased, humored by Deborah Ann gawking at him.

"Huh? Oh!" She girlishly grinned. "Girl was I staring?" She asked, unable to contain her school girl gaze.

"Yeah Deborah Ann you was." Effie Mae said smiling.

"I'm sorry Anthony if I made you nervous—"

"It's okay Deborah Ann, you didn't make me nervous."

"Well Anthony it was nice meeting you."

"Same here Deborah Ann." He shifted his eyes to Effie Mae in response to Deborah Ann again staring at him.

"You can close the door Deborah Ann." Effie Mae said laughing.

"Oh, okay girl." She looked at Effie Mae then again turned to Anthony fixating her eyes on him. "If you need me just call." His eyes widened in response to her peculiar statement seemingly directed at him. "Oh, that was meant for Effie Mae." He blushed, flattered by Deborah Ann's obvious attraction to him. Effie Mae giggled.

"Bye Deborah Ann."

"Huh? Oh, okay girl." She girlishly chuckled as Effie Mae again broke her gaze at Anthony. "Was I staring again? I'm sorry Anthony."

"It's okay Deborah Ann." He said shifting his eyes briefly to Effie Mae then back to Deborah Ann, watching as she slowly closed the door. He again turned to Effie Mae.

"Baby?"

"Yeah Anthony."

"You want to tell me what that was all about?"

"That was about Deborah Ann thinking you the finest man she ever laid eyes on." She laughed.

"And what do you think Baby?" He asked embracing her in his arms.

"Am I including Huck?" Anthony's mouth flung open. Effie Mae giggled.

"Baby?"

"I'm just teasing with you Anthony." She said continuing to laugh, even though she did believe Huck's attractiveness far outweighed most men she'd ever seen. "I think Deborah Ann's right." He looked at her with skeptical eyes.

"Why is it I feel you're not being entirely honest?"

"Thank you for coming Anthony." Effie Mae said redirecting their conversation.

"Thank you for inviting me Baby." He placed a quick kiss to her lips then looked around the apartment.

"So is this where I'll be staying?"

"Yeah Anthony . . . I know it's kind of small but yeah this is where we gon be staying." He looked at her with perplexed eyes.

"Baby—we? Do you think that's a good idea?"

"Why not Anthony?" Effie Mae said intimately kissing him, prepared to pick up where they left off in Mississippi. "You don't want me to stay here with you?"

"Baby I would love that but—" She smooched him on the lips.

"But what Anthony?" He shifted his eyes down at her protruding belly. Effie Mae giggled.

"I'm pregnant Anthony—not sick!"

"I'll keep that in mind." She again kissed him. Anthony embraced her in his arms and began seductively kissing her on the neck, cheeks and lips.

"Anthony—"

"Yes Baby?" He said continuing his kisses.

"I promised J.R. when we got back together he would be the only man I'd be with." Anthony stopped.

"Baby?"

"What Anthony?"

"Are you sure getting back with J.R. is the right thing to do?" He looked in her eyes seeing some reservation.

"I don't know Anthony."

"Baby have you ever been only with J.R. since you married him?" She smiled when remembering the five monogamist years of her and J.R.'s marriage.

"Yeah Anthony—once." He again kissed her.

"Baby?"

"Yeah Anthony?"

"Are you and J.R. back together now?" An enticing smile appeared on his face. Effie Mae blushed.

"Boy, there you go with that smiling again!" He kissed her gently on the lips. "Maybe we should just get started on business Anthony."

"Business?" Anthony stared momentarily at her, surprised by her response then kissed her lightly on the lips. "Okay Baby—" He stated placing a quick kiss on her lips. "—if that's what you want then business it is." Effie Mae thought of Blue's *end of life* opinion regarding her relationship with Anthony, and now wondered if she could keep her promise. "I love you Baby." Anthony stated believing this to be his opportunity to win her back. They gazed into each other's eyes then passionately kissed.

---

Melvin hurried from the storeroom and headed in the direction of the front door in response to the knocking of an early morning visitor. He looked through the peephole.

"It's me Melvin." Huck said. Melvin opened the door and allowed him to enter. "What's up Melvin?"

"I ain't gon lie, it's been hard running the place without Tyrell." Huck's attention drew to the man seated at the bar in front of a stack of papers. He did a double take when identifying him a Anthony then looked at Melvin.

"Effie Mae up yet?" Huck asked glancing over at Anthony, curious of his presence.

"I ain't seen her this morning Huck, we been busy working on the inventory and—" Huck interjected.

"We?" Melvin shifted his eyes to Anthony then again turned to Huck.

"He showed up here sometime last week." Melvin said speaking underneath his breath, alerting Huck with his eyes of Effie Mae's intimate involvement with him.

"Damn!" Huck said in a low tone, disappointed by the news. "Let me go talk to this girl—see what's going on." He again shifted his eyes to Anthony then hurried up the stairs, knocking on the apartment door. "Effie Mae you woke girl?" The door gradually opened. Effie Mae stood on the other side wearing a white silk robe covering a hot pink negligee.

"Hey Huck." He looked at her with frustrated eyes then followed her inside the apartment. She walked over to the kitchen and began removing breakfast dishes from the table, putting them in the sink of soapy water—convicted by Huck's chastising eyes.

"What Huck!" Effie Mae said raising her voice.

"Ain't that Anthony downstairs?"

"You know that's him." She stated, offensively. "He came here to help me run this jazz club—he smart." Huck slightly tilted his head.

"Is that right?"

"Anthony's an accountant Huck—"

"And he also in love with you Effie Mae—what you doing girl?"

"What?"

"You know what." He asjed agitated. "What's going on with you and Anthony?"

"What you mean what's going on with me and Anthony? I told you Anthony's an accountant and him being here is good for the club." Huck grabbed hold of her arm.

"Good for the club Effie Mae—" He snatched open her robe revealing the negligee. "—or good for you?" She quickly pulled it closed. "I thought you and J.R. was working on getting back together?"

"This ain't got nothing to do with J.R." Huck looked at her with aggravated eyes.

"I can see that." He glanced around the room. "Anthony staying here with you Effie Mae?"

"You asking me that for J.R. or you?" Effie Mae said staring him in the eyes. "Anthony was my fiancée and the man I was living with before Blue got sick."

"And J.R.'s your husband and it's his baby you carrying."

"Well ain't nothing been decided yet." She stated, minimizing Huck's words. "And as far as this being J.R.'s baby, I got five other babies by that man, so being pregnant with another one ain't nothing new." Huck shook his head.

"Damn shame . . . that man." Effie Mae jerked her arm away from his hold then continued putting dishes in the sink. "So you just lied to Ol' Blue—had my brother believing you was getting back with your husband, getting pregnant, going on dates—all that." He again shook his head. "You hurt me girl."

"This ain't got nothing to do with you Huck!" She yelled.

"I guess you already forgot about Ol' Blue?" Tears erupted from Effie Mae's eyes. "Girl my brother loved you so much on his death bed he wrote you a love letter!" Huck stated, infuriated. "Wanted the whole world to know just how much he loved you—"

"Stop it Huck!"

"Ol' Blue left you everything he owned in this world." His anger surged. "My brother's barely cold and you already replaced him with Anthony—got him living up here in her in my brother's place!"

"Can't nobody replace Blue!" Effie Mae shouted as she wept. "You think you the only man got a right to lay in Blue's bed?" She yelled. A guilty look formed on Huck's face.

"Come here girl." He said taking her in his arms, laying her head onto his chest.

"I miss him so bad Huck." Effie Mae stated, unable to control her tears.

"I know—I miss him too." He kissed her lightly on the forehead.

"Why did Blue have to die Huck?"

"I wish I could answer that Effie Mae." He said as tears ran down his handsome face.

---

Effie Mae and Anthony sat at a table in the jazz club the following morning reviewing documents of the day to day operations of the club. They looked in the direction of the front door when hearing the knocking of as unexpected visitor.

"I got it." Melvin said hurrying from the kitchen. He looked over at Effie Mae and humped his shoulders, uncertain of who it could be. He arrived at the door then looked through the peephole seeing J.R. on the other side. He turned quickly to Effie Mae.

"Effie Mae—" He said in a low voice.

"Yeah Melvin."

"It's J.R."

"Let him in Melvin." He shifted his eyes to Anthony then back to Effie Mae.

"You sure?"

"Yeah Melvin it's okay." Melvin's anxiety grew as he opened the door with apprehension.

"Hey J.R., how you doing this morning?"

"I uh, I'm good." J.R. said as he entered.

"Hey J.R." Effie Mae said emotionally preparing herself for his discovery of Anthony.

"Effie Mae." J.R. replied shifting his eyes over to the man seated at the table with her.

"How's it going J.R.?" Anthony said looking up from the multitude of papers. J.R.'s mouth dried, shocked by his presence. He coughed. "Uh, Anthony . . . when did you uh, get here?" J.R. shifted his eyes to Effie Mae with inquiry. She quickly intervened.

"J.R., Anthony's gon run the jazz club for me." J.R.'s mouth slightly opened. He shifted his eyes to Anthony then back to Effie Mae.

"Run the jazz club? So uh, is this permanent or temporary?"

"Since Effie Mae doesn't know how to run a business, it looks like I'm here to stay." Melvin quickly intervened.

"Can I fix you some breakfast J.R.?" He asked trying to lessen the tension. J.R. glanced over at him, but gave no reply.

"You here to see me J.R.?" Effie Mae said trying to divert his attention from Anthony.

"Uh, yeah . . . if you uh, have time to see me." He again shifted his eyes to Anthony then looked at Effie Mae.

"I'll be back Anthony—I'm gon take J.R. upstairs so we can talk." She said seeing the hurt in J.R.'s eyes.

"Okay Baby." Anthony stated applying a kiss to her lips. J.R. looked over at Melvin watching from the bar, embarrassed by the intimate exchange between his wife and her former fiancé. Melvin's dread amplified.

"You sure I can't get you something to eat J.R.?" He asked trying to diffuse the awkward situation. J.R. remained speechless. "Well if you change your mind I got a ham baking in the oven and it's just about done." Melvin nervously chuckled. "All I have to do is add some eggs, grits—" J.R. cut him off.

"I'll uh, keep that in mind Melvin uh . . . thank you." J.R. watched as Effie Mae rose from the table then again shifted his eyes to Anthony.

"Come on J.R."

"Uh, Anthony it was uh, good seeing you."

"Same here J.R." Anthony said looking up briefly from the stack of business papers. Melvin watched with apprehension as Effie Mae and J.R. walked up the stairs. He humped his shoulders before walking away returning to the kitchen to check on his ham.

---

"Is uh, Anthony living here?" J.R. asked visually scanning the apartment as they entered — his eyes quickly being drawn to the men's pajamas thrown across the bed.

"Yeah for now J.R."

"Are you uh, living here with him?" J.R. asked unsure if he really wanted to know.

"If you asking if me and Anthony living together J.R., yeah we are." He stared at her, uncertain exactly how to digest the news.

"I thought we uh—"

"J.R. . . . me and Anthony talked and we decided we gon stay together and get married like we planned before Blue got sick." J.R.'s heart pounded in his ears as he listened to Effie Mae's coldhearted words. His mouth dried. He coughed. She ignored the pained looked in J.R.'s eyes.

"So uh, when did you plan on telling me Effie Mae?" He asked looking at her with angry eyes. "After the wedding? Or did you expect me to give you away to Anthony too?"

"I wouldn't do that J.R. —"

"But you'd do this?"

"Do what J.R.?" Effie Mae said raising her voice.

"Let me believe we getting back together —" He looked down at her pregnant belly with doubt. "You uh, sure that's my baby Effie Mae or is that one Anthony's too?"

"Yeah J.R. this your baby you know that!"

"Do I Effie Mae?" J.R. looked at her with enraged eyes. "No, I don't!" He shouted. She turned away unable to face him. "Look at me Effie Mae." She slowly turned and looked into J.R.'s disappointed eyes.

"Us getting back together was what Blue wanted not me." J.R. sarcastically chuckled, not surprised by her betrayal.

"So uh, that's it?" He said struggling to control his temper. "What uh, happened to you being faithful to me Effie Mae?" J.R. suddenly noticed Anthony's engagement ring on her finger. "Is uh, that Anthony's engagement ring?"

"J.R. I love Anthony!"

"Do you Effie Mae?" He stated cynically. "Do you even know what that word means?" Effie Mae looked t him, but gave no answer. J.R. stared angrily at her then took a deep breath before speaking. "I remember you telling me you loved Blue then you left here and started a life with Anthony . . . saying he was good for you." He said mocking her. "Then you left Anthony and came back here and married Blue." Effie Mae maintained her silence as J.R. began angrily pacing through the apartment. "And all the while you telling me you coming back home to be with me and the children." He suddenly stopped and looked her in the eyes. "And Huck—where uh, exactly do he fit into all this?"

"Blue told me to stay away from him." Effie Mae said trying to add humor to the situation.

"And did you?" J.R. yelled, unamused. She looked in his reprimanding eyes but gave no reply. "I came here this morning Effie Mae to see if you was ready to come home and I find you here—playing house with Anthony." His eyes drew to her purple negligee lying slightly beneath Anthony's pajamas. "I'm threw with you Effie Mae!" J.R. shouted. "I want you to sign them divorce papers so I can move on with my life!" Her eyes widened with fear, shocked by his readiness to end their marriage. "I got six children at home that need their momma, but that don't seem to matter to you." J.R. looked at the woman he loved and for the first time saw an end to their chaotic marriage. "The only thing that's important to you Effie Mae is what man you got in laying in your bed!" Effie Mae's mouth abruptly opened.

"I didn't hear you saying nothing J.R. when you was the man I was lying with in bed with—now was you?" She yelled. He sarcastically chuckled in response to her childish reply.

"I'm your husband Effie Mae!" J.R. hollered out, appealing to her inability to understand what that truly meant. Effie Mae stared at him, clueless to the significance of her being his wife. "Maybe one day the good Lord will see fit to send me a good woman, one that won't mind being a real wife and mother to my children."

"My babies already got a momma, J.R.!" Effie Mae screamed.

"Do they Effie Mae?" He bellowed.

"You know they do!"

"When Effie Mae?" J.R. asked enraged. "When you ain't entertaining some man in your bed?" Effie Mae looked away in shame when hearing J.R.'s demeaning opinion of her.

"You wrong for saying that J.R."

"Am I?"

"I'm a good momma to by babies." He half-heartedly laughed.

"Do you really believe that Effie Mae?" J.R. said in response to her unproven belief. "You ain't got a clue of what that mean."

"Don't be judging me J.R. you ain't perfect!" He chuckled through his anger.

"And you ain't even close."

"What you want me to say J.R. — I'm sorry? Okay then . . . I'm sorry." Effie Mae said afraid of losing her children. He shook his head with pity.

"Ain't them the same words you said when after I found out my son's was really Anthony's?" Tears ran down Effie Mae's cheeks, hurt by J.R.'s cruel reminder. "Bye Effie Mae." He said unsympathetic to her tears as he headed towards the door.

"J.R. wait!" He stopped and again faced her.

"What I'm waiting for Effie Mae? For you and Anthony to realize y'all ain't right for each like Blue already told you?"

"You leave Blue out of this!" Effie Mae shouted, sobbing. "You can't keep my babies from me J.R.!" He forced a chuckled remaining unmoved by her again playing the victim.

"You know where your children at Effie Mae — m" J.R. looked at her with sarcasm. "—whenever you can make time to see them." A sigh of relief showed on Effie Mae's face. "I won't stop you from seeing the children Effie Mae, but I can stop them from being a part of you and Anthony's house playing."

"Why you doing this J.R.?"

"If you think I'm gon let you interrupt my children's lives again like you did when you decided to play house with Anthony —" She looked into J.R.'s bitter eyes. "—think again."

"You can't stop me from having my babies J.R. . . I'm gon get me a lawyer!" Effie Mae screamed. J.R. ignored her empty threat.

"And don't you dare ask me if Anthony can be a part of my children's lives, the answer is no — do you understand me Effie Mae?" He shouted turning to leave. J.R. suddenly stopped and faced her, unable to walk away from the woman he loved. "Effie Mae —"

"What you want J.R.?" She yelled.

"If you ever decide you want a life with me and the children —" He looked her squarely in the eyes. "—my door is always open, but don't you come to me unless you sure that's really where you want to be." Effie Mae watched as he stormed out the apartment, slamming the door.

---

"Good morning Baby." Anthony said awakening Effie Mae with a gentle kiss to her lips as he sat on the side of the bed. A huge smile displayed on her face.

"Good morning Anthony." He again kissed her.

"I'm on my way downstairs to get started on the books."

"It's too early Anthony, I want you to stay up here with me." Effie Mae whined. He placed a quick kiss on her lips.

"Baby, we have a business to run." He again kissed her. "You know what Baby—"

"What Anthony?"

"I think it would be a great idea if I trained Melvin on some of the more important things, that way he could be more efficient in his role as manager." Effie Mae smiled impressed by Anthony's professionalism.

"I don't care what Huck say." She giggled. "I told him you was smart." He looked at her, puzzled by her statement.

"Did Huck say that I wasn't?"

"Not exactly—" Effie Mae sat up.

"So Baby, what exactly did Huck say?"

"Don't worry about it Anthony." She smiled. "That was just his jealousy talking—" She quieted when seeing the worried look in Anthony's eyes.

"What?"

"You look tired Baby."

"I am Anthony, I think I'm gon stay in bed today—get some rest."

"Aww my poor Baby." He kissed her lightly on the forehead. "I guess being pregnant makes you kind of tired huh?" She noted the look of disappointment in his eyes.

"What's wrong Anthony?"

"I guess I can't help wishing that was our baby you were carrying."

"I'm sorry Anthony, it's just that at the time you was wanting us to have a baby—" He interjected.

"It's okay Baby there's still time." Anthony smiled then placed an affectionate kiss to her lips. "I have lots of work to do, but I should be back in—" He looked at his watch. "—about three hours to check on you, that should be just about lunch time okay?"

"Okay Anthony."

"It's the least I can do for the woman I love." He said placing a quick kiss on her lips. Effie Mae smiled. "Did you want me to have Melvin fix you some breakfast? I've heard how you pregnant women are always hungry with these strange cravings." Anthony said teasing.

"Just having you here with me Anthony is enough." She stated recalling J.R.'s biting words.

"Everything okay Baby?" Anthony asked when noticing the uneasy look in her eyes.

"Yeah Anthony I'm fine." She said masking her hurt.

"You sure?"

"Yeah Anthony I'm sure." Effie Mae forced a smile. "I don't know what I would do without you Anthony." She said electing not to tell him her altercation with J.R.

"I love you Baby." Anthony said applying another kiss to her lips.

"I love you too Anthony." He walked over to the door then stopped, looking at her with an enormous smile on his face. Effie Mae blushed.

"What?"

"Right now Baby I feel like the luckiest man in the world." She smiled. "I'll see you at lunch time." He opened the door to leave.

"Bye Anthony."

"I'll be back before you get a chance to miss me." She giggled, watching as Anthony exited the apartment then climbed quickly out of bed and hurried over to the dresser removing the photo of Blue kept hidden in the top drawer underneath some clothes. Her eyes watered.

"I love you Blue." She stated, placing a light kiss on the photo. "I can't wait 'til Lil' Tyrell Lee Jones come in this world." Effie Mae rubbed her pregnant belly. "I'm gon love that little boy just as much as I love you Blue."

"Effie Mae!" Melvin said through the closed door. "Anthony said you wanted some breakfast."

"Just a minute Melvin." She again kissed Blue's picture then put it back in the drawer and swiftly got back in bed. "Come in Melvin." He opened the door then entered.

"Anthony wanted me to make sure you ate breakfast—" He silently gazed at her. Effie Mae blushed.

"What?"

"Tell me something Effie Mae."

"Tell you what Melvin?"

"How in the hell you manage to look so good this early in the morning?" He stated flirtatiously. Her blushing smile widened.

"Thank you Melvin, but right now I feel like a mother hen waiting to lay a big fat egg." She said rubbing her growing belly, giggling.

"Well to me you look like a woman I could wake up to every morning and lay down with every night—pregnant or not." He seductively smiled. Effie Mae again blushed.

"Thank you Melvin."

"Now that I got that out of the way, was it something in particular you wanted to eat for breakfast sweetie?"

"Right now Melvin the only thing my stomach gon let me keep down is grits." Melvin quietly chuckled.

"Did you know that was Tyrell's favorite breakfast? That boy knew he loved him some grits!" Melvin said continuing to laugh. Effie Mae beamed. "He use to put so much butter in them things—" Melvin abruptly silenced. He looked at Effie Mae with questioning eyes. "You sure that ain't Tyrell's baby you carrying Effie Mae?"

"I done wished a thousand times Melvin this was me and Blue's baby I'm carrying." Effie Mae looked down at her protruding abdomen. "But I'm gon love Lil' Tyrell Lee Jones—" A puzzled look formed on Melvin's face.

"Tyrell Lee what?"

"Tyrell Lee Jones—that's what I'm gon name my baby boy." Melvin's eyes widened.

"Boy?"

"Yep." Effie Mae said, assured. "Somehow Melvin I know I got a little boy growing inside me."

"Well I hope you right Effie Mae." Melvin said humoured. "Because I'd hate to see a little girl named Tyrell Lee Jones." Effie Mae giggled. "Grits rights?"

"Yeah Melvin."

"You sure that's all you want Effie Mae?"

"That's all this little boy gon let me eat!"

"Okay . . . grits it is." Melvin half-heartedly chuckled. "I'll be back in a few minutes then with some grits." He turned to leave then again turned back. "Effie Mae I'm bringing you some orange juice and milk, you need that sweetie if you want Lil' Tyrell to be a healthy baby boy." A caring look showed in Melvin's eyes. Effie Mae smiled.

"Okay Melvin." He stared momentarily at Effie Mae before exiting the apartment to prepare her grits.

• • • •

Effie Mae climbed out of bed and hurried in the bathroom to wash her face as she waited for Melvin to return with breakfast. She rushed back out when hearing the phone rang.

"Hey Momma."

"Effie Mae . . . you doing alright child?" Millie asked concerned.

"Naw Momma everything ain't alright why you asking?" Effie Mae said sensing her momma's call had something to do with J.R. Millie hesitated, trying to think of how to approach the subject of her eldest daughter's current living arrangements.

"What's wrong with me Momma?"

"What you talking 'bout what's wrong with you child?"

"Momma me and—"

"What's going with you and J.R., Effie Mae?"

"J.R. told you about me and Anthony?"

"You know he did!"

"What he calling you for Momma? If I want to be with Anthony—" Millie cut her off.

"Is that what you want Effie Mae or what Anthony want?"

"Momma, Anthony came here to help me run this jazz club."

"Well J.R. seem to think it's much more than that."

"It is Momma." Effie Mae briefly paused. "Me and Anthony back together." Millie sighed with disappointment.

"Effie Mae do you love J.R.?"

"I don't know Momma . . . all I know is right now I need Anthony."

"Need him for what child?"

"Anthony love me Momma."

"And so do your husband, Effie Mae!"

"It ain't the same Momma."

"What happened to you and J.R. getting back together?" Millie subtly scolded. "Ain't y'all got another child on the way?"

"Yeah Momma but—"

"But what Effie Mae?"

"I want Blue!" Effie Mae cried out as her eyes watered.

"Effie Mae that man's gone baby."

"I don't want him to be gone Momma!"

"I know you don't child, but you being laid up with Anthony ain't gon bring him back."

"I know that Momma!"

"Blue's gone Effie Man and ain't nothing in this world gon bring him back."

"Don't say that Momma!" Millie's eyes widened, frightened by Effie Mae's disturbing words.

"Effie Mae!"

"What Momma?"

"Do you hear how you talking child?"

"What Momma?"

"Tyrell Lee Jones is gone Effie Mae—" Millie stated firmly. "—and all the wishing, hoping and pretending in the world ain't gon change that one bit!"

"I know that Momma!" Effie Mae said raising her voice.

"Then talk like it!" Millie stated, upset with worry. Effie Mae gave no reply. "Did you hear me child?" The silence continued. "I guess I'm gon need to talk to Anthony—let him know my daughter seem to be losing her mind thinking she can bring back the dead by wishing—" Effie Mae interjected.

"Momma don't tell that man that!"

"I know losing Blue seem like the most painful thing in the world." Millie said empathizing with her hurting daughter. "I know well how pain can destroy you if you let it." Millie's eyes slightly watered. "Doctor said it was pneumonia took my Frank from this earth, no different than that cancer took Blue." Effie Mae attentively listened—hearing the circumstances of her father's death for the first time. "After losing the man I loved, the hurt seem like it wasn't ever gon leave my heart, but I couldn't give up, I had two little girls that needed their momma, and needed me to be strong—"

"I ain't like you Momma."

"Like me or not Effie Mae . . . it's time for you to move one, but with your husband not Anthony—"

"I don't know if I want to do that Momma."

"Effie Mae your husband love you child—"

"I know that Momma!"

"Then act like it!" Millie yelled. "Anthony's your past child and it's time you stopped living in it."

"That ain't what I'm doing Momma."

"You told me yourself you and Anthony done changed so much you just like strangers."

"That's changing Momma."

"Then tell me this child . . . what you and Anthony got in common besides being in bed together?" Effie Mae's jaw dropped in response to Millie's blunt words.

"Momma!"

"I'm listening but I don't hear you speaking."

"I'm thinking Momma."

"Well while you thinking answer me this."

"What Momma?"

"What is it you and J.R. got in common besides all them babies?" Millie asked chuckling.

"I don't know Momma."

"Well maybe it's time you thought about it."

"Momma when I married J.R. I hated that man!" Millie gasped.

"Effie Mae!"

"What Momma I did—you know I didn't love J.R, an when he was talking 'bout taking me away from you and Annie Mae—"

"And I'm sorry for that Effie Mae—n" Millie shook her head with remorse. "—but I didn't know what else to do with you."

"But you know what Momma . . . after me and J.R. started having babies—" Effie Mae's face lit up. "—when my Millie Ann was born, J.R. was right there waiting on his baby girl to come into this world." Millie delighted in hearing Effie Mae's recollection of the birth of her first born child. "I still see the look on J.R.'s face every time Ms. Ida pulled one of them baby girls out of me." Effie Mae's smile grew. "But the day Lil' J.R. was born J.R. was so excited Momma I thought he was gon smoke one of Mr. Daniel's pipes." Effie Mae laughed.

"You know that's the first time I ever heard you speak on J.R. as a wife should speaks on her husband."

"Momma I done so much wrong to J.R." Effie Mae said sounding repentant. Millie silently rejoiced in hearing the responsible words coming out of her daughter's mouth. Effie Mae again recalled J.R.'s recent threat to find another wife. "Maybe J.R. need to go head on and find him another wife--somebody better than Effie Mae Reed." She said thinking out loud. Millie quietly giggled.

"I think J.R. just fine in keeping the wife he already got."

"Thank you for saying that Momma."

"You welcome child."

"Bye Momma."

"Bye child."

---

Effie Mae stood early morning outside of Huck's apartment door excited about telling him of her plan to reunite with her husband, fulfilling Blue's dying wish. She also wanted to ask if he would let her move in with him until she could again win J.R back. She knocked and waited for Huck to answer. He peered through the peephole then tilted his head, stunned when seeing Effie Mae standing on the other side. A cunning smile formed on his face as he opened the door wearing only his navy blue, silk boxers.

"Hey Effie Mae." He said stroking his finely groomed chin hairs in anticipation of the reason for her unexpected visit. She looked at his half naked, masculine physique and blushed. "What you blushing for?" Huck said smiling. "You seen me in less." She giggled.

"Well I didn't come here for that."

"You sure?" He teased.

"Yeah Huck I'm sure, now let me in." He stepped aside and allowed her to enter.

"Okay now Effie Mae I'm warning you girl." He said closing the door.

"I need to talk to you Huck."

"Talk I'm listening."

"J.R. came over and saw Anthony." Huck tilted his head.

"Is that right? I tried to tell you about that didn't I Effie Mae?"

"I see now Blue was right."

"You hard headed Effie Mae—"

"Anyway—"She said ignoring Huck's chastising words. "—after talking to Momma she made me see the only thing me and Anthony got in common is we both like having a good time." She giggled. Huck frowned.

"I ain't trying to hear about you and Anthony, Effie Mae."

"Well it is!"

"You something else." He grinned.

"But if I keep living with Anthony, I ain't ever gon get J.R. back."

"Now you worried about that huh?"

"Yeah Huck I am, but right now J.R.'s so mad at me over Anthony I ain't even sure he want me no more."

"So what you want me to do Effie Mae? I ain't getting in that man's business."

"I ain't asking you to Huck—" She looked at him with pleading eyes. "—I just need a place to stay away from Anthony and the only place I got to go is here." His eyes widened.

"What you mean here?" Huck gazed in her desperate eyes. "Effie Mae . . . you think that man don't know about me and you?"

"What?"

"You know what!"

"Yeah he know, but you ain't trying to marry me Huck—Anthony is."

"How you know I ain't?" He seductively smiled. "I asked you once before didn't I?"

"Come on Huck I ain't got no place else to go!"

"So you just gon ignore me huh?"

"Huck I'm trying to get my husband back!" He half-heartedly laughed, amused by her desperation.

"Calm down girl." He said giving in. "If I say yeah Effie Mae I ain't coming home and finding Anthony in my house you understand me girl? Or old Daniel."

"What about J.R.?" She teased.

"I'm okay with J.R." Effie Mae's eyes widened, surprised by his unexpected reply. "I know that man won't do nothing to disrespect my house." A serious look displayed in Huck's eyes. "When you talking about moving in?"

"Let me talk to Anthony first then I'll let you know."

"Effie Mae!"

"What Huck?"

"Don't tell that man where I live!"

"I ain't." She giggled.

"I mean it Effie Mae!"

"I said I ain't Huck." He gazed at her and again stroked his chin hairs.

"What's in it for me?" An enticing smile stretched across his handsome face. Effie Mae blushed.

"What you mean what's in it for you?"

"You staying here in my house like you my wife, I might want to play husband one night." She giggled.

"We'll see." Huck tilted his head.

"Is that right?" He winked.

---

"It looks like we have another full house tonight, Baby." Anthony said entering the apartment. He inhaled the aroma of the dinner Effie Mae had prepared.

"Mmm . . . that's smells delicious Baby." Anthony said, his stomach growling as he walked over and embraced Effie Mae from behind. his eyes exploring the oven cooked barbeque chicken, scalloped potatoes, and fried cabbage on the stove. He placed a kiss on her neck. She giggled

"Baby, should you be standing on your feet like that?" Anthony asked turning her around, kissing her on the lips.

"I'm pregnant Anthony not sick."

"Well thank you for the delicious meal." He again kissed her. "I only have a few minutes to eat then I've got to get back downstairs." Anthony said releasing his hold then picking up a spoon off the stove, scooping a mouthful of the scalloped potatoes from the casserole dish putting them in his mouth. Effie Mae wrapped her arms romantically around his neck and kissed him lightly on his chewing lips.

"Stay up here with me Anthony."

"I would love to do that Baby except money seems to have a way of disappearing when the club gets really busy."

"Huh?" A stunned look appeared on Effie Mae's face. "You think somebody's stealing it Anthony?"

"Baby, of course somebody's stealing it."

"Stop Anthony!" She said trying to taked the spoon from his hand as he continued eating from the casserole. "I was gon fix you a plate."

"I've asked Melvin to keep a closer eye on the cash register and let me do the meeting and greeting of customers." Anthony said embracing Effie Mae from behind when she turned to fix his plate. "I love you Baby." He kissed her softly on the neck. She giggled.

"I love you too Anthony." Her mind raced as she tried to think of how to tell him of her plan to reunite with her husband. "You love running the jazz club don't you Anthony?" He turned her head around and kissed her on the lips.

"Yes Baby I do—thank you."

"I'm glad you do Anthony, but are you doing it because you love it or because I asked you too?"

"Both." He placed another kiss on her lips.

"Would you keep doing it Anthony—" She turned away to avoid looking him in the eyes.

"If what Baby?"

"If I went back to J.R.?" Anthony slowly turned her around then removed the plate from her hand, sitting it on the kitchen counter. He took a deep breath and blew it out through his mouth then looked Effie Mae in the eyes.

"Baby, are you trying to tell me something?" He asked fearful of her impending reply.

"I was just thinking Anthony—maybe I should try and see if I can—" He interjected.

"Can what Baby?" He said looking at her with disappointed eyes. "What . . . be a good wife to J.R.?" He looked at her, believing J.R. to be the reason for her sudden change of mind. "—Is that really what you want Baby?"

"I don't know Anthony."

"I thought we decided we were going to move forward with planning our wedding and getting married?"

"I ain't sure that's what I want no more Anthony."

"Baby, is J.R. pressuring you about the two of you getting back—" She cut him off.

"Naw Anthony, I talked to Momma and she thinks—" He looked up at the ceiling and took a deep breath then stared at Effie Mae, trying to read the confused look in her eyes.

"Is that where all of this is coming from Baby?"

"Anthony, Momma made good sense." He shook his head, displeased with her momma's meddling.

"And just what was it your momma made good sense about Baby?"

"She helped me see the only thing we got in common is—"

"Is what Baby?"

"You know what Anthony." Effie Mae blushed.

"Oh, that!" He smiled. "So Baby what is it that you're saying?"

"What I'm saying Anthony is as much as I like us having a good time—" She giggled.

"It takes more than that to make a marriage work?" Anthony said reluctantly accepting her momma's truth.

"Yeah Anthony." He glanced around the apartment.

"So then tell me Baby, what was the reason for all of this . . . us living here together, becoming re-engaged and me running the jazz club?" She looked at him with apology.

"I'm sorry Anthony I thought this was what I wanted, but after talking to Momma—" He cut her off.

"So tell me Baby, is there anything else your momma said that I need to know?" Effie Mae slid his arms around her waist and kissed him. "Do you love me Baby?" Anthony asked hoping to change her mind.

"Yeah boy you know I love you." She again kissed him. "It's just that I ain't seventeen years old no more Anthony."

"Baby . . . that's silly nobody stays seventeen forever."

"It ain't just that Anthony, I got a husband and seven babies that need me." Effie Mae said speaking as a responsible adult.

"Baby you know I don't mind helping you with the kids."

"I know Anthony, but being with J.R. and my babies is where I belong." She looked in Anthony's disappointed eyes. "You understand don't you Anthony?"

"Yes Baby I'm afraid I do." He said looking at her with saddened eyes. "I'll miss you Baby, but I want you to do what you believe is best for you and your kids." He hesitated. "And J.R." An odd look formed on Anthony's face. "Did I just say that?" Effie Mae giggled.

"Yeah Anthony you did."

"So I guess this means I'm on my way back home?"

"Noooo Anthony I need you . . . who gon run the jazz club?"

"Baby, I thought you wanted me to leave?"

"Naw boy, I was just saying you can't be my fiancé no more because I'm trying to get back with my husband." Effie Mae thought about what she'd just said and giggled.

"If you're sure you want me to stay Baby—I'll stay."

"You mean that Anthony?"

"Yes Baby I mean that . . . I'll stay here and run your jazz club." He kissed her lightly on the lips. "If it means I'll get to spend time with you and our son of course I'll stay." Effie Mae wrapped her arms around Anthony's neck and gazed in his eyes.

"Thank you Anthony."

"You're welcome Baby, so I guess you'll be moving in with J.R.?"

"Nope." A confused look showed on Anthony's face. "Right now J.R.'s so mad at me Anthony he probably wouldn't let me sleep on his back porch." Effie Mae laughed.

"Wow, now that is mad." He said placing a kiss her on her forehead. "My poor baby."

"I'm hoping I can get J.R. to love me again." Anthony looked at her with optimistic eyes.

"Baby, I don't think he ever stopped."

"You didn't see him Anthony!" Effie Mae stated. "The last time I saw J.R.that mad was when he found out Lil' J.R. wasn't his son."

"Ouch, I'm sure that hurt." Anthony said. "Well if he could forgive you for that then—"

"Anthony J.R. said he wanted me to sign the divorce papers!" He laid Effie Mae's head on his chest. "He didn't really mean that Baby, you said he was really upset didn't you?"

"Anthony he said he was gon find him another wife."

"Baby—" Anthony said, doubtful.

"What Anthony"

" J.R.'s not going to find another wife." He stated disturbed by J.R. frightening Effie Mae with his idle threat. "Do you want me to talk to him Baby?"

"Naw Anthony that ain't gon do nothing but make him even madder." She felt mocked when seeing the smile on Anthony's face. "It ain't funny Anthony!"

"I know Baby."

"Then why you smiling?"

"To be honest Baby, I was just taking pleasure in the reality of J.R.'s son actually being mines—that's all." A triumphant look displayed on

Anthony's face. Effie Mae looked at him, unamused. "So Baby you never said where you'd be living once you move out, since it obviously won't be with J.R." Her anxiety heightened as she prepared to answer Anthony's question.

"I already know what you gon say Anthony—"

"Oh no, that doesn't sound good Baby."

"I'm only going there because I ain't got no place else to go Anthony—" He interjected.

"Baby?"

"I'm gon be staying with Huck, Anthony." His mouth opened to speak, but nothing came out. "I already asked him and he said yeah." Anthony's eyes filled with fret, alarmed by her unsavory decision.

"Baby?"

"What Anthony?"

"Think about what you're saying."

"What Anthony?"

"Baby, do you think living with Huck is better than living here with me?"

"Naw . . . yeah, I don't know Anthony."

"Baby, this is the same man that traded you off to some madam to be a whore in a whorehouse!"

"I know Anthony, but Huck's my friend."

"Friend!" He said raising his voice in upset. "No Baby, Huck's not your friend!" She looked at him with childlike eyes. "For goodness sake Baby, the man was once your pimp or have you forgotten that?"

"Naw Anthony I ain't forgot." A desperate look appeared on Effie Mae's face. "But if I keep living here with you Anthony I'm gon lose my husband."

"Would it be so bad Baby if you got stuck with me?" She looked at Anthony sympathizing with the look of rejection on his face.

"I'm sorry Anthony that ain't what I meant." She placed a smooch on his lips. "I'm gon always love you boy no matter what." A huge smile showed on Anthony's face. "And me, you and Lil' J.R. gon always be a family." His smile widened. Effie Mae intimately kissed him.

"Baby if being a wife to your husband is what you truly want, I accept that." She again kissed him. "So when did you plan on moving out and in with—" Anthony swallowed the newly formed lump in his throat. "—Huck?"

"I don't know Anthony." Effie Mae's eyes filled with tears as she reminisced on her life with Blue in the apartment.

"Baby what's wrong?" He asked when seeing her tears.

"Me moving out of here is more than just me leaving Anthony, I got a lot of memories of me and Blue living in this apartment."

"Aww Baby." Anthony said lightly stroking Effie Mae's hair, placing a gentle kiss on her forehead.

"Anthony did I tell you Blue passed away in here?" He looked mystically around the apartment.

"No Baby I didn't."

"We was laying right there in the bed when my baby took his last breath." A uneasy look displayed on Anthony's face.

"Baby?"

"What Anthony?"

"Could you spare me the details please?" He said shifting his eyes over at the bed.

"Do that bother you Anthony?" A lump formed in his throat.

"A little."

"I'm sorry Anthony."

"No Baby, it's okay." Anthony swallowed the enormous lump. "If talking about Blue makes you feel better—then talk." He said placing a quick kiss on Effie Mae's lips before again shifting his eyes over at the bed.

"Thank you Anthony."

"You're welcome Baby." Effie Mae blushed when seeing the seductive smile on his.

"What?"

"Your memories in that bed with Blue won't keep us from having a good time will they Baby?" He asked dismissing her graphic recollection of Blue's end of life in the bed they now shared.

"Naw Boy." Effie Mae said sounding much like seventeen years old Effie Mae Reed. "But after I move Anthony we can't be having no more good times."

"Fair enough." He said smiling. "Baby?"

"Yeah Anthony?"

"Can you take your time moving out?" She giggled.

"Yeah boy, but you got one week Anthony." His mouth abruptly opened in response to her short timeline.

"Baby, one week!"

"Anthony!"

"Okay Baby, if you say one week then one week it is." He again seductively smiled.

"There you go again with that smiling." Effie Mae said blushing. Anthony kissed her on the lips—intimately moving his lips to her neck and shoulders then again returning to her lips. They passionately kissed.

"Okay Anthony—two weeks." Effie Me said unable to resist his tantalizing persuasion. "And that's it." They again kissed.

"I love you Boss." He teased. She giggled.

"I love you too Anthony." He continued applying enticing kisses to her lips and neck as he led her over to the bed. "Anthony I thought you said you had to get back downstairs."

"A few missing dollars won't break us."

# Chapter Twenty-Nine

"I love French fries Daddy." Lil' J.R. said stuffing a handful of fries in his mouth as the family ate a dinner of chili burgers, hand cut French fries and canned peaches.

"I know Lil' J.R., but slow down before you choke."

"Okay Daddy."

"These chili burgers taste really good Daddy." Sarah said biting into the large bun, stuffed with the red flavorful mixture of ground beef and Manwich sauce."

"Well I'm glad everything tastes good." J.R. said merely responding to his children's voices—his mind occupied on his last bitter conversation with Effie Mae.

"Daddy when is Momma coming over and eat dinner with us again?" J.R.'s ears deafened to his daughter Billie's voice.

"Daddy!"

"Huh?"

"I said when is Momma coming over here again?"

"Well Billie I uh, guess only your momma can answer that." He said masking his anger with Effie Mae from the children. "She's uh, pretty busy these days with her new business." J.R. stated as his thoughts drifted to the day he saw Anthony's pajamas thrown across his wife's bed.

"Daddy how come when Momma and Anthony come over they only pick up Lil' J.R.?" Lena asked looking at him from across the table.

"Have you uh, forgotten Lena . . . Anthony's Lil' J.R.'s father." J.R. said speaking without thinking—his words guided by hurt.

"No he ain't!" Lil' J.R. shouted. "You my Daddy!"

"Calm down Lil' J.R., let's not talk about that right now—" J.R. silenced when he noted Mahalia's unusual quietness. "Mahalia are you feeling alright baby?"

"I wanted to go and see D.J. with Millie Ann, but Mr. Daniel said they was going to the hospital to see Ms. Geraldine today and I couldn't go."

"I don't uh, think it was because he didn't want you to go Mahalia, I think you uh, might not be old enough."

"Yes I am Daddy!"

"Let me uh, talk to Cousin Daniel and see if he knows." J.R. said as his mind again drifted to the argument with Effie Mae over her son fathered by Daniel. "And if uh, you're not old enough, maybe we can ask Cousin Daniel if D.J. can uh, come over here the next time he goes to the hospital." A large smile appeared on Mahalia's face.

"Okay Daddy."

"Sounds like Millie Ann's back." J.R. said when hearing footsteps on the back porch. He rose from the table and walked over to the back door, looking out seeing Millie Ann—carrying D.J.

"Hi Daddy." She Millie Ann said walking pass him as she entered the house. "Say hi to Daddy, D.J." The toddler looked at J.R. with unfamiliarity and smiled then giggled. J.R. forced himself to look at his cousin's son before noticing Daniel's car parked outside.

"Millie Ann is uh, everything alright? Geraldine okay?" He asked, curious of Daniel's continued presence." Millie Ann's ears deafened to her daddy's questions as she inhaled the aroma of dinner.

"Oooh! We having sloppy Joes for dinner Daddy?"

"Go wash your hands."

"Okay."

"Let me hold D.J., Millie Ann." Mahalia said reaching for him. She placed the toddler in her sister's awaiting arms then hurried over to the kitchen sink to wash her hands.

"You hungry D.J.? Mahalia asked seeing him reaching for the food on her plate. J.R. silently stood at the back door watched his cousin's parked car. His mouth slightly opened when seeing the driver's side door open and Daniel emerge and began walking towards the house. The two men looked one to the other from the distance as both psychologically prepared themselves for the awkward union. Their mutual gaze intensified as Daniel stepped on the back porch and stood on the other side of the screen door.

"How you doing J.R.?" He asked, nervous.

"Cousin Daniel." J.R. replied somberly. "Everything alright?"

"If you asking about Geraldine, she's as well as she can be after having a massive stroke."

"That uh, sounds like good news—I hope." J.R. looked at hm and waited for Daniel to disclose his reason for being there.

"Can I talk to you for a minute J.R.?"

"Uh, okay." He said looking at his *disloyal* cousin as he opened the door allowing him to enter. Daniel's heart raced as he walked past J.R. on his way inside.

"Hi Mr. Daniel!" Lil' J.R. yelled. "We eating French fries!"

"Smells good too." Daniel said.

"Hi Mr. Daniel!" The other children greeted.

"Hey Kids."

"We can uh, talk in my room." J.R. said closing the back door. "Uh, Millie Ann . . . me and uh, Cousin Daniel's going in my room to talk."

"Okay Daddy." She said standing at the stove dumping chili meat onto the open bun on her plate.

"I need you to uh, keep an eye on Lil' J.R. and your sisters."

"Okay Daddy."

"If you need me—" She cut him off.

"I said okay Daddy!" He shifted his eyes discretely over at D.J. sitting on Mahalia's lap before exiting the kitchen. Daniel followed. His anxiety mounting as they entered J.R.'s room, promptly closing the door, shielding the children from whatever verbal altercation they were about to have—a discussion J.R. knew would be about his estranged wife.

"How's Effie Mae doing?" Daniel asked unable to resist.

"To be honest Cousin Daniel, I uh, don't really know." J.R.'s mouth dried. He coughed. "The uh, last time I saw her she was uh, back with Anthony."

"Anthony?" Daniel said thinking back to the conversation he'd had with Effie Mae regarding Anthony coming to New York, and her being in denial about his prediction. "So you and Effie Mae's ain't—"

"Getting back together." J.R. looked at him. "I uh, guess not." Daniel noted the hurt in his eyes. "If uh, Anthony is who my wife chooses to be with then I guess uh, I can't stop her now can I?"

"Yeah, I guess you right J.R."

"But you know Effie Mae—" J.R. sarcastically chuckled. "—she uh, wants what she wants . . . no matter who gets hurt, right?"

"You gon be alright J.R.?" Daniel asked, surprised by his pessimistic words.

"Alright?" J.R. shook his head. "No Cousin Daniel, I uh, think maybe it's time for me to move on with my life—let Effie Mae live hers." Daniel masked his renewed hope for a future with his cousin's wife.

"Move on?" He asked pretending to be worried.

"I uh, had my attorney prepare some new divorce papers since Effie Mae seem to have left the others in Mississippi." Daniel forced a look of sympathy as he looked in his perceived rival's distressed eyes. "You sure that's what you want J.R.?"

"I don't think what I want matters much." J.R. said cynically chuckling. "But you know what Cousin Daniel, I don't think it ever did." Daniel's ears deafened to his cousin's emotional words as he though only of he, Effie Mae and D.J. as a family. "And as foolish as this might sound —" J.R.'s mouth dried. He coughed. "I would uh, love to have my wife back here with me and the children."

"I guess it ain't easy to shake that kind of love off." Daniel said speaking on his own behalf. The two cousin's looked one to the other both being fully aware they were in love with the same woman.

"You uh, said you wanted to talk Cousin Daniel?"

"Yeah J.R., the reason I wanted to talk to you it's Geraldine —" A troubled look appeared on J.R.'s face.

"Is she uh —"

"Dying?" Daniel said completing J.R.'s thought. "Naw J.R. that woman to ornery to die." Daniel half heartedly chuckled. "She want to see Effie Mae." A bewildered look showed in J.R.'s eyes.

"Geraldine wants to uh, see Effie Mae?"

"I think she want to apologize to Effie Mae for taking her baby from her the way she did." J.R.'s mouth slightly opened.

"Apologize — to Effie Mae?"

"I know, sound crazy don't it?"

"Yeah it does."

"That crazy woman's convinced herself if she hadn't took D.J., she would've never had that stroke." Daniel shook his head. "I tried to tell her J.R. that ain't had nothing do with nothing, but she stubborn and won't listen." J.R. refrained from voicing his opinion. He'd always believed Geraldine's decision to take Effie Mae's son, fathered by her husband, would have definite consequences.

"I wish I could help you Cousin Daniel, but uh, Effie Mae and I ain't talked much since she uh, set up house with Anthony." J.R. paused. "She's uh, wearing his engagement ring again." Daniel's head pounded as he listened to J.R.'s report on his forewarning Effie Mae that this would happen.

"So I guess she really do plan on marrying Anthony this time." Daniel said camouflaging hiw own agitation felt over Effie Mae's re-kindled romance with Anthony.

"I guess only she can answer that Cousin Daniel."

"I guess I'll find out when I go to see her tomorrow — tell her Geraldine want to see her."

"Uh, when you talk to her Cousin Daniel—" He looked in J.R.'s pleading eyes. "—could you uh, tell Effie Mae . . . her children miss her."

"I sure will J.R."

"And uh, Cousin Daniel—"

"Yeah J.R.?"

"Would you uh, tell her that I uh—that I love her?" Daniel nodded in agreement, uncertain if he would keep his promise. "Thank you Cousin Daniel."

---

Effie Mae watched from the sofa as Huck entered his apartment carrying a large box, sitting it on the floor next to the several other boxes and her two suitcases.

"You sure that's everything Effie Mae?" He asked exhausted.

"Yep." Huck took a deep breath then looked at the multitude of *things* she brought from Blue's apartment.

"I guess I need to get started putting this stuff in my room." She said standing up.

"Sit down Effie Mae." Huck stated. "I'll put it up later, you don't need to be trying to lift that stuff . . . you hear me girl?"

"Yeah I hear you Huck."

"I mean it Effie Mae—you know you pregnant." She loocked down at her extended abdomen.

"I can see that Huck." She said smiling.

"What you smiling about?"

"I never thought I'd see the day when I'd be living with Henry Lee White Junior." She teased. He blushed.

"What's that suppose to mean Effie Mae?"

"Nothing." Effie Mae giggled.

"I see you already getting started."

"Do you cook Huck?"

"When I want to."

"I got to see this." Effie Mae said grinning.

"What?"

"Huck cooking?"

"I know how to cook—I had too if I wanted to eat!"

"What about your momma Huck?"

"Effie Mae you met my momma." He shook his head. "Only thing Momma ever picked up was that bottle of scotch." He chuckled then momentarily gazed at her. She blushed.

"What?"

"You ain't gon believe this Effie Mae."

"Believe what?"

"You the first woman I ever let live with me."

"You lying Huck, I don't believe that!" Effie Mae said laughing.

"I ain't lying girl!" Huck cunningly smiled. "Ol' Huck had too many women to pick just one."

"So why you letting me stay here?"

"You tell me." They looked at each other and blushed. Effie Mae's blushing smile widened.

"What you smiling about this time Effie Mae?"

"I ain't gon have to be worrying about you coming in my room at night am I?"

"Only if you want me to." He blushed then looked intimately into her eyes. She blushed.

"What?"

"How long you plan on being here Effie Mae?"

"Why—you tired of me already Huck?" She teased.

"I get use to you being here—" He looked at her with seriousness. "—I might not let you leave . . . if J.R. don't want you I do."
Effie Mae tilted her head.

"Is that right?" They laughed. Huck stared at her as he imagined her being a permanent fixture in his life.

"Well Effie Mae—" He said ending his gaze. "— I'm getting ready to make a move, you need anything?"

"What you got to eat Huck? You know I'm eating for two now." She giggled.

"It's something in there you can make a sandwich with." Effie Mae's mouth flung open.

"A sandwich?"

"Effie Mae, I ain't gon be gone that long!" He said amused. "Make yourself a sandwich girl and I'll bring you something back—what you want?"

"That too much food Huck!"

"You said you was eating for two didn't you?" She giggled then smiled.

"Thank you Huck." He gazed into Effie Mae's as he placed two fingers underneath her chin and slightly tilted her head romantically kissing her.

"You welcome Effie Mae." Huck stated applying a quick kiss to her lips before walking away and exiting the apartment.

# Chapter Thirty

"Anthony you know I don't understand all them accounting words." Effie Mae said as she listened to him  discussing the club's finances in accounting terms, a language beyond her comprehension.

"Okay Baby I'll put it this way—Blue's Jazz Club is doing great, and the profits are impressive. She smiled, looking around their newly constructed office, located just left of the steps leading to the upstairs apartment.

"I love your new office Anthony."

"Not mines Baby—yours I'm just sharing it with you, remember you're the proprietor of this jazz club." Effie Mae smiled as she absorbed Anthony's words. "And speaking of that, I recommend you give Melvin a raise he's doing an excellent job here."

"Okay Anthony if you think so."

"I do." He kissed her quickly on the lips. "I also think you need to get more involved in the business." He said, again kissing her.

"Anthony!" Effie Mae looked out the office hoping his kiss hadn't been seen. Her eyes met with Melvin's as he wiped off tables. He silently chuckled. "Anthony you can't be kissing me like that boy!"

"Why not?" He placed another kiss on her lips.

"Anthony! What if the staff see you?"

"You're right, I'll only do it only when the office door is closed." Anthony kissed her again.

"I'm serious Anthony, you can't keep kissing me like that you know I'm trying to get back with my husband."

"Okay Baby I'll try not to do that, but I won't promise." He kissed her a fifth time.

"Anthony!" Effie Mae again looked out and into the prying eyes of Melvin still watching. He grinned.

"So Baby how's thing going with you living there with Huck?" Anthony asked bothered by her undesirable living arrangements.

"If you asking if me and Huck's sleeping in the same bed, the answer is no Anthony." A surprised look formed on her Effie Mae's as she reflected on her answer.

"What's that look for Baby?"

"Huck?"

"What about Huck?"

"He been a perfect gentleman Anthony and that ain't like Huck."

"Now that's scary." He said skeptical of Huck's idea behavior.

"Scary? What you mean Anthony?"

"Huck . . . the perfect gentleman?" Anthony's skepticism grew. "Baby does that even sound right to you?"

"Naw Anthony it don't, but Huck trying to give me time to—" He interjected.

"Do what Baby, make your way into his bed or him in yours?"

"I'm telling you Anthony—" Effie Mae looked at him with sincerity. "—Huck ain't tried to do nothing to me."

"Give him time." Anthony said unconvinced. "How's things goings with J.R.?" He asked redirecting the conversation. "Have you and he talked yet?"

"Not yet Anthony but I am—"

"Before or after Huck gets you in his bed?"

"Anthony!"

"Call J.R., Effie Mae."

"I said I am."

"Don't just say it Baby do it." Anthony watched, waiting for her to pick up the office phone. "Now!" He said insisting. "Before it's too late." She giggled.

"Okay Anthony I'm gon do it." Effie Mae picked up the phone and dialed then hung up.

"Baby, why did you do that?" A look of uncertainty displayed in her eyes.

"I don't know what to say Anthony?"

"Baby I don't think you'll have to say anything once J.R. knows it's you."

"You think so?"

"Yes Baby I think so." Anthony again kissed her. "And if J.R. won't talk to you, remember I'm still here." Effie Mae looked in his engaging eyes and blushed.

---

A month after finally agreeing to meet with Ms. Geraldine, Effie Mae entered through the hospital doors accompanied by Daniel, neither spoke a word as they stepped onto the elevator and headed up to the third floor. Effie Mae nervously watched as the elevator arrived at its designated floor and the doors opened. She suddenly backed in the corner and refused to come out.

"You gon be alright Effie Mae?" Daniel asked, troubled by her panicky behavior.

"I don't know Daniel—" She stated nervously."

"Mr. Daniel."

"What?" She said confused.

"When you talk to me in front of Geraldine call me Mr. Daniel."

"Take me home Daniel!" Effie Mae shouted, angered by his selfish request.

"Come on now Effie Mae." He pleaded. "You know if Geraldine hear you calling me Daniel it's gon upset her."

"Take me home Daniel!" She demanded. The elevator doors again closed.

"Wait a minute Effie Mae." Daniel said trying to calm her down. "I know you nervous but—" She cut him off.

"What else I'm gon be not knowing why Ms. Geraldine want to see me!" Effie Mae shouted. "How I know she ain't wanting to hurt me?" Daniel humorously grinned. Effie Mae's anger heightened. "It ain't funny Daniel!"

"Calm down girl."

"How am I gon calm down Daniel when I got a crazy woman waiting to see—" He interjected.

"Come on now Effie Mae, call me Mr. Daniel."

"Take me home!" She bellowed. "Open that door so I can get off this elevator!" The elevator doors again opened—still on the third floor. Effie Mae move swiftly to exit. Daniel quickly caught hold of her arm.

"Effie Mae."

"Turn me a loose Mr. Daniel." She said looking him angrily in the eyes, her fury magnified by fear.

"Come here girl." He said pulling her gently into his arms, embracing her. "Do you think I would let Geraldine hurt you?"

"You allowed her to take my baby boy, so don't ask me what I think you would let your wife do Mr. Daniel!" She pulled out of his embrace.

"Effie Mae—" Daniel again tried to take hold of her. Effie Mae pushed him away. "—if I thought Geraldine was even thinking about hurting you, I would've never brought you out here you know that." She looked at Daniel with mistrust as he moved his lips towards hers in hopes of a kiss. His eager lips landed on the back of Effie Mae's head as she quickly turned away. "I guess I had that coming."

"I guess you did Mr. Daniel." He looked at her as the elevator doors again closed.

"Let's just go see what Geraldine want then we can go to my house so you can see our boy and we can talk okay?" Effie Mae pushed him away as he again tried to kiss her then pushed the "open" button on the elevator's wall panel—the doors abruptly opened. Daniel watched as she stepped out of the elevator and headed down the elongated corridor. He followed. "It's the second room on the right Effie Mae." He stated, speaking just above a whisper. Effie Mae shifted her eyes nervously at the nurses sitting in the Nurses Station as she walked past—stopping at the second door on the right. She turned and looked ar Daniel as je approached her. He nodded assuring her everything would be okay. Effie Mae trailed him inside the room watching as he walked over to the bed then leaned down placing a kiss on Ms. Geraldine's cheek. Her eyes opened.

"I brought Effie Mae with me Geraldine." Daniel said speaking softly. She nodded. He looked over and into the terrified eyes of Effie Mae. "Geraldine want you to come over to her. Effie Mae subtly shook her head no.

"Co-o-o-me—ere. " Ms. Geraldine said speaking through her semi crooked mouth. Effie Mae looked at her then turned to Daniel.

"Go on." He urged. She slowly walked towards the bed then stopped just to the left of Daniel and gazed upon the partially paralyzed face of the woman who'd stolen her baby boy—wondering what she had to say. The two women looked one to the other before Effie Mae abruptly walked away, fretful of the hurtful words Ms. Geraldine might say.

"Ef—fie—Mae?" She again turned, looking briefly at her then shifted her eyes to Daniel. He intervened.

"Yeah Geraldine it's Effie Mae." Ms. Geraldine peered through her right eye then gradually raised her unaffected right hand, beckoning Effie Mae with her fingers to come to her. Effie Mae remained frozen.

"Go on Effie Mae." Daniel again urged. "She can't hurt you—she ain't strong enough." Ms. Geraldine silently chuckled, amused by Daniel's words. He took hold of Effie Mae's arm and guided her over to the bed.

"Ow—you—do—in?" Ms. Geraldine asked.

"I'm doing fine Ms. Geraldine." Effie Mae said shifting her frightened eyes to Daniel. He nodded. She again turned to Ms. Geraldine. "Mr. Daniel said you had a stroke?" Effie Mae said glancing nervously over at him. Ms. Geraldine nodded. "Mr. Daniel said you wanted to see me?" Effie Mae said shifting her eyes briefly to Daniel. Ms. Geraldine nodded.

"D.J.—get—bi—ev'time I—I—see im." Effie Mae's eyes met with Daniel's unable to understand her muttered words.

"Oh, she just said D.J.'s getting bigger every time she see him." He chuckled. "I always bring her pictures when I come out here—Geraldine know she loves seeing how big that boy's getting.

"Yeah Ms. Geraldine he growing like weeds alright." Effie Mae said forcing a smile, looking quickly to Daniel. Ms. Geraldine used her right hand to point at Effie Mae's stomach then shifted her eyes over at Daniel, visually asking him if he'd fathered Effie Mae's unborn child. His anxiety magnified, guilt-ridden by his continued lust for Effie Mae. Daniel shook his head no.

"Ou—preg—gin?" She asked chuckling. Effie Mae looked over at Daniel for clarification.

"She said she see you pregnant again, wanted to know who the father was." A large smile formed on Effie Mae's face as she remembered the many times Ms. Geraldine remained at her side during the birth of her many children—even Daniel Jr.

"This one is definitely my husband's, Ms. Geraldine." She said giggling. Ms. Geraldine's eyes dampened.

"I'm—so-o-o-ry." She said trying to extend her weakened right hand to Effie Mae. Daniel quickly intervened, raising his wife's hand, extending it to his one time mistress. Effie Mae's fear mounted as she remained cautious about taking hold of the hand of her long time adversary.

"Go on Effie Mae." Daniel stated. "She ain't gon hurt you." She looked in Ms. Geraldine's tearful eyes, searching for signs of lingering animosity before apprehensively reaching out her right hand, allowing Ms. Geraldine to take hold. She gently squeezed Effie Mae's hand as she wept. Daniel's eyes moistened as he watched—pleased to witness the two women in his life finally come to a long awaited *truce* as tears emerged from both their eyes.

"I'm the one who should be apologizing to you Ms. Geraldine." Effie Mae said weeping. "I don't know why I did what I done." Ms. Geraldine hugged her with her right arm then laid Effie Mae's head on her chest, forgiving her for the affair she had with her husband and the son she bore.

"I—ove—you—Ef—fie—Mae."

"I love you too Ms. Geraldine." She placed a light kiss on Effie Mae's cheek then released her. Daniel watched Effie Mae as she rose from the embrace, continuing to weep. He longed to take her in his arms and comfort her. Ms. Geraldine's heart pounded in her ears when seeing the lingering love her husband still had for Effie Mae. She realized at that moment his love for the mother of his son had grown and nothing she could say or do would ever take that away.

"Dan-iel."

"Huh?" He said breaking his gaze at Effie Mae. "You call me Geraldine?" She nodded then pointed to the box of Kleenex on the nightstand next to her bed. "Oh, okay." Daniel pulled a few tissues from the box then reached over, preparing to wipe away Effie Mae's tears. She quickly removed the tissue from his hand, prohibiting him from displaying his affection in the front of his wife.

"Thank you Mr. Daniel." Effie Mae said wiping her tears.

"Okay uh, you welcome Effie Mae."

"Dan-iel."

"Huh?" He again turned to his wife. "You need something Geraldine?" She nodded and again pointed to the nightstand.

"I gave Effie Mae the tissue already." She continued pointing. "You need something else?" Ms. Geraldine nodded. "What you need me to get?" She aimed her finger at the top drawer of the nightstand. "You want me to get something out of that drawer?" She again nodded. "He walked over and pulled open the top drawer. Effie Mae watched as he retrieved a large white envelop folded in half. "I forget you had me bring that out here Geraldine." Daniel handed it to her. She shook her head no. "Huh?" He said puzzled by her refusal to take it. She pointed to Effie Mae, instructing him to give it to her. Effie Mae stared at the mysterious envelope, apprehensive about taking it. Her slightly trembled as she removed it from Daniel's hand and prepared to open it. She unfolded the envelope and carefully pulled out the paper inside. Effie Mae looked at the document, identifying it as a birth record. Her eyes brushed over the document in search of the written words naming of the infant and its parents. She gasped when seeing the newborn being identified as Daniel Lee Jones Jr. Her eyes quickly glanced down to the signature line searching for the mother's name. Effie Mae again gasped when seeing her name listed as the birth mother. She looked at Ms.

Geraldine with gratitude then leaned down and hugged her. The two women once rivals—embraced and cried as friends.

———————————

Effie Mae entered J.R. church for the first time after Blue's funeral seeing him in the sanctuary speaking with a male member of his congregation. A huge smiled appeared on his face when he noted her standing in the vestibule. He held up one finger indicating he'd be with her in a few minutes as he continued in conversation with his member. Tears suddenly erupted from Effie Mae's eyes as her thoughts drifted to the day of Blue's funeral. J.R. briefly shifted his eyes over at her becoming alarmed when seeing Effie Mae sobbing uncontrollably.

"Uh, Brother Williamson would you uh, excuse me I uh—" J.R. hurried from the sanctuary into the foyer. Brother Williamson watched with curiosity as J.R. embraced Effie Mae in his arms and attempted to console her.

"Effie Mae what's going on?"

"Everything alright Pastor?" A Deacon exiting the bathroom, located just off the foyer asked when witnessing his intimate embrace with the unfamiliar female.

"Uh, Deacon Green could you uh, go ahead and finish speaking with Brother Williamson . . . make sure you get his wife's hospital room number?" Deacon Green glanced briefly in the sanctuary at Brother Williamson then turned his focused back to J.R. and his female companion. "I really need to uh, take care of this."

"Okay Reverend—" Deacon Green scrutinized the intimate embrace his reverend shared with the pregnant female. "—did you want us to go out to the hospital and pray with Sister Williamson too?" He asked, stalling.

"Yes Deacon please do." J.R. said upset by Effie Mae's weeping.

Deacon Green looked at her, taking note of the wedding ring on her finger. He assumed she lived in the neighborhood and might possibly be seeking counseling for her wayward husband.

"Is that young lady gon be alright reverend?" He asked, snooping. "If you need me to see about her so you can tend to Brother Williamson—" J.R. interjected.

"No, I'll take care of her." Deacon Green's nosiness heightened.

"You sure?"

J.R. ignored the inquisitive deacon as he escorted Effie Mae from church and out to his car parked in front. Deacon Green watched through the glass doors of the church as J.R. assisted Effie Mae in the car then climbed and drove away.

"I wonder what that was all about?" Deacon Green said to himself.

• • • •

J.R. assisted Effie Mae out of the car and into his house as her crying persisted. "You came to the church Effie Mae—what's going on?" He asked as they entered the living room being seated on the sofa. She looked in his worried eyes, but gave no reply. "You and uh, Anthony having problems?" J.R. asked hoping she'd say yes. "You uh, need me to call him and try to fix whatever's broken?"

"I ain't with Anthony no more J.R." Effie Mae said decreasing her crying to a sniffle. "That's over."

"Uh, over?" He said containing his excitement. "When uh . . . when did this happen?"

"About a month ago."

"A month ago?" J.R.'s curiosity mounted as he wondered where she'd been living. His mouth dried. He coughed. "So uh, where have you uh, been staying?" He asked hoping she wouldn't say with Daniel.

"I know what you gon say J.R., but it ain't like that." His mouth again dried. He coughed then took a deep breath and slowly blew it out.

"Okay so uh, what is you know I'm gon say?"

"I'm staying with Huck."

"Huck?" He said shocked.

"Yeah J.R. but it ain't what you think.

"Then tell me Effie Mae what it is you think I'm thinking?" J.R. said trying to remain calm.

"J.R., me and Huck ain't nothing but friends."

"Effie Mae why didn't you just come home?"

"I didn't think you wanted me here."

"What made you think that?"

"You said you was moving on with your life—"

"I was hurt Effie Mae!" J.R.'s said feeling remorseful. "I could never get mad enough where I wouldn't want you here with me and the children." He suddenly silenced, looking at her with surprised eyes.

"Effie Mae—Huck?" A childlike innocence displayed in her eyes. "I ain't had no place else to go."

"You always have a home here with me Effie Mae no matter what." She looked in J.R.'s sincere eyes, comforted by his welcoming words.

"You think you could love me again J.R.?"

"Effie Mae I never stopped." His eyes moistened. "I have loved you from the very first day I saw you, and when you said you'd be my wife I truly felt blessed." She smiled. "And when you started giving me all them beautiful children it seemed like the blessings wasn't ever gon stop coming." J.R. beamed as he reminisced.

"Then I messed everything up."

"No Effie Mae, we messed it up."

"You ain't the one who was out there making babies with somebody else J.R."

"No I wasn't." He kissed her on the forehead. "But I'm the one who walked out on my wife and children because I couldn't find it in my heart to forgive." J.R. looked up and shook his head. "A man of God struggling to forgive." He said chastising himself. Effie Mae laughed.

"What?" He stated in response to her out of place laughter.

"Seem we both had a problem with that J.R."

"Huh?"

"You was having a trouble forgiving me for being with another man—" He interjected.

"Men not man—" Effie Mae's jaw dropped. "—did you forgot about Jimmy?" She giggled.

"Naw J.R., I ain't forgot about Jimmy." She smiled. "I'm gon have to introduce you to him one of these days." A triumphant look appeared on J.R.'s face.

"I uh, actually wouldn't mind meeting the man I stole you from." He smiled. Effie Mae giggled.

"I had trouble forgiving you too J.R."

"For uh, taking you away from Jimmy?"

"Not Jimmy—Anthony." J.R.'s mouth dried. He coughed.

"Anthony? You uh, sure you and he are over?"

"Yeah J.R. I'm sure." She stated knowing that in her heart Anthony still held a significant place.

"So uh, here we are many years . . . and men later." Effie Mae's jaw dropped.

"Men?" She said stunned by him referencing to her many indiscretions.

"There was uh, Blue your husband—" J.R. corrected himself. "—your *spiritual* husband, Anthony your fiancé and the father of my son, Cousin Daniel, father of your second son—" Effie Mae laughed, amused by his teasing. "And a Huck!" J.R. said with inquiry. Effie Mae continued laughing. "And now you're a widow, even though we was never legally divorced—you and your fiancé just called it quits, and you have another child on the way that I'm praying is mines and not a Blue Jr." Effie Mae's mouth abruptly opened. "To say that life with Effie Mae Reed has been a journey—" She interjected.

"I told Momma I didn't want to meet you in the first place, but Rev. Hill kept on trying to get me to—"

"Not Rev. Hill, it was me who insisted on meeting you." Effie Mae lowered her head.

"If you want a divorce J.R.—"

"No Effie Mae I don't want a divorce." J.R. quietly chuckled. "I don't think a divorce would change anything that I—" He paused. "—we been through."

"If you divorce me J.R. maybe you can find the right woman for you." He looked in her frightened eyes.

"Effie Mae, baby you are the right woman for me."

"How can you say that J.R. after all I done to you?"

"Come home Effie Mae."

"I would love to come back home with you and our babies J.R., if you sure that's what you want."

"Yeah Effie Mae, I'm sure that's what I want." She looked at him and thought of the Blue's question—"*Do you think you could ever fall in love with J.R.?*"

"I love you J.R." Effie Mae said answering Blue's question out loud, realizing her love for him had grown, but knew it could never take the place of her love for Blue. "You sure Effie Mae?"

"Yeah J.R. I'm sure." They gazed at each other then passionately kissed.

# Chapter Thirty-One

"You ate already Effie Mae?" Huck asked when seeing her sitting on the living room sofa as he entered the kitchen from his bedroom. He noticed the huge smile on her her face.

"What you smiling about?"

"He still love me Huck."

"Who?"

"My husband!" She giggled. "Who you thought I was talking about?"

"I never know with you Effie Mae, it could've been anybody—Anthony, old Daniel, Melvin?" He joked. A tell-tale look displayed in Effie Mae's eyes as she giggled. Huck tilted his head.

"Melvin?" She recalled Melvin's recent proposal and blushed. "You blushing." Huck said looking at her with curious eyes—he again tilted his head. "Melvin?"

"Naw, but he did ask me if he could take Blue's place." Huck again tilted his head.

"Is that right?" He stroked his chin hairs and grinned. "I see Ol' Melvin slicker than roller skates on ice." He quietly chuckled.

"Well, I wasn't talking about Melvin I was speaking on my husband." Effie Mae said holding out her hand displaying her wedding ring, once again adorned on her finger. Huck humorously smiled.

"You something else Effie Mae." She giggled. "So I guess that means you moving out?"

"Yeah Huck I am." A look of gratitude displayed in her eyes. "Thank you Huck." He smiled.

"You welcome Effie Mae."

"Naw, I mean it Huck!"

"Okay Effie Mae I believe you." Huck said continuing to smile.

"You let me stay here in your house—" She suddenly silenced then giggled.

"What you laughing for?"

"It's just that you been acting like the perfect gentleman—" He quickly interjected.

"Perfect Gentleman?" His eyes widened. "What's that suppose to mean?"

"You never tried to get me in your bed—play husband or none of that."

"Effie Mae don't you tell nobody that!" A boyish smile formed on his handsome face. "Might have the ladies thinking Ol' Huck's done lost his game." They both laughed. "Huck's reputation with the ladies is what keeps Ol' Huck in the game."

"I got something else to be happy about too." Effie Mae said eager to share her information.

"What's that Effie Mae?" She picked her purse up from the sofa and opened it, removing the folded document. "This!" She said holding it up.

"What's that?" Huck asked, watching as she unfolded it.

"It's my baby's birth record Huck." He titled his head.

"Old Daniel's boy?"

"Yep."

"Where you get that from Effie Mae?" He asked, suspicious. "And what you do to get it?" He looked at her and again tilted his head. She giggled.

"Nothing!"

"Nothing?"

"I just went to the hospital to see Ms. Geraldine—" He cut her off.

"Old Daniel's wife?"

"Yep." Her eyes beamed as she fixated on D.J.'s birth record. "Daniel came and told me Ms. Geraldine wanted to see me." Huck noticed her calling him Daniel.

"See you for what?"

"Daniel said she was feeling guilty 'bout taking my baby boy from me, so I went to go see her." Effie Mae stated, electing not to tell Huck of her immense fear in doing so. "Then Ms. Geraldine said she forgave me for what happened with me and Daniel."

"Forgave you?" Huck stated in disbelief. "Why?"
"Daniel said she thinking that was why she had her stroke—" Huck interjected.

"Daniel?" He said suspicious of the status of her relationship with Daniel. "Effie Mae you messing with old Daniel again?"

"Naw—why you say that Huck?"

"I see you calling him Daniel instead of Mr. Daniel." Effie Mae giggled.

"It's just that he be wanting me to call him Daniel instead of Mr. Daniel." Huck laughed out loud. "I see Ol' Melvin ain't the only one roller skating on ice." Effie Mae smiled. "What old Daniel's wife say about that?"

"Nothing."

"Nothing?"

"I didn't call him that in front of Ms. Geraldine—I ain't crazy Huck!" He laughed.

"You ain't?" Huck titled his head. "You sure about that Effie Mae?" He teased. She laughed.

"Yeah Huck I'm sure I ain't crazy."

"I don't know Effie Mae—"

"Let me finish telling you Huck!"

"Talk, I'm listening."

"Ms. Geraldine told Daniel—" Huck chuckled underneath his breath as he listened. "—to give me this big yellow envelope she had in the drawer next to her hospital bed . . . and when I pulled the paper out inside I saw it was my baby D.J.'s birth record."

"And?"

"And it had my name on it Huck!" She said elated. "Naming me as my baby boy's momma!" He nodded.

"I'm glad for you Effie Mae I know how much you love that boy."

"So Huck after you help me move all my stuff over to J.R.'s house, I need you to take me to get my baby boy." A look of surprise formed on Huck's face. He tilted his head.

"Is that right?"

"What you mean?"

"Effie Mae did that woman say you could have that boy?"

"That's my baby Huck!" She said raising her voice. "And if I want him I'm gon get him."

"What about old Daniel, Effie Mae?"

"What about him?" A perplexed look formed on Huck face, stunned by Effie Mae's coldness.

"That's his boy too Effie Mae—you think old Daniel gon let you just walk in there and take that boy?"

"He can't stop me Huck—" She held up the birth record. "—this paper right here say I'm that boy's momma."

"It ain't that easy Effie Mae!"

"How come it ain't?" Her agitation mounted. "It was that easy for Ms. Geraldine to take my baby boy from me!"

"Old Daniel love that boy Effie Mae." Huck said in Daniel's defense.

"I love my baby boy too!"

"I know you do Effie Mae, but your boy's the only child old Daniel got."

"No he ain't Huck what about them babies he got with Sadie Ann?"

"Effie Mae those ain't old Daniel's kids!"

"Yes they are Huck."

"Naw Effie Mae that's what Sadie Ann led that man to believe, used it to get old Daniel's money."

"How you know Huck?" Effie Mae shouted. "You just saying that."

"Effie Mae . . . Sadie Ann had both those kids by number man Curtis."

"Who? Curtis?" She said confused.

"By the time old Daniel made his way over to that girl, she was two maybe three months pregnant by Curtis—her husband." Huck stated having first hand knowledge. "Effie Mae don't neither one of those kids belong to old Daniel!"

"You lying Huck, you just don't want me to have my baby boy!"

"Effie Mae I wouldn't lie to you girl, not about that!" Tears erupted from her eyes as began weeping.

"Mr. Daniel can't have my baby Huck!"

"Oh, so now it's Mr. Daniel."

"Take me to get my baby Huck!" Effie Mae yelled.

"I can't do that Effie Mae."

"Why not? Mr. Daniel don't even like you."

"Wrong is wrong Effie Mae, and what you trying to do is wrong." She glared angrily at him.

"That's alright Huck, you ain't gotta take me I'll find way."

"Think about what you doing girl, taking that boy gon kill that man."

"I don't care if it do!" Huck tilted his head.

"Is that right?"

"Don't try to stop me Huck!" Effie Mae stated with tear-filled eyes. "He always trying to get me in his bed . . . okay I'll lay down with—" Huck interjected.

"Effie Mae, girl you better than that!"

"Am I Huck?"

"Think about what you saying girl!"

"I am!" She screamed out in fury. "And I'm thinking 'bout how Mr. Daniel and his wife stole my baby boy from me!"

"Let it go Effie Mae."

"I can't do that Huck—I'm going over here and get my baby boy and if you won't help me I'm gon have Anthony do it."

"Anthony?" Huck looked in Effie Mae's determined eyes. He shook his head. "Damn shame."

"I want my baby Huck!"

"I know you do Effie Mae, but that ain't the way to do it."

"I don't care if it ain't, only thing I care 'bout is getting my baby boy back."

"Effie Mae—"

"What Huck?" She shouted.

"Have old Daniel ever stopped you from seeing your boy since that time I had to talk to him?"

"Naw, but he shouldn't have him in the first place!" Effie Mae yelled. "That woman stole my baby Huck!" She bellowed.

"I know Effie Mae and old Daniel and his wife was wrong but—"

"But what Huck!" She hollered out. "That boy grew inside of me not Ms. Geraldine—"

"I know Effie Mae but you wrong girl." Huck said trying to reason with her. "Okay Effie Mae I'll take you." He stated sympathetic to her tearfulness. "I can see now I ain't gon be able to stop you." He took a deep breath, angry with himself for giving in. "Ain't no point in getting Anthony involved in this—that man didn't come up here for all l that."

"Let's go Huck!" She shouted.

"I said I was taking you Effie Mae—" He looked at her with disappointed eyes. "—after I eat." He looked around the living room at her many boxes, still scattered about. "But J.R. gon have to come get all this stuff, I ain't getting ready to break my back." Effie Mae giggled through her tears.

———————————————

Huck pulled up to the curb several houses away from Daniel's and parked. He looked over at Effie Mae seated next to him, hoping she would change her mind.

"You sure I can't talk you out this Effie Mae?"

"Nope."

"How you gon explain having your son to J.R.?"

"You let me worry about that." She hastily opened the door and got out. Huck watched as she walked quickly down the sidewalk, stepping up on Daniel's front porch.

"Damn shame—that girl ain't never satisfied." Huck said to himself. Effie Mae knocked on the door and anxiously waited for Daniel to answer. The door quickly opened. He stood on the other side, a large smile on his face. Her mouth suddenly dired as she looked into Daniel's eager eyes. Effie Mae's mind raced as she tried to think of how to remove her baby boy with little to no resistance from Daniel.

"How you doing Effie Mae?" He asked through the enormous smile on his face.

"I'm doing just fine Daniel." She said seductively flirting. His smile widened—delighted in her calling him Daniel. "You gon let me in or leave me out here standing on the porch?" She girlishly giggled.

"Oh naw, come on in Effie Mae." Daniel said stepping aside, allowing her to enter. "You came to see D.J.?" He asked hoping by some miracle she'd come to share his lonely bed. Effie Mae gave no reply as her ears deafened to Daniel's voice as she now thought only of her recently rekindled relationship with her husband. "I just put that boy down for a nap and—"

"Huh?" She said, again tuning in his voice.

"I say I just put D.J. down for a nap." His noticed the occupied look in Effie Mae's eyes. "You alright Effie Mae?" She silently stared at him, ambiguous about the decision she faced. On the one hand, she knew being intimate with Daniel would betray the trust restored between her and J.R. On the other, she believed walking away with her son warranted it. "The last time we talked you said you was moving in that with that monster Huck . . . how's that working out?" Daniel asked probing to see if she'd shared her bed with him yet.

"Close the door." Effie Mae stated in a suggestive tone.

"Huh?" Daniel's eyes widened in response to her inducement. He kept his lustful eyes fixated on her face as he slowly closed the door. Effie Mae forced a smile as she convinced herself that sharing in intimacy with Daniel would be the only way she could walk away with her son, unchallenged.

"You ain't gon kiss me Daniel?" She said masking her guilt as she prepared for their inevitable, intimate rendezvous.

"Huh?" Daniel said seemingly mesmerized. Effie Mae wrapped her arms intimately around his neck.

"Kiss me Daniel."

"What you doing Effie Mae?" He asked gazing in her eyes, debating within himself if giving into Effie Mae's advances would result in consequences.

"You don't know Daniel?" She said whispering in his ear, placing an seductive kiss on his willing lips.

"Wait a minute Effie Mae." He stated, uneasy by her eagerness. "What's this all about? I thought you was trying to get back with J.R.?"

"Well I ain't back with J.R. yet Daniel—now am I?" She giggled then kissed him softly on the ear. "Hearing all your talk about your lonely bed made me miss us." Effie Mae said applying repeated kisses to his neck and ears—working her way to his awaiting lips.

"Come on now Effie Mae." Daniel said trying to resist the urge to submit to her seduction. She continued gazing in his eyes then passionately kissed him.

"You sure about this Effie Mae?" He asked no longer able to resist.

"You want me or not Daniel?" Effie Mae said as she applied another kiss to his compliant lips.

"You know I do." Daniel stated, aggressively kissing her. She looked at him with alluring eyes as she took hold of his hand and guided him in the direction of her old bedroom. He followed with helpless anticipation, dismissing the fact that she continued to be his cousin's wife. A gigantic smile displayed on Daniel's face as his fantasy of sharing in long awaited intimacy with the woman he loved—became reality.

• • • •

Huck glanced at his watch twenty five minutes after Effie Mae left. He looked in the direction of Daniel's house, hoping he'd see her on her way back—without her baby boy.

"Damn!" He shouted, convinced Effie Mae had included her body in her plan to gain custody of her son. "That girl took that old man to bed." Huck shook his head as he made himself comfortable on his leather seats and awaited Effie Mae to carry out her *plan of deceit* to seduce Daniel and walk away with her son without resistance.

• • • •

He quickly sat up, forty minutes later when seeing Effie Mae hurrying down the sidewalk headed towards his car carrying D.J. on her right hip—strapped across her left shoulder dangled an over-stuffed diaper bag. She swiftly opened the car door and climbed inside, closing it quickly behind her.

"Let's go Huck."

"Effie Mae what you doing girl?" Huck asked hoping to talk her into returning her son.

"Let's go Huck!" Effie Mae said raising her voice.

"Girl take that baby back in that house."

"Nope, I got my baby back and I'm keeping him—now let's go!"

"I can't do that Effie Mae."

"Okay then—" She stated with defiance. "—I'm gon walk." Huck tilted his head.

"Is that right?" His attention drew to Effie Mae's toddler son sitting on her lap looking at him with unfamiliarity. "Hey little man, tell your momma to take you back in that house." D.J. looked at him and smiled then giggled.

"I ain't playing Huck!" Effie Mae threatened. "If you don't drive me away from here I'm gon take my baby boy and walk." He looked at her with disapproving eyes and shook his head then started the engine.

"Close the door and put your seat belt on." He momentarily stared at her before putting his car in gear. "Where you want me to drop you?"

"Take me to J.R.'s house." She said dismissing the frustrated look in his eyes as she closed the door, putting the seat belt around both her and her toddler son. Huck stared briefly at her then pulled from the curve and drove off on his way to J.R.'s house.

---

"Come on sweet baby." Effie Mae said extending her open arms to the toddler as she sat on the living room floor at J.R.'s house. He walked unbalanced being cheered on by his sibling—all watching as he wobbled towards his momma, losing his balance after only six steps then plopping down on his rear end. D.J. looked around into the excited eyes of his siblings and giggled.

"Get up D.J." Millie Ann said raising him to his feet. Effie Mae's attention drew to the kitchen when hearing the sound of the ringing phone. She knew for certain the caller would be Daniel. J.R. answered.

"Hello . . . uh, Cousin Daniel how are you?"

"How you doing J.R.?"

"I'm uh, I'm good." J.R. said looking in the living room at Effie Mae, pleased to have her home.

"Is Effie Mae anywhere around J.R.?" Daniel asked hoping she'd not taken his son over to Huck house—but prepared to go there if it meant getting his son back..

"Uh, Effie Mae yeah she's right here." J.R.'s heart nervously pounded, uneasy by Daniel's call. "Effie Mae—" He said trying not to let his insecurity show. "It's uh, Cousin Daniel." J.R. sat the phone on the kitchen counter then hurried in the living room to assist Effie Mae up from the floor.

"Thank you J.R." He kissed her lightly on the lips then rubbed her pregnant belly.

"No baby, thank you." J.R. said applying a kiss to her cheek. Effie Mae smiled as she tried to think of what she would say to Daniel in response to what she knew the conversation would be. Effie Mae maintained her calm demeanor as J.R. picked up the phone and handed it to her.

"Hey Mr. Daniel."

"Why you do that to me Effie Mae?"

"You were sleeping so good, I didn't want to wake you up."

"Why you do that to me girl?"

"I guess chasing behind D.J. all day really tired you out." She said forcing a giggle.

"Effie Mae bring my boy home."

"We was just in here watching this little boy trying to walk." She glanced over at J.R. being careful with her words. "I guess it won't be long before he walking by his self.

"Effie Mae please bring my boy back!"

"I want to thank you Mr. Daniel for taking me to see Ms. Geraldine—next time you speak to her tell her I said thank you for what she done for me." Effie Mae said smiling as she looked in J.R.'s inquiring eyes trying not to arouse his suspicion.

"Effie Mae it would tear Geraldine apart if she came home and that boy wasn't here."

"Yeah I know, but she gon be alright."

"Effie Mae I love that boy more than anything in this world, please bring my baby back!"

"I know you do Mr. Daniel and I'm sure gon tell that little boy his daddy said he love him." J.R. shifted his eyes over at her when hearing her reference to Daniel as D.J.'s daddy.

"Tell me what I need to do Effie Mae." Daniel pleaded.

"I know you miss him Mr. Daniel—" Effie Mae said ignoring his pleading words. She glanced over at J.R. and smiled trying to maintain her calm outward appearance. "But you trying to care for D.J. and Ms. Geraldine—" He cut her off.

"Effie Mae please! please! please—"

"Is more than you need to be dealing with by yourself!" She again shifted her eyes to J.R. "We don't want you having a stroke too." Effie Mae half-heartedly chuckled, looking briefly at J.R. "Just let me know when you want to come see this little boy Mr. Daniel—J.R. can cook dinner so we can eat together as a family." Daniel's frustration surged.

"Girl if I had known messing with you I was gon lose my boy, I would've never touched you Effie Mae!" He said raising his voice.

"I know how much you like pork chops." She said giggling. "So I'm gon be sure to have J.R. cook pork chops on that day just for you." J.R. looked at her and smiled.

"Effie Mae don't take my boy from me . . . please!" Daniel shouted. J.R. quickly turned to Effie Mae in response to hearing his cousin's raised voice.

"Is uh, everything alright with Cousin Daniel?"

"Yeah J.R., Mr. Daniel's fine—he just missing his baby boy is all." Daniel continued pleading.

"Effie Mae please!"

"Well Mr. Daniel you just keep on caring for your wife." Effie Mae said forcing the words out her mouth. "D.J. gon be just fine over here with his family." J.R. nodded in agreement.

"Effie Mae please give me back my boy."

"So ain't no cause for you to be worrying about this little boy—I'm going in here right now and give him a big kiss for you."

"Effie Mae don't do me like this girl—please!"

"Bye Mr. Daniel." She handed J.R. the phone. "Hang this up for me J.R."

"Is uh, everything okay?" He asked returning the phone on its base.

"Mr. Daniel just worried 'bout how he gon explain to Ms. Geraldine he ain't got D.J. no more."

"I'm sure uh, she'll understand." J.R. said assisting her back in the living room then lowering her down on the floor.

"I guess he gon find out." Effie Mae said turning her attention back to her toddler son—watching as he again pulled himself up and attempting to walk. "Come on D.J. baby." Effie Mae coached.

———————————

"I'll be back Anthony." Effie Mae said watching from the office as Melvin opened the front door allowing Huck to enter, his angry eyes fixated on her. Anthony looked out in the club seeing Huck headed for the office.

"Baby, is everything alright?" He asked suspicious of Huck's early morning arrival Effie Mae stood.

"Yeah Anthony I must've left something at Huck's house when I moved out."

"Something like what Baby?"

"I guess Huck gon let me know when I talk to him." She said forcing a chuckle, not wanting Anthony to know what she knew would result in an altercation.

"Okay Boss." Anthony teased.

"I'll be right out Huck." Effie Mae said removing the impending conversation from within earshot of Anthony. She walked hastily from the office, meeting Huck mid-center of the club.

"Sit down." He demanded. "How you sleep last night Effie Mae?" Huck asked staring in her eyes as she sat.

"I slept just fine Huck." She stated rebelliously. He tilted his head.

"Is that right?" His attention drew to Melvin when noting him eavesdropping from the bar area as he stocked alcohol in preparation for the night's expected crowd of patrons. He again turned to Effie Mae. "Ol' Blue sure would be hurt if he was here to see what you done to old Daniel—taking his son from him like that."

"Don't be putting Blue in this!" Effie Mae said shifting her eyes in the direction of the open office door. "Besides, Blue always took me to go see my babies—" He cut her off.

"To see them Effie Mae, but Blue never would've let you walked away with them kids."

"What you trying to be Huck—my daddy?" He gazed at her, hurt by her verbal attack. "Ms. Geraldine took my baby from me the day that boy was born." Effie Mae said attempting to justify her actions. "I ain't done nothing but took back what was already mine—" Melvin interrupted.

"Hey Huck—" He called over from the bar. "—can I get you some scotch man?" Melvin said trying to run interference when seeing the fury in Huck's eyes directed at Effie Mae. Huck glanced over at him, ignoring his offer.

"So I guess you thank y'all even huh?"

"Yeah Huck I do." Effie Mae stated without remorse. "You saw how they done me Huck." He looked at her, refusing to sympathized with her vengeful actions. "That's my baby Huck and I'm keeping him!" She raising her voice. Melvin quickly looked over seeing the agitated look on Effie Mae's face.

"Can I fix you a bowl of grits Effie Mae?" He asked attempting to diffuse the heated discussion. "It won't take me but a minute to put a pot on." Effie Mae shifted her eyes over at him but gave no reply. She resumed her eye to eye gaze at Huck.

"Your baby huh?" Huck said shaking his head, disappointed by her disregard for Daniel's love for his son.

"Yeah Huck my baby."

"What about old Daniel, Effie Mae?"

"What about him Huck?"

"He didn't have nothing to do with that boy being here?"

"What you want Huck?"

"I want you to give that man back his son, but I know what I want don't matter."

"Nope it don't."

"Damn shame." Huck looled at her trying to hold back his temper.

"Why you worried about Mr. Daniel anyway? He don't even like you." Effie Mae stated childishly. Huck sarcastically laughed to himself, let down by her out of character callousness.

"I guess Ol' Blue didn't know the woman he loved at all." He said shifting his eyes briefly over at Melvin as he continued watching from the bar. "Don't look like I know you either." Effie Mae ignored the look of displeasure in Huck's eyes. "J.R. know what you doing Effie Mae?"

"Why? What you gon do Huck, tell him?" She stated rebelliously.

"I might."

"Stay out of this Huck!" She shouted. Melvin looked over with concern. He worried of the effects Effie Mae's agitated state would have on her pregnancy and unborn child.

"You sure I can't get you that bowl of grits Effie Mae? I'm sure Lil' Tyrell would love a warm bowl of buttery grits right about now." He said, humored. Effie Mae ignored him. Huck tilted his head.

"Lil' Tyrell? I thought you said that was J.R.'s baby?"

"Don't you worry about whose baby this is!" She yelled. "And don't be worrying about what's going with me and my husband either."

"J.R. know you tricking again Effie Mae?" Huck asked verbally lashing out. "Or did he ever know? Maybe I should tell him." Effie Mae's eyes filled with shame.

"Tricking?"

"Yeah, tricking." He looked at her with judgmental eyes. "What you call using your body to get you what you want?"

"I call it taking back what belong to me in the first place."

"Girl what you done with old Daniel wasn't no different than what you was doing over at Ms. Norma's." Effie Mae tilted her head mocking him.

"Is that right?"

"Ol' Blue would roll over in his grave if he could see you now, Baby girl."

"I told you to leave Blue out of this Huck!" She bellowed. Anthony rose from his desk in response to her loud voice, walking over to the door, standing in the doorway. His concern heightened when seeing the angry look on Huck's face as he stared at Effie Mae.

"Baby, did you find out what it was you left at Huck's house?" He asked.

"Yeah Anthony she found out." Huck said answering on Effie Mae's behalf.

"Good, I'm glad to hear it." Anthony said shifting his eyes to Melvin noting the tensed look on his face. He again turned his attention to Effie Mae.

"Baby, are you alright?" Huck looked at Effie Mae and tilted his head in response to Anthony referencing to her as—Baby.

"Yeah Anthony, Baby's doing fine." Huck stated sarcastically, preventing Effie Mae from responding. She turned to Anthony.

"I'm fine Anthony—just a little tired."

"Maybe you should go upstairs and lay down—" She cut him off.

"I will Anthony after I finish talking to Huck." Anthony noticed the distressed look in her eyes. "I'm okay Anthony, go back to what you was doing."

"Are you sure?"

"Yeah Anthony she sure." Huck said shifting his eyes to Effie Mae, warning her of his intent to hurt Anthony if he didn't back off. Melvin's anxiety magnified in response to the bone chilling glare in Huck's eyes.

"Go back to what you was doing Anthony." Effie Mae said not wanting Huck to hurt him.

"If you're sure you're alright." Melvin quickly interjected in lieu of calling the police.

"Yeah Anthony, she's fine . . . I was just getting ready to fix her a bowl of grits." He said, nervously chuckling. Anthony slowly turned and entered the office leaving the door open, watching as Huck's contemptuous eyes remained locked onto Effie Mae—angry with himself for participating in her betrayal of Daniel.

"Bye Effie Mae." Huck said shifting his eyes briefly at Melvin before standing. Effie Mae watched with defiance as Huck walked away, exiting the club.

"Effie Mae?" Melvin called over to her.

"What Melvin?"

"Telephone—it's Daniel."

"Tell him I'm busy." She said staring at the club's front door, uneasy by the hurtful argument she'd just had with her good friend Huck. Her eyes suddenly drew to Melvin's unrelenting gawk as she stood.

"What Melvin?" She yelled.

"You alright sweetie?"

"I'm fine Melvin." She said walking towards the stairs. "If Anthony asks for me tell him I'm upstairs with my baby." Melvin watched with worry as Effie Mae headed up the stairs.

"Oh, Effie Mae—" She stopped and looked at him.

"What Melvin?"

"Could you send Deborah Ann back down? I need her to help me set up for tonight." Effie Mae momentarily stared at him then continued up the steps.

---

Melvin hurried to the front entrance of the jazz club when seeing Daniel standing just inside the door, visually searching through the crowded establishment in hopes of seeing Effie Mae.

"Hey Daniel!"

"How you doing Melvin?"

"I see you back again tonight, I guess you here to see Effie Mae—or did you stop by this time to actually enjoy the music, good food and strong drinks?" Melvin said trying to cheer him up. Daniel's ears deafened to Melvin's friendly conversation.

"Is she in tonight Melvin?"

"Yeah she here." Melvin said looking over at the closed office door. "Did you want me to let her know you here?"

"If you don't mind."

"You know she probably ain't gon see you right?"

"I know Melvin, but I ain't gon stop trying until she do."

"Must be something real important you been up here six nights straight." Melvin said, subtly probing as he sympathized with the apathetic look on Daniel's face.

"Yeah Melvin it is."

"Well while I'm doing that, why don't you go ahead and take your usual seat . . . what you drinking tonight? Whatever it is you know it's still on the house."

"You can bring me a beer again tonight Melvin." Daniel said being seated at a lone table, left of the front entrance. Melvin obtained eye contact with a bar maid and beckoned her over.

"Tap right?" He said as the she headed over.

"Did you need something Melvin?"

"Yeah, look here Celia bring my friend Daniel here a beer—it's on the house."

"Alright." She looked at Daniel and smiled then walked away.

"Tap!" Melvin called out. She nodded. "I'll let Effie Mae know you here." He looked at Daniel with concern and wondered what dilemma brought him back every night.

"Thank you Melvin."

"No problem Daniel." Melvin said headed in the direction of the office. He glanced back at Daniel when arriving at the door then knocked. Melvin hoped by some miracle Effie Mae would meet with Daniel to resolve whatever issue weighed so heavy on him.

"Yeah Melvin."Anthony said in response to the knock.

"I need to speak with Effie Mae."

"Come in Melvin." She said certain it had something to do with Daniel. Melvin entered—an apprehensive look on his face. "What you need Melvin?"

"Daniel's out there again Effie Mae, what you want me to tell him?" Melvin shifted his eyes over at Anthony then turned back to Effie Mae.

"I'll be out."

"Huh?" Melvin said, uncertain he'd heard her right.

"I said okay Melvin." Effie Mae stood. "I'll be back Anthony."

"Okay Baby." He looked at her and smiled then turned quickly to Melvin catching him before he exited. "Oh Melvin . . . could you have the kitchen make me a corn beef sandwich?" Anthony said rubbing his stomach. "All this work, I forgot I hadn't eaten since breakfast.

"Corn beef? Okay." Melvin shifted his eyes to Effie Mae then turned again to Anthony. "I'll put that order in right now—let me know if it's anything else you need Anthony."

"I'll be sure to do that Melvin, thanks." Anthony resumed working on payroll and inventory. He stopped and looked at Effie Mae seconds afted Melvin left the office.

"I'm sorry Baby."

"For what Anthony?"

"I forgot to ask if you wanted Melvin to bring you something from the kitchen."

"I ain't hungry Anthony."

"Not hungry?" He looked at Effie Mae's enlarged abdomen. "Baby you're pregnant."

"I know that Anthony." She giggled.

"I'm calling the kitchen right now and tell them to fix you a ham and cheese sandwich— okay Baby?" She smiled.

"Okay Anthony." Effie Mae said turning to leave. She again faced him. "Make sure they put plenty of pickles on that sandwich Anthony."

"Pickles?" He frowned. "On a ham and cheese sandwich?" She giggled.

"I'm pregnant Anthony, remember?"

"Well I won't be asking for a bite of that."

"Good, that mean I can eat my own sandwich this time." His mouth slightly open. Effie Mae laughed then left the office.

• • • •

Daniel's eyes lit up when seeing her emerged from the office. He watched with hopeful eyes as Effie Mae walked in the direction of his table. Melvin observed from bar, taking note of their awkward eye exchange.

"How you been doing Effie Mae?" Daniel asked, humbled. She lowered herself in the chair across the table from him. "How my boy doing?" Effie Mae stared into his eyes, ignoring his question. "Effie Mae please let me see my boy!" Daniel pleaded.

"Here's your beer Sir." Celia said sitting the mug in front of him.

"Thank you baby." Daniel looked briefly up at her then resumed his gaze at Effie Mae.

"Hey Effie Mae how you feeling tonight?" Celia asked looking down at Effie Mae's pregnant belly. "Gril I hardly ever see you outside of that office these days." Effie Mae looked up at her and rubbed her rounded abdoment, masking the tension thickening between her and Daniel.

"I'm just waiting on this little boy to get here."

"Boy? Effie Mae how you know it's a boy?" Celia asked looking at her protruding abdomen with curious eyes. "I've heard people sometimes say if the belly high it's a girl, and if sits low—it's a boy." A confused look appeared on Celia's face as she thought for a moment. "Or is it the other way around—well anyway I just want you and Blue to have a healthy happy baby, I know that's what Tyrell would've wanted." A glowing smile displayed on Effie Mae's face, delighted at the thought of having a child by Blue.

"Thank you Celia." She stated electing not to tell Celia, Blue hadn't fathered her unborn child.

"Well let me get back to work, Melvin don't like me spending too much time talking to customers . . . he like for me to keep them drinks rolling!" She said laughing.

"Melvin bet not say nothing bout you talking to me!"

"I wasn't talking about you Effie Mae—girl you the boss." Celia again laughed. "It was good talking to you Effie Mae."

"You too Celia." Effie Mae again turned to Daniel as Celia walked away. She noted the mug of beer in front of him.

"Beer? You drinking now Daniel?"

"I might have a beer every now and then, but that's it." Effie Mae stared at him, annoyed by his presence. "How's my boy?" Daniel again asked.

"My baby boy's doing just fine."

"I miss that little boy too!" Daniel said reaching over, gently touching Effie Mae's hand. She snatched it away. "You know Effie Mae, us being together again really brought back a lot memories." He said looking in her lackluster eyes. "But if I had known for one minute it was gon cost me my boy—" Daniel shook his head with regret. "—I would've never touched you girl!"

"I guess it ain't good to want nothing that bad, now is it?" He lowered his head in shame. "I told you already, you ain't getting my baby boy, Daniel." He looked at Effie Mae in awe when seeing the bitterness in her eyes.

"You hate me that much Effie Mae?"

"I don't hate you Daniel, you my baby boy's daddy." Daniel half heartedly smiled.

"Then tell me why you doing this Effie Mae?"

"I remember you once telling me you loved me Daniel—" He quickly interjected.

"I still do Effie Mae!"

"Then why you let your wife steal my baby boy then wouldn't let me lay eyes on my boy." Daniel again reached over taking hold her hand.

"Effie Mae—" He gazed into her eyes. —I loved you then and I still love you girl!" She listened without compassion. "And I know somewhere in your heart you still feel something for me too."

"That's over Daniel."

"Naw Effie Mae it ain't over." He shook his head, unconvinced. "You say that, but when we was together a few weeks . . . we both know it was some love still there." She snatched her hand away.

"You ain't getting my baby boy Daniel!"

"Effie Mae please give me my boy back!" Daniel begged. "I know what me and Geraldine done was wrong and I regret ever letting her take that boy." Effie Mae listened with cynical ears.

"Your regret can't take back the hurt you and your wife put me through, now can it?" Daniel took a sip of the beer trying to think of how to reply.

"First time you and me got together Effie Mae—" He paused. "—it wasn't love I was looking for." She abruptly rose from the table.

"Bye, Daniel."

"Effie Mae wait!" Daniel called out. "Please, just hear me out." Effie Mae stared briefly at him then again sat. "What I'm saying Efffie Mae is I fell in love with you girl, and after that everything just got complicated." Daniel stated. "I started questioning my love for Geraldine, and when you got pregnant it scared the hell out of me!" A look of confusion appeared on his face. "And when Geraldine found out—" Effie Mae interjected.

"How you think I felt Daniel!" She said raising her voice. "You wasn't the one had a baby growing inside of you!"

"I know Effie Mae—"

"J.R. took my babies and left—seem like after that bad things just kept happening."

"Bad things!" Daniel's eyes filled with rage. "You mean that damn Huck turned you into one his whores—" He yelled." —that's the bad thing that happened!" Effie Mae quickly looked around, hoping Daniel's words had not been heard over the band.

"Then I got beat me half to death—"

"Yeah by that monster Huck!" Daniel stated with fury. Effie Mae looked at him, but gave no reply. "I know it and you know it . . . I could kill him for that and I should've!" Effie Mae's mouth abruptly opened, shocked to hear Daniel's violent words.

"I ain't planned on getting pregnant Daniel." She stated with apology. Daniel again took hold of Effie Mae's hands, enveloping them inside his own.

"I know you didn't Effie Mae, but I'll never say t regret you having that little boy." Daniel stated with tatherly pride as he thought of his son. "But you knew I had a wife Effie Mae—" She again snatched her hands away.

"You wasn't thinking 'bout your wife Daniel when you was crawling in my bed every night after she had done gon to sleep, now was you?" He briefly lowered his eyes.

"Yeah you right Effie Mae I wasn't." He stared at her with guilty eyes. "I wasn't trying to hurt you Effie Mae, only thing I could think about was how bad I had hurt Geraldine." Daniel took another swallow of beer. "I guess I never thought once how I was hurting you, and I'm sorry for that Effie Mae." She looked at him with unsympathetic eyes.

"Now you know how that kind of hurt feel."

"Don't hurt me like this Effie Mae." Daniel pleaded. "That boy means the world to me and it's gon kill me not to have him!"

"I got my baby back Daniel and I'm gon keep him."

"Effie Mae please I'm begging you girl—don't take my boy from me!" She looked in his pained eyes then stood.

"Bye Daniel.

"Effie Mae wait!"

"I got a club to run."

"Effie Mae please!" Daniel watched with helplessness as Effie Mae walked away, reentering the office then closing the door. Melvin sympathized with Daniel's obvious hurt as he watched from the bar seeing him guzzle down the remainder of his beer then slamming the mug down on the table. Melvin concluded things hadn't gone as Daniel had hoped. He retrieved another mug, filling it with beer from the tap then headed over to Daniel's table.

"Hey Daniel your glass look empty man, we don't like seeing empty glasses in the house." Melvin said chuckling as he sat the new mug of beer on the table.

"Thank you Melvin."

"You get everything squared away with Effie Mae? Or do I need to reserve this table for you tomorrow night?" Melvin said lightly chuckling as Daniel took a swallow of beer.

"What's that they say about a woman scorned Melvin?" Melvin quietly grinned then joined Daniel at his table.

"You look like a man with a whole lot of stuff to get off his chest." Daniel looked at the closed office door and took another swig of beer.

"Yeah Melvin I do."

"Well, my customers seem to think I'm a pretty good listener." Melvin said curious to hear Daniel's story.

• • • •

"Your vitals were pretty good this morning Mrs. Jones." The nurse said peering over her glasses, shifting her eyes briefly over at Daniel seated in the chair next to his wife's bed. Ms. Geraldine nodded and smiled. "And how are you today Mr. Jones?" The nurse asked as she charted the results.

"I'm doing well, thank you for asking." Daniel said trying to mask his troubled state of mind from his wife.

"Your wife continues to be showing improvement Mr. Jones—and that's always good." Daniel forced a smile.

"I'm glad to hear ot."

"If there's anything she needs just let us know."

"Okay, I sure will do that."

"I'll see you later Mrs. Jones." The nurse said smiling as she exited the room. Ms. Geraldine shifted her tired eyes over to Daniel, unconvinced by his words. She knew him well enough to know something serious occupied his mind.

"Wha—wron—Dan—iel?"

"Nothing . . . ain't nothing wrong Geraldine." Daniel stated, unable to hide his obvious unrest.

"Ef—fie—Mae— too—ba—by?" Ms. Geraldine asked through her partially paralyzed mouth. Daniel burst into tears. Her eyes moistened as she sympathized with her husband's hurt.

"Ow?" She asked already knowing the answer.

"You already know how Geraldine." Daniel said lowering his head in shame. "I'm sorry Geraldine." She nodded. "That girl knew I couldn't turn her away, and after I went to sleep—" He looked in Ms. Geraldine's comforting eyes. "—she took my boy Geraldine!" She extended her unaffected right hand to him. Daniel took hold of it, placing it inside his own. Tears trickled down Ms. Geraldine's face as she again experienced the hurt from her husband's betrayal—with Effie Mae.

"I'm sorry Geraldine." He said shaking his head with remorse. "I guess I'm just weak!"

"She—bri—ba—by—baaack."

"Naw Geraldine." Daniel said looking at her with doubtful eyes. "I've lost my boy forever." Ms. Geraldine shook her head no.

"She—bri—im—bac." She nodded with certainty.

# Chapter Thirty-Two

Melvin sat on the edge of the stage and waited for Effie Mae to arrive to work the following morning. He watched as she opened the door and entered, closing it behind her.

"Make sure you lock that." He said startling her. "Like Huck said, you got all kinds of critters crawling up in here." Melvin laughed. "Good morning Effie Mae."

"Hey Melvin . . . I didn't see you sitting there." Effie Mae stated looking over at the closed office door. "Anthony up yet?"

"I ain't seen him this morning, did you want me to call upstairs and see?"

"Naw that's alright Melvin I can wait for him to come down."

"You sure?" He asked preparing himself for the non-confrontationally discussion he planned to have with her regarding information he'd received from his conversation with Daniel.

"I know that Anthony said he was gon be working late doing the payroll—" Melvin interjected.

"And he was too!" He said chuckling. "Effie Mae I had to finally make that man go to bed—he was keeping me up!" She giggled. "I'm just gon let him sleep then." Melvin silently gazed at her.

"What?" Effie Mae said blushing. He chuckled and smiled. "What Melvin?"

"I dreamed about Tyrell last night." He said delighted by *the dream*. Effie Mae's blushing smile widened.

"What about Blue, Melvin?" She asked, anxious to hear his dream. "Tell me Melvin . . . whaat you dreamed about my husband?"

"In this dream Effie Mae I saw Tyrell just as clear as I'm seeing you now." Melvin smiled as he recalled *the dream*. "That boy was smiling just like I seen him do so many times before when he looked at you." Effie Mae found comfort in Melvin's well chosen words. "Yeah, my cousin knew he loved him some Effie Mae." Melvin stated leading up to the true message. Effie Mae's eyes moistened.

"And Effie Mae loved her some Tyrell Lee Jones."

"You know what else happened in that dream Effie Mae?" A peculiar looked formed on Melvin's face. "Tyrell said something to me that didn't make a bit of since—" He looked in Effie Mae's eager eyes. "—but he said *ask my wife she'll understand.*"

"Me?" Effie Mae said smiling. "If you ain't understand it Melvin what make Blue think I'm gon understand?" She giggled.

"I'm just telling you what Tyrell told me Effie Mae." Melvin stated, humored.

"So what else did my baby say Melvin?"

"Let me see if I can remember how he said this." Melvin pretended to be recalling *the dream.* "Oh yeah now I remember . . . he said your love for him would override any past hurts and wrong doings, and he knew in the end you would do what you knew was right?" Tears emerged from Effie Mae's eyes in response to Melvin's *dream.* "Let see, Tyrell also told me to tell you he loved you girl." Melvin corrected himself. "I mean—Baby girl." A caring smile displayed on his face. Melvin knew the words he spoke would touch her heart if she believed they'd come from Blue. Effie Mae lowered her head and wept. She knew Blue's message meant her to giving her baby boy back to Daniel. Melvin came down from the stage and embraced Effie Mae in his arms, resting her head on his chest. "I guess Tyrell was right when he said you'd understand."

"Yeah Melvin he was." Effie Mae looked at Melvin as he wiped her tears with his hand. "Well the next time you see Blue, you tell Tyrell Lee Jones his wife said—" She smiled. "—she love him back."

"I sure will do that Effie Mae." Melvin said kissing her lightly on the forehead.

"Everything alright?" Anthony said standing at the bottom of the stairs seeing Effie Mae embraced in Melvin's arms, weeping.

"Everything's fine Anthony." Effie Mae said continuing to cry. Melvin ended their embrace.

"I'm gon let you take over from here Anthony." He said. Effie Mae looked at Melvin and smiled. He nodded. Anthony hurried over and took her in his arms.

"What's going on Baby?" He asked shifting his eyes to Melvin, requesting an explanation.

"I was just telling Effie Mae about a dream I had about Tyrell."

"Oh, okay . . . that explains the tears." Anthony said kissing her on the forehead. "Are you alright Baby?"

"Yeah Anthony I'm alright." She glanced over at Melvin and wondered if the message supposedly given by Blue originated in his heart. He looked at her with ambiguity. On the one hand, he scolded himself for deceiving her. On the other, he knew his story in reference to Blue was one she needed to hear.

"Can I fixed you some breakfast Anthony?" His eyes lit up.

"That would be wonderful Melvin, I'm starved."

"You want me to fix you something too Effie Mae—some grits?"

"Naw Melvin not right now I—" Anthony intervened.

"Baby your pregnant, you need to eat."

"I know I'm pregnant Anthony, but right now—"

"Come on Baby . . . let's go in the office so you can sit down." He said guiding her in the direction of the office. He looked back at Melvin and nodded, requesting he go ahead and fix Effie Mae some breakfast. Melvin nodded then headed for the kitchen.

———————————

J.R. looked around the kitchen table at his man children and smiled. He momentarily watched as Effie Mae held D.J. on her lap using her finger to feed her eager baby boy the sweet potatoes prepared for dinner.

"I don't like cabbage." Lil' J.R. whined as he picked at the light green vegetable lying on his plate.

"Then just eat your chicken and sweet potatoes Lil' J.R." Effie Mae stated.

"Okay." He lowered his head. "Can I have some French fries?"

"If you eat all your cabbage Lil' J.R. I'll have your daddy cook French fries for dinner tomorrow, okay baby?"

"Oooh! Okay Momma." He grabbed a handful of cabbage from his plate and stuffed it in his mouth.

"Slow down Lil' J.R. before you choke." J.R. stated. Lil' J.R. opened his mouth, allowing the slightly chewed substance to drop back onto his plate. All heads turned in the direction of the back door when hearing the knocking of an unexpected visitor.

"I uh, wonder who that is?" J.R. said looking at Effie Mae. She gave no reply. He rose from the table and walked over to the back door peeped through the curtain. "It's uh, Cousin Daniel." He said shifting his eyes to Effie Mae, uncomfortable by his cousin's presence.

"You gon let him in J.R. or leave the man standing out on the back porch?" Effie Mae teased. J.R. hesitated then opened the door.

"Uh, Cousin Daniel everything alright?"

"Yeah J.R. everything's fine." A huge smile spread across Daniel's mature face when seeing his beloved baby boy.

"I guess you uh, came to see D.J." J.R. said glancing over at Effie Mae in response to Daniel's unexpected drop-in.

"Huh?" Daniel said unable to remove his eyes from the toddler. "Oh, yeah . . . I've missed that boy too, place ain't been the same without him." He said chuckling. Effie Mae's stomach rumbled with butterflies as she prepared to give her baby boy back to his daddy.

"Mr. Daniel came to get this little boy J.R., take him back home." She said masking the emotional hurt burning in her heart. Daniel's mouth slightly opened, stunned by her unanticipated announcement. He looked at her with questioning eyes.

"Nooooooo!" Millie Ann cried out. J.R. quickly turned to his oldest daughter in response to her sudden outburst.

"To uh, stay Effie Mae?" J.R. asked confused by her upsetting news.

"Yeah J.R."

"Nooooooo!" Millie Ann again yelled.

"Calm down Millie Ann." J.R. said disturbed by her upset over D.J. leaving. He again looked at Effie Mae for explanation.

"With this baby almost here J.R., and me running the jazz club, caring for two babies is gon be too much for me to handle." She said trying to explain her 'Melvin persuaded' decision to relinquish custody of D.J. back to Daniel.

"I can take care of him Momma!" Millie Ann said crying, not wanting the toddler to leave.

"I know you can baby, but you got school Millie Ann."

"Please Momma!" She begged through tear filled eyes.

"Uh, I'll do it." J.R. said trying to resolve the dilemma. "I uh, don't mind watching D.J. while Millie Ann's at school—"

"J.R., Mr. Daniel's been caring for this little boy since he was born."

"Mr. Daniel's too old to take care of D.J., Momma." Mahalia said angered by her big sister's tears. J.R.'s eyes widened, surprised by her rudeness.

"Mahalia!"

"What Daddy?"

"Eat your food." He said shifting his eyes to Daniel, embarrassed by his young daughter's spoken truth.

"Millie Ann baby I'm gon be needing your help when this baby get here okay?" Effie Mae said hoping to appease her eldest daughter. Millie Ann reluctantly agreed.

"Okay Momma—can D.J. come over every day?" Daniel intervened.

"Not every day baby, but I'll bring him over anytime your momma say it's okay—alright Millie Ann?"

"Yeah." She said gradually calming. Daniel looked over at Effie Mae and thanked her with his eyes.

"Uh, Cousin Daniel would you like to uh, join me and my family for supper?"

"I'd love to sit down with my cousin and his family J.R." Daniel said as he sat down at the table—humbled by his offer.

"I guess you can finished feeding this little boy then Mr. Daniel." Effie Mae said handing him the toddler. Daniel's heart raced as he took his son in his arms and lovingly hugged him then placed a kiss on his forehead.

"Daddy missed you boy!" He said kissing him on the cheek. Effie Mae watched as the toddler looked up at his daddy and smiled then gently laid his head on Daniel's chest and yawned. "You look like you sleepy boy—is daddy's boy sleepy?" D.J. looked at him and smiled then cooed. J.R. noted the pained look in Effie Mae's eyes as Daniel bonded with her baby boy.

"Mmmm, that smells good J.R." Daniel said as J.R. placed a plate in front of him. He again looked at Effie Mae, his eyes filled with gratitude knowing returning her son wasn't easy.

"Feel like this little boy laying on my bladder again." Effie Mae said rubbing her sizeable belly, trying desperately to think of an excuse to leave the room.

"Uh, boy?" J.R. said chuckling.

"Ooooh! You got a boy like me and D.J. in your stomach Momma?" Lil' J.R. said with widened eyes. J.R. quickly intervened.

"Uh, your momma's not sure about that yet Lil' J.R."

"Boy or girl—seems like the bigger this baby get the more I got to pee." Effie Mae said forcing a giggle as she struggled to get up. J.R. hurried over when noticing her unsuccessfully trying to stand, weakened by her decision to surrender her baby boy.

"Uh, let me help you." He said taking hold of Effie Mae's arm, assisting her to her feet.

"Thank you J.R."

"Can you uh, make it?"

"Yeah J.R.—" She forced a smiled. "—I can make it." Effie Mae walked hastily from the kitchen and headed down the hallway—her eyes erupting with tears as she entered the bathroom and immediately closed the door. Effie Mae lowered herself into a sitting position on the floor, clasping her hand over her mouth as she uncontrollably wept in silence.

---

Effie Mae looked anxiously out the back door as Millie got out of J.R.'s car and began walking towards the house. J.R. trailing Millie, carryimg her suitcases.

"Hey Momma!" Effie Mae said flinging open the door seconds after Millie stepped on the porch.

"How you feeling child?" Millie asked embracing her eldest daughter, kissing her on the cheek.

"Can't you tell Momma?" Effie Mae said pulling open her pink silk robe, exposing her enlarged abdomen, now nine months pregnant. "Look at you Momma!" Effie Mae said when noticing Millie's new and improved look.

"I got tired of wearing that old ponytail, thought I'd let my hair down and throw a few curls in it—" J.R. interjected.

"Well it uh, looks good Ms. Millie." She blushed.

"Thank you J.R."

"If I uh, wasn't already married to the greatest woman on this earth, I'd have to ask you out on a date." J.R. teased. Millie smiled, flattered by his playful words.

"Is that lipstick you got on Momma?" A girlish smile formed on Millie's face.

"Look like I got here just in time." She said redirecting the subject, uncomfortable by all the attention. "Child you look like you a sneeze away from popping!"

"It won't be long now Momma—" Effie Mae silenced when noticing her momma's gaze.

"What Momma?"

"You know Effie Mae—" A motherly smile formed on Millie's face. "—this the first time I ever seen you pregnant and you look just beautiful!" Effie Mae's eyes widened.

"Beautiful? Momma I look like I swallowed a watermelon."

"Yeah, but just wait until you done gave birth to that beautiful baby boy." Effie Mae's mouth flung open.

"Momma how you know it's a boy?"

"I don't know how I know Effie Mae." She placed her hand on Effie Mae's belly. "I just know." Effie Mae beamed.

"You hear that J.R.? If Momma right, it look like Lil' Tyrell Lee Jones gon be coming in this world!"

"Jones-Smith." J.R. said correcting her. Effie Mae glanced over at him, but gave no reply.

"Who? Millie said confused. "Tyrell Lee Jones?"

"Jones-Smith." J.R. repeated. Millie shifted her eyes over at him then turned to Effie Mae.

"Wasn't that—"

"Yeah Momma that's Blue's name." Effie Mae said sensing Millie's objection. "I know what you thinking Momma but this baby belong to my husband." Millie raised an eyebrow.

"Then why you naming J.R.'s son after Blue?"

"Momma, me and Blue—" Millie interjected.

"You and Blue?"

"See Momma that's why I didn't tell you."

"Seem to me J.R.'s son ought to be named after J.R. not Blue." J.R. quickly intervened seeing Effie Mae's growing anxiety.

"Uh, Ms. Millie—" He sat her luggage down on the kitchen floor. "—we uh, decided to honor Blue by naming our son after—"She cut J.R. off.

"Honor Blue for what?" Millie frowned. "Ain't no honor in a man laying up with another man's wife." J.R. embraced Effie Mae in his arms and placed a comforting kiss on her lips before addressing Millie's hurtful words.

"Uh, Ms. Millie nobody could ever deny how much my wife loved Blue." Effie Mae looked at him and smiled. "So uh, when she asked me if it we could name our son after Blue—" Millie looked at Effie Mae, bothered by her request. "—I uh, had no problem saying yes."

"You got somewhere you can put my bags J.R.?" Millie asked wanting to end the three person conversation and speak with her eldest daughter alone.

"You'll uh, be sleeping in Millie Ann's room." J.R. said realizing she wanted to speak with Effie Mae alone. "I'll uh, take them in there." He lightly chuckled. "When uh, Millie Ann heard you were coming she uh, volunteered to give her Grandma Millie her bedroom." He stated proudly. "But that's uh, Millie Ann—always willing to help others." J.R. shifted his eyes to Effie Mae then picked up Millie's luggage and exited the kitchen.

"Let's go in the living room Momma so we can sit down." Effie Mae said as J.R. headed down the hall to Millie Ann's room.

"Good, the sooner I get off these feet the better . . . feel like I'm walking on rice." Millie said giggling as she sat down on the sofa glancing around the cozy four bedroom home. She smiled. "Ain't I always said J.R. was a good man?"

"Yeah Momma you did, but I already knew that."

"Then why you naming that man's son after Blue, Effie Mae?" Millie said speaking just above a whisper.

"Momma if it ain't bothering J.R. none—"

"That man love you Effie Mae, he'd name that child anything you asked him—" Millie abruptly silenced when seeing J.R. emerge from Millie Ann's room on his way back to the living room.

"Ms. Millie we uh, all know Lil' J.R. was fathered by Anthony—" Millie's mouth quickly opened, shocked to hear J.R. freely speak on his wife's past indiscretion. "—so I guess if we can uh, call Anthony's son Lil' J.R., we can certainly name my son Tyrell Lee Jones-Smith." A warm smile formed on Effie Mae's face. "But—" J.R. added. "—we won't be calling my son Lil' Blue." Effie Mae giggled. J.R. looked at her with seriousness. "Alright Effie Mae?"

"Okay J.R." She said continuing to giggle. Millie raised an eyebrow. "Did you hear your husband Effie Mae?"

"Mr. Daniel gon be bringing my baby boy over later on Momma." Effie Mae said diverting from the conversation.

"Mr. Daniel?" Millie thought for a moment. "Ain't he that old man you had your last child by?" J.R. quietly chuckled, amused by Millie's description of his cousin.

"And don't forget Ms. Millie he's also my cousin." He joked. Millie looked at Effie Mae and raised an eyebrow. "Uh, Ms. Millie we have uh, put all that behind us, so if it's okay with you we'd uh, like to—" Millie cut him off.

"If it don't bother you none J.R., I sure ain't gon let it bother me."

"Thank you Momma." Effie Mae said pleased. "Momma wait 'til you see my baby boy—he walking and everything!" A grandmotherly smile displayed on Millie's face.

"Awww . . . I can't wait to see him Effie Mae."

"But first Momma I want to take you to my jazz club."

"Jazz club?" Millie scowled. "I don't need to be sitting up in no jazz club Effie Mae."

"Come on Momma, I want everybody to meet Ms. Millie Reed." Effie Mae said giggling.

"Well, I guess it won't hurt none for me to go in there for a few minutes—" Millie said feeling honored. "—but I sure ain't gon be doing no drinking!"

"I know that Momma."

"Rev. Hill wouldn't know what to say he knew I was up here in New York sitting in a bar." Effie Mae and J.R. laughed.

"Ms. Millie since you uh, already breaking one of the Ten Commandments—" Millie's jaw dropped. "I guess uh, you coming to church won't be a problem." J.R. teased.

"Stop it J.R." Effie Mae said, amused. "Don't be making my momma feel like a jezebel cause she coming to my club." Millie's eyes widened.

"I'm uh, sorry Ms. Millie you know I was only teasing." She looked at him then raised an eyebrow.

"I know that son, and I would love to come to your church J.R."

"And I would uh, be honored to have you there Ms. Millie." Effie Mae looked at her momma and smiled.

"I love you Momma."

"I love you too child."

————————————

Anthony hurried from the office when seeing Effie Mae, Millie and J.R. enter the jazz club. Millie shifted her eyes to Effie Mae and raised an eyebrow when seeing him.

"It's just business Momma."

"Good . . . keep it that way." She said looking at Anthony with suspicion as he approached.

"How's everybody doing?" Anthony asked extending his hand to J.R. The two men shook.

"Good morning Anthony." Effie Mae said girlishly smiling.

"Good morning Effie Mae." He replied slightly blushing. She giggled, humored by Anthony abstaining from his usual greeting of *Baby*. They shared an intimate smile observed by Millie and J.R.

"It's good to see you again Ms. Reed." Anthony said suddenly hugging her. Millie's eyes abruptly widened in response to his unanticipated embrace.

"How you doing Anthony?" She said shifting her eyes to Effie Mae then back to Anthony.

"I'm fine . . . things couldn't be better." He looked at Millie with peculiarity. "You look different Ms. Reed—better!" Effie Mae giggled.

"Thank you Anthony." Millie said eased out of Anthony's hold. "I see you still hanging around with my daughter." He shifted his eyes to Effie Mae then again to Millie.

"It's strictly business Ms. Reed." Millie looked over at Effie Mae with skepticism.

"You sure about that Anthony?"

"Yes Ma'am." He said looking in J.R.'s inquiring eyes. Effie Mae again giggled. "She wouldn't have it any other way Ms. Reed."

"My daughter?"

"She wants to keep it professional and I respect that." He said looking briefly at Effie Mae. She blushed.

"You gon introduce me to that lovely lady standing next to you Effie Mae?" Melvin asked as he headed towards the group. Millie looked in the direction of the compliment. Effie Mae's jaw dropped.

"That's my momma!" She said uneasy by Melvin's flirtatious words.

"You gotta be kidding me." He grinned. "Ain't no way that young lady's your mother!" Millie blushed. Melvin extended his hand then quickly took hold of Millie's when she reached to shake. He raised it to his lips and gently kissed it. A girlish smile formed on Millie's face. Effie Mae watched with an open mouth, shocked by Melvin's advances on her momma.

"How you doing Effie Mae's momma?" He said kissing Millie's hand a second time. She shifted her eyes over to Effie Mae, captivated by Melvin's charm.

"My name is Ms. Reed—Millie Reed, I guess my daughter so use to calling me momma . . . she forgot I do have a name other than momma."

"Ms. Reed it's a pleasure to meet you." Melvin said kissing her hand a third time. Millie's smile grew. "We ain't seen too many of Effie Mae's family members up this way, so it truly is a pleasure to meet you Ms. Reed. Millie continued blushing.

"Thank you uh—"

"Melvin Jones." He said glancing briefly over at Effie Mae and again to Millie before kissing her hand a fourth time. She girlishly giggled.

"It's a pleasure to meet you too Melvin."

"Momma—Melvin is Blue's cousin."

"Is he?" Millie said flattered by Melvin's attention. "I only met Blue once but he seemed like a really nice man, and he seemed to love my daughter." She said trying not to stare in Melvin's enticing eyes. "I'm truly sorry for your loss Melvin."

"Thank you Ms. Reed." Melvin looked at Effie Mae. She smiled. "We all loved Tyrell and his passing was a huge loss for all of us especially Effie Mae." Effie Mae's eyes filled with tears. Anthony and J.R.'s filled with envy.

"Mind my manners Ms. Reed." Melvin stated.

"Millie." She said correcting him. He smiled then reluctantly released her hands.

"Can I fix you some breakfast Millie?"

"As a matter of fact Melvin—" Millie said blushing. "—some breakfast would do me just fine."

"Give me forty minutes and I'll bring you the best breakfast you ever ate!" He said smiling.

"Well when it's ready I'll be right here waiting for it Melvin." Millie flirted.

"I guarantee you'll be glad you did." He winked. J.R.'s mouth slightly opened as he watched Melvin walked away to prepare Millie's breakfast. J.R. looked at Effie Mae, puzzled by what had just taken place. Anthony paid little attention to the flirtatious encounter.

"Come on Momma let's sit down."

"If you need me I'll be in the office Ba—oss." Anthony stated, quickly correcting himself. Millie raised an eyebrow. "It was good seeing you again Ms. Reed." He said preparing to return to the office.

"It was nice seeing you too Anthony." Millie said being seated mid-center of the club. "Next time you speak to Betsy, be sure and tell her Millie Reed said hi."

"I sure will Ms. Reed." Anthony said shifting his eyes to Effie Mae. She smiled. J.R. watched as Anthony walked away, uneasy by his playful behavior with his wife.

"Uh, boss?" J.R. said, unamused.

"Anthony just teasing with me J.R., that boy know he the real boss around here." Effie Mae giggled then joined J.R. and Millie already seated at the table.

"Melvin can cook can't he?" Millie whispered. Effie Mae and J.R. laughed.

"Yeah Momma, Melvin can cook." Effie Mae's laughter ended she heard a knock at the door. Millie look at her with concern.

"Effie Mae y'all open this place up this early?"

"Naw Momma we don't, but that don't stop people from showing up here."

"I uh, I'll get it." J.R. said getting up from the table. He walked over to the door opening it to a crack seeing Huck.

"How you doing J.R.? If you here that means Effie Mae in there too."

"Uh yeah, she is."

"Who is it J.R.?" Effie Mae asked.

"It's me Effie Mae." Huck said. Her anxiety heightened as he entered. Millie watched, curious of his early morning arrival.

"How you doing Ms. Reed?"

"I'm just fine Henry Lee." Huck smiled, amused by her still referencing to him by his birth name.

"I need to talk to you Effie Mae."

"I'm with my momma Huck." She said worried he might again confront her about deceiving Daniel.

"This ain't gon take but a minute." He said, his eyes subtly demanding.

"I'll be back Momma." Effie Mae stated. J.R.'s eyes displayed inquiry as he wondered of the urgent need for Huck to speak his wife. "If Anthony come looking for me tell him I'm upstairs." A worried look appeared on Millie's face when looking at the large number of stairs.

"Child you don't need to be climbing all them steps." J.R. looked over at them.

"I uh, think Ms. Millie's right, maybe you should uh, go to your office?" Effie Mae shifted her eyes to Huck and awaited his permission. J.R. noted Huck's slight nod of the head.

"Let me go talk to Anthony." She said getting up from the table heading in the direction of the opened office door. Huck followed. Millie and J.R. looked on, puzzled by Huck's insistence. Anthony looked up when seeing Effie Mae and Huck walking towards the office.

"Good morning Huck." He said as they approached.

"How you doing Anthony?"

"I'm not exactly sure—" He said shifting his eyes to Effie Mae trying to read the look on her face. "You're the second surprise I've had this morning." Huck glanced over at Effie Mae—his patience lessening.

"I need to talk to Huck for a minute—"

"About?" Anthony said. Huck shifted his eyes to Effie Mae in response to Anthony's response.

"I was gon go upstairs Anthony, but Momma didn't think I should be walking up all them steps." Effie Mae said seeing the fury in Huck's eyes. Anthony noted it as well.

"Is there something I can help Huck with?" Anthony asked, troubled by the nervous look in Effie Mae's eyes. She quickly intervened.

"Naw Anthony this ain't gon take long."

"I guess that means you want me to leave?"

"Yeah Anthony just for a minute." His frustration heightened in response to the frightened look in Effie Mae's eyes.

"Okay . . . and you're sure everything's alright?" He shifted his eyes to Huck then back to Effie Mae. Huck looked at Effie Mae, his fury magnifying. He interrupted.

"Yeah Anthony everything alright—" Huck shifted his eyes to Effie Mae. "—for now." Anthony ignored the subtle threat.

"I'll leave, but if you need me—" Huck cut him off.

"She won't."

"It was good seeing you again, Huck." Anthony said getting up from his desk, looking him in the eyes. Huck again looked at Effie Mae—warning her with his eyes.

"Did you want me to close the door?"

"Yeah you do that Anthony." Huck said watching as Anthony placed a light kiss on Effie Mae's cheek as he prepared to leave. He looked at Huck, his eyes giving him warning.

"Thank you Anthony." Huck mocked as Anthony exited the office closing the door behind him. Effie Mae turned to Huck, curious of his *thank you*.

"What you thanking Anthony for?"

"For not making me have to whip his ass." He said grinning. "It's too early in the morning for that." Effie Mae chuckled through her fear.

J.R. and Millie eyes displayed worry as Anthony joined them at the table.

"I uh, wonder what that's all about?" J.R. asked as the three looked at the closed office door.

• • • •

"What you want Huck?" Effie Mae said preparing herself for another verbal battle with her friend.

"Sit down." He demanded. She momentarily stared at him, hesitating before lowering herself into Anthony's black leather chair.

"If you came here 'bout me taking my baby boy from Daniel, I already gave him back." Huck tilted his head, surprised.

"Is that right?"

"Yeah that's right!"

"That's good to hear, but that ain't why I'm here." A confused look showed Effie Mae's eyes.

"Then why you here?"

"You don't know?" He again tilted his head.

"Naw Huck, I don't!"

"What's wrong with you Effie Mae?"

"What you talking about—ain't nothing wrong with me."

"Yeah Effie Mae it is." She looked at him with rebellious eyes. "What you did to get your son back—" She interjected.

"I did what I had to do!"

"Did you Effie Mae?"

"Yeah I did Huck!"

"Naw Effie Mae . . . you did what you wanted to? You didn't have to lay down with old Daniel—" He tilted his head. "—I guess once a whore always a whore." Effie Mae jaw dropped—she looked away, shamed by Huck's angry words. "Girl if you wanted to get back in the business all you had to do was say so, you know Ol' Huck can always make that happen, right?" He sarcastically winked. She quickly stood.

"Get out of my office Huck!"

"Sit your ass down." Effie Mae stared briefly at him then again sat. Huck glanced around the office.

"Look around—" He said admiring her professional work environment. "—Ol' Blue left you his life, everything he owned in this world." He suddenly chuckled. "I imagine if he could've left you his soul, Ol' Blue would've gave you that too." Effie Mae's eyes erupted with tears.

"Why you doing this Huck?"

"And you gon throw all this away—tricking."

"You ain't had no problem with me tricking when it was putting money in your pockets now did you?" She said raising her voice. He gave no reply, convicted by Effie Mae's biting words. "In case you forgot you was the one started me to tricking in the first place."

"I love you girl." Huck said, softening his demeanor.

"What?"

"I said I love you Effie Mae."

"Huck you know I'm back with my husband."

"Naw Effie Mae I don't mean it like that—" He cunningly smiled. "—I do, but I respect what you and J.R. got."

"Then what you talking 'bout?"

"I'm saying I love you enough to want what's best for you, and I know tricking ain't it—" An apologetic look entered his eyes. "—it never was." He gently took hold of Effie Mae's face and gazed in her eyes. "Don't ever disrespect yourself like that again . . . you hear me girl?" Effie Mae nodded. "I know you wanted your son back and I understand that." He thought of his own estranged children. "But that wasn't the way to do it Effie Mae." Her eyes displayed shame. "You told me a long time ago you didn't do that no more—you remember?"

"Yeah Huck I remember." She quietly laughed. "I also remember you beating me half to death for telling you that."

"Now I apologized to you for that Effie Mae!" He said with remorse. "I was wrong and I told you that girl."

"But your apology ain't took not one lump off my head." Effie Mae said laughing. "Now did it?" Huck grinned.

"You pulled through." Effie Mae mouth flung open.

"Only because Ms. Geraldine and Mr. Daniel took care of me!"

"Next time I see old Daniel I'll thank him for that." Huck teased. Effie Mae giggled. "I'm glad you pulled through Effie Mae.

"I'm glad I pulled through too Huck, my babies needed me!"

"You may not know this Effie Mae, but you stuck with me girl."

"What?"

"I'm serious Effie Mae . . . you stuck with me for the rest of your life." He looked in her eyes and smiled then kissed her softly on the lips. "I know you said I can't be loving on you—" Effie Mae's jaw dropped.

"I mean that Huck!" He cunningly grinned.

"I can respect that Effie Mae, but I also want to be able to respect you." He looked at her with chastising eyes. "Don't do that no more Effie Mae." She looked at him, but gave no reply. "I mean that girl!" A *ceasefire* smile displayed on his face. "We still friends?" Effie Mae giggled.

"You gon always be my friend Huck you know that." He grinned then placed two fingers underneath her chin and slightly tilted her head. Effie Mae closed her eyes as she allowed him to kiss her briefly on the lips.

"Naw I need more than that—get up." He assisted Effie Mae to her feet, embracing her in his arms then passionately kissed her. They gazed in each others eyes as the kiss ended. "Blue would be proud of you Effie Mae—" An enormous smile formed on her face. "—you and J.R. getting back together, you running his jazz club—" She interjected.

"Anthony running his jazz club." She teased. Huck grinned.

"I'm proud of you Effie Mae." He placed a quick kiss on her lips. "I'm especially proud of you for giving old Daniel back his son." He took hold of her hand. "Come on."

"Come on?" She said surprised. "Where we going Huck?"

"Just come on girl I want you to see something." He guided her over to the office door, opening it partway. He looked out at J.R., Anthony and Millie as they talked amongst themselves. "Look at that man out there, he loves you to death."

"Which one?" Effie Mae said, humored. Huck quietly grinned.

"Girl you something else." He closed the door. "I'll be around Effie Mae so you might as well tell your kids to get use to calling me Uncle Huck." Her mouth quickly opened.

"Uncle Huck?"

"That's right, unless you want them calling me daddy." He cunningly grinned. Effie Mae's mouth again opened as Huck embraced her in his arms and intimately kissed her.

"Bye Effie Mae."

"Bye Uncle Huck." She giggled. He winked then opened the door to leave. Millie, J.R. and Anthony looked quickly in the direction of the office when seeing the door open. Huck exited, walking through the club.

"Y'all take care." He said as the trio watched him open the front door and exit.

"Here you go Millie." Melvin said startling the group as he arrived with her breakfast.

"If you'll excuse me." Anthony said swiftly standing. "I need to go check on Effie Mae, make sure my Baby's alright." J.R. eyes widened. He turned quickly at Anthony, bothered by his intimate words regarding his wife. He stood.

"I think I uh, should be the one to—"

"No!" Anthony yelled. "I'll take care of her." J.R.'s jaw dropped. He looked at Millie. She raised an eyebrow.

"Effie Mae's my wife—" J.R. said paraphrasing Blue's last words to him. Anthony ignored his marital claim to Effie Mae as he hurried in the direction of the office.

"Ms. Millie—" J.R. said watching Anthony as he entered the office. She looked at her frustrated son-in-law . . . loss for words. "Would you uh, tell my wife I'll be at the church—praying." A clueless looked showed on Melvin's face as to what had just taken place as he stood holding the enormous breakfast he'd prepared for Millie. He watched as J.R. stormed out the front door then humped his shoulders before again turning to Millie.

"Let's see now Ms. Reed." Melvin corrected himself. "I mean Millie." He winked. She blushed. "I brought you some sweet ham, eggs over easy, fried potatoes, buttered grits and two slices of toast—with the strawberry jam already on top." He sat the plate of food on the table.

"It looks and smells delicious Melvin." Millie said inspecting the enormous meal. A look of self-achievement beamed on Melvin's face. "Thank you Melvin."

"You welcome Millie." She again blushed. "Anytime you want a home cooked meal all you got to do is ask." Millie giggled.

"I'm gon hold you to that too." She said blushing. Melvin's attention drew to Effie Mae as she exited the office, returning to the table.

"Effie Mae you want me to fix you some breakfasts?" She looked at the full plate of food in front of her momma then turned to Melvin.

"Just bring me a plate Melvin, I think Momma got enough food to feed me, her and J.R." Effie Mae said noticing her husban's absence. "Momma where J.R. at?" Millie looked at her and raised an eyebrow.

# *Chapter Thirty-Three*

Push Mrs. Smith!" The delivery room nurse coached as Effie Mae glistened with beads of sweat and prepared to give birth to her eighth child. J.R. stood patiently to her left and hoped Millie's intuition would hold true, and he and Effie Mae would soon be welcoming a son of their own.

"Ahhhhhhhh!" Effie Mae cried out, giving a final push—thrusting her newborn infant into the world, assisted by the doctor.

"Mrs. Smith." The doctor said clamping and cutting the umbilical cord of the crying infant. "What were you and your husband hoping for?"

"A boy!" They both stated in unison.

"Then congratulations—you've just given birth to a healthy baby boy!" J.R. leaned down and kissed Effie Mae lightly on the lips.

"Thank you Baby." He stated, overjoyed.

"Look like we finally made us that boy J.R.!" Effie Mae said elated, not only because her and J.R. now had their own son, but because he entered the world in honor of Blue.

"I love you Effie Mae." J.R. stated, again kissing her.

"I love you too J.R." They smooched.

"Do you already have a name for your son?" One of the nurses in the delivery room asked as she cleanedthe infant off with a large white towel. Effie Mae's looked at J.R., eager to make the announcement.

"We gon name that little boy—" J.R. quickly intervened.

"Tyrell Lee Jones Smith." He stated proudly.

"That's quite a name." A second nurse in the room said.

"Yeah it is." J.R. chuckled. "But the man we named him after—" He looked in Effie Mae's moistened eyes. "—was quite a man."

"Well let me introduce you to your son Mr. and Mrs. Smith." The nurse said looking at J.R. for assistance in pronouncing the elongated name.

"Tyrell Lee Jones Smith." He stated with fatherly pride as she handed the handsome baby boy to Effie Mae.

"Welcome to this world Tyrell Lee Jones Smith." Effie Mae said.

---

Millie cradled two month old Tyrell Lee Jones Smith in her arms as she sat on the front pew in J.R.'s church. Seated to her right sat Sissy Hill, glaring sporadically at Daniel located to her far right, holding his toddler son on his lap. Sissy looked over at him with disgust then leaned towards Millie's ear and whispered.

"Look at him Millie—Cousin Daniel ought to be ashamed of his self!" She said turning to him and rolling her eyes. "Old man." She scoffed. "I can't believe he had a baby with his own cousin's wife and at his age, Millie!" Sissy said angrily gawking at him. He ignored his cousin's rude behavior. She again whispered in Millie's ear. "Girl just look at him, sitting down there looking like that baby's granddaddy." Millie quietly chuckled.

"Hush now Sissy that man gon hear you."

"I don't care if he do Millie—I want him to hear me!" She said resuming her unrelenting stare. Daniel looked at her then took hold of his son's chubby hand and waved. Sissy quickly looked away. "Old man."

"Sissy what you messing with that man for? Millie asked as she admired her new grandson.

"It just makes me sick Millie knowing I trusted my baby brother's care to Cousin Daniel . . . you know, as a man he could look up too, show him what being a good husband was all about." She again glanced over at him. "Snake!"

"Sissy!"

"What Millie he is." She turned to her cousin and scowled. "Any man that would climb in bed with own cousin's wife ain't nothing but a snake, you know I'm right Millie!"

"From what I heard Sissy, him and J.R. already made amends—" Sissy interjected.

"Millie you know how my baby brother is . . . just let people walk all over him, been that way every since he was a child." She shifted her eyes quickly to Daniel. "That comes from Momma and Daddy spoiling that boy—you know they was old as Abraham and Sarah in the Bible when Momma birthed him." Millie quietly chuckled.

"Sissy!" She whispered.

"What Millie they were . . . Momma and Daddy know they were too old to be having a baby."

"How's Fannie Mae Parker doing these days?" Millie asked, diverting from Sissy's persecution of her cousin Daniel.

"You mean besides her messing around with Deacon Davis?" Sissy whispered. "But you didn't hear that from me girl."

"Sissy that woman been widowed for years now, and so has Deacon Davis . . . if they want to date—" Sissy cut her off.

"Millie you a widow." She adamantly pointed out. "And girl you ain't had nobody since Frank died back when your girls were just babies." Millie gave no reply, electing not to discuss her current relationship status with her gossiping friend.

"Don't let Rev. Hill hear you in here discussing them folks business, you know how he feel about you and all that gossiping." Sissy's jaw dropped.

"Gossiping!" She stated innocently. "Millie I ain't gossiping." She looked around the sanctuary noting Lil' J.R. sitting on Anthony's lap, one row back. "Millie I know Effie Mae's your daughter, but girl she sure did make a mess out of her life especially with those sons.

"Well Sissy with this one she got it right."

"But Milli she named my brother's son after some old boyfriend."

"Well Sissy I met that old boyfriend and—" Sissy interrupted.

"Millie you never told me that—when? How come I never met him?"

"I didn't know you was interested in meeting your sister-in-law's special men friends." Millie raised an eyebrow.

"You know that ain't what I'm saying Millie."

"Blue was a good man—"

"Blue?" Sissy frowned. "Now what kind of a name is that for a grown man Millie?" She said. "Blue . . . that's the color of a crayon not a man."

"It don't matter what they called him Sissy, that man was the best thing to come into my daughter's life and he loved Effie Mae until the day he died." Sissy's mouth flung open.

"Now how gon say that Millie? My baby brother was a good to Effie Mae!" She shifted her eyes again to Daniel and shook her head then turned back to Millie. "And he loved that girl just as much as that Blue person did."

"I never said he didn't Sissy, but I remember warning you and Rev. Hill both long before J.R. ever met Effie Mae she was gon be too much for him to handle."

"Now how you gon sound Millie?" Sissy said glancing over at Daniel seeing him playing *patty cake* with D.J. She frowned. "Snake!"

"Sissy leave that man alone!"

"Why Millie? Cousin Daniel sitting his butt in here in my brother's church flaunting that child, knowing Effie Mae's that boy's momma." Sissy discreetly glanced around. "Now what you think J.R.'s member's gon think when they find out?"

"That ain't got nothing to do—" Sissy interjected.

"I tell you what they gon think Millie—" She looked around. "—they gon think if their pastor can't run his own wife how in the heck he gon run the church, that's what they gon think girl!"

"Sissy you gon give yourself a stroke worrying about something don't neither one of us have power to change."

"If I could—I tell you one thing Millie, I wouldn't let my baby brother marry Effie Mae again that for sure." She looked at Millie with unapologetic eyes. "I hate saying it girl, but you seen how Effie Mae treated my baby brother."

"Sissy you and me both know when J.R. married Effie Mae, he didn't even know my daughter and she didn't know him."

"Millie that ain't no excuse for how Effie Mae done my poor brother—that's why I never wanted my him marrying Effie Mae's trifling—" Sissy abruptly silenced the turned her attention briefly to Daniel and D.J.

"I'd be the first one to say how my daughter treated J.R. wasn't right—"

"You damn straight it wasn't right Millie!" Millie's eyes widened in response to Sissy's language.

"Don't forget you in church." She said looking at her old friend with chastising eyes. "If Rev. Hill heard you talking like that—"

"I'm sorry Millie but you know yourself Effie Mae done my baby brother wrong."

"I ain't ever said it wasn't Sissy, but what's done is done."
Sissy's agitation grew.

"How you gon say that Millie? My baby brother still trying to live down the shame Effie Mae brought on him!"

"Don't look to me Sissy, J.R.'s the one trying to do so." Millie raised an eyebrow. Sissy ignored Millie's truthful words as she scrutinized her newborn nephew with suspicion.

"Something wrong Sissy?"

"You said you met the man Effie Mae named my baby brother's son after?" Sissy asked continuing to visually examine the infant.

"If you thinking this child belong to Blue—don't."

"What? I didn't say that Millie."

"But you was thinking it."

"Well if I was Millie can you blame me?"

"I guess I can't, but I'm telling you now this baby don't bear no resemblance to Blue."

"Millie you know that baby look just like Effie Mae." Sissy said shifting her eyes to Anthony and Lil' J.R. "Is it ever gon end Millie?"

"Is what ever gon end?"

"Effie Mae shaming my poor baby brother."

"All I can say Sissy is let's just pray that it do."

"That's easy for you to say Millie, but—"

"Maybe when you get back home you should have your husband preach you a sermon on stone throwing." Sissy's jaw dropped.

"Now how you gon say that Millie, I ain't throwing stones at Effie Mae for how she humiliated by baby brother having babies by stray men—" Sissy silence when looking in the reprimanding eyes of Millie.

"Before you sit here and throw another stone at my daughter, you need to remember something."

"What's that Millie?"

"We all got skeletons hanging in our closets." Millie looked at her with an accusatory eye. "Now don't we?" Sissy's mouth abruptly opened.

"Now Millie that was a long time ago, and you swore you'd never tell a soul."

"And I never have." Millie's attention drew to her sleeping grandson as he stretched. A grandmotherly smile appeared on her face before she again turned to Sissy. "But the next time you go looking to judge my daughter—open your closet and take a peek see what's in there." Sissy turmed away saying nothing further, She looked at Daniel engaging him in a visual standoff. Rev. Hill stepped in the pulpit observing the obvious conflict between his wife and her cousin.

"Ahem" He cleared his throat breaking their mutual gaze. Sissy looked into her husband's chastising eyes then focused her attention to her newborn nephew lying across Millie's lap.

"Good afternoon brothers and sisters, I'm Rev. Otis Hill and I'm here from Mississippi to officiate the vow renewal of your Pastor, Rev. J.R. Smith and his lovely wife Effie Mae." The word 'Amen' echoed through the church. "Now I'm sure many of y'all probably wondering who I am, and why I came from so far away to officiate a wedding." Rev. Hill lightly chuckled. "Truth is—Rev. Smith is my brother-in-law, he's the baby brother of my wife Sissy—stand up honey." He said knowing if he didn't introduced his wife to J.R's congrefation, the ride home to Mississippi would be intolerable. Sissy stood displaying a proud look on her face as she glanced around the sanctuary making certain to be seen. Rev. Hill shifted his eyes to Millie. She raised an eyebrow. "You can sit down now honey." He said in response to her prolong standing. All eyes looked in the direction of the sanctuary's entrance when the sound of the wedding hymn filled the church's acoustic and the husband and wife prepared to make their grand entrance.

To the right of the sanctuary the sweet sound of the piano played the traditional hymn. To the left, the organist harmoniously complimented the pianist. Dressed in a charcoal Black tuxedo accented with a white shirt and Black bow tie, J.R. proudly escorted his beloved wife—Effie Mae Smith, adorned in a chiffon, cream silk wedding gown handmade by one of J.R.'s patrons down the aisle. Complimenting her wavy black, dangling hair displayed a floral band of *Baby's-breath*. The eyes of the many onlookers followed J.R. and Effie Mae up to the altar where they stood, committed to renewing their marriage vows. Seated in the rear of the sanctuary on the very last pew sat Huck.

# Chapter Thirty-Four

Millie, the Hill's, Pete, Annie Mae and the children convened in J.R. and Effie Mae's backyard for a Saturday evening barbeque before their returned home to Mississippi the following morning. J.R. accompanied by Pete, stood to the left of the backyard grilling ribs, hot dogs and hamburgers. Millie, and the Hill's convened at a wooden table near the back porch. All eyes looked in the direction of Daniel's car when seeing it pulled to the curb and parked. Sissy watched with sympathetic eyes as Daniel assisted Ms. Geraldine from the car and into her wheelchair then removed his toddler son from his car seat in back and sat him on Ms. Geraldine's lap before pushing the wheelchair towards the house.

"You got him Geraldine?" Daniel asked seeing the toddler squirming on her lap, secured only by her right arm. She nodded then kissed D.J. on his cheek. He looked at her and giggled. Sissy shifted her eyes across the table at Millie and Rev. Hill, subtly shaking her head with disapproval.

"Geraldine you remember my cousin Sissy don't you?" Daniel asked as they approached. She looked at Sissy with unfamiliarity. "That's J.R.'s sister—you remember her don't you?" Rev. Hill observed Ms. Geraldine's confused state of mind with compassionate eyes.

"Watch out for that little fella!" He yelled when seeing D.J. reaching for his daddy.

"Geraldine ain't gon let that boy fall Rev. Otis." Daniel said amused by his overreaction. "Let me get this boy Geraldine before Rev. Otis have a heart attack." He chuckled then removed the reaching toddler him from her lap, kissing him on the head. "Daddy love you boy." Sissy shifted her eyes to Millie then turned back to Ms. Geraldine.

"Ow—you—doing Sis—sy?" Ms. Geraldine asked hugging her with her right arm.

"I'm fine Geraldine, how you doing?" Sissy looked at her with pity. Ms. Geraldine nodded indicating she was fine. "After all these years we finally see each other again . . . last time I saw you Geraldine it was at you and Cousin Daniel's wedding." Ms. Geraldine lowered her head.

Sissy grasped hold of Ms. Geraldine's right hand and gently squeezed it seeing the hurt in her moistened eyes.

"It's gon be alright Geraldine." Sissy said believing her emotional hurt to be caused by Daniel's betrayal with Effie Mae. Ms. Geraldine again raised her head and looked into Sissy's understandable eyes.

"J.R.—is—won—erful—man." Ms. Geraldine said smiling. "I love— im—so—much."

"Momma and Daddy raised that little boy right!" Sissy said boasting. "Thank you for saying that Geraldine, but my poor brother—"

"Ahem!" Rev. Hill cleared his throat warning his wife not to get started. Sissy glanced over at him and again hugged Ms. Geraldine. The two women shared a smile.

"And that man right there Geraldine—" Daniel pointed to Rev. Hill. "—that's Sissy's husband, Rev. Otis." Rev. Hill stood then walked over to her.

"It's a pleasure to meet you Geraldine." He said patting her lightly on the back. "They tell me you had a stroke?" She nodded. "We'll certainly be praying for you." Ms. Geraldine smiled and nodded. He gave her a second pat on the back then returned to his seat. Rev. Hill took note of her afflictions and wondered how Daniel could have allowed himself to commit an act that brought so much hurt and shame to his wife of many years. He believed the consequences of Daniel's moment of weakness would one day bring him a season of regret.

"And this lady right here—" Daniel hesitated. "—that's Effie Mae's momma, Ms. Millie." Ms. Geraldine's eyes filled with tears as Daniel pushed her over to Millie. She looked at Millie then reached out to her requesting a hug. Millie looked at her with ambiguity. On the one hand, she felt guilty about Effie Mae's affair with Daniel producing a son. On the other, she couldn't help but empathize with the pain Ms. Geraldine had inflicted upon Effie Mae by taking her son.

"I'm—or—ry for—ow—I treat—Ef—fie Mae." Ms. Geraldine said weeping. Millie reached over and hugged her.

"Don't start all that mess Geraldine!" Daniel snapped." Ms. Millie came here to enjoy herself, she ain't trying to hear about all that stuff from yesteryear." Ms. Geraldine continued crying. "I told you about beating yourself up over all that old mess." Daniel looked at her, numb to her tears. Millie's eyes erupted with tears in response to Ms. Geraldine's sincere remorse.

"I can't be mad at you Geraldine for how you felt about my daughter laying down with your husband and having his child." Millie saw the hurt deepen in Ms. Geraldine's eyes. "You ain't done no different than what a lot of women would've done had it been they husband." Ms. Geraldine took hold of Millie's right hand and held it against her cheek. "Being Effie Mae's momma, it's me who should be apologizing to you."

"You hear that Geraldine?" Daniel said hoping Millie's words would lessen his wife's guilt. Millie looked up at him, troubled by his insensitive words to his wife then again turned to Ms. Geraldine. "Maybe one day before she leaves this world she can forgive herself."

"Geraldine my daughter had some real bad things happen to her before she married J.R." Sissy glanced quickly to Rev. Hill in response to what she believed would finally be an explanation for Effie Mae's dramatic change in behavior at age sixteen that resulted in her sexual promiscuity. She swiftly turned away when seeing the disciplining look in her husband's eyes. Millie continued speaking.

"If I had listened to my child when she was having her problems instead of worrying 'bout what folk was saying about her —" Sissy again glanced over at Rev. Hill. He ignored her judgmental gaze as he listened to Millie's heartfelt words. " —maybe she could've faced what it was guiding her ways." Millie eyes filled with tears. "My daughter was broken, and marrying J.R. or no other man wasn't gon fix her." She gazed in Ms. Geraldine's sorrowed eyes as both women quietly wept.

Rev. Hill looked at his wife and raised a scolding eyebrow, reminding her of how she served as the main source of the gossip about Effie Mae in the church.

"You gon be alright Ms. Millie?" He asked, understanding the weight of the burden she'd carried all those years.

"I'm gon be just fine Rev. Hill." Millie said picking up a paper napkin from the table, wiping her tearful eyes. "For the first time in years I finally feel free." She chuckled through her tears. "I guess that's what the good book mean when it say *the truth shall set you free.*

"It sure will Ms. Millie." Rev. Hill nodded. "It sure will."

"Whe—Ef—fie—Mae?" Ms. Geraldine asked, releasing Millie's hand.

"She's in the house with her new baby." Millie said handing her a paper napkin.

"Ta—me—in—ouse." Ms. Geraldine said looking up at Daniel, dabbing her eyes. He again sat D.J. on her lap. The toddler looked up at her and smiled as she secured him with her right arm.

"You got him Geraldine?" She nodded. Daniel looked at the steps leading up to the back porch and tried to figure out the best way to take the wheelchair up.

"Here . . . let me help you Daniel." Rev. Hill said hurrying over. "I can lift it from the front if you grab it from behind."

"You gon be able to lift it Rev. Otis?" Daniel asked.

"Don't worry about me lifting, you just make sure that baby don't fall." Rev. Hill said looking at the squirming toddler held by Ms. Geraldine's good right arm. "Is your wife gon be able to hold onto him?"

"Geraldine ain't gon let that boy fall—she can crack walnuts with that right arm, it's pretty strong." Daniel stated, chuckling.

"Then let's go." Rev. Hill grabbedthe front of the wheelchair, as Daniel lifted it from behind. The two men carried it up the stairs onto the back porch.

"Thank you Rev. Otis." Daniel said opening the back door as he prepared to push his wife inside.

———————————

"What's going with you and Pete, Annie Mae?" Effie Mae asked as she cradled her infant son in her arms, seated on the living room sofa with her baby sister. She giggled.

"Don't be laughing Effie Mae it ain't funny."

"I thought you and Pete had a perfect marriage." Effie Mae teased.

"Pete gon have to stop treating me like I'm his child." Annie Mae said pouting. "I ain't sixteen no more Effie Mae, I'm a grown woman."

"Did you tell Pete that little girl?"

"Yeah I told him."

"I know Pete Parker didn't like hearing you say that."

"Naw he didn't." Annie Mae paused. "He started crying when I told him."

"I know Pete Parker ain't cried!" Effie Mae said laughing. "I didn't think Pete's eyes even made tears no more."

"Stop making fun of my husband Effie Mae." Annie Mae whined.

"Ef—fie—Mae." Effie Mae's laughter abruptly ended when hearing Ms. Geraldine's voice before seeing Daniel pushing her in the living room in her wheelchair, stopping in front of Effie Mae. Annie Mae's mouth slightly opened when observing the look of fear on her big sister's face. A loving smile showed on Effie Mae's face when seeing D.J. sitting on Ms. Geraldine's lap. The toddler looked at her with familiarity then reached. Daniel removed the fidgety toddler from his wife's hold as he continued reaching for his momma. Annie Mae's mouth flung open in response to the look of love in Daniel's eyes as he looked at her big sister, still standing behind his wife's wheelchair. He noted the look in

Effie Mae's eyes, nonverbally asking if Ms. Geraldine knew about her taking D.J. from him and the means by which she'd done so.

"I—see ou—and—J.R. finely—got tha—boy." Ms. Geraldine said teasing. Effie Mae and Daniel's mutual gaze abruptly ended.

"Yeah . . . J.R. finally got his little boy." She said forcing a chuckle before again turning her attention to Daniel and D.J.

"Let—me old—im." Ms. Geraldine muddled. Daniel noticed the apprehensive look in Effie Mae's eyes in response to Ms. Geraldine's request.

"It's okay Effie Mae." He said. "She can still use her right arm." Ms. Geraldine cradled her arm and prepared to receive the infant. Effie Mae gently placed him in her hold. An endearing smile formed on Ms. Geraldine partially paralyzed face as she admired the newborn then observed Annie Mae staring at her.

"Tha—you—sis—ter." She asked looking briefly away from the infant to Annie Mae. "She ook—like—you."

"Yeah Ms. Geraldine that's my baby sister Annie Mae." Ms. Geraldine nodded.

"How you doing Ms. Geraldine?" Annie Mae said. Ms. Geraldine smiled and nodded then turned her attention back to the newborn.

"Ms. Geraldine did you see my momma outside?" Daniel intervened.

"Yeah Effie Mae they talked." He said gazing lovingly at her, turning away when noticing Annie Mae watching him . . . watching her big sister.

"Hey D.J." Effie Mae said. The toddler smiled and squirmed at the sound of her voice, continuing to reached for her. Daniel handed her the active toddler.

"You see your baby brother D.J.?" He said pointing at the infant. D.J. looked at Daniel and giggled. "His name is—" Daniel looked at Effie Mae and waited.

"Tyrell Lee Jones Smith." Effie Mae stated proudly. Annie Mae continued her gawk at Daniel as he gazed at big sister persisted.

"Effie Mae I'm gon run out here and see what Momma doing." Annie Mae said anxious to tell her momma of Daniel's obsession with Effie Mae.

"If you thinking Melvin out there Annie Mae, he ain't." Effie Mae said giggling. "That man don't ever leave that jazz club." A puzzled looked formed on Annie Mae's face.

"What Melvin got to do with Momma?"

"Never mind little girl." Effie Mae said quietly grinning. "You just go see 'bout Momma." Annie Mae rose from the sofa and walked pass Daniel and Ms. Geraldine on her way through the kitchen. She looked back at Daniel before hurrying out the back door and off the porch approaching Millie and the Hill's.

"Momma!"

"What's wrong with you child?" Millie asked when seeing her overly excited state.

"You should see how that old man in there looking at Effie Mae!" Annie Mae said scowling. "I don't see how Effie Mae could've ever laid down with that old man!" Millie silently chuckled.

"Ahem!" Rev. Hill cleared his throat seconds after Sissy shifted her self-righteous eyes over to him.

"You see Otis . . . I ain't the only one who feels that way." She said, feeling justified.

"That's your sister business Annie Mae." Millie stated in Effie Mae's defense.

"Momma you should see—" Sissy intervened.

"But you right Annie Mae, Cousin Daniel ought to be shame of himself . . . know he old enough to be Effie Mae's daddy." Rev. Hill looked at his wife and shook his head then stood.

"Let me go on over here with J.R. and Pete before me and my wife end up leaving here before I get a chance to eat."

"What Otis? I ain't doing nothing but speaking the truth." He walked away ignoring her words then joined J.R. and Pete over at the grill. Rev. Hill glanced back at his wife and shook his head.

"Careful Sissy don't let your mouth 'cause Rev. Hill to leave here without you.

"Girl I ain't paying Otis no mind." Sissy said looking over at him, rolling her eyes. "It's my mouth and I'll say what I want to say."

"It's a lot of women would love to be the wife of a pastor." Millie said teasing.

"Girl, Otis ain't going nowhere . . . and you right Annie Mae—" Sissy said continuing to voice her opinion on her wayward cousin. "—that snake had the nerves to stand his old behind at my baby brother and Effie Mae's wedding reception last week and tell me and Millie how he loved Effie Mae." Sissy said looking in Annie Mae astounded eyes. "And how he would've loved to have married my brother's wife." Annie Mae's mouth abruptly opened.

"Marry?" Annie Mae said raising her voice. "That man said he wanted to marry my big sister, Ms. Sissy?" Annie Mae looked at Millie. "Momma!" Millie raised an eyebrow.

"Yeah Annie Mae that's what that snake said alright." Sissy said frustrated. "Then had the nerves to say it wasn't meant to be—" She looked at Millie then again turned to Annie Mae. "He damn right it wasn't meant to be!" Millie looked at her old friend with chastising eyes.

"Sissy!"

"I'm sorry Millie but it makes me so damn mad seeing that old snake lusting after my baby brother's wife."

"Look like I'm gon need to get Rev. Hill back over here."

"For what Millie?" Sissy glanced over at her husband seeing him taking a hot dog off the grill biting into it. "Otis know better than to mess with me when I'm having one of my fits—" She again turned to Millie. "—you see he got up and left . . . and he did the right thing Millie."

"Maybe I need to go over there with the men." Millie said disturbed by Sissy's continuous harsh judgment of her cousin.

"I'm sorry Millie, but I'm mad girl."

"Well you being mad Sissy ain't gon change a thing."

"I know Millie but how could Cousin Daniel do his poor wife like that?" A sympathetic look displayed in Sissy's eyes. "You saw that woman didn't you Annie Mae?"

"Yeah I saw her."

"Poor thing can barely speak."

"Well that poor woman ain't always been that way Sissy." Millie stated cynically. Sissy's agitation grew.

"Cousin Daniel knew he was married Millie!And he knew Effie Mae was his own cousin's wife . . . I don't know what he was thinking!" Sissy paused. "Yeah I know what he was thinking—like most men think with his—"

"Sissy!" Millie said quickly cutting her off.

"What Millie, he was."

"Ms. Sissy how old is that man?"Annie Mae asked bothered by him being intimate with her big sister.

"Let's see . . . Cousin Daniel's got to be about two or three years older than me." Sissy said recollecting.

"Careful Sissy you keep talking you gon give your own age away." Millie giggled. "I know you don't want folks in the church to know you ain't the spring chicken Rev. Hill thinks he married." Millie raised an eyebrow.

"Older than me . . . and that's all I'm gon say." Sissy said. Their attention suddenly drew to the candy apple red Cadillac pulling up to the curb and parking. J.R., Pete and Rev. Hill's attention also drew to the shiny red car. All eyes watched as the male inside got out. Sissy and Annie Mae's mouths slightly opened when recognizing the driver as Huck. He took note of their gazing eyes as he headed towards the house. He discretely blushed. Pete noted Annie Mae gawking at Effie Mae's extremely handsome friend, seemingly unable to remove her eyes from his face.

"Annie Mae!" Pete called out trying to break her stare.

"What Pete?"

"Come here girl." Millie chuckled when seeing her son-in-law's obvious insecurity.

"Gone child . . . go see what your husband want." She said grinning. "Cause that look on that boy's face say he ain't please at how you looking at your sister's friend."

"Annie Mae!"

"What Pete?" She said continuing her gaze.

"How you ladies doing?" Huck asked looking into the gazing eyes of Annie Mae and Sissy then ultimately to Millie.

"We doing just fine Henry Lee." Millie said amused by her young daughter and the *Reverend's wife's* as they continued to gawk. "If you looking for Effie Mae she in the house."

"Thank you Ms. Reed." Huck stated shifting his eyes at his two admirers, flattered by their endless stare.

"Daniel and his wife just went in to see her and the new baby." Millie said. Huck tilted his head and silently chuckled.

"Is that right?" He noted J.R., Pete and Rev. Hill observing from over at the grill. He greeted them with a nod of the head then turned back to the ladies. "Y'all take care." He said blushing as he walked away, stepping onto the back porch then entering the house.

"Y'all can stop all that staring now." Millie stated.

"Oooh Momma that man is so good looking." Annie Mae said still looking at the back door.

"Annie Mae!" Pete again called out.

"Here I come Pete." She said seeing the demanding look in his eyes. "There he go again Momma treating me like I'm his child."

"Go head on child." Millie said giggling. "Go see what your husband want."

"Pete don't want nothing Momma."

"I think Pete want your eye on him and off Huck." Millie raised an eyebrow. Annie Mae's mouth opened. "Remember Annie Mae the grass ain't always greener on the other side."

"Millie girl if the grass on the other side look anything like man, I think I'd have to give that grass a run for his money!" Sissy stated with excitement. Millie's eyes widened, shocked by her friend's naughty words.

"Sissy!"

"What Millie?"

"Look like Rev. Hill gon have to keep a closer eye on you."

"Millie you telling me that man don't look good to you?"

"That man too young for me."

"That ain't what I ask you girl and you know it." Sissy thought for moment. "Oh that's right you prefer a man just a little older like Melvin." Millie blushed. Annie Mae's jaw dropped.

"Momma!"

"What's taking J.R. so long to cook that meat?" Millie said deflecting from the topic of Melvin.

"Millie girl . . . it looks like Otis gon have to keep a eye on all of us!" Sissy said bursting into laughter.

"Annie Mae!" Pete hollered out.

"I'm coming Pete." She looked briefly over at him then turned to Millie. "Momma we gon have to talk about this Melvin."

"You just go talk to your husband, that's all the talking you need to be doing."

"I'm gon go see what Pete want—" Annie Mae said walking away. "—then we gon have to talk Momma." Millie chuckled as her excitable young daughter joined her husband over at the grill.

"You called me Pete?"

"We okay ain't we Annie Mae?"

"What you mean?"

"We still working on us ain't we?"

"Yeah." She said in a child-like manner. He place a quick smooch her on the lips.

"I'm doing better ain't I?"

"Yeah . . . long as you don't start treating me like a child again." He again kissed her.

"I didn't do that did I?"

"Well—" He cut her off.

"I love you girl and I'm gon make us work!" Pete took Annie Mae in his arms and romantically kissed her.

"Millie if I was a little younger and single—girl I'd give that good looking man a run for his money!" Sissy said grinning. "Yeah girl I sure would." She said looking in the direction of the back door.

"You better be careful what you let roll off your tongue Sissy."

"What Millie . . . I'm just being honest girl." Sissy looked over at her husband seeing him biting into a bunned hotdog. She lowered her voice. "Girl back in the day before I met Otis—" A lustful smile stretched across Sissy's face as she reminisced. "—I use to love being in the arms of a good looking man and I had my fair share of them too!"

"Sissy—"

"What Millie?"

"Don't you let Rev. Hill hear you over here talking like that!" Millie scolded. "And forget you his wife now."

"I ain't forgot Millie, I said if I was single." Sissy again shifted her eyes to the back door. "Girl they don't make men that good looking no more!"

"Sissy!"

"What Millie?"

"Don't let Rev. Hill hear you over here lusting after my daughter's friend."

"Millie I ain't worried about Otis hearing me . . . he couldn't hear thunder in a rain storm." The two women laughed.

• • • •

Huck stood just inside the kitchen, unseen as he entered. He silently laughed as he observed Daniel's continued gaze at Effie Mae.

"Hey Effie Mae." He said breaking Daniel's stare. Ms. Geraldine looked around when hearing his voice, watching as he walked through the kitchen on his way to the living room.

"How you doing Daniel?" Huck said looking at him as he approached. Daniel's mouth quickly dried, ill at ease by Huck's presence. "You here to see Effie Mae's baby?" Huck asked taunting him.

"My wife—" Daniel's anxiety magnified "—she wanted to see Effie Mae and the baby." His shifted his eyes to Effie Mae then again to Huck.

"Is that right?" Huck said tilting his head then looked over at Effie Mae and winked. She smiled. "How you doing girl?"

"Hey Huck."

"Well Effie Mae—" Daniel said nervous. "—I guess me and Geraldine's gon head on outdoors and eat, let her enjoy the sun before time for her to go back to this nursing home." He glanced briefly into

Huck's gazing eyes then turned back to Effie Mae. "I'll go ahead and take D.J. so you can get the baby from Geraldine."

"Just let me kiss my baby boy goodbye." Effie Mae said applying a kiss to the toddler' cheek. "Momma loves you D.J." He looked at her and smiled then laid his head on his momma's chest. Effie Mae kissed him on the forehead then handed the toddler to Daniel. Huck watched, amused by Daniel's inability to resist his display of affection for Effie Mae despite being in his wife's presence.

"It was good seeing you Ms. Geraldine." Effie Mae said ending her mutual gaze with her former lover.

"I love—ou—too—Ef—fie—Mae." She said extending her right arm, requesting a hug.

"I'll get him." Huck said removing the infant from Ms. Geraldine's cradled arm allowing her and Effie Mae to embrace. Daniel continued his gaze at Effie Mae as she and his wife affectionately hugged, Ms. Geraldine gently placing her right hand against Effie Mae's cheek.

"Than—ou." Effie Mae shifted her eyes to Daniel, puzzled by his wife's *thank you.*

"Oh, she talking about that thing with D.J." He said, quickly shifting his eyes to Huck then back to Effie Mae trying to obscure the details of their conversation. "Come on Geraldine I'm hungry!" Daniel said, impatient. She released Effie Mae.

"I—un—gry—too." She said chuckling.

"You ready for this boy Geraldine?" Daniel asked preparing to sit D.J. on her lap. She nodded. "You got him?" He said sitting the toddler on her lap Ms. Geraldine kissed the toddler on the top of his head. "Yeah, I want to get on out here before Rev. Otis start eating!" Daniel said laughing. Ms. Geraldine quietly grinned. "I've seen that man sit down at a dinner table before—" He looked at Effie Mae. "Rev. Otis ate everything but the tablecloth!" He burst into laughter. Effie Mae's mouth slightly opened.

"Mr. Daniel!"

"What Effie Mae?" He continued laughing. "Rev. Otis ain't got that big from just looking . . . that man can eat!" D.J. looked at his daddy amused by his laughter. He giggled.

"See there Mr. Daniel . . . you got my baby laughing at Rev. Hill."

"Say bye to your momma, D.J." Daniel said staring at Effie Mae.

"Bye my sweet baby." She said kissing him on the cheek. He looked at her and smiled then squirmed, again reaching for her.

"Be still boy!" Daniel said alarmed by his sudden movement. "You got him Geraldine?" She nodded. Huck watched through envious eyes as Effie Mae and Daniel shared time together with their son. He intervened.

"Your wife said she was hungry Daniel." He said looking at him. Daniel shifted his eyes over at Huck then again looked at Effie Mae.

"Alright Effie Mae . . . I'm gon get Geraldine on out here so she can eat then we gon move on."

"Ou—and—J.R.—ake care—tha—ba—by." Ms. Geraldine said smiling.

"We will Ms. Geraldine."

"You know you can come get this boy anytime you want Effie Mae." Daniel said concerned the new baby might take Effie Mae's attention away from his son . . . and him."

"I will Mr. Daniel—bye D.J." Effie Mae said waving at the toddler. Daniel turned the wheelchair in the direction of the back door and pushed. Huck quietly chuckled, humored by Daniel's uneasiness by his presence.

• • • •

"Girl what's going on with Annie Mae and Pete?" Sissy asked probing. "The way she was looking at that good looking man—" Millie interrupter her.

"The way she was looking at him?" Millie raised an eyebrow. "You wasn't exactly blind to him yourself Sissy." Sissy half-heartedly chuckled.

"Girl you know I didn't mean nothing by that, I was just running my mouth is all." She said trying to minimize the verbal lust she'd repeatedly expressed for Huck.

"Annie Mae's young and naïve, you ain't either one." Millie raised an eyebrow. Sissy's jaw dropped in response to her old friend's blunt words.

"I saw how she could barely take her eyes of that man—just ignored poor Pete."

"Look like Annie Mae got it in her head it's more to life than Pete." Sissy's mouth quickly opened.

"Millie girl you think Effie Mae putting that mess in her head?"

"Effie Mae got enough mess in her own head to be worrying about her sister's."

"Uh-hum." Sissy looked at Millie, unconvinced.

"My daughter's growing up is all it is, but she say Pete want her to stay sixteen forever." Sissy's eyes widened.

"Girl what's wrong with Pete?" She looked over at him and shook her head. "People change Millie . . . how can Pete expect that girl to stay sixteen forever when he was always filling her up with babies?" Millie's mouth abruptly opened.

"Sissy!"

"What Millie? You know I'm right!" She shifted her eyes over at Annie Mae, still held in Pete's embrace. "Every time I saw that poor child she looked like she'd swallowed a beach ball."

"Well they both wanted a big family—" Sissy interjected.

"Then they got what they wanted, six times."

"And neither Annie Mae or Pete would change a thing."

"I tell you one thing Millie—" Sissy looked at her with warning. "—Pete keep that mess up he gon run that girl out of his bed and into another man's bed."

"They working on it." A skeptical look displayed on Sissy's face. "After what I saw today, Pete may be working on it but it looks to me the only thing Annie Mae's working on is her way out of that marriage!" Sissy nodded confirming her belief. "You just wait and see Millie."

"Annie Mae ain't going nowhere cause Pete ain't gon let—" Sissy cut her off.

"Let her? Girl he ain't gon be able to stop her—" Sissy silenced when seeing the silver Lincoln Continental pull up to the curb and park. "You know who that is Millie?" She asked in response to the enormous smile forming on her old friend's face. Millie gave no reply as she watched the driver's side door opened and the male driver got out and began walking towards the two women. Sissy's mouth quickly opened. "Millie girl ain't that the man who called me ma'am at Effie Mae and J.R.'s reception?" She said frowning. "Like I was a old woman or something." Millie's blushing smile grew.

"Yeah that's Melvin."

"Millie I know it ain't none of my business, but what's going on with you and that man?" Millie ignored her probing question. J.R., Pete, Annie Mae and Rev. Hill's attention turned to Melvin, watching as he walked over to Millie with a huge smile on his face. Her smile widened.

"Hey woman." Melvin stated intimately.

"Hey Melvin." Millie said unable to mask her fondness for him. He glanced over at Sissy.

"How you doing Sissy?"

"I don't know how I'm doing seeing you leading my friend astray." Melvin ignored her opinionated words as he again turned to Millie.

"What time you heading back home?" He asked gazing in her eyes.

"We suppose to be leaving in the morning." She said unable to stop blushing.

"I was hoping to spend a little time with you before you left." Millie giggled.

"That would be nice."

"I just need to check with Effie Mae make sure I can go in a little later tonight."

"Well as Effie Mae's momma you got my permission to take all the time you need." They chuckled.

"I can appreciate you saying that Millie, but unfortunately you ain't my boss . . . at least not at the jazz club." He winked. Millie giggled. Sissy's jaw dropped. "Can you get away for a minute, come ride with me?"

"I sure can." Millie stated. Sissy's jaw again dropped. "Then let's go." Melvin took hold of Millie's hand as she stood to her feet then placed a light kiss on her cheek. Sissy's self-righteous eyes widened.

"Millie girl don't you let that man talk you into doing something you gon regret." She said troubled by Millie's obvious infatuation with Melvin. Melvin intervened.

"Sissy, I have the utmost respect for this woman." He looked at Millie and smiled. "It ain't too many women like Millie still around." Millie continued blushing, flattered by Melvin's complimentary words. "To me Millie's like a rare jewel." Sissy shifted her eyes over at Millie, disturbed by her receptiveness to a man she barely knew. "In fact, I can see myself marrying this woman."

"Marrying her?" She said raising her voice. "You don't even know Millie!"

"I know her well enough to know she's the perfect woman for—" Sissy cut him off.

"How!" She yelled, shifting her eyes to her old friend, angry by the passive look on her face. "How the hell can you know Millie in a only few weeks?"

"Because I made it my business to know this woman when I realized she was somebody I could spend the rest of my life with."

Rev. Hill watched with troubled eyes as his wife continued her ongoing bickering with Millie's suitor. He too shared her concern.

"I've had my fair share of women over the years—" Sissy shifted her eyes to Millie, a skeptical look on her face. "—but the one thing I ain't ever had is a good woman." He turned to Millie and winked. She girlishly giggled. "And now that I do, if she'll have me I plan on marrying this woman!" Sissy's frustration grew.

"Now how you gon marry Millie with her living all the way in Mississippi and you living here in New York? Because I know my friend and she ain't getting ready to leave Mississippi for you and no other man!"

"Well I think you should know Sissy . . . I'm a determined man." He turned to Millie and again winked. She again giggled.

"I see you over there giggling Millie, but I hope you ain't done nothing that's gon make your girls ashamed of you." Melvin interjected.

"I would never do anything to bring shame on this woman!" He said insulted by Sissy's accusation. "I learned from my father a long time ago—you don't treat a diamond like glass." Melvin said, again looking at Millie. "And this woman right here, she's my diamond." Sissy looked at Millie and smirked. "So I'm telling you now Sissy, I ain't going nowhere and you gon be seeing me again . . . either here or in Mississippi because it's my intention to make Millie Reed my wife." He kissed Millie lightly on the lips. Annie Mae's mouth flung open.

"Momma what you doing?" She shouted from across the backyard before quickly hurrying over.

"Uh-hum." Sissy said in response to Annie Mae's reaction. "You see what I was talking about Millie." Melvin watched as Annie Mae approached.

• • • •

"You happy girl?" Huck asked Effie Mae. A girlish smile formed on her face.

"Yeah Huck I am."

"You sure?" He teased. She giggled. "What about Anthony, he gon be alright?"

"There you go again worrying about Anthony."

"It ain't Anthony I'm worried about . . . I'm making sure this is what you want." He looked at her with concern in his eyes. "I ain't trying to come to the club one night and hear about you living up there with Anthony again." Effie Mae giggled. "I'm serious Effie Mae.

"You ain't got to worry about that Huck." He tilted his head.

"Is that right?"

"I'm back home with my husband and this is where I'm gon stay.

"What about Anthony's boy? How's that working?" Effie Mae chuckled.

"Why you acting like you my daddy Huck?"

"Somebody need too—you hard headed Effie Mae!" Her mouth slightly opened. "You are!"

" Look like Lil' J.R. don't want nobody being his daddy except J.R." Huck tilted his head.

"Is that right?"

"I been trying to get Anthony to spend more time with his son so he can get use to him, but Anthony ain't doing nothing but spoiling that boy."

"It ain't gon happen overnight." Huck smiled then silently stared at her. Effie Mae blushed.

"What?"

"I'm happy for you girl." He stated shifting his eyes to the newborn cradled in his arms. "Tyrell Lee Jones Smith." Huck quietly chuckled. "That's a lot of name for one boy." Effie Mae's eyes dampened.

"The man little boy named after was a whole lot of man."

"I know Blue—" Huck corrected himself. "—Tyrell . . . and I know he would be honored." He gazed at his brother's *namesake* then handed the infant back to Effie Mae. She kissed her sleeping son on the forehead then laid him in the bassinette next to the sofa. "What's going on with you and old Daniel?" Huck asked, amused. "Man act like he love sick or something." Effie Mae giggled.

"He'll get over it." Huck tilted his head and smiled.

"Is that right?" He grinned. "Girl you something else."

"I know."

• • • •

"Momma what you over here doing with that man?" Annie Mae yelled.

"How you doing Annie Mae?" Melvin asked, politely.

"I don't know you!" She shouted.

"You don't remember me?" He asked. "I'm Melvin."

"I don't know you Melvin and neither do my momma!" She said continuing to yell, upset by the affection he displayed towards her momma. Pete also approached. He looked at Melvin with suspicion then turned to his mother-in-law.

"You alright Ms. Millie?" He shifted his eyes to Melvin.

"I'm fine son."

"Melvin?" Pete said recognizing him. "The bartender, right?"

"Yeah man . . . how you been doing Pete?"

"I'm doing okay Melvin, but my wife ain't too happy about seeing you over here kissing on her momma."

"I love your mother-in-law Pete—" Annie Mae intervened.

"You don't even know my momma!" She said infuriated.

"Me and Millie's been getting to know each other since she's been here." He looked at Millie and smiled. She blushed. "Your mother-in-law invited me to come see her in a couple weeks so that we can keep getting to know one another."

"What you mean by that?" Pete said uneasy by Melvin's statement.

"Not like that man." Melvin stated. "I respect Millie no less than my daddy respected my momma, and he would've gave his life for that woman." Pete again looked at Millie.

"Ms. Millie what you got to say about that?" She looked at Annie Mae before speaking.

"I lost my husband many years ago son and I ain't looked at another man since that time." She turned to her enraged daughter. "I guess I never thought there was a man alive could ever take Frank Reed's place." A smile formed on Millie's face as she looked at Melvin. "But I see in Melvin what I saw in my Frank—a kind and gentle man; a man who truly loves me for me." She said shifting her eyes to Sissy. "A man who made my today's happier than my yesterdays and made me look forward to seeing my tomorrows." Millie again looked at Melvin. "I know Melvin's a man that's gon love my family as his own." He smiled. "And he can cook!" Millie stated humorously. Melvin laughed then intervened.

"Like I said, I'll be coming to Mississippi in a couple weeks and I look forward to getting to know you and your wife Pete, and I want y'all to get to know me." Sissy looked across the yard at Rev. Hill. He stared back, a shocked look in his eyes as he watched in awe. J.R. sporadically glanced over at his mother-in-law and Melvin between flipping hamburger and turning over hot dogs still cooking on the grill.

"You ready Melvin?" Millie asked, smiling. He looked at Annie Mae and Pete before shifting his eyes over at Sissy, noting her inquiring eyes.

"I'm just gon take Millie out and wine and dine—" Annie Mae cut him off.

"Wine?" She shouted. "My momma don't drink!"

"Then we can just have dinner, if that's alright with you Annie Mae." She looked abruptly to her momma.

"Remember Annie Mae—" Millie looked her in the eyes. "—I'm your momma you ain't mine." She raised an eyebrow then walked away with Melvin. All eyes watched as he assisted Millie in his car, closing the door then hurrying to the driver's side and getting in. He honked his horn twice then drove off. Annie Mae's anger accelerated.

"I'm going in this house right now and tell Effie Mae about her friend Melvin—trying to get with my momma." Annie Mae stated rushing in the direction of the house, running up the stairs. Sissy maintained her silence as she wondered of the extent to which Millie had submitted herself to Melvin.

• • • •

Effie Mae and Huck looked in the direction of the back door as Annie Mae rushed in. They noted the distraught look on her face.

"Effie Mae you better talk to your friend!" She yelled. "What you talking about Annie Mae? What friend?"

"Melvin!"

"Melvin?"

"That man just left here with Momma!" Huck tilted his head and cunningly grinned.

"Is that right?" Annie Mae ignored him.

"What you talking about Annie Mae, Melvin don't ever leave that jazz club."

"Well he left there today because he was just out there kissing on Momma!" Effie Mae's eyes widened.

"What you mean he was kissing on Momma?"

"That man was out there talking about he was gon marry Momma!" Huck silently chuckled, amused by Annie Mae's overly exaggerated reaction.

"Annie Mae, you know Momma ain't getting ready to marry Melvin or nobody else."

"You didn't see him Effie Mae!" Annie Mae whined. "That man said he was coming to Mississippi in two weeks so he could get to know Momma better." Effie Mae's eyes again widened. Huck quietly chuckled.

"What he mean by that?"

"That's what Pete asked him."

"Pete?"

"Yeah, Pete wanted to know why he was kissing on Momma and—" Effie Mae interjected.

"What Momma say Annie Mae?"

"She said something about not having a man since Daddy died." Huck's quiet chuckle progressed into laughter.

"Annie Mae you sure that was Melvin?"

"Yeah I'm sure . . . he even said his name was Melvin!"

"Let me call Anthony—see what's going on." Effie Mae said looking at Huck with puzzled eyes. "I ain't ever seen Melvin leave that club."

"I'm gon go talk to Ms. Sissy, Effie Mae . . . see if Momma told her where that man was taking her." Annie Mae said pouting.

"Yeah Annie Mae you go do that." Huck said teasing her. She looked at him and rolled her eyes then hurried back through the kitchen and out the back door. "Sound like your momma and Melvin gon be in trouble when they get back." Huck said continuing to laugh.

"I know Melvin been cooking for Momma and asking me a bunch of questions 'bout her, but she ain't said nothing about them getting together like that."

"I see Ol' Melvin's slicker than I thought." Huck said grinning.

"I ain't ever seen Momma talking to a man like that."

"Look here Effie Mae I'm gon go ahead make a move, see what Buckeye's up to . . . he been calling me all day woke me up early this morning—I think it's his sister's birthday or something." Effie Mae's mouth opened, astonished.

"Sister? I ain't think Buckeye had no brothers and sisters." She stated then looked at him with suspiciousness.

"Naw Effie Mae, Buckeye's sister ain't ever been my woman." Huck said reading the look in her eyes. " Peggy like a little sister to me."

"How many brothers and sister do Buckeye got?"

"It's just them two." Huck stated then seductively stared at Effie Mae, stroking his chin hairs.

"Kiss me." Her mouth flung open in response to his unexpected request.

"Huck!" Effie Mae said looking through the screened backdoor.

"Come on Effie Mae ain't nobody looking."

"Huck, I'm in my husband's house."

"Come on now Effie Mae I ain't asking for nothing but a kiss." She blushed.

"Just one and that's it."

"That's it for now." He teased. Effie Mae's mouth again flung open.

"Huck you know I'm back with my husband."

"Tell that Anthony, he ain't giving up on you." Huck stated with certainty then placed two fingers underneath Effie Mae's chin, slightly tilting her head. He gazed in her hazel brown eyes and passionately kissed her. He continued his gaze as the kiss ended. Effie Mae blushed.

"What?"

"For the first time in my life I wish I was in another man's shoes."

"What?" She said looking at him with curiosity. "Who's?"

"J.R.'s." Effie Mae's mouth slightly opened stunned by his unexpected words.

"What about Blue, I thought you wanted to be in his shoes?"

"I ain't trying to hurt your feelings Effie Mae, but Blue never really had you."

"What you mean?"

"In all these years you been J.R.'s wife and he been your husband." Effie Mae listened, surprised by his words. "It ain't Blue's family you got or Blue's son you just had, it's J.R.'s and that man love you girl with everything he got in him." She smiled.

"I guess you could be right."

"Naw Effie Mae I know I'm right, it ain't every man that's gon let you do to them what you done to J.R. and still love and respect you." Huck said continuing his embraced. He romantically kissed her. "Bye Effie Mae."

"Bye Huck."

"I'll be around."

"You better be." She said teasing then watched as he exited out the back door. Effie Mae turned her attention to her sleeping newborn son and smiled. "I love you Tyrell Lee Jones Smith." She paused. "Lil' Blue." Effie Mae giggled.